A Blazing Gilded Age

EPISODES OF AN AMERICAN FAMILY AND A VOLATILE ERA

THE AUTHOR

Rich DiSilvio is an author of both fiction and nonfiction. He has written books, historical articles and commentaries for magazines and online resources. His passion for art, music, history and architecture has yielded contributions in each discipline in his professional career.

In *A Blazing Gilded Age*, DiSilvio has crafted a fictional narrative entwined with historical facts and famous American figures that is entertaining and educational. DiSilvio's previous works include his historical novel *Liszt's Dante Symphony*, and his historical tome on Western civilization, *The Winds of Time*.

DiSilvio's work in the music and entertainment industries includes commentaries on the great composers (such as the top-rated Franz Liszt Site), and the *Pantheon of Composers* porcelain collection, which he conceived and created for the Metropolitan Opera. The collection retailed throughout the USA and Europe.

His artwork and new media projects have graced the album covers and animated advertisements for numerous super-groups and celebrities, including, Elton John, Engelbert Humperdinck, Pink Floyd, Yes, The Moody Blues, Cher, Madonna, Willie Nelson, Johnny Cash, Miles Davis, The Rolling Stones, Jethro Tull, Eric Clapton and many more.

He has also worked on projects for historical documentaries, including *Killing Hitler: The True Story of the Valkyrie Plot*, *The War Zone* series, James Cameron's *The Lost Tomb of Jesus*, *Return to Kirkuk*, *Operation Valkyrie*, and many others.

Rich lives in New York with his wife Eileen and four children.

A Blazing Gilded Age

EPISODES OF AN AMERICAN FAMILY AND A VOLATILE ERA

Rich DiSilvio

Cover art and interior book layout by © Rich DiSilvio.
Photographs & images are from purchased collections or courtesy of Wikipedia's public domain images.

ISBN-13: 978-0-9817625-5-5

DV BOOKS
Digital Vista, Inc.
New York, USA

www.DVBooks.net

EPISODES

1

The Hellhole

June 30, 1881

The cage-elevator rattled as Marcus Wozniak and the morning crew descended 1,200 feet into the mineshaft at Huxley Coal, just outside of Pittsburgh. Reaching bottom, the metal-grated door slid open as Marcus carefully lit the head torch strapped to his cap and then snorted. The stagnant air was dank, while droplets of water, oozing in from underground springs, turned the mineral dust on the ground into pungent puddles of black goo. The crew began treading through this slop when Marcus gazed at his portly buddy. "Hey, Chucky, so today's your birthday!"

Chucky cracked a lazy smile as his fat, stubby finger picked the sleep out of his eyes. "Yeah, thanks, Marcus. But I don't feel no better, now that I'm fourteen."

Marcus chuckled. "And with those silly new whiskers, you don't look any better, either!"

Chucky grimaced and nudged Marcus into the path of a mule hauling a pit car loaded with coal. Marcus quickly averted the collision, while their pal Jimmy chimed in, "Hey, Chucky, you shouldn't push him like that. Even though he's only twelve, Marcus ain't like his scrawny, older brother Tasso.

No, no," he said as his voice echoed down the dark tunnel, "Marcus is stronger than me and my brother put together!"

Chucky waved his meaty hand dismissively. "Oh, don't fret none, Jimmy. Marcus is one of my bestest buddies. Right, Marky-puss?"

Marcus shook his head with a half-hearted smile as they navigated deeper into the mine, knowing that the nickname wasn't derogatory; it referred to his cute face. "Sure, Chucky. We've been working together here since I was nine!"

A rugged middle-aged miner scowled as he gazed down at Marcus. "How in hell does Huxley have the gall to hire nine year olds? The legal age is twelve, for Christ's sake. That's downright criminal!"

"Yes, sir, I reckon it is," Marcus replied respectfully. "But, you see, my family needs the money, and my pa's pay just isn't enough. So he had Doctor Galton sign some paper, called an affa-David, or something, to say that I was older than I really was."

The miner sighed sympathetically. "I know doggone well whatcha mean," he said as he swung his pickaxe onto his shoulder and veered around a miner lighting his head torch. "I hear many folks have to do the same deplorable thing. It just ain't right. We slobs earn pennies a day while Huxley makes millions! This whole system stinks! But ain't you got any brothers to pitch in?"

The three boys swerved closer to the marching man, as Marcus replied, "Yes, I do, sir. But, you see, my oldest brother Stanislaw lost his leg when a pit car loaded with coal knocked him to the tracks—the flanged wheel sliced his right leg completely off."

The man cringed, while Marcus swallowed hard. "So, Stanislaw stays home with my mom. And, well, my middle brother Tasso, he's...he's a—"

"He's a troublemaking loafer!" Chucky blurted.

Marcus frowned, as Chucky and Jimmy chuckled.

Jimmy looked over at Marcus. "Yeah, I reckon Tasso is your pa's dark and dirty piece of coal, while you're his glittering diamond!"

The man gazed at the heckling youths and then back at Marcus. "What's with this brother Tasso of yours?"

Marcus glanced heatedly at his two friends, and then up at the man. "Tasso might be a troublemaker, sir, but you see, he was a sickly kid. So he was never able to do what Stanislaw and I could. I reckon that must have been pretty hard on him. And while we were working, he was getting ribbed for being a loafer by imbeciles like Chucky." Chucky grimaced, as Marcus added, "But Tasso finally got himself a job here nine months ago as a breaker boy. And just two months ago, he got moved down here with me and my pa."

As Marcus craned his neck, trying to locate his wayward brother amid the chaotic change in shifts, Jimmy interrupted, "Breaker boy—bah! Even though the breaker house is above ground, I hated that job. All we did was sit hunchbacked over that stupid long chute, removing debris from the stream of coal that zipped past us, which dropped into the grinder and then landed in the hopper cars way down below. My back still aches from that crappy ol' job!"

"Yeah, and you kinda look like Quasimodo, too!" Chucky jibed with a hefty cackle.

Jimmy straightened his back. "Ah, shut up, Chucky! At least I got promoted to a driver, and direct these dumb mules to haul all of our coal. You're still a silly *nipper!*"

Chucky's smile vanished. "Well, if we nippers didn't open and close those huge metal doors for ventilation, we all would suffocate, you idiot! Or we might even get blown up, if the firedamp ain't released from these chambers!"

As Jimmy rolled his eyes, the man nodded. "He's right, son. That invisible firedamp is methane gas. And it's mighty flammable." He gazed down at Marcus. "So, what position do *you* hold here, baby blue eyes?"

Marcus' lips twisted, not relishing the perpetual comments about his baby face. "I happen to be a *laborer*, sir. Just like all of you *adults!*"

The man adjusted the battered pickaxe on his shoulder as he looked at Marcus' deceptively sweet little face, then down at his strapping little body. He smiled. "Indeed! You're a mighty fine specimen, specially for a tyke your age."

"Much obliged," Marcus replied. "And I have ambition, too, sir. In fact, I just might become a driller before you!"

The man chuckled. "Yeah, you just might, son. I appear to be just another tool to Mr. Huxley. And quite frankly, I'm sick of chiseling rocks with this dang-ol' pickaxe. I'd just love to get my paws on one of Joseph Fowle's nifty new jackhammers. Hell, they work on compressed air and can pummel stone faster than ten of us back-breaking laborers."

As the morning crew dispersed into different tunnels, making their mundane exchange with the outgoing drones, Marcus turned and waved good-bye to Jimmy—who waved back and grabbed the mule from the night-shift driver. He petted the mule on the forehead. "Listen, Donkey Dan, you better not shit on my foot again today. Do you hear me!?"

As they all chuckled, Jimmy grabbed the reins and head slowly down tunnel 9. The animal snorted and obediently followed—ready to begin another monotonous round of hard labor, once again.

The man gazed at the youths and winked. "Now you boys all try to have yourselves a good day!"

As he began strolling down tunnel 12, Marcus called out, "Hey! Excuse me, sir. But, what's your name?"

The man turned. "Larry. Larry the laborer!"

As the subjugated herd of miners continued to shuffle down their dark, dreary tunnels, Marcus bent down and began filling his Davy lamp with oil. As he did, his long golden-brown hair fell into his sparkling-blue, crystalline eyes. Whipping his head back, he smiled. His father Jedrek had instructed his sons to cut their hair short—like his—as a safety precaution. Yet little Marcus, in a rare moment, was the only one to ignore his pa's plea. Not to be defiant or spiteful, but to assert his independence as a young man.

Meanwhile, Chucky yawned and began waddling lethargically down tunnel 13. His head turned. "Well, I reckon I'll catch you later at lunch time."

Marcus gazed up and chuckled. "Sure thing, Chucky. That's your favorite time of day!"

Chucky spun around and raised his precious metal lunch box as he walked backwards. Lovingly, he kissed it, and then pivoted rather clumsily to continue onward. As he and 40 others straddled over tracks and past young drivers pulling mules and their cargo, Chucky could see the series of metal doors that were still being erected to control ventilation. His door, however, was right in front of him, and he placed his lunch box down. Taking his station, Chucky grabbed the metal door, awaiting instructions.

One crotchety old sod walked past and elbowed him. "Look alive, tubby!"

Chucky flinched. "Yes, sir! *I am* alive."

"Just keep that door open, blubber boy! We got some heavy drillin' goin' on down here, and we can't have no firedamp buildin' up!"

"*I know*, sir," Chucky grumbled as he brazenly stuck his tongue out at the old prune—quite safely, after he passed.

Chucky smiled and sank slothfully to the floor as he pulled out his set of jacks. Yet as he tossed them, he heard a jackhammer squeal, and a *spark!* Instantly, a violent explosion erupted! With hellish fury, the blazing fireball illuminated the darkness and shattered the silence! Chucky was blown backwards as he watched the old man and seven others light up like torches and drop like charred match sticks. Frantically, he tried to get up to close the metal door, but the raging wave of fire engulfed him. Chucky screamed to no avail as his fat, oily skin flared up and sizzled like bacon.

Over 100 yards back, Marcus heard the deafening blast and harrowing screams. A disquieting chill ran up his back, fueling a surge of tears in his eyes. His head dropped, profoundly aware that his dear friend Chucky had seen his last birthday, while *he* would never see Chucky again. Purging the wretched thought, he immediately looked up, and with a sniffle, began scanning the mine's dark, craggy walls—aiming to regain his bearings amid the labyrinth of tunnels. Frantically, he reached down to make sure the wire mesh covering his Davy lamp was secure—knowing that an open flame would ignite the methane. But a far greater fear now wracked his mind: where were his father Jedrek and brother Tasso?

As Jimmy and a throng of miners ran feverishly towards the main exit, Marcus turned and yelled, "Hey, Jimmy, have you seen my pa or brother?"

Jimmy slowed down. "No, but I doubt you'll find Tasso. Hell, when he ain't slacking off hiding in a nook somewhere he's usually getting into trouble."

Marcus nodded nervously. "Yes, I know. Tasso's a handful, Jimmy, but I must find him and my pa."

"Jesus—you remember what happened to Jake and Eddy!" Jimmy exclaimed as he rejoined the fleeing crowd. Gazing back with fear in his eyes, he cried, "So, come on, let's go! Besides, I bet Tasso was the first one to reach the surface."

"I doubt it," Marcus replied as Jimmy vanished into a turbulent stream of bodies and mounting smoke.

As Marcus' heart pounded to the ominous rumble and harrowing screams, he pondered Jimmy's chilling reminder about their two little buddies. Jake and Eddy had both died in one such blast two months ago—their mangled bodies being scraped off the ground with flat shovels after being squashed by fallen shale. Marcus twitched; not so much by their gruesome deaths, or even Chucky's, but by the disturbing fact that he was now growing immune to all of these terrible calamities. Yet the fatalities of friends were one thing; family was a different matter. His mind flashed back to Tasso. He knows his brother has only been underground for two months now (having replaced their poor, dead friend, Eddy) and isn't too swift. With a steadfast gleam in his eye, Marcus reached up and extinguished the makeshift torch strapped to his cloth cap. Although standard issue, these candled caps are often deadly at times like this, and he knew the protocol. Rising to his feet, Marcus quickly began pacing down the main tunnel, carrying the large Davy lamp in his right hand. Being only 4-feet, 6-inches tall, little Marcus did all he could do to keep the unwieldy lamp from hitting the ground.

As he ran against the tide of fleeing miners, he came across one of the old-timers; a man the crew calls Homer. That's because of the thick cataracts covering his eyes, which made him nearly as blind as the famous Greek author. Actually, Marcus always thought his reptilian-clad eyes were rather creepy looking, and figured Homer to be almost as old as the ancient scribe. But Homer is a pretty sharp fellow, just like his namesake, and doesn't seem to mind his limited vision. As the old man once said, "What the hell's the difference? I'm down here like a damned mole for 14 hours a day and then rise up to the surface only to see the stars and moon. So, who needs light or sight?"

Marcus lifted his lamp. "Homer, did you see my pa or brother?"

Homer turned his head slightly, not even making eye contact, as is his custom. "No, Marcus. But from the sound of that explosion and those screams, I suggest you make your way to the cage. Get your little arse elevated to the surface, but quick!"

Marcus shook his head firmly. "Can't do that, sir," he replied in his typically respectful tone. With his free hand, he yanked up his heavily stained and oversized trousers, and added, "I'm sorry, Homer. But I must find them!"

With that, Marcus quickly grabbed a pickaxe nearby and began pacing down the main tunnel.

Homer's head swiveled toward the sound of his footsteps. "You danged fool! You're running the wrong way! Listen to me, son. There's no telling what might happen next!"

As Marcus continued his search, he peered down each artery that branched off the main tunnel, but didn't see a sign of either one. With each step, Marcus was growing more and more concerned, yet more and more determined.

Back at tunnel 13, the fiery blast was gaining momentum. A miner gasped at the horrific sight of eight of his buddies' charred bodies and Chucky's deformed carcass some 20 yards up ahead. Immediately, he lunged forward and began pushing another set of large metal doors closed, hoping to contain the fire, but the courageous miner was too late. The mischievous methane gas had already seeped into the next and far larger chamber. Instantaneously, an enormous fireball erupted, blowing the metal doors off their hinges and vaporizing the paltry obstruction of flesh and bones. The fiery mass grew swiftly in volume and now began raging through the mine's tunnels, igniting every molecule of methane it could find. Winding its way through a labyrinth of tunnels, the blazing wave of terror made no distinction—incinerating everything in its hellish path. As it entered the main tunnel, 18 diggers, 11 timber men and 14 mules froze in utter fear as they helplessly watched the fiery wall of death rapidly approach. In an instant, they were engulfed. Their screams of agony and honking yelps were earsplitting, yet brief, as the scorching inferno cremated their bodies and continued its frenzied course.

Trapped and petrified, other miners and young nippers scurried to take cover in nooks, behind doors or even pit cars. One miner squeezed behind a metal door, yet as the fire raged through it pinned him against the tunnel wall. Standing with his face and hands pressed against the metal slab, he began to sizzle as the metal door began to glow—frying him like a huge skillet.

Nearby stands the main airshaft; it is the all-important lifeline, supplying miners with oxygen. At the top of that 1,200-foot duct sits the enormous fan house. As the fire twisted its way through the tunnels, like a devilish snake seeking air, it instinctively made its way toward the blustery air source.

Up above, one of the mechanics was performing a routine valve repair, when suddenly the fan's motor began to labor. Curious, he began to walk closer to inspect it, when, to his surprise, huge twisting-tongues of fire blew out the top of the fan. The motor choked, and the entire unit blew straight up, through the roof, and into the clear blue sky. The mechanic was blown backwards to the ground—staring in disbelief at the geyser of fire as chunks of the fan's cowling and motor crashed down all around him.

Down below, the intense heat and bright light stunned and blinded the trapped moles, so accustomed to darkness.

Jedrek Wozniak's eyes, however, widened, as he saw his good friend, Bill "Rusty" Mulvaney, blasted off his feet, landing face down on the tracks.

Bill is a brawny Irishman with a ruddy, freckled complexion that is partially covered with a thick rusty beard and mustache, hence the nickname. He also stands a good 6 inches taller than Jedrek at a towering 6-feet, 5-inches, yet he now lay flat and moaning on the ground. Rusty had been standing behind a fully loaded pit car filling it with aggregate; however, his two work mules had the misfortune of standing in front of the metal cart, literally in the line of *fire*. Now their huge carcasses lie smoldering on the ground—looking like an oversized pig roast. Although to Rusty and Jedrek, the horrid stench was nowhere near as pleasant. Rusty now began trying to push himself off the tracks as the huge wave of fire burnt most of itself out, being followed by a thick drifting veil of black smoke.

Grabbing his Davy lamp, Jedrek rushed forward, yet, as he did, he saw a timber support post, which was shoring up a loose portion of the ceiling, start to give way. Jedrek stopped briefly as the vertical member snapped and keeled over—pinning Mulvaney's body to the tracks. Amid a mounting shroud of smoke, Jedrek turned up the wick on his Davy lamp, fairly certain that the lantern's safety mesh would prevent the flame from igniting anymore of the volatile firedamp. Placing the lamp down, Jedrek grabbed his pickaxe with both hands and swung it hard and deep into the rough-hewn chunk of timber. Firming up his grip, Jedrek then jammed his heels into the sides of the iron rail. Leaning back with all his weight, he began to slide the hulking mass of splintered wood off Mulvaney's back.

Just then little Marcus appeared out of the black mist, wide-eyed and badly shaken. "Pa! Are you alright?"

Jedrek's head turned. "Marcus, stay put!" came the firm command in Polish; unable to speak fluent English like his son.

"Let me help you, Pa. Please!?"

"*Żaden!*"

With a nervous huff, Marcus placed the Davy lamp down as he wiped his sooty face with the ragged sleeve of his oversized shirt.

As Jedrek struggled to pull Mulvaney free, terrifying sounds of massive cave-ins and shrieking screams echoed throughout the dark chambers, sending an eerie chill down Marcus' back. As far as he was concerned, his daily work site was now beginning to feel like a creepy catacomb or, worse yet, Hades. During his search, Marcus had stepped over the dead bodies of men and mules, but now the rancid smells of burning flesh mixed with noxious gases were pushing his neophyte senses to the limit. As he covered his nose and mouth with his hand, all he could think of was his father's safety and where his older brother might be.

Anxiously, he squalled, "Come on, Pa. Hurry! Let's go! We have to find Tasso."

"Jed minuta!" his father snapped.

As Rusty rose to his feet, he hugged Jedrek, thankful for being set free and for sustaining no fatal injuries. Yet Rusty knew his Polish friend would have little problems lifting the heavy beam off his back. Jedrek was uncommonly strong and was well known for having punched a disobedient horse, sending it to its knees; hence gaining the utmost respect of Mulvaney and many fellow miners.

Jedrek wrapped his arm around Rusty's waist and began to escort him toward Marcus, who was still standing impatiently by the exit. The two strapping men shuffled their way over the tracks, while Jedrek instructed Mulvaney to continue on to make sure the cage elevator was still operational. As Rusty nodded and disappeared into the dark mist, Jedrek turned to reach for his pickaxe; yet, as he did, another tremor rocked the tunnel, sending an even larger beam of timber crashing down, missing his shoulder by mere inches. Jedrek looked down at the fallen timber and then over at Marcus—a smile of relief etching his masculine face. Calmly, he brushed the dust off his shoulder and began picking the debris out of his eyes when, unexpectedly, another beam snapped and let loose—this one knocking Jedrek on his back and landing squarely on his chest. Jedrek looked quickly at Marcus and yelled in his typical, Polish tongue, "*Zatrzymaj się!* Stand back! I got this."

Marcus tried desperately to obey his father, but his body was instinctively fueling his muscles to move forward. Somehow, he managed to harness the charge, but Marcus was now trembling with anxiety. Adding to his frustration were the drifting waves of thick black smoke that were marring his vision, yet he was still close enough to see his imperiled father.

Jedrek closed his eyes and took a deep breath, praying to the Lord not to take his life, especially not now in front of his youngest and most cherished son. As he exhaled, he pushed hard. But the splintery member merely budged a few inches, landing back on his muscular chest.

As Marcus worriedly took a small step forward, Jedrek barked "No! Stay back!" He took another deep breath as adrenaline pumped through his body like needles of steel. Releasing a deep, warrior like grunt, Jedrek pushed with all his might. This time the massive beam miraculously flew off his chest as if it were a piece of lath. Jedrek looked over at his son and, in his typical, rugged manner, winked.

A wave of relief washed over Marcus as a delightful grin lit up his adorable, cherubic face. Proud of his father's Herculean feat, Marcus grabbed his lamp and jubilantly lifted it—honoring his father's triumph. Jedrek humbly acknowledged the tribute with a nod, and began brushing the dirt off his chest while rising toward an upright position. Meanwhile, Marcus had noticed the flickering glow of his lantern on the ceiling, forcing his sparkling blue eyes to drift upward. But, suddenly, *they froze!* A large fissure was spreading rapidly across the width of the tunnel.

Heightening his sense of dread was the low and menacing rumble that swiftly reached a most frightful pitch. Helplessly, Marcus watched as a massive slab of shale broke loose from the ceiling. Jedrek moaned like a grizzly caught in a bear trap as the tonnage of rock came crashing down on his legs, crushing them like grapes under a steel press.

Marcus turned ashen as he felt his tiny heart pounding rapidly inside his chest. A numbing haze washed over him, so much so that he felt faint. But somehow, Marcus managed to shake it off. Instinctively, he lunged toward his father, and began gouging away at all the rocks and small bits of lumber. What he unraveled, however, was horrifying. Marcus clenched his hands into fists and stared in disbelief. The vision before him of his beloved father—trapped under a mass of rock and revealing only his upper torso—was worse than any nightmare he had ever experienced. His body began to shake as conflicting feelings of terror, heartbreak and helplessness stormed through his veins. Tears rushed into his eyes, but Marcus bravely summoned the will to dam them. He had to show his father that he was strong, just like him. Jedrek was a rock; just like the ore he dug and, now, quite chillingly, comprised half his body. His father was a workhorse, an exemplary byproduct of his Industrial Age. He was a practical man who knew life was tough, and the only way to survive was to be even tougher. Crying was simply not an option, at least not for a real man.

Marcus' lips tensed up as he grabbed his father's pickaxe and began chipping away at the large chunk of shale. As he swung, a maelstrom of confusion beclouded his mind. He could understand the deaths of other people, but *his* father? Jedrek was invincible; a good man, a devout Catholic that did everything right. So this didn't make sense. The only logical explanation was that God placed his father's salvation in his hands. As such, Marcus' swings became more frenzied, until, that is, his father waved his hand.

In broken English, Jedrek uttered, *"Zatrzymaj się!* (Stop!), Marcus, please!"

Marcus kept swinging as he yelled, "Don't worry, Pa. The Lord placed you in my hands. I'll get you out!"

"Marcus! Enough!" he commanded in his Polish brogue. "It appears God has other plans. Please, my son, come here."

Marcus' windmill-like stride slowly came to a halt as his pickaxe slipped through his fingers and hit the ground. Marcus fell hopelessly to his knees and covered his face, pushing his little fingers into his eyes to keep the tears at bay. Taking a deep breath, he lowered his coal-stained hands. He leaned toward his father, who then pulled Marcus close to his chest with his one free arm.

Jedrek's once powerful voice was now frail and wracked with pain. "It's no use, Marcus. Please, do not risk your life for nothing. Always remember that. Fight the good fight, but never waste your valuable energy on lost causes."

The sound of those harsh, fatal words on his tender, young ears was too much to bear, and tears began to stream down like acid; burning his face, heart, and soul. "Pa, you're *not* a lost cause. You could *never* be, *never!* I can find help, and get you out of here. I can, I swear I can!"

Jedrek knew that his legs were irreparably crushed. Moreover, the iron rail digging into his back had clearly broken his spine. Even if he did survive by some miracle, he'd be a cripple, just like his oldest son Stanislaw. And to burden his wife with two invalids was unthinkable.

"Marcus, you must listen to me. You must find your brother Tasso and get out of here before it's too late."

"But, Pa—"

"Please! Shush!" Jedrek demanded with a gurgle and a choke. As small rocks and dust continued to stream down all around them, he added, "Tell your mother I love her. *You,* my precious son, will have to be strong. Take care of your mother and two brothers. You have always been my pride and joy, Marcus. You have a great little mind and a good, pure heart. It grieves me to put such a burden on you, but I know you can handle it. You, Marcus, are now the man of the Wozniak house."

Marcus' eyebrows pinched as he wiped the tears from his smudgy, charcoaled face. "But, Pa, I'm the youngest!"

Jedrek coughed. As he spoke, blood began to ooze out the corner of his mouth, "Marcus, Stan is crippled and can never work again. And as for Tasso, well, he has given many indications that he might very well be a lost cause. God forgive me, but I cannot leave this world in peace if he was to watch over my flock. So, promise me that you will fulfill my last wishes."

Marcus looked into his father's bloodshot eyes. They looked horrifyingly different. The once sparkling orbs of sapphire blue were now dark gray and sullen, like the distant moon in a gloomy, cloud-filled sky about to fade from sight. Yet they were unnervingly penetrating, deep with import, as if his father's thoughts and soul were being transported into his own.

Marcus summoned the courage to nod, while his father mustered the strength to smile. Aware that the magical spark of life was quickly fading, Jedrek struggled to leave his son the last bit of wisdom he would ever relay. "You must get a good education so that you can rise out of this tomb and into the sunshine of American prosperity. You must get out of this dirty business, this dirty town, this dirty slave penitentiary. I'm sorry; I brought you all here for a better life, but failed. But all my hopes ride on you, Marcus. I know you can do what I never could. You have the best of your mother and me. So, please, abandon our past. We do not live in Poland anymore. We are now Americans. Speak the language; learn the culture. No more Stanislaw, Tasso and Marcus. You must be Stan, Ted and Marc! Do you hear me?"

Marcus forced out a smile to comfort his father, having heard that last bit of instruction many times recently. "Yes, Papa," came his tearful reply, "Americans we three shall be. So help me God."

He bent over and embraced his father's sturdy torso— grabbing his shoulders as if never wanting to let go. With a sob, he pushed his soft fledgling checks into his father's tough, leathery face. Jedrek grabbed his son and hugged him with a passion that heretofore he was never able to display. Regrets filled his mind about how he never physically expressed his love; but the hellhole they lived in called for stoic strength and prevented love from fully blossoming. However, Jedrek was darn glad to have this brief moment— this beautiful gift. The lump of love and pride that now welled in his throat was from 12 years of pent-up and unspoken bliss in watching his son grow, and now all his hopes rested in poor little Marcus' hands. Tears trickled out of the corners of his eyes, melding with his son's—evoking an almost spiritual bond.

The blood from Jedrek's lips soiled Marcus' face as he kissed his precious son's cheek. He grabbed the nape of his son's neck and pressed their faces even tighter together in a last embrace—he, too, wishing never to let go; yet painfully aware that he had only seconds to cherish the fleeting moment. The savory feeling of his son's warm, human flesh against his would soon be gone forever, leaving Marcus with a cold carcass—frigid and lifeless as the shale crushing his lower body. The thought of slipping away from his son into the cold, black abyss of death was horrifying—unbearable. His heart began to weep in a twisted knot of excruciating sorrow mixed with utter dread as he murmured, "Now go! Fetch your brother...and get back to the cage. Get out. And you...must...visit...Cal—"

Jedrek expired just as Tasso arrived unexpectedly, panting, frazzled, and late as usual. "Marcus, is that you?"

Painfully, Marcus lifted his head and turned. "Yes, but I think pa is—"

"Oh, my God!" Tasso squealed as he placed his Davy on the ground. "Pop! I'll get you out."

Tasso began to dash over, but slid quickly to a halt. He wasn't prepared for what he saw. His father's torso perplexingly ended, meshing into a heap of rock. As his eyes cascaded up to his face, his pickaxe slipped through his fingers—falling to the floor. All he saw was a cold, blank stare; his father's mouth was partially opened. But most unnervingly, his entire body was dead still. Tasso screamed as his chapped fingers dug into his sooty face.

Marcus turned back to his father, his tiny lips quivering at the dreadful sight. The guiding light in his life was extinguished. That magnificently strong and courageous soul, so full of life and vitality, was now unfathomably gone; his body now motionless; his eyes, lifeless; his deep, commanding voice, now painfully silent. Marcus gazed down at his father's prematurely weathered, but still handsome, face. With a sniffle, he wiped the hair out of his eyes, and he took extra care this time to take a long, hard look—scrutinizing and memorizing every chiseled feature of his father's face. Marcus had to imprint it in his mind—just like a carving by Michelangelo that would stand the test of time and last forever.

A call rang out, startling them both.

It was Bill Mulvaney; he had cleared a path to the cage and returned to escort his good friend and children to safety.

"Come on, lads!" he said with a grin. "That danged ole cage is still working. It's the only way out. Call your pa, we m-must get g-go—" Rusty's voice painfully crumbled to a halt as his eyes landed on Jedrek's corpse. His face twitched nervously, while his head fell awkwardly. Stroking his grisly red beard for an odd moment, he then seemed to snort like a horse as his head snapped up. He reached over and grabbed both their arms. "Keep a good hold on them lamps, boys!" He then pivoted them around and began walking them quickly towards the cage.

Tasso screamed as he flailed his arms—breaking himself free. "Leave me alone! I can't leave my father down here." As rage turned his brown eyes red, he yelled, "And *you* can't leave your best friend down here. Can you?"

Mulvaney's well-trained nose could smell the deadly firedamp amid the coal dust that wafted through the dark toxic tunnel, and he coldly dispensed with sympathy, opting for survival. "Shut your damned mouth, son! We can't get your pa's body free, and this confounded mine is right likely to blow! So, move your ass, boy, and follow us."

With that, Rusty pulled Marcus forward as he made a dash for the cage. Marcus' head spun around to see if Tasso was following and, as sure as a frightened kitten, he was right there on their heels. As the three stormed toward the cage, they watched the mesh-covered elevator begin to rise steadily up the shaft. It was chock-full of miners, and to Tasso, it appeared that they were being left behind. Panic-stricken, Tasso ran headlong and leapt onto the rising pen, his fingers desperately trying to maintain their grasp on the grating.

Meanwhile, the ascending miners scorned the frantic youth, hollering, "Get the hell off, boy!"

Another barked, "You'll get sliced in two once we enter the shaft, you danged fool. Jump, son, JUMP!"

One 15-year-old buddy bellowed, "Tasso, the cage *will* come back…now JUMP!"

Tasso's jittery eyes gazed at his friend as fear now fueled a steady stream of tears. With the deepest of regrets, he released his grip, falling to the floor. Like a wound-up tension spring just released, Tasso bounced up to his feet and frantically began racing in erratic directions—his eyes desperately seeking another exit.

"Ted! Listen to me," Marcus yelled commandingly. "They said the cage would come back down. So calm down, we *will* get out!"

Tasso, however, was now hysterical and he began to hyperventilate—his breath short and gasping, his heart pounding like a piston.

Mulvaney stepped over and cracked him good, right across the face. "Snap out if it!"

Marcus glared at Rusty, his eyes radiating a mixture of utter surprise and discontent.

"Listen up, Marcus," Mulvaney said in his rough, raspy voice, "I ain't trying to be a mean son-of-a-bitch, but it's the only way I know to break him out of it."

As they both turned toward Tasso, his hysteria had stopped, but to their chagrin, he now wielded a pickaxe. Tasso took a broad step toward Mulvaney and—with eyes ablaze—began rocking his deadly weapon to and fro. "No one but my pa hits me! Got that, *Billy boy?*"

Mulvaney's lips twisted. "And no snot-nosed kid is gonna threaten *me* with a pickaxe! Got THAT—*Tasso?*"

Rusty and Tasso never clicked, and Marcus wanted to peacefully disarm this conflict mighty quick, especially now that his father was no longer around to protect Tasso from his perpetual mischief. He stepped forward and said tactfully, "Mr. Mulvaney, my father's last wish was that we be called Ted and Marc from now on. So, please, no more Tasso!" Distracted, Mulvaney now gazed at Marcus, as he in turn, looked at his brother. "And, Ted, please put down that damned pickaxe! Rusty is only trying to help us. We can't panic, and we certainly shouldn't be fighting with each other. We all need to pull together; otherwise, we'll never get out of here."

Rusty looked at the wise little youth and nodded. "You're a smart boy, Marc. Just like your pa always said." Then turning toward Ted, he added with a mixture of frustration and disgust, "Unfortunately, the same can't be said about you, Teddy! So, what'll it be, hothead? If you got the nerve, give it a shot. Otherwise, put that goddamned thing down before I rip it out of your scrawny little arms and give you a good shellacking! Something your pappy should have done a hell of a lot more of!"

Ted's nostrils flared as he lifted his pointy battle-ax and charged. Mulvaney stood patiently still, and then at the last second, strategically stepped aside, whereby allowing him to grab the handle and whip Ted to the ground. Ripping the pickaxe out of his hands, Mulvaney shook his head angrily, like a bull-sized matador that just ripped the horns off a man-sized bull. "I hate to be so hard on you, boy, but you better pull yourself together. You're pa is no longer here to patch up your mistakes or pay for them. You've been nothing but a frightful nuisance to that good man ever since you were born." As Mulvaney continued to scold the wayward youth an additional layer of disgust deepened his raspy voice as thoughts of past misdeeds fired up his red-hot temper. "And I know damned well it was *you* who set the Mullins' barn on fire. It was also *you* who beat up that little Chink, Danny Chang, just because he had them slits for eyes. Now I sure as hell don't like these damned Chinks stealing our jobs, and think we ought to ship most of their tiny asses back home, but beating that kid up for no good reason is another matter. You got a mean streak in them scrawny bones, boy, and your pa did all he could to keep all your shenanigans hush, hush. But now you got no one to protect your spoiled little ass. So my advice, *Teddy boy*, is grow up and start acting like a man!"

Ted sat on the ground sniveling as he tried his hardest to wipe away the tears and suck up the mucus that now embarrassingly betrayed his manhood. He wanted desperately to get up and kill Bill Mulvaney, but he now knew he couldn't. Besides, the scruffy man's harsh words did have a ring of truth to them, and that gave Ted pause to rethink his actions, more specifically, how those actions must have burdened his poor dead father. He never looked at it from another perspective, especially from an adult's point of view. He was too concerned with his own miserable life. He never wanted to work in this dark, dingy rat hole, and certainly not 12 long, grueling hours a day. He was tired of blowing coal dust out of his nose every day and irritated by the fact that he now had what miners called "red tips"— that is his fingers turned red from sorting all the sulfuric ore, thus causing them to painfully crack and bleed.

And, sure, he knew some people called him unruly, lazy, or a daydreamer, but he also knew how Archibald Desmond Huxley lived. He had seen his huge estate sitting so picturesquely on top of Huxley Hills, and photographs of other tycoons' mansions. They paraded around with their fancy clothes and rode the best purebred horses and most luxurious carriages. Life for the elite was simply grand. Not that Ted had any intentions of working so hard, especially from a mental standpoint, but he did have aspirations of appearing on stage as a flamboyant cowboy. His mother had shown him newspapers that heralded the great new stage sensations Buffalo Bill and Texas Jack in *The Scouts of the Prairie*.

This new Wild West type of show was gaining tons of good press, and best yet, making tons of money. And the work surely didn't look too difficult. In fact, despite being a sickly kid who was prevented from doing most activities, many knew that Ted was the best little horse rider in all of Pittsburgh and Westmoreland County. While his two stronger brothers began doing chores almost as soon as they could walk, he, on the other hand, was allowed to ride the neighbor's pony and eventually their horse. His silent wish had long been to one day steal that horse and ride off to meet Buffalo Bill. There he could shine in the lights, and get all the attention, praise, and money he ever wanted, and rightly deserved.

Breaking Ted's reverie, Rusty kicked the sole of his dirty worn-out shoe, poking his bare foot through the hole. "Snap out of it, boy! The cage is already on its way down."

Marc was looking up the shaft, when he eagerly looked over. "It's true, Ted. Here it comes!"

As the metal cage reached the floor, Marc unlocked the gate and slid it open. Mulvaney walked over to his toolbox and mindfully picked it up, suspecting that a major cave-in was almost certainly imminent. "Let's go, boys!"

As the three entered the cage, Marc turned and slid the gate closed. With a jerk, the sturdy heap of metal began its ascent. Ted looked down at his swollen and cracked fingertips—coated with dried blood—and angrily closed his eyes. Then eagerly, he looked up. With a sigh of relief, his eyes gazed through the grating at the beautiful blue sky far above. *I swear*—his mind vowed with determination—*I'm never coming down here again.*

No sooner had his mind uttered those words, did another explosion rock the mine. An ominous tremor rattled the entire shaft as the cage bounced violently and came to an abrupt stop. They each turned and looked at one another, eyes wide, and hearts pounding. It was now some 20 feet off the ground and, to their further dismay, the steel cables were beginning to squeal and moan under immense stress. Evidently, a small seam of shale had been blasted loose, and it now protruded into the elevator shaft. The top of the cage had rammed into the jagged obstruction, and the motor was now straining to lift what was clearly impossible to move.

"Be prepared!" Rusty exclaimed, "this baby's gonna drop!"

The rigid steel cables could no longer bear the stress and snapped—the cage barreling down and smashing hard into the bedrock. Their three bodies bounced haphazardly and tumbled to the floor like lifeless scarecrows as the metal pen bobbed several times before coming to a most fateful stop.

Ted broke out into a mean sweat, his clammy skin turning pale gray. He jumped to his feet and tried to slide the gate open, but it was too badly mangled to budge. As he began pounding the grating, Rusty diligently opened his toolbox and fetched his wire cutters.

"Step back, red tips!" came the firm command. "You'll only split open those cracked pieces of bloody meat and make more of a mess."

Marc grabbed his brother's arm and pulled him away. "Come on, Ted, let him through."

As Mulvaney began snipping the wire mesh, Ted's eyebrows pinched—he suddenly recalled what Rusty had said earlier. His face, again, flushed with fear. "But you said this was the only way out!"

Rusty spun his head around and gazed into Ted's eyes as he kept snipping. "I meant the only *easy* way out. This ole cage was our best choice, small fry." Turning his attention back to his task, he added, "But we sure as hell can give the escape shaft a shot. Some of them stairs were covered with rubbish, last I saw it, but I'm just praying this recent blast didn't cause more damage."

With a last snip, the twisted gate broke free. Mulvaney took a step back and rammed it open with his hefty shoulder. "Okay, now, each of you boys grab a lamp and a pick. I'll fetch the toolbox and shovel."

As the threesome gathered their gear, Mulvaney stepped out of the cage and started to quick-pace toward the escape shaft. "Come on, boys! I need me some light. Step it up!"

Catching up to his side, the three ran abreast down a series of dark, smoky tunnels. Hopping over debris and squeezing past pit cars that blocked their path, they eventually came to a dead end. The tunnel was completely destroyed by the cave-in. They would have to backtrack and try another artery. As Mulvaney paced quickly towards the alternative tunnel, Ted looked at Marc with his hopeless brown eyes.

"Don't worry," Marc whispered, "if he doesn't get us out of here, I will!"

Ted looked at his younger brother and rolled his eyes, yet, as he did, he tripped—he and his lamp crashing to the ground as the Davy's safety mesh unraveled. The open flame quickly flared up trying to devour more oxygen.

Ted sat up and gazed into the bright light, entranced. "Ah, that's better. More light!"

"NO!" Marc cried. "It could set off more firedamp!" Quickly, Marc grabbed the lamp and carefully began turning down the wick.

Mulvaney had already stopped and was now giving Ted one hell of a stare. "Damn you, small fry! You trying to get us ALL fried?"

Ted's upper lip curled as he retorted acidly, "No, *Billy Bourbon*. I tripped!"

Ted was well aware of Mulvaney's secret nickname, which no one but his close friends would ever dare mention to his face. Well, except for Jimmy O'Doul, that is. But Jimmy paid dearly for that mistake when Rusty hauled off and broke his jaw with one shot, and then cracked his ribs with another. Ted had even witnessed O'Doul's thrashing for disobeying this golden rule, but Ted's bad temper always found a way to trump good sense.

Mulvaney's brow twisted. "If you wasn't Jedrek's son I'd have me a picnic tanning your dirty no-good hide, you little varmint." Angrily, he shook his head. "And that's a mighty typical excuse you got there. I'm supposing that's why you figured an open flame was *better. More light!* Right?

Ain't that what you said?" With a look of disgust, Rusty added, "Very bright. Very *bright*, indeed!"

Ted's frown revealed more than just being caught in a white lie; he hated Mulvaney—emphatically. The red-bearded brute had too often encouraged his father to take a harder line with him when he had gotten into trouble, and Ted had always resented it. Moreover, he didn't think the old oaf was so bright himself—never attending so much as one day in school, while he had done four years. So who was *he* to talk?

Marc stepped over, aiming to divert the conversation. He extended his hand down to help lift up his brother. "So, what did you trip over, you silly clod?"

"Who the hell knows?" Ted grunted as he grabbed his brother's hand and hoisted himself up. As he turned to pick up his lamp, Ted noticed the vague image of the meddlesome obstruction. Irritably, he squinted and bent over to get a closer look. There before his eyes was a bloody arm sticking out of a mound of rubble.

"AHH!!!" Ted yelped as he recoiled and fell awkwardly backwards—landing on his buttocks. Staring at the bloody stump, he cried, "That ghoul just tripped me!" Jumping to his feet, he added, "This is downright creepy!"

Marc giggled. "Besides being a pain in the rear, you can also be quite funny."

"Well, I didn't mean to be that time," Ted said as he wiped his brow, "I'm serious; this is getting awfully gross and morose."

Marc smiled. "Yes, I forgot, Mr. Gross Morose. Breaker boys aren't used to seeing things like this up on the surface. But when you've been down here as long as I have you sort of get used to grisly sights like this."

The only close deaths Ted had experienced were his two younger siblings, each dying in childbirth—both of whom, he was told, were summoned by God, who had other special plans for them in Heaven. But the deaths down here were gruesome and sadistic tortures that just didn't register in Ted's young and flighty mind. "Well, I don't care to ever work down here again or get used to gruesome ghouls lurking in the dark," Ted moaned. "This is like one of those scary Grimm's fairy tales that mom used to read to us, and I hated them, too!" Ted scratched his chin, trying to devise another suitable rhyme as he added, "Grimm's ghouls are for fools, and Huxley's cave is for—"

"The *brave!*" Marc interjected, with a smile and a puffed out chest—filling in Ted's loss for words.

Ted didn't like his little brother's quicker wit or his insulting insinuation, but neither did Mulvaney find the juvenile banter or breather amusing. "BOYS! We need to get a move on. Now snuff out that danged lamp, Ted. We can't be risking our necks like this with an open flame. Save the oil for your brother's Davy. We sure as hell will need it. Now, *let's go!*"

Over three grueling hours passed as they crawled over debris and dug their way through mounds of shale and ore that blocked their path. The previous sounds of men screaming, mules honking, and combustible gas exploding had all vanished, leaving them in an eerie silence, where only their panting breaths and footsteps could be heard. As they continued their strenuous journey through a maze of cloudy darkness, noxious smells, and occasional dead bodies, Marc's lamp was beginning to die. It had already been refilled with Ted's fuel, so they were now at the proverbial end of the road.

"Once that lamp goes out, we'll be left in total darkness!" Ted wailed. "Then what? We'll never get out of here!"

Marc shined the dim lamp in his brother's direction—its luminosity was little more than the brilliance of a match. "Ted, we can't think like that. Let's just try to find the escape shaft. I'm sure we should be able to see some daylight from there."

"That's right," Rusty interjected, "and I'm suspecting it ought to be mighty close. So hang on to your wits, Tass—uh, Teddy."

Ted rolled his eyes as he turned and mumbled, "And you hang on to your nit wits—Rusty the Retard!"

"What was that?" Mulvaney inquired.

"Oh, nothing, Big Red," Ted said as he adjusted his suspenders and continued walking.

With the lamp's glow now down to a mere 4-foot radius, Marc suggested to Rusty that he should hold the Davy lamp, while they, in turn, would grab onto the back of his shirt as he navigates their way through the abyss.

Mulvaney winked at the astute youth and grabbed the dying Davy as they latched onto his shirt. Moving along one step at a time, Rusty hunched over and held the lamp close to the ground to spot any obstructions. Progress was painstakingly slow as they swerved around fallen chunks of shale and stepped over twisted pit car tracks and burnt or broken timber. Most unsettling, was seeing the tools and melted lunchboxes of dead or deserted miners. After groping around for another 45 minutes—not seeming to make any headway—even Marc was beginning to get concerned. The flame had further diminished in size—its paltry luminance now down to a disturbing 2-foot radius.

The fact of the matter was, Rusty had lost his bearings in the utter darkness, and didn't wish to tell the boys—his own nerves beginning to fray.

Just then Ted stepped on something soft that squeaked. He jumped and squealed, "Oh, my God! What was that?"

Rusty turned and laughed. "You sure are a frightened little Mary, aren't ya? It's probably a rat. Them rodents seem to get more brazen—or just plain stupid—when there's less light down here. I've stepped on quite a few myself over the years."

Ted did his typical rolling of the eyes as he thought, *and I wish I was Paul Bunyan, so I could step on* YOU—*you stupid, red rodent!*

Meanwhile, Marc was becoming wary of Mulvaney's navigational skills, and asked him how much farther they would have to go to reach the escape shaft.

"Well, I'm a reckoning it's just up ahead about 100 feet or so," came Rusty's white lie as he wiped the mounting sweat off his brow. "But, I'm afraid we got ourselves a b-bigger problem than that, b-boys." Mulvaney's voice was marred with foreboding, and it had crackled with stress, finally revealing his own inner fears that he had managed so well to conceal, until now.

Rusty didn't have to say another word as all three watched the precious flame wither, getting smaller and smaller. A disturbing wave of dread welled inside them as they watched their comrades' petrified faces begin to fade. Instinctively, their pupils began to devour their irises, desperately trying to receive the slightest bit of luminance to project an image of humanity on their retinas—as if sensing the coming gloom. They were now painfully aware that this might very well be the last vision of life they will ever see again. Ted and Marc gripped Mulvaney's shirt tighter as they watched the flame dance on the wick like a dying sprite, its tiny glow getting darker and darker as it made a final flicker and died. The world, as they knew it, went black.

Marc and Mulvaney could hear a sniffle and then a disquieting crescendo of the most wretched whimpering. Ted was losing it. As far as he was concerned, all three of them were as good as dead. Worse yet, Ted's fear was now conjuring up further perils that the dark mine would now present. His mother had recently relayed to her sons William

Foulke's startling discovery of a large prehistoric lizard, which scientists were now calling dinosaurs, this one in particular being labeled a Hadrosaurus. It was just another piece of evidence that was supporting Darwin's theory of evolution, and Ted was now panic-stricken. "Marc, what if a Hadrosaurus attacks us!? Foulke found those bones deep underground!"

"Ted, dinosaurs lived a long time ago," Marc replied, "they're all dead."

"We don't know that for sure," Ted cried, "but I'm damned sure of one thing—pretty soon *we'll* all be dead!"

With that, Ted broke down and bawled. Marc could feel his brother's body sliding down next to him, finally reaching the ground. The sobs grew more and more wrenching and uncontrollable.

Marc, too, was shaking. It was as if fear were a small army of soldiers hauling tiny needles into his nerves, yet Marc took a deep breath and used his mind as a shield to ward off the attack. His brother needed help and his father's dying words were to watch over the family. He had to be strong. The once private first class was now a general, whether he liked it or not. Yet he was quite aware that his drastic leap in rank was in name only; he knew he hadn't any experience or training. Marc was momentarily lost in thought; he had to think of something that would comfort his poor brother, who pathetically was now falling apart. Just then a recollection came rushing into his mind. Marc knelt down and felt around for Ted's shoulder. Making contact with his brother's boney bicep, Marc pulled Ted into his muscular little chest and hugged him tight. "Ted, don't let the darkness scare you. Just make believe it's bedtime, and mom turned off the oil lamp."

Ted had all to do to speak as he stammered, "B-but when t-the light goes out, we still h-have moonlight. I can't even s-see you—and your chest is right in my face!" As he took another whimpering breath, he snorted. "But I sure as hell can smell you. Christ, you smell like a danged fart mule!"

As Ted pushed him away, Marc laughed as he replied, "Fart mule, huh? Well, that's because I work harder than you, you lazy sloth. But that's it, Ted. Keep up the sense of humor, even if you didn't mean to be funny."

"I sure as hell didn't," Ted grumbled as he reached for his nose in the dark, pinching it closed. Then in a nasal voice, he said, "There's nothing funny about your smelly armpits. Gee whiz, they're curling my nose hairs. Get those god-awful things away from me!"

Meanwhile, Rusty was having one heck of a hard time dealing with the kiddy theater, which had gone from whimpering melodrama to infantile comedy. Mulvaney didn't have any children, and his understanding or compassion, especially for those entering adolescence, was quite limited. He much preferred spending his time at the watering hole downing a few good shots of whiskey, gin or bourbon with his buddies—or sitting on his dilapidated back porch with his wife Maureen doing more of the same. One could say that Rusty and a bottle were mighty close. But then again, it was his only escape from the drudgery called his life, other than his occasional tussles in bed with Maureen.

Marc sensed Rusty's loss of patience by his silence. He felt around for his pant leg and tugged. "What do you suggest we do now, Mr. Mulvaney?"

"I'm thinking, Marc," came Rusty's indecisive and emotionally distraught response. Thoughts of Maureen and all his buddies now flooded his worried mind. The sobering realization that he would never lay eyes on them again, hear their drunken laughter, or feel Maureen's soft body pressed up against his struck Rusty hard, like a jackhammer to the forehead. God, how he wished he had a drink now!

"I have an idea," came Marc's voice out of the darkness. "How about we continue on by touching the wall and walking slowly—you know, feel our way along? You said the escape shaft should be just up ahead—right, Mr. Mulvaney?"

"Listen, Marc," Mulvaney uttered somberly as he reached down, clutched his shirt, and pulled him up. Feeling for his face, Rusty grabbed Marc's little head, spun it sideways, and leaned over to whisper in his ear, "The fact is I ain't got a clue where we are, and I don't wanna alarm your lily-livered brother."

"What!?" Marc exclaimed, shocked. Yet he didn't appreciate Rusty's jibe either, as he added, "And that's not nice!"

"What's not nice?" Ted's voice sounded.

"Nevermind," Marc snapped. He was getting annoyed at Rusty's poor leadership and finally had enough. Yet he wanted to remain respectful. Diplomatically, his voice rose with calm and steady determination, "Listen, you two. Let's feel our way along the wall until we reach the escape shaft. We don't need eyes to do that. So, *get up*, and *let's go!*"

Despite his grave reservations, Rusty couldn't help but be impressed by Marc's commanding resolve and resourcefulness. His eyes rolled in the blackness, searching his soul for the same fortitude. Sure they were lost, but doing nothing was a sure way to cash in one's chips, and Rusty won many hands at poker bluffing his way to victory. So, he thought, perhaps he could bluff his way out of this godforsaken mine, too. Rusty spun around and reached out to touch the wall. Making contact, he barked, "Very well! Latch on to me, boys. Let's move out!"

Marc thought the command sounded militaristic, and he adjusted his cap and shouted, "Company...*march!* One! Two–Three–Four...One! Two–Three–Four..."

Ted's lanky body was still trembling, but he actually managed to chuckle, gaining some relief from his brother's cadence. He reached out and clutched onto his brother's shirt, while, Marc, in turn, grabbed onto Mulvaney's.

The grizzly-faced leader even joined in as all three chanted a selection of military cadences and marched step-by-step toward God knows where.

The three blind mice marched over mounds and stumbled over rocks as they stepped in time and barked in unison. However, after groping around for another 35 minutes their breathing eventually became labored and their echoing voices more muted and listless. Marc sensed that it was more than just fatigue.

"Just a minute," Marc said, feeling a bit lightheaded. He recalled his father telling him that it was harder to breathe in tunnels that are too far away from the airshaft. He had said the best way to conserve oxygen was not to talk. As such, Marc suggested that they should stop the marching chants.

"Suits me," Rusty said, realizing, most painfully, that he had led them in the wrong direction once again. His huge lungs just couldn't get enough oxygen to fuel his massive body, and he no longer wished to pursue the futile expedition. Opting to let the three of them rest peacefully until they lost consciousness and then drifted off quietly into the netherworld, Rusty summoned up the deceptive words to end their trek and their lives. "I think maybe a rest stop might do us some good, boys. You've done good, real good. So take a load off them legs and be still."

"I'm for that," Ted moaned, utterly humiliated and exhausted. "Besides, I don't care to sing those silly marching tunes anymore. There's no sense to it."

As the two slid wearily down to the ground, Marc remained standing. "Well, Ted," his voice resonating with an air of optimism, "Mom told me that the Romans were the first army to use cadences. Something about how it kept them organized, upbeat, and in tune with one another. It's kind of like their emblem—a bunch of sticks. I think it was called faces or fasces or something like that. Anyhow, held together the sticks can't be broken. Yet separate them, and they snap easily. The same is true for us; together we'll have the strength to get out of here. We will. I know it. But we just can't quit!"

"You're a mighty courageous little lad, Marc," Rusty uttered with respect, yet in a voice tainted with gloom and fatalism. "And one hell of a smart boy, too," he added.

"Well, my mom says I'm a good listener, if you can call that smart," came Marc's cheerful response as he thought about his mother. "She knows an awful lot about history, and my pa, well, my pa knows how to live off the land and work harder than ten horses. I saw him bend a rod of iron and even break a hefty piece of lumber with the stroke of his steel-fisted hand." As Marc continued his voice unexpectedly began to crack, "He is the strong…est man a-live. I mean…*was*."

Ted's head dropped as he began sobbing. The harrowing cries echoed in the darkness, sending a disturbing chill down Marc and Rusty's back.

"Aw, shucks," Marc whimpered, "I should have kept my stupid mouth shut. I guess I'm not so smart after all, am I?"

Rusty reached over, feeling around for the two youngsters. Grabbing a shirt and a pant leg, he gave them a firm shake. "Listen, boys, your pa was a great man. Jedrek Wozniak was a man of honor and a true blue friend. And once we get out of here, I promise to keep an eye on things."

Rusty had no idea where that foolish burst of insanity came from, knowing very well that they'd soon run out of oxygen, while Huxley's dreary mine would aptly provide their bodies with a suitable tomb. At that sullen moment, a dark capricious thought entered his mind; namely, would Huxley send Maureen a bill for the burial plot? Knowing Archibald Huxley, as he does, he wouldn't be surprised.

"Thanks Mr. Mulvaney," Marc replied, waking Rusty out his macabre foray. "We sure could use your help. Right, Ted?"

Ted said nothing, and continued to sob.

However, Marc and Rusty could hear that Ted's sobs were turning softer and sluggish, morphing into faint sniffles and eventually fibrillating snores. He had exhausted himself out, physically and emotionally.

Marc felt around for Rusty's shoulder—touching his furry head instead.

Rusty flinched. "Is that you, Marc?"

"Yes, sir," Marc replied softly as he leaned over and drew his head towards where he suspected Rusty's ear would be. He then whispered, "Mr. Mulvaney, like I told you, our air is running out, and that means we must be far from the airshaft and escape shaft. I'm glad Ted didn't pick up on that when I mentioned it before, but I think it's best if you stay here with him and I go look for one of those shafts."

Mulvaney reached out and felt around for Marc's head. Patting him tenderly, he whispered, "You're a brave little soldier, Marc. I'll try to keep Ted as calm as a catfish if he wakes up, but there's no guarantees. As you know, we two are like firedamp and a spark, so if he wakes, I reckon you'll hear us no matter where you might be."

Marc chuckled. "Yes, I know," he whispered. "I'll be back as soon as I find a shaft. And if Ted does wake up, just tell him something to calm his nerves."

"Sure thing, Marc. Now you be careful, and good luck!" Rusty scratched his head. "But I don't see how you'll ever find us?"

"Well, that shouldn't be too tough. You see, I felt the fork in the tunnel 234 steps back, but you took the left fork. I intend to go back and take the right fork."

Rusty chuckled. "You say 234 steps!?"

"Yes, sir. I counted every step we took, and remember several obstructions and some of the tunnel's features we came across, including that fork."

"Well, damn, boy. I don't know why you'd do such a silly thing, but it sure makes sense to me now. Get a move on! And watch your *counted* step!"

Marc giggled. "I will, Mr. Mulvaney!"

Marc traced his steps, carefully stepping over all the obstacles they had encountered, and eventually found the fork, right where he counted it—234 to be exact. Turning right, he walked slowly along the tunnel, feeling his way and trying to record any irregularity that could help him get his bearings. Unfortunately, what he came across next was not something he could feel, but rather smell. He had stepped into a mushy mound of excrement—the foul smell of feces and urine being very familiar. Mines did not have lavatories, nor could miners squander precious time going up to the surface for such a trivial task as internal waste removal. Pinching his nose, he paced off another 500 steps when he saw a 3-inch, vertical sliver of light. It was the result of a partially opened metal door blocked by a mound of fallen shale. Excitedly, Marc peered into the crack. But all he saw were the bodies of nine dead miners. One of them was Larry the laborer! His heart dropped. What's more, the Davy lamp inside flickered, and also took its last breath— aptly bathing the nine extinguished lives in darkness.

Marc pounded the door, and cried, "Why, God? Why?"

Left once again in a total void, Marc's faith and hopes began to crumble, as he thought: *this mine is a godforsaken hellhole!* Several lonely minutes passed in gloomy silence, until thoughts of Ted and Rusty beckoned him to carry on.

Resuming his blind journey, Marc paced off well over 100 steps, when his navigational hand hit a timber post. As he moved his fingers over the roughly milled chunk of wood they hit an object, making a familiar sound. Curious, Marc's little fingertips excitedly examined the metal artifact, his mind instantly recognizing the shape. It was a Davy lamp!— hanging patiently on a hook, just waiting to be lit.

Please, God, make it have oil! His mind reeled as he excitedly pulled the lamp off the hook. Marc's heart fluttered with anticipation as he gave the lamp a good, solid shake. A delightful grin etched his cute little face as he heard the precious liquid splash around inside. He felt around for the flint block and, with trembling hands, attempted to ignite a spark. But to his utter grief, the block was worn smooth and not a single spark could his eager eyes see. Marc spun around and leaned helplessly against the tunnel wall. Staring into a black void of cold and unsettling nothingness, Marc could only hear the trickle of moisture dripping from the ceiling. He closed his eyes, but it didn't matter. All was black, either way, just like his hopes. It then hit him; his brave quest was over, their fates were sealed. Like all the dead miners and his beloved pa, they, too, were trapped in a cave that would become their catacomb.

Hopeless and dejected, horrific thoughts about his father's death crept back into his troubled little mind; worse yet, how he and his two mates would soon follow his father through the threshold into the frightening unknown. Marc tried to purge these vexing thoughts from his head, but it was just too overbearing. His legs inevitably gave out, and he slid slowly down the craggy wall, his back being scratched on the way down. As his little buttocks hit the ground, his awkward cap slid down over his eyes. Sitting for several long and lonely minutes in the pitch-black abyss, a tear welled in his eye and then trickled down his cherubic cheek. Memories of his father crowded his mind, haunting him about the tragic loss, and taunting him about his own loss, his loss in the quest for life. Then, quite unexpectedly, a startling vision of his beloved mother appeared out of the blackness of the tragic theater in his mind. As if an actress on an eerie spot lit stage, Marc saw his mother being pushed out onto the street—with Stan wheeling along at her side—alone, crestfallen and penniless. The landlord, the infamous Archibald Huxley, cackled with a sinister shrill as he slammed the door of their tenement shut, causing Marc to flinch. The vision was jarring. The burden he would heap upon his family, if he gave up, suddenly became a battle cry for survival. His father's last words once again resounded in Marc's little head like a bugle call. He had to take care of his mother and his brothers. Somehow he would find a solution. With resolve, Marc defiantly wiped his tears away. As he did, his hand hit his clumsy hat, falling into his lap—the awkwardly attached torch hitting his thigh.

At first, nothing registered, but then, like the once luminous candle on his cap, Marc's mind lit up; *Of course!*

Excited, he reached down and grabbed his cap. Feeling around for the match—which he kept tucked behind the mounting strap—Marc impatiently pulled it out. He knew the torch was useless—having earlier burnt itself out—but he now had a nearly full Davy lamp sitting right next to him. Eagerly he struck the match and shoved it into the wick. In utter rapture, Marc saw the world slowly begin to reappear as his eyes danced to the warm glow of light.

"Yahoo!" he bellowed as his voice reverberated down the empty, craggy tunnel.

Lifting the lamp, Marc hopped to his feet and spun joyously around in a circle.

After completing a brief victory dance, Marc diligently began scoping out the tunnel. Regaining his bearings, Marc scurried toward the escape shaft. As he paced along the winding tunnel, he almost tripped over a rodent, which, evidently, also seemed happy to see the light. Marc smiled, wondering if it was the same rat Ted had stepped on earlier. Pacing off another 200 steps, Marc's eager eyes suddenly saw a beautiful sight. Up ahead, golden rays of sunlight were shining down, hitting the mine's floor and making a most delightful pattern. As he approached, Marc was overcome by the spectacular sight. It appeared like a luminous oasis in the middle of hell, offering salvation. He peered up the semi-obstructed shaft and marveled at the beautiful sight of white cumulus clouds floating in a peaceful cerulean sky. It took a few moments before Marc painfully realized that the lovely vista was only visible through tiny apertures; the escape shaft was partially obstructed by fallen chunks of shale. Thoughts of his brother and Rusty suddenly rushed into his mind. Excited, he turned and made a dash to retrieve them.

Meanwhile, back in the lightless void, Ted had awoken from his slumber and was back in typical form; badgering Mulvaney with questions.

"I don't believe you!" Ted cried as he blindly reached out and grabbed a hold of Rusty's pants. "You said Marc found help, but *if* he did, why did he come back and then leave again? Huh? Tell me? Why?"

"Like I told you, TassO," Rusty retorted, losing his patience, "he called out from over yonder." Rusty was not too swift with creating a tale as he added, "I don't know why he did that, but just hang on and stop using up our air!"

Ted huffed and started to feel for the wall as he unsteadily rose to his feet. As he started to walk blindly, he tripped over Mulvaney's foot—crashing to the floor.

"OUCH!" Ted yelped as he could feel the blood oozing out of the cracks of his red-tips. "Damn you, Rusty! Get your big stupid hoof out of my way?"

"Watch your tone, boy. Or I'll ram this big hoof right up your bony little butt!"

"Try it, you big, clumsy ox!" Ted blasted, "I'll bet you can't even find me." With that, Ted took several steps backward.

Rusty heard his footsteps, stood up, and lunged through the abyss, grabbing Ted by the shirt. As he began to rattle his lanky body, Ted yelled, "Wait! Hold on! I think I see something!"

"Yeah, you're gonna see stars," Rusty growled, "after I crack you in that naughty little skull of yours!"

"No! I'm not kidding!" Ted exclaimed, "I really think I see something. It looks like a flicker of light!"

Rusty suddenly thought he saw the faintest image of Ted's delighted face before his eyes. He waved his free hand in front of his face, just to make sure, and, lo and behold, the dark, hazy image disappeared and then reappeared. "By golly, I think you're right! I can see your ratty little mug!"

"Very funny, Rusty brain!" Ted snapped. "Turn around and look over there—to your right!"

"Just then a faint Oriental voice echoed throughout the cavern, "Hello! Anybody here?"

"Yes!" Mulvaney yelled as he pondered the distinct voice. "Is that you, Ying?"

"Ah! Big Rusty," the voice replied as it gained in volume. "Yes, yes, it Ying."

"Is there a way out down there?"

"No, no. No can find. And Davy no more bright."

Ying's Davy lamp was emitting the luminance of a small candle as he walked slowly closer. Mulvaney and Ted grabbed their pickaxes and began to walk towards the faint shimmer of light.

As they approached, Ying spotted Ted's face as it emerged out of the darkness. "Ah, YOU! You bad! You hit son. Yes, yes. Very bad!"

Mulvaney stepped in front of Ted. "Hold your horses, Ying. This boy just lost his pa, and you know how good a man Jedrek was. Besides, we all need to get our duffs out of here, and mighty quick!"

Ying's lips twisted, his revulsion too hard to suppress. "Still say, Tasso *no good!*" Ying then looked at his Davy. "But can you no see? Oil almost gone. Then we no see!"

As the three looked at the faltering flame, they were perplexed that the smaller the little yellowish flutter got the brighter the tunnel became.

Just then a voice rang out, "Hey, fellows! I found the escape shaft!"

As they turned, there was little Marc heading their way with a big smile and a brightly burning Davy in his hand.

"Well I'll be a pickled beet!" Rusty rejoiced, "I knew you'd do it!"

Ted's gaunt face lit up as he ran over to hug his brother. As he did, Ying's eyebrow furled. Gazing at Rusty with his almond-shaped eyes, he said, "Still say, Tasso *bad!*"

As Ted hugged Marc, he glanced back, catching Ying's harsh stare, and then looked over at Mulvaney. His head dropped as his hands fell to his sides. Looking at the ground, Ted muttered, apparently to all, "I'm sorry."

As far as Rusty was concerned, he had already intervened and done more than he should have. He smirked and swung his pickaxe over his shoulder. "Let's get a move on! Time's a wastin'. Lead the way, Marc."

With that, the group gathered their gear and began to follow their little knight in shining armor, or rather their knight with shining lantern.

Ted peered over at his brother; his eyes for the first time showing a smidgen of remorse. "I really am sorry. I reckon I never should have clobbered Danny."

Marc glanced at Ted with perturbed, twisted lips. "Ted, never mind saying sorry. Just do the right thing in the future, so you don't ever have to say you're sorry again."

"Sure, that's easy for you to say," Ted snapped, his crotchety temper already restored. "You're ma and pa's perfect little darling, aren't you? Yet, all I ever get is a kick in the ass."

Marc shook his head. "Maybe because you deserve a good kick in the ass!"

Ted wiped the partially hardened mucus off his nose and frowned. Pulling up his sagging pants, he started to march onward, using his upside-down pickaxe as a cane, and making sure not to trip over any more dead bodies or step on any disoriented rats.

Meanwhile, Ying held up his Davy lamp as it finally gave its last flicker and died. He turned and looked up at Mulvaney. "Ah, good thing Marcus here, yes?"

Rusty nodded, realizing that Marc was leading them in the opposite direction of where he had misled them earlier. His mind sighed; *you got that right. Thank God for Marc!*

As they reached the base of the escape shaft the foursome came to a halt. With a sense of relief, Ted and Marc gazed up the long stairwell at the long-anticipated, and most beautiful, light at the end of the tunnel.

"It don't look all that bad," Rusty said happily. "Let's go! Start breaking up these big boulders, boys, while me and Ying haul the chunks behind us."

Swinging their pickaxes into the fallen rock, Marc and Ted gnawed away at the stone in unison, while Rusty and Ying heaved the large chunks of debris. Their renewed sense of hope had fired up their fatigued muscles like a spark igniting an internal combustion engine. And like a well-oiled machine, the foursome burrowed through the rocky debris for nearly an hour, eventually reaching the surface.

Upon exiting the dark shaft and the hellhole below, they all squinted as they stepped into the bright sunlight. The mixed emotions of relief and joy were too much for even a tough mule like Rusty as tears welled in his eyes, and they all embraced. Turning around, they all took deep breaths of fresh air as they relished the beautiful sights of green grass, mountains, trees, birds and blue skies. Looking upward, they each counted their blessings in their own unique ways.

Off in the distance, black smoke still rose out of the airshaft, while a repair crew was already patching up the roof of the blown-up fan house. Workers were scurrying all around trying to assess the extent of the mine's damage, while others sat tending the wounds of the injured. Meanwhile, Jack Hastings, the mine supervisor, was pressing miners for answers, making detailed damage reports, and compiling a list of casualties. He had already

received word of Jedrek's demise, and now spotted
Mulvaney, Ying and the two Wozniak boys. A crowd of
joyous miners, including little Jimmy, surrounded the
survivors and they patted their mates on the back, while
they walked semi-dazed with a mixture of relief and grief.
Hastings looked down at his clipboard and checked off the
names of the four additional survivors. Looking back up
he motioned for Rusty to come over.

Mulvaney excused himself and walked over, dutifully
standing before the supervisor as he brushed the soot off his
disheveled shirt. Hastings gazed at him through his round
clip-on spectacles with a touch of sympathy. Jack may not
have been the most compassionate man in the world, but
next to the Arctic freeze of Archibald Huxley, Hastings was
like a Franklin stove.

Hastings glanced over at the two little Wozniaks, and
back at Mulvaney. "Best you take the boys home. I reckon
you being so close, and all, you'll do me the kindness of
extending our regrets to the Mrs."

"Sure thing, Mr. Hastings," Mulvaney said somberly.
"But seeing that the company coach ain't running, just yet,
could you favor us with your carriage?"

Hastings' left brow rose. "Actually, as you can see, Bill,
we lost us more workers than just Jedrek. So I sure can't give
up my personal carriage as I have me a hell of a long list of
things to do, including the unpleasant task of contacting Mr.
Huxley, he's out of town. But why don't you head on over to
the stable and tell Stokowski that I authorized you to borrow
two horses."

Rusty lowered his head in gratitude. "Much obliged, sir."

As Mulvaney spun around and started to head toward
the stable, Hastings added, "Just make sure you get them
horses back here in the morning; safe and sound, and bright
and early. Otherwise, Huxley will have both our hides!"

Rusty glanced back and nodded. "Sure thing, sir."

2

The Wozniak Cell Block

June 30, 1881

Mulvaney collected the two horses from Stokowski (who was a lanky old man with a hunched back and only two teeth, both rotted), and he saddled them up. Gazing out toward the northern horizon, Rusty contemplated the journey home. The trail was a good 20 miles long, but it was an awfully pretty ride. The panorama of wooded mountains and green valleys was always a pleasant sight to behold, especially when the dewdrops glistened—radiating a colorful spectrum of colors. Yet Rusty knew all too well what lay ahead at the end of that rainbow, and it wasn't gold—at least not for him and his ilk. Miners were like insignificant carpenter ants; their entire life and purpose was simply to bore through hard substances, whereby destroying nature and themselves in the grueling process. Meanwhile, men like Huxley, Carnegie and Frick were the very select few who were reaping in the gargantuan rewards of gold, or in this case, coal and steel.

Rusty looked at Stokowski with a poignant gaze, hoping not to look that haggard when he reaches his age. He then waved over the two Wozniaks, and they mounted their steeds.

On their journey home, the three strolled along with their heads down, wearing long sullen faces. Mulvaney was mounted on a beautiful young, brown Arabian stallion, while Ted manned the reins on an adult, black and white roan, with Marc seated behind. Mulvaney had no idea how to break the dreadful news to Sophia, knowing her to have been very much in love with Jedrek, and having an emotional vein running through her passionate Neapolitan heart, which in matters dealing with love and war could ignite just like firedamp.

Meanwhile, little Marc was beginning to feel the weight of his father's last words. To be the man of the Wozniak house was going to be extremely difficult. He and his brother only earned pennies a day, while his mother had no option but to care for poor, crippled Stan. *How*, he thought, *can we possibly survive?* Adding to Marc's troubled little mind was his father's unfinished last sentence, "You must visit Cal—" Marc was baffled. Cal—what? Callensburg? California? Where? Moreover, and most importantly, Marc just couldn't fathom a world without his father. It was unthinkable, unbearable. Marc felt himself sinking into a deep, melancholy mist when, quite unexpectedly, Ted yelled, "Come on *Billy boy!*" as he glanced at Mulvaney's stallion. "I'll bet this old mare and I can beat both your molasses asses home!" With that, Ted kicked the sides of his old lady as the spotted roan bolted forward.

Marc was thrust backward and barely managed to grab onto Ted's waist as his face twisted with anger. "What in blazes are you doing?"

"What do you think? Showing that rusty old oaf that I can blaze home faster than he can, even with you strapped on my back!"

Marc looked back at Mulvaney, who was now a good 12 yards behind, his face beet-red mad, and his furry red beard blowing wildly in the wind. "Slow down, you blaming idiot!" Rusty bellowed. "These horses ain't ours to mess around with. They belong to Mr. Huxley!"

Marc turned forward and, not knowing what else to do, pinched Ted's stomach. But Ted just grinned and cackled like a naughty hyena, "Hee, ha! Nice try, Marc. So, who's the brave one now?"

"Ted, don't be silly! That was because I know you're afraid of the dark. This is not being brave, this is just *foolish!*"

"Well, I prefer things that are foolish, not ghoulish— remember? So just hang on and enjoy the ride!"

As their horse's head rocked with each galloping stride, Marc held on tight to Ted's waist as he gazed at the rapid blur of Magnolia trees passing by. His mind raced equally as fast, trying to figure out how else to stop Ted's reckless romp. Ted's heels were still pounding the horsemeat as he used the reins like a whip to slap the mare's neck. As they darted through a thicket of trees, with branches slapping their shoulders, Ted ducked quickly as a branch tore a swath off Marc's shirt.

"Okay, enough!" Marc yelled as he looked at the bruise on his arm. "This is *not* funny."

Just then they emerged upon a clear vale. Yet Ted showed no signs of stopping. It was then that a risky proposition crossed Marc's mind. *Please work!* He thought as he placed his hands over Ted's eyes.

Unfortunately, that only dared Ted to go faster, and, once again, his hyena cackle shrieked, "Yahoo! What a ride! I bet Buffalo Bill would be mighty taken with this blind stunt."

"Ted! *Slow down!*" Marc blasted as his fingers now dug into Ted's eye sockets. "There's a creek up ahead!"

"Who's the fool now, Marc?" Ted snapped as he whipped his head to and fro. "Let go of my eyes, and I'll slow down."

Just then a rope came flying over their horse's head as Mulvaney tugged hard—wrenching the mare's neck sideways. The animal's body twisted as it stumbled to the ground—Ted and Marc flying off its back and into the creek. Mulvaney dismounted quickly and ran to the edge of the stream. "You boys alright?"

Marc looked up, peeved and drenched. "My rump's sore, and my arm is bleeding, but I reckon I'll survive."

Ted sprang up with a demented smile plastered on his wet, wayward face. "Yee-ha!" he shouted as he began ringing out his shirt, "that was one hell of a ride."

Marc turned and looked in astonishment. "And one hell of a fall!" His eyes then noticed the large, jagged rock in the middle of the creek that Mulvaney diverted them from hitting. "Look at that, you idiot! We could have been killed!"

Mulvaney angrily crossed his arms, and blustered, "Not to mention we both warned you to stop! I don't get what makes that little brain of yours tick, Teddy boy, but it sure ain't much!"

Petulantly, Ted twisted his lips as he thought: *What makes it tick? You make it tick—you tick me off!* He then gazed down and continued to wring out his shirt, only this time imagining it to be Rusty's neck. But as he did, blood, quite shockingly, began to ooze out of it! A bit spooked, Ted yelped and let go, only to realize that it was his own blood. His red-tips had cracked, once again. Relieved, Ted bent over and began rinsing his hands in the rippling water.

Meanwhile, Mulvaney hadn't lost a beat as he continued, "Besides, as I told you—you thick stubborn mule—my neck is on the line for these two danged horses. I have me a good mind to tan your hide till it bleeds like your ratty little red-tips!"

Ted gazed up, his eyes piercing like daggers. "Tan *my* hide? You're the one who tripped our horse!"

"And a mighty good thing I did—you blundering idiot! Look at them jagged rocks in the creek!"

Ted slapped the water, his face gnarling with contempt. "I would have jumped right over them…if Marc didn't cover my eyes!"

Marc rose up and blasted, "I wouldn't have covered your eyes, Ted, if you listened to me!"

Ted's upper lip furled with disgust. "Sure, right! I'm always the bad guy." Gazing deep into his brother's eyes, he snarled, "*You*; you're always the perfect one, the smart and cute, wonderful Wozniak." Then gazing up at Mulvaney, he added, "And, *you*; you're always the big, dumb brute. The one who always told my pa to tan my hide. Well, now's your chance." Ted's devious eyes had already mapped out a course of action as he boldly dared, "Of course, that's *if* you can catch me—*Billy Bourbon!*"

With that, Ted made a dash for dry ground as Mulvaney trod over to catch him. Just as Mulvaney was about to grab his shirt, Ted cupped his hand and splashed a good pint's worth of cold creek water in his face. As Rusty flinched, Ted pivoted quickly and made a beeline toward Mulvaney's horse. Before the big, red-bearded giant could react, Ted had already leapt onto a rock and sprang onto the stallion's back.

Grabbing the reins, he yelled, "I'm through with all of you! I've had it. I don't need me another pa, Rusty, and I don't need a little brother telling me what to do. Good riddance!" With a hard kick to the young Arabian's flanks, Ted pulled the reins to the right as the stallion changed direction and bolted.

Marc couldn't believe his eyes. "Ted! Stop! Come back. You'll really get in trouble this time."

Seething with anger, Rusty's lips twisted as he punched the palm of his hand. "Aw, let the spoiled rascal go! As they say, all you need is one bad apple to spoil the bushel. And he's one Macintosh I'd just love to squash!"

Marc certainly didn't think the situation was funny, but he couldn't resist laughing. "He sure is, isn't he?"

Mulvaney cracked a modest smile, his wet mustache parting from his curly beard, revealing his large amber-colored teeth. He wiped his brow rather pensively, trying to mask his inner thoughts, as he concernedly walked over to inspect the legs of the fallen mare for breaks.

Meanwhile, Marc's smile quickly vanished as he gazed down at the stream of water rushing around his ankles. He could see the golden rays of the sun breaking through the mounting gray clouds and sparkling on the rippled crests of liquid, as the yellow orb, reflecting in the water, slowly edged its way toward the rocky crests of the Appalachian Mountains. He just couldn't understand all the hardships this day had so cruelly brought upon him. How was it that just that morning everything seemed so bright, warm, and sunny, and now everything was topsy-turvy—being painfully dark, cold, and cloudy? How could life change so quickly and so profoundly? And why? As he made his way onto the pebbly soil, water squished out of the seams and holes of his muddy leather boots. His eyes gazed aimlessly at the ground as he approached Mulvaney.

"Well, it looks like we're in luck," Rusty said, somewhat relieved. "This gal seems to be fine—just a few bruises here and there, but otherwise, she's good to go!"

Marc gazed slowly up at the horse and then over at Mulvaney. "But, what, in God's name, are we going to do about Ted and Huxley's Arabian stallion?"

"Never you mind about that," Mulvaney said with quasi-confidence, "Ted may be a wild card, but he ain't no royal flush! He'll be coming home in a day or so when he ain't got nothing to eat and no place to rest his rotten little head. And as for the stallion, well, that poses a bit of a problem, but I'm betting Ted will return in a day or so."

Mulvaney straightened out the saddle, jammed his boot into the stirrup, and hauled himself up. Extending his left hand down, he said, "Now come on, Marc. Time's a wastin' and that sun will soon be setting."

Riding over the rolling hills and through the lush valleys they finally came upon the smoggy city of Pittsburgh. Off in the distance, factories churned and belched black soot as the glow of ore being smelted into steel could be seen through the string of windows that stretched across their red-bricked facades. Seemingly endless miles of hopper cars, loaded with coal, rolled slowly over the Philadelphia and Reading Rail Road's web of tracks, while black iron horses blew steam out their nostrils as they laboriously pulled the cargo to their loading docks.

As they strolled through the narrow cobbled streets, lined with brick-faced storefronts and wood-clad tenement buildings, town folk were still busy conducting transactions and loading goods onto horse-drawn carts. Cautiously, Mulvaney weaved the horse through the frenzied streams of bodies but almost hit Calvin Pendleton, the gregarious blacksmith. He was riding his favorite toy—a penny-farthing bicycle with its odd and excessively large front wheel.

Pendleton overreacted and sharply turned the awkward little handlebars, thus tipping over the tall vehicle. As he crashed to the ground, Marc didn't even notice, being lost in a gloomy fog, while Mulvaney cried out, "Pardon me, Calvin! You alright?"

Pendleton righted himself and, with a bit of difficulty, his cumbersome contraption. He then began brushing off his precious derby. "I'll live, Rusty, ole boy," he said with a chuckle. "But you put an awful nasty dent in my new bowler."

Pendleton was a colorful soul, who while relishing the capitalistic fervor of a young and restless America still had a nostalgic reverence for his old Britain. Then looking at Marc, he added, "And where, good heavens, might your pa be? I have a frightfully long list of projects stacked up, and he has shown himself to be a damned good iron worker."

Mulvaney was hoping to pass through town without much fuss for Marc's sake, but knowing that Jedrek had begun working four hours every night at Pendleton Iron Works, he had to turn his horse around.

Little Marc clutched onto Mulvaney's waist and buried his somber head into his back. His mind was elsewhere and his heart heavy.

Meanwhile, Mulvaney gazed at Pendleton with cheerless eyes. "Well, Calvin, I hate to be the bearer of bad news, but you see, there's been another explosion at the mine. And, well," Mulvaney's voice cracked, "J-Jedrek didn't m-make it."

Pendleton rubbed his partially baldhead in shock, and then placed his derby squarely on his head. "My Lord, Rusty, that's awfully dreadful news, alright." His eyes drifted over to little Marc, whose head was still buried in Mulvaney's back. "Listen, little fella, your pa spoke very highly about you, even telling me that you'd make a damned good iron worker yourself, if you want to. So, when you feel up to it, by all means, drop in on me, you hear? There's nothing better to clear the mind and soul than keeping busy with a good day's labor."

Marc turned his head slightly; revealing one eye, as he respectfully nodded, and replied with a melancholy whimper, "Much obliged, sir."

Rusty pulled the rein and spun the mare around as he gazed down at Pendleton and nodded. "That's mighty nice."

Pendleton winked and waved him on. "Sure, now you go on. And if Mrs. Wozniak needs anything—and by Jesus, I do mean anything—you let me know?"

"Will do. You're a mighty special man, Mr. Pendleton, and you make living in this crummy old town danged bearable."

Pendleton nodded in appreciation and waved him on; empathetic to the trauma little Marc was suffering.

As they trot down the street, the flickering glow of gas lampposts lit up the street. Meanwhile, 360 miles off to the east, Thomas Edison toils in his laboratory to perfect the electric light bulb and his dynamo generator, which he claims will light up America and revolutionize the world—making gaslight obsolete. Nearby, however, and off to the west, the sun had finally slipped behind Mount Washington, which only five years previously had been aptly called Coal Hill.

Amid the onset of twilight, Mulvaney spotted the Wozniak abode just up ahead. It was situated in the dankest part of Pittsburgh. The ramshackle tenements, all without plumbing, were where the majority of miners were corralled, being indentured servants of the Huxley slave machine. Surrounding these dilapidated "cell blocks" were rows of factories with large smoke stacks billowing black soot—defiling the twilight sky. The air was thick and noxious, and many a heart and lung skipped a beat or breath. Steamships and barges added their waste to the mix as they busily traversed the confluence of the Monongahela and Allegheny rivers, which surround the Pittsburgh peninsula. The city had become the crucial epicenter of activity in the heavily industrialized Midwest, and it had quickly gained the worst reputation for air quality, even surpassing the longtime industrial leader, London.

However, viewed from another set of eyes, Pittsburgh was the coal-burning firebox of America; it kept the nation's boiler fired up, as it steamed feverishly uphill in its quest to become a global dynamo. The young nation, which had suffered setbacks with a bloody Civil War, leaving over half a million dead, was just now breaking out of its Reconstructionist malaise and steaming toward a brighter future. A miraculous burst of creativity and innovation spurred capitalists to build large industrial networks, which would supply the resources needed by ambitious architects to build taller buildings with steel or vast steel-cabled suspension bridges, such as the Brooklyn Bridge (which presently was two years away from completion). It would likewise supply scientists such as Edison, Westinghouse, Tesla and Bell with wire, glass, rubber, and metal for their electrical facilities or new telephone system, which the city of Pittsburgh had also just been wired with, albeit only for those who could afford it. It was a luminous time of great excitement and miraculous wonders, and capitalists had little restraints to hold them back.

All this, however, mattered little to Rusty and the far larger number of laborers. They were the mere cogs and grease in this massive machine; toiling away day and night to keep the engine running, only to be cast out like refuse once spent.

Mulvaney tethered the spotted mare to a post, and then escorted little Marc to his first-floor apartment.

Marc looked up at the tall woolly-faced pillar for support, while Rusty placed one hand on his shoulder and opened the door with the other. As Marc slipped through the weathered threshold, Stan came wheeling towards them in his makeshift wheelchair. His father had built the contraption out of a standard oak chair—cutting off portions of the legs and mounting on a set of iron wheels he had deftly crafted at Pendleton's iron shop.

"Marcus, what are you doing home so early?"

Marc stood frozen like a chunk of ice, yet the burning pain inside began to melt his cold façade—a tear dripping down his face.

Before Stan could say another word, their mother came running into the small and sparsely furnished room. "You were supposed to work a double-shift today. I hope you're not being docked pay? Are you hurt or sick?"

Marc remained mute as tears streamed down his little cheeks. Sophia curiously looked up at Mulvaney; she didn't like his expression either, nor did she like the looks of their soiled clothes—Marc's being wet, torn and muddy.

"Sophia," Rusty stammered, "I t-think you ought to s-sit down."

Sophia's eyes widened as one hand covered her heart and the other her gapping mouth. She mumbled, "Where's Jedrek? And Tasso?"

Marc ran into her arms, burying his head into her chest. "Momma," he whimpered, "papa is dead. And Tasso, he ran off."

Sophia staggered as Mulvaney rushed over and guided her and Marc gently onto the worn, floral-printed sofa.

Meanwhile, Stan screamed, "What!? This can't be! Please, God, tell me this can't be?"

As Sophia bellowed a mournful cry, her sons joined the heart-wrenching dirge. Stan wheeled himself closer, and the three hugged and wept uncontrollably. Their hearts were crushed by the cruel loss, while their minds couldn't imagine what their lot in life would now be. Rusty did his best to console his dear friends, while the clanking chain and gear of the cuckoo clock ticked for an hour. The boys began reminiscing about their father, while Sophia gazed at the small and blurry photo she had of her and Jedrek in her heart-shaped locket. It was when they had first arrived in America for a new and better life. Her eyes then surveyed the small room; the used sofa they had bought from their neighbor Janet, who had moved when her husband died last year at the mine; the crooked and peeling walls in dire need of paint; the portrait of Chopin, Jedrek's favorite Polish composer; the potbelly stove that Jedrek repaired, and the cracked front door, which whistled in winter when the harsh, cold nor'easters came howling down from Canada. Her ears then drew her eyes to the noisy yet beautifully crafted Swiss cuckoo clock—a family heirloom that Jedrek received from his father before leaving Poland. She thought of how it accompanied them on their long journey across the Atlantic and precisely counted their eight years here in America, from their joyous and hopeful landing right up to the very second Jedrek died in the mine.

Mulvaney noticed Sophia looking at all their meager possessions, deeply lost in thought. Rusty happened to be just as rusty on financial and legal matters as his nickname, but he knew how other people had fared after suffering losses, and he posed the question. "Well, Sophia, I reckon the state is gonna come looking to get their share of Jedrek's possessions. I heard they take an arm full."

Sophia awoke from her hazy daydream with startling vigor. "Over my dead body!" she retorted irritably as she blew her nose. Wiping her face with a white handkerchief, edged with lace, she gained some composure, and continued, "Although I do need to check up on the laws. My little sister Filomena attended Vassar College, and she keeps me well informed of such goings on." Then with a proud sparkle in her tear-filled eye, she added, "Did you know, she's an activist, and now works with Elizabeth Stanton and Susan B. Anthony?"

Mulvaney's ruddy face turned milky white as he shrugged his hulky shoulders. "Nope, but to be quite honest, Sophia, I ain't never heard of them two gals."

Sophia shook her head. "Never heard of them? My dear Lord, where have you been, besides in a dirty mine or a filthy saloon!?"

Sophia was unpredictable, sometimes gentle, intelligent and loving, and other times explosive and unwittingly sarcastic. It irked her how Rusty and so many other men wasted their lives away without trying to expand their horizons, or do something productive beyond their admittedly hard slave labor. She explained to Rusty how Stanton, Anthony and her sister were extremely vocal with their Women's Christian Temperance Union, which in addition to campaigning for women's rights, happened to advocate outlawing liquor and closing down saloons. Something, she believed, Rusty should pay heed to—not out of cruelty, but out of concern.

As Mulvaney smirked, Sophia's passion was again rising. "As you know, Rusty, our government has fallen dreadfully short of delivering rights to us women. It's appalling how they only recognize our husbands. Yet, once they die, they fly in like vultures to devour our possessions as if *they* were the widows. It's like we women don't even exist!"

Rusty could see that Sophia was going to boil, and knew she often would go on long-winded tangents in her fits of rage. And Sophia did just that, as she blustered, "And for that matter, they even treat us Italians like dirt! My sister Filomena and her friends have been reviled in New York City and Boston as dark-skinned infestations that are despoiling the rich Anglo-Saxon heritage of this country. Even the newspapers liken us Italians to dimwitted grease monkeys!" As Rusty tried to get a word in to calm her down,

Sophia continued with animated gestures, punching the air, "And did I ever tell you that my brother Mario had been beaten to a pulp by those animals at Tammany?" As Rusty barely shook his head, she went on, "Well, he was. He was only sixteen at the time. They broke his nose and ribs with sticks. And do you know why?" Again Rusty only had a second to shake his head, no, as Sophia added, "Because the *Dago* tried to sell vegetables on the wrong street, or what I like to call Anglo-Saxon Lane! My poor brother returned to Italy after that flogging."

Rusty thought he had an opening. "Well, my—"

"And," Sophia trampled onward, "they even had the gall to take their Anglo-Saxon axe to my family's name! No sooner had they arrived on the shores of Manhattan, did the clerk chop off the vowel and disfigure our name. What was once Parselli is now Parsell! And they have mutilated every Italian name in the history books—as Petrarca became Petrarch, or the great explorers Cristoforo Colombo became Christopher Columbus and Giovanni Caboto became John Cabot. It's utterly insulting!" Sophia bellowed. Before Rusty could mention how his Irish Catholic kin were currently being slapped with anti-immigration laws due to their massive influx after the potato famine, Sophia stood up with a huff and patted Marc and Stan on their backs. "Go on, I am upset, and there is no need for you boys to hear my tirades." Gazing at Marc, she said, "Why don't you go clean up." Then looking at Stan, she added, "And you, Stanislaw, continue cutting up those peppers and onions in the kitchen."

Stan rolled his eyes with a mixture of embarrassment and humiliation—his kitchen chores not being the manly role he had envisioned for his life's calling. His once rock-hard, coal-miner's torso was now just a frail frame, with one boney twig of a leg, and one missing limb. All that remained of his former self, as far as he was concerned, were his muscular arms, which now had the duty of propelling his decaying body along with the heavy iron-wheeled-contraption his father crafted for his useless carcass. Irritably, Stan began wheeling himself toward the kitchen.

Meanwhile, Marc gazed up at his mother. "Pa said he doesn't want us to use those names anymore, Momma."

Sophia nodded. "Yes, I know. His wish was for your boys to blend in, and I suppose we ought to respect his wishes. But as much as I want to see you become a full-blooded American, I also fear what the end result might be."

Sophia gazed pensively into space. She knew Marc had to assimilate in order to be successful in America, yet she also knew that, oftentimes, maintaining a connection to one's roots is as important as retaining a bond with one's family. There are unique histories and assets in one's past that shape an individual, which allows them to bring new ideas to the table, or, in this case, add to America's diverse melting pot. The British had been remarkably successful at colonizing North America, yet they failed miserably in maintaining their colony. Sophia was an avid reader and her father and sister both helped to feed her insatiable appetite for knowledge. As such, she knew that the Romans maintained their empire for over a thousand years, and it was precisely because they welcomed all other ethnic and religious groups, and gave their acquired provinces all the glories that Rome itself had, namely forums, marketplaces, immense public baths, sports arenas and, of course, citizenship. Despite the imperial nature of the Empire, it had unquestionably been the most civilized and liberal beacon of hope in its day, for outside its borders were hordes of savage barbarians without culture, who only sought warfare and reveled in lawlessness. And that America was inciting ethnic conflict with bigoted snobbery and exclusionary laws, as well as exploiting its working class, was a powder keg waiting to explode.

Meanwhile, Sophia was a bit disillusioned by the so-called riches to be found in the fledgling nation called America. She had come from a fairly wealthy family that nurtured education, her father being a history teacher. Sophia had even learned several languages, all spoken fluently, and had lived a comfortable life. Having met up with Jedrek, who was touring Italy, akin to Lord Byron, they had fallen in love and married. They moved back to his native Poland, yet lack of work forced them and their young family to make the bold voyage across the Atlantic, seeking the riches in the New World that so many Europeans spoke of and desperately sought. The hysterically heralded Gold Rush some 30 years ago had blinded many poor slobs to leave behind family and friends for a chance at sifting out a fortune, only to leave the vast majority broke while others only found their gravesites. Sophia was also well aware of how barbaric America could be, knowing firsthand how 8,000 Italian children had been kidnapped and sold in America at private auctions for anywhere from $100 to $500 each. She had even read the article about this dirty racket, which appeared in *The New York Times* eight years ago in 1873, just as they were landing on America's shore.

But, more importantly, during those past eight years, Sophia had witnessed her husband being treated no better than an animal himself, working long hours at a grueling job for crumbs, while fat gluttonous tycoons leaned back and laughed over their lavish dining tables. Jedrek's death now shocked her like a lightning bolt to the head; galvanizing all that was wrong with America. She always had high hopes for her sons, and knew the importance of not repeating the mistakes of history. As a young girl, living in the Neapolitan village of Sorrento, Sophia's father had taught her well, and it stuck hard in her mind and soul. Moreover, the fact that her rich heritage boasted of so many great achievements by so many brilliant minds is what prompted her to name two of her sons after famous Italic figures. Torquato Tasso was a 16th century genius from Sorrento who was now one of the most widely read poets in modern day Europe. Tasso had achieved fame in his own day, yet had tragically succumbed to mental illness, suffering torments for years. Only a few days prior to his receiving the highest honor "King of Poets" by the Pope, Tasso tragically died. His tale inspired many artists during the 19th century, including Lord Byron and the famous Hungarian composer Franz Liszt, who created two powerful symphonic poems, which sang of Tasso's triumphs and tragedies.

Meanwhile, Marcus Aurelius was the renowned Roman Emperor who also happened to be the greatest philosopher of his day. His profound words and valiant deeds held the Empire together as it suffered endless waves of barbaric incursions. Sophia had long wished for Marcus to go off to college and become that wise philosopher—one who could walk the halls of government and rectify these grave injustices. But now it seemed her entire world and bountiful dreams, along with those of her children, had all been horrifically squashed and brutally ground to pulp. With a sad reflective frown, Sophia now realized that little Marc would have to be shackled to the mine, slaving like her husband had to make ends meet. Her vexed mind then suddenly realized, for the first time, how her son Tasso painfully mirrored his namesake, being prone to misfortune. She hadn't given the tragedies of Tasso's life as much consideration as his literary triumphs, and she now felt superstitiously guilty. Yet, she still believed that somewhere in her son's troubled little mind he, too, could rise up to gain respectability for something. Just what that something was, however, eluded her, as Rusty's voice shattered her thoughts, "Sophia! Are you alright?"

Sophia shook her head. "Oh, why, yes. Yes, of course. Excuse me." She looked around half dazed, not realizing that Marc had left the room long ago. She gazed back at Rusty. "What were you saying?"

Mulvaney empathetically took her hand and gently escorted her to the double-hung window (its six panes of crown glass being remnants of the earlier 1790s structure, which Archibald Huxley had no intentions of updating). Gazing through the distorted circles of glass, Mulvaney pointed to the Pendleton Iron Works building down at the far end of the street. "Cal said if there's anything you need, anything at all, just let him know." As Sophia nodded, rather mechanically, Mulvaney added, "And it appears he took a liking to Marc. I think the boy might even get himself a good job, if he wants it."

Sophia gazed up at his hazel eyes with a look of unshakable will as she snarled through her clenched teeth, "Oh, he'll want it! Believe me." Then, as if fire were injected in her veins, she spat, "I'm through with Huxley and his cursed coal mine. He's taken my son's leg, and now my husband's life, he'll never rob me of anything again!"

Mulvaney had never gotten used to Sophia's quick mood changes and, once again, was caught off guard by her volatile flare up.

Sophia, once more, looked out the window, her eyes shifting feverishly to the left and right. "So, tell me, where do you think Tasso ran off to?"

Clumsily, Rusty shrugged his huge shoulders. "Ain't got a clue. But you can bet he'll be right back, mighty quick, as soon as his little stomach starts crying for momma's home cooking!"

Sophia's eyes remained glued to the horizon. "Actually, Tasso has run away before; once for ten days. I grant you, he may not be the smartest or strongest little fellow, but he does have spunk."

Mulvaney smiled. "That he has! Along with a nasty attitude and foul mouth."

Sophia turned and peered right into Mulvaney's skull with her blaring brown eyes. "Knowing at his age that I'd be slammed in a dark, filthy cave and forced to dig and slog the rest of my life for pennies a day would make *me* pretty darn ornery, too!"

Mulvaney's head jerked back as he said with a chuckle, "Indeed it would! And I'd be willing to bet it would make you a hell-of-a-lot more than just ornery. More like *lethal!*"

Sophia actually managed to crack a smile as Mulvaney added, "I can see mighty clearly where Marc gets his brains and Ted his hot-head. All from one, two-sided source!"

A reflective gleam sparkled in her eye, recalling how her father used to point up to Mount Vesuvius and say, "Sophia, my darling, you are like that mountain—most often beautiful and intriguing, yet, in rare moments, ugly and terrifying."

Sophia looked up at Mulvaney. "Yes, my papa had said that was because I was a Gemini."

Rusty's bushy brows pinched. "I thought you were Italian?"

Sophia chuckled. "No, no. Gemini is a sign of the Zodiac. You know—astrology!"

Mulvaney squinted, perplexed and somewhat embarrassed. "Uh, yeah, sure—" he uttered, trying to mask his ignorance. But then, by a stroke of luck, a recollection came flowing into his rusty head, "Ah, yeah, ain't that got something to do with the stars looking like animals and crazy stuff like that?"

Sophia nodded politely. "Yes. Just like how people call you Rusty because of your red traits, ancient people believed the stars had some say as to how we were made, giving each of us that were born in the same month similar traits and, likewise, a specific name. Yet these zodiac signs tell us about much deeper traits than just our looks, Rusty, things that exceed what the eye can see."

Rusty smiled as his head bobbed. "Ah, yeah, that's right. I think old man Homer talks about this nonsense, too. I mean, how do little flickering lights in the sky have the smarts to control things all the way down here?"

Sophia smiled. "Well, astrology is based on a lot of guess work, Rusty. But then again, so is religion. How do we really know that Jesus rose from the dead, or healed the blind? Were those ancient scribes honest witnesses, fallible mortals, or even blind fanatics? And how can the Trinity physically exist or, like those crazy little stars, control things all the way down here?"

"I'm not a religious man, Sophia," Rusty said straight-faced, "but that's the Word of the Bible. That's dangerous talk, what you're saying."

"Perhaps it is," Sophia replied. "But I'll tell you what *is* dangerous—that damned coal mine! And I intend to look into this mess and get some answers, along with retrieving Jedrek's body. My husband deserves a decent burial."

Rusty hung his head, a tear blurring his vision. "Indeed he does. He was a good man, your husband—honest, brave, and hardworking." Looking back up into her eyes, he added, "I can see Jedrek's spirit in your little Marc, too, I can."

Unexpectedly, tears streamed out Sophia's eyes as her fiery will gave way to her tender, grief-stricken heart. Her trembling hands covered her face. "Yes, Marcus, for as long as I can remember, was his favorite. How Jedrek could feel that way, I don't know. Lord knows, I could never pick just one myself; I love them all the same. But there *was* a special bond between those two."

Mulvaney was at a loss for words. Uncomfortably, he gazed at the floor.

Sophia wiped her face with her handkerchief and blew her nose. Her face, however, once again, began its typical Gemini transformation—turning from tender grief back to fiery rage. "Do you realize this is the third explosion in seven months!?" she said, her eyes ablaze. "Christ! Funerals are becoming more popular around here than baptisms. And Archibald Huxley is to blame. He's a reckless and ruthless monster!"

"I agree!" a voice rang out behind them.

As they spun around, there was little Marc, still filthy and unwashed, yet his face was stern and radiating resolve as he marched to his mother's side.

"Why didn't you clean up?" Sophia asked with paternal gravity.

"Momma, I had more important things to do. I might as well tell you. Pa's dying wish was that I should be head of the family."

Sophia smiled affectionately as she gently stroked his hair and replied with a touch of condescension, "My dear, you are only twelve years old. Furthermore, you are the youngest in this household. I will handle such matters. Therefore, sweetie—"

"*Therefore*, you are disobeying Pa's *will!*" Marc interjected, commandingly, "and the *law!* And by doing so you will jeopardize our estate and inheritance. Widows get practically nothing under the law! Yet with me as the executor, I might be able to work some loopholes to our advantage."

Sophia and Rusty recoiled at the youth's erudite remarks as Sophia grabbed both his shoulders and stared deep into his eyes. "Marc, where did you learn those big words?"

Marc's face suddenly had a different look to it. Sophia had seen Marc act mature beyond his years in many instances, but he now looked like a pint-sized man with unshakable determination—like a mini-Napoleon, if anyone could possibly be much smaller.

"Momma," he said, "I was down the street talking to Mr. Pendleton. Oddly enough, pa's last words were that I must visit Cal—yet he never finished the word. But then I realized it wasn't a place, like California, it was a name— *Calvin*, Calvin Pendleton. And it is a good thing I did go, because not only did Cal give me a job, but his lawyer, Mr. Donnellson, happened to be there. Anyhow, that gentleman gave me some very good advice, Momma."

Sophia's face lit up with a grin as she hugged and kissed her little prodigy.

Marc smiled as he looked up at Rusty, who winked, and then back at his mother. "You see, Mr. Donnellson told me that widows must surrender two-thirds of the estate and one-half their personal property to the government."

Sophia gasped. "Dear Lord! That's utterly insane. Are you sure?"

"That's what he said. You can ask him yourself tomorrow."

Rusty nodded as he looked down at Marc. "I think you might be right. I heard that's what happened to Kate McCrery when Jack died last December in the mine. They came like a thieving pack of bandits and collected the lion's share of everything Jack owned." He turned his gaze to Sophia as he scratched his beard. "I recall years ago how Jack even sold Kate's dress to buy himself a good bottle of rum one night. Feisty ole Kate tried to make a court case out of it, but the judge ruled that she belonged to Jack, and it was in his right to sell whatever he owned."

Sophia snarled, "Do you see what I mean? This country treats us women like mere possessions, no better than a piece of clothing to be used or abused; however a man chooses. And it won't stand!"

"Well, Sophia," Rusty retorted, "women may be treated like clothes, but damn, Huxley treats us men like dung! Anyone who slacks off or makes a mistake gets a trouncing, docked pay, or even fired, and every single one of us faces danger every day of our lives in his stinking mine!"

"You're absolutely right," Sophia replied as she refocused her thoughts. "Huxley is just a cold-hearted brute! He seems to care more about his precious pet, Rex, than his workers' lives and safety." Sophia's eyes oscillated as her mind reeled and fed her fury. "They say a dog is a man's best friend, but I think *both are dogs!*" Gazing down at Marc, she added, "We had better speak to that lawyer tomorrow— not only about our personal affairs, but also about seeing to it that that mangy, no-good mutt doesn't get away with this. We must stand up and do something!"

Marc nodded firmly, his confidence further boosted by his inclusion in managing the family's affairs.

Mulvaney interjected, "And if I can help in any way, I'll be at your side quicker than a jackrabbit."

Sophia turned and placed her hand on Rusty's arm in appreciation. "Thank you, Rusty," she replied thoughtfully. Yet her face, once again, began to morph with rage as she seethed, "But mark my words, Huxley *will* pay for this great loss, one way or another!"

3

The New Huxley Mansion

June 30, 1881

Earlier the same day, and some 350 miles east of Pittsburgh, Archibald Desmond Huxley had been at the construction site of his new summer mansion on the north shore of Long Island. Archibald is a prime example of the other side of life in America, and he is currently engaged in yet another extravagant project. The beautiful hilly coastline of the island had enamored him after taking a sojourn there last year with his rich friends. Only Bayard Cutting and Vanderbilt, with his Idle Hour hunting retreat, had built Tudors on the south shore, while the other moguls procrastinated about building on the remote island. Huxley, on the other hand, was the pioneer who now blazed a northern trail, which in 30 years time would become known as the famous Gold Coast of Long Island. Vanderbilt, Frick, Coe and other industrial tycoons would all in due time carve their splendid estates into the hilly terrain, leaving their indelible mark of lavish opulence as each tried to outdo the other.

As carpenters sawed and fastened huge dental trim moldings, and masons laid their assortment of colored travertine and imported marble, Archibald's wife Penelope was working her own magic. She was fitted in her new pink taffeta dress with a bustle; a revived fashion statement that was now back in vogue. The protruding bustle drastically exaggerated Penelope's buttocks, looking more like a caboose, while her tight corset accentuated her narrow waist, curved hips, and otherwise average breast, thus achieving that utopian hourglass figure. Penelope was endowed with exceptionally attractive features, had the royal pedigree of the Stuart clan in her Scottish blood, and was well educated at the highly selective all-women's Wellesley College. But, most importantly, she knew it, as her haughty air could be so odious at times as to make even the most learned and refined scholar roll their eyes.

Penelope walked up the unfinished grand flight of marble stairs, alongside Philippe Dutoit, a prominent purveyor of fine art. Dutoit was a petite man with a mousy voice, round spectacles, a thin mustache with curled-up waxed edges, and a well-manicured goatee, whose Madison Avenue gallery catered to the elite. Arriving on the top landing, Philippe placed his hefty valise down as they both gazed up at the large blank wall before them.

"You see, Madame Huxley," he squeaked, "this spot is the focal point—the most vital. So, I strongly suggest a Renoir for this magnificent location. His works are the rave of Paris and the world—naturally, along with Monet and Degas."

Penelope shook her head. "Philippe, Renoir's works are indeed avant-garde and very pretty, as are those of Monet and Degas, but I wish to have a painting that will amaze and arrest every guest that enters the main entrance below. Those new impressionists may be the talk of Paris today, but I want artwork that is technically supreme and timeless."

Penelope swung her arm around, pointing at all the architectural details being constructed. "As you can see, my house is designed on the ancient Greco-Roman order; consequently, those loose dabs of paint simply do not fit the refined atmosphere of Huxley Manor. The artists I seek are Alma-Tadema, Leighton, Gerome and my absolute favorite, William Bouguereau."

An expression of resignation etched itself on Philippe's face. "Madame, I do not confide my personal opinion to many people, for my job is to sell the works of artists who can supply the demand. In other words, Bouguereau is indeed highly praised and eagerly sought in Paris today, but—" Philippe paused as several construction workers passed by them. As they trampled down the stairs with hammers and chisels in hand, he peered left and right to confirm their privacy, and continued, "But *maître* Bouguereau requires a bare minimum of one full month to create a single masterpiece. Meanwhile, Monet and Degas, for example, are both capable of executing four to eight paintings in the same time!"

Penelope shook her head. "My dear Philippe, only the most naïve cannot see the difference between high art and décor, and, unfortunately, too many are easily swept up in this degenerate craze of praising and collecting these substandard crafts. I'll be the first to admit that I relish being at the forefront of patronizing the avant-garde, but I daresay that I am far too educated to fall prey to such whimsy."

Philippe smiled. "Yes, Madame," he said as he bowed his head. "I can see that you are a most educated woman, hence my humble and honest confession." As his eyes reconnected with hers, he eliminated all his usual histrionics of salesmanship, and continued, "I run a business, Madame Huxley, and as you surely know, those who can supply me with a fast and steady flow of art are the ones that allow me to amass the most profit. Thus, that explains why all my peers have rallied so hard to promote these impressionistic artists. Their works are indeed pretty to behold, and do have a place in the world of art, but the impressionists are simply nowhere near the caliber of all those fine artists you've mentioned." Philippe licked his fingers and twisted the waxy ends of his pointy moustache as he added, "Four to eight sales per month versus one is simple arithmetic that any child learns in grade school, so, please, excuse my capitalistic bent. May I rectify my faux-pas by showing you a fine selection of works by Bouguereau?"

Having won her ground and made her point, Penelope nodded, as Philippe eagerly snapped open his valise and pulled out his Bouguereau portfolio. As his toothpick arms struggled to hold and open the large book, he gazed at her, his eyes dancing and eager to reveal more of his secrets. "Please, Madame, do not mention what I am about to say to anyone. But just last week, I had presented Monet and Degas with a most pointed and prophetic question. Namely, whom did *they* think would be hailed as the greatest artist of our age in a hundred years from now? Can you guess the response of both of these great artists?"

Penelope's face remained just as fixed as the imported Carrara marble she stood on as she replied dryly, "William-Adolphe Bouguereau."

Philippe's plump, jovial expression deflated. "How could you have guessed? Even my most erudite colleagues all suggested Renoir or Monet himself."

With a partial smile, Penelope replied, "That was simply the correct answer. Furthermore, talented artists can always recognize their superiors. That Monet and Degas were so honest to admit as much is the truly miraculous part of your little secret." Penelope lifted her nose slightly, her tone now professorial. "I do believe that true talent always rises to the top—eventually. Do you realize that Columbus was overshadowed by Vespucci and countless others, and was forgotten for two whole centuries?"

Philippe shook his head gently in the negative as Penelope added with a haughty twang, "And Wolfgang Amadeus Mozart was likewise overshadowed by Antonio Salieri and his peers during his lifetime, only to be recognized as the brightest talent of his day several decades after his death."

Philippe now recognized that he had met more than his match. With a nervous twitch, he nodded, as if knowing such information, and pointed his finger at the first photograph in the catalog.

Penelope looked down. She shook her head and waved her hand as Philippe turned the page. Philippe turned seven more pages, receiving a similar response, until finally, she stopped his hand. Penelope's eyes widened as she pointed obsessively at Bouguereau's *Birth of Venus*.

"Ah, yes," Philippe said, his eyebrows rising with admiration, "the master completed that just two years ago. It's a beauty, indeed. This colorless photograph does it no justice, for the original is a sight to behold." Yet, his face suddenly radiated concern as he added, "However, it has many collectors clamoring for it, Madame."

"I *must* have it!" Penelope demanded in utter rapture. "It's divine!" she said, spinning around and looking up at the vacant wall. Flanking each side of the whitewashed void stood tall roman-styled columns with Corinthian capitals, majestically framing the all-important focal point. She gazed back at Philippe. "It's simply perfect for this spot! When can I get it?"

Trepidation afflicted Philippe's already mousy voice, which now leapt to a stuttering shrill, "W-well, it may have already been s-sold, Madame Huxley. But, I will—"

"You WILL get it for me!? Correct, Monsieur Dutoit?" Penelope insisted with a bewitching grin.

Philippe couldn't resist her sudden charm and effervescent smile. Being a lover of beautifully crafted works of art, as surely Penelope's face was, Philippe blurted spontaneously, "I will indeed do my best to secure this lovely piece for a most lovely lady."

Penelope patted Philippe's shoulder several times. "I know I can count on you," she said, as she wiped the golden-red locks out of her eyes. "And price is not a concern, so I'll hear of no excuses. I shall not be outbid by *anyone!* Is that understood? And that includes John Pierpont Morgan!"

Philippe looked at her most warily. "But Madame, Monsieur Morgan is proving to be a formidable collector of fine art." He swallowed hard. "Moreover, is Monsieur Huxley aware of this limitless ceiling you now propose and place at my disposal?"

Penelope smiled as her index finger rose vertically to buckle her luscious lips closed. Then slipping her finger away, she whispered, "That will be our little secret!" With a wink, she lifted up her long and fluffy dress, turned, and descended the stairs with an ecstatic bounce in her step.

Left standing at the top of the landing, Philippe closed his eyes and began stroking his v-shaped goatee. The thoughts of the difficult task before him and the very real prospect of failure were not pleasant. Nor was spending a lofty sum of money that Archibald was not privy to, for his ruthless reputation was well-known.

Meanwhile, Penelope skipped through the busy foyer, teaming with painters and finishers, and exited the unfinished mansion. With a confirmed sense of prowess powering her every step, Penelope floated over the lawn (strewn with a dizzying array of debris, cement vats and busy masons), looking like a self-propelled mannequin as her umbrellalike dress hid her moving legs while she oddly glided over the uneven terrain. Reaching her final destination on the rear lawn, Penelope stood beside Charles McKim, of the fledgling architectural firm McKim, Mead and White. They had just built the Newport Casino, which while not offering gambling did feature a billiards room, dancing hall, and space for other activities, including the new American pastime for the elite: the competitive sport of lawn tennis. The casino even held the National Championships, soon to be called the U.S. Open.

Penelope relished the sport, and now pointed to McKim's plans, waving her finger to move the proposed fountain and gardens several yards to the west in order to accommodate the suitable lawn space required for the game.

McKim shook his baldhead, while his bushy mustache flapped resolutely with every syllable, "Mrs. Huxley, please. I understand your concern for a recreation area, but the fountain and gardens *must* be directly behind the rear exit. Symmetry is key to the purity of your mansion's aesthetics."

After having put Philippe in his place, Penelope was in no mood to be challenged, and since McKim and company had yet to begin what would become a stellar career, she questioned his judgment, "Charles, as it is, you persuaded me—quite craftily, may I add—to approve this Beaux-Arts structure of yours, when every other new estate I see is either a Tudor or Queen Anne. This Greco-Roman order, which you claim will hold thrall over my peers, is indeed a gamble, especially for a Stuart with royal Scottish blood. However, I can certainly recognize the style's perfection, historical impact and longevity. Therefore, as I told you, this dwelling must be grand and magnificent—it must not incite the slightest bit of mockery. Nay, it must crush the ambitions of the weak while also plaguing our formidable rivals with doubt as to whether or not they could even come close to achieving the magnificence of Huxley Manor."

Astutely, McKim switched his thinking from architectural maven to consummate salesman. "I assure you, Madame, that your three-story Beaux-Arts palace, sporting 70 glorious rooms, will be the envy of all. But the fountain and gardens must be centrally located. Look for yourself," he said as he pointed to the huge set of double doors that were symmetrically flanked by a row of towering fluted-columns. "The nine-piece sculpted fountain, out here, featuring Neptune at the center, surrounded by two horses and six dolphins, will be seen by all your guests as they dine inside. And once the double doors are open, they will have access to this beautiful, circular basin sporting a most impressive re-creation of Roman antiquity." He then stepped sideways and pointed back to the horizon. "Then as your guests round the fountain they can walk down the central path that will recede some 600 feet back to the spectacular shoreline, which overlooks the Long Island Sound." McKim pointed back down to his plans and directed her vision with his moving index finger. "We will then construct a square grid with perpendicular pathways that will branch off every 50 feet. Lush topiary gardens with all sorts of exotic flowers, plants and shrubs will be planted in such a way as to give even Hadrian's Villa, that grand archetype of all others, a resolute trouncing."

Penelope appreciated McKim's enthusiastic vision; yet her uppity nature simply dictated that she score at least one victory of her own. "Very well, Charles, have it your way with the centrally located fountain, but I simply abhor a square, geometric grid for something so natural as a garden. I would much prefer to see a series of winding paths."

McKim's brief smile—in regards to his victory over the fountain—faded quickly as his fastidious mind scrambled to find a solution to Penelope's chaotic request—which now shattered his crystal clear and mathematically precise vision. His eyes oscillated feverishly, searching his mind for several seconds, until finally stopping. "Wait! I have a better idea!" he exclaimed. "How about a labyrinth?"

Penelope's left eyebrow rose, her mind seething over McKim's phrase 'I have a better idea.' Such insolence, she thought, that he, a mere scribbler of lines, could trump every idea her lofty head conceived. This brash, little hired hand was now becoming most intolerable.

McKim, however, could read a face like a book, and Penelope's unhappy story was exceedingly succinct and blunt. Quickly adjusting his delivery, McKim continued *his* story, yet with a bit of Penelopian drama, "Yes, *your* labyrinth will be the talk of the town, Penelope. I can see it now in the *New York Tribune*—'Huxley Manor slays viewers with its utter magnificence, while its lush labyrinthine garden devours stragglers.' It will be an absolute triumph— worthy of Caesar himself! In fact, I can even envision the headline: 'Penelope came, saw, and conquered!'"

Penelope could not resist being amused, and actually cracked a slight smile, while McKim continued his minstrel show. "You said you wish to decimate or dishearten your rivals. Correct Mrs. Huxley?" As she nodded and playfully twisted her lips, he continued, "So what better way to get them lost in thought about how grand your palace is than to get them lost in a magnificent maze?"

Penelope nodded somewhat reluctantly and waved her alabaster hand. "Oh, very well! A labyrinth it shall be. Just so long as it is not that dreadfully boring square grid you first proposed. That was simply hideous!"

McKim bowed his head with a sagacious grin, recognizing her need to stick a thorn in her olive branch. Feeling a bit magnanimous, McKim looked up and asked,

"So where would you like me to put the open lawn space for tennis?"

Penelope looked at him with guarded eyes.

"No, no! Seriously," McKim implored, "I shall place it anywhere your heart desires."

Without hesitation, she replied, "Fine. Then place it on the roof?"

McKim squinted as another rush of anxiety gripped him—his face now marred with trepidation. "You don't truly expect me to lay grass on your roof, Mrs. Huxley, do you?"

Penelope smiled, having duped the brilliant draftsman. "I suppose I could force you to come up with a workable solution to achieve such a fanciful idea, but no, Mr. McKim," she pointed to her right, and added, "just over there beyond the imported Linden tree will be sufficient. However, it is imperative that the ground be level."

"Well, I'm a level-headed man, Mrs. Huxley," McKim said as he gleefully slipped his pencil behind the top of his ear. "So you may count on that!"

With congenial smiles on both their faces, McKim nodded politely as she blinked her acceptance. Penelope was about to take her leave, when he added, "Oh, yes, I've been meaning to tell Mr. Huxley. The imported marble sculptures from Florence for the terrace will be delayed about three weeks. Furthermore," he said with a relapse of anxiety, "the mahogany bar for his recreation room went a tad bit over budget. The hand-carved figures of buffalos cost us $350 more than anticipated."

Penelope's smile vanished as her nostrils flared with rage. "Who does this artisan think he is? Rodin!" Her voice climbed another octave. "Tell him that he can keep the damned piece of wood for all I care!"

"Mrs. Huxley," McKim pleaded nervously, "we cannot back out now, we commissioned him for this custom crafted work of art. Furthermore, it is not just wood, but includes a sculpted granite top, brass railings and bar mounts, which are in the shape of buffalo heads, and ample shelving to hold over 200 bottles of liquor. It truly is an exquisite piece. Perhaps you should see it first, before making such a rash decision. I'm sure you'll agree that this bar is worth every extra penny."

"I'll drink to that," came Archibald's reply as he rode up on his black stallion, decked out in his flamboyant hunting gear.

Archibald cut a striking figure; having served under General George Custer in the Civil War, he adopted his idol's flare for self-promotion and flashy attire. At that time, Archie even tried to claim credit for shooting and killing J.E.B Stuart in the Battle of Yellow Tavern, seeking his own quick rise in rank and quest for fame. However, John Huff proved that it was indeed his shot that killed the famous Confederate cavalryman and received his rightful acclaim. Archie had even worn his golden wavy locks very long, like his brave yet reckless commander, but after Custer's slaughter at Little Bighorn in 1876, Archie cut his prematurely gray hair short and kept it neatly combed— making the fiery coal tycoon look more like a doctor than an avid big-game hunter, despite the fact that his prey today was duck.

Penelope pivoted around, not pleased with her husband's flippant salute to wasteful spending. "Archie, you must be drunk! We can find a dozen artisans that would jump at this project. I don't care how many buffalos it features, it is only a bar for Christ's sake! I'm absolutely befuddled. You squeeze and save every penny out of every dollar earned, and you ration out those pennies to your miners just as carefully, yet you are now willing to allow a little insignificant flea like this walk all over you?"

Archibald released one of his many bellicose cackles, this one with a sarcastic bite. "My dear, Penny. I certainly would not spend a penny more for a nagging wench like you, but when it comes to my toys, there is little I would not pay to possess them."

Penelope's face turned red, her pride and dignity almost too deeply wounded to respond. Yet she knew Archie all too well. He was never to be challenged in public, tolerating her rebuttals, only sometimes, in private.

It was very much a man's world, especially in America. The old stories Penelope's mother relayed to her about their feisty female Scottish ancestors had a markedly different flavor to them, being that their lineage stretched back to Queen Mary of Scots. Yet, knowing of her relative's bloody demise at the hands of Queen Elizabeth, she opted to use her head rather than lose it, so Penelope demurred. "You're a cad, Archie. An utter cad!" With a huff, she added, "As it is, you have how many of those disgusting buffalo heads hanging around, so who needs carvings of them, too?" Then waving her hand, she added, "But do what you please!"

Irritated, Penelope turned and began to march away as Archie retorted brutishly, "I *always* do what I please. Remember that—my dear, petulant Penny!" Then with a final dose of venom, the ruthless brute spat, "So, tend to your fineries or frilly décor, or better yet the kitchen. But I will *not* tolerate an Ellen Sherman in *my* house!"

Archie's last remark was in reference to the wife of the great Union General William Tecumseh Sherman. Despite the general's prowess of ruling the battlefield, he was but a mere private at home, being under the firm command of his wife Ellen.

McKim was utterly taken aback by Archibald's crude manhandling of his wife. Nervously, he looked up at the mounted barbarian—sporting a large hunting knife strapped to his waist and two rifles mounted on his horse—and asked, "So, I take it that means you will pay the extra $350?"

Huxley's eyes peered over at his feisty boxer, Rex, who was running to greet him, as he cackled, once again, "Of course not! Hell, I'll gladly pay for my toys, Charlie. But I'm not a goddamned chump!" As Rex excitedly reared up, standing on his hind legs and licking Archie's boots, Huxley bent over and patted his loyal companion on the head. However, his smile quickly turned sour as he instructed Rex to heel, and gazed back at McKim with menacing eyes. "And I won't tolerate being taken for a fool!"

Archie grabbed a dead duck from his pouch and tossed it high into the air, directly over McKim's baldhead. Instantaneously, he pulled out his Winchester shotgun from its scabbard, cocked it, and fired three rapid shots—disintegrating the bird. As a plume of bloody feathers wafted to the ground (some deflecting off McKim's slick head), Rex scurried to retrieve whatever remains he could find.

The shaken architect recoiled from the spectacle as his mind now stumbled over a pressing thought: how would he deal with this unpredictable and deadly swindler? "But, Mr. Huxley, I cannot—" McKim caught his nervous faux pas, knowing that Huxley did not tolerate being challenged, expecting only a subservient reply, and he altered course, "Or should I say, what is it that you'd like me to do, sir?"

Archie gazed down at McKim, the confident glare in his eye like a silver bullet that could remedy any adverse situation. "I need not have to say, Charlie. You know what must be done. Furthermore, I expect delivery of the piece to be on schedule, or else *he* will be subject to *my* late fees! Is that understood?"

Now sweaty and nervous, McKim ran his finger around his stiff collar as he tried to swallow. Meekly, he nodded.

Huxley pulled back on the reins and pivoted the horse around. "Excuse me, but I must pay President Garfield a visit about some truly important business. So, please, Charlie, tell me that you're capable of handling a minor nuisance like this?"

McKim wiped his moist brow and stood erect. "Most assuredly, Mr. Huxley. You can count on me."

"Oh, I do *count* on you, Charlie. I count every penny you spend. So you best not go one penny over budget, or else I'll have to start counting how many bullets I intend to put in that bald, little head of yours!"

The blood in McKim's face fled quicker from his veins than a scared Angora cat, leaving him as pale as the white animal, as well. Before he could even muster a response, Huxley laughed, "Relax, Charlie!" However the dark unsettling tinge in his voice didn't offer McKim much comfort as he added, "Just get the job done. I have two daughters and a son that are dying to get into their new bedrooms. I'll catch up with you in about a week or so."

With that Huxley whistled for Rex to follow as he kicked his stallion's loins. As the *three* animals rode toward the recently completed carriage house, McKim pulled out a handkerchief and wiped his sweaty baldhead. An uneasy feeling swept over him, while his limbs continued to shake uncontrollably. As he watched Huxley hop into his lavish carriage and begin to ride off, he sighed. *Thank God!*

The frazzled architect turned quickly and summoned his project manager. He instructed him to pay the artisan $350 out of the company expense account and hire 10 more men to speed up production. Huxley had pulled several stunts previously, costing McKim over $6,000 out of his own pocket, and he wanted this nightmare to come to an end...before his business came to an end...or, God knows, his life, too, for that matter.

Forty-five minutes later, Huxley arrived on the shores of Brooklyn and boarded a ferry. As the little steam-powered ship sliced through the turbulent waters of the East River, he gazed up at the city's new marvel. The Brooklyn Bridge exemplified the grand ambitions of the young American nation and Huxley's chest inflated with pride, knowing that his coal mining enterprise—at a rudimentary level—was the key ingredient that allowed the steel mesh of cables to keep the large expanse hovering over the mighty river.

Disembarking, Archibald stepped upon the small island of Manhattan, whose solid, rocky footprint not only allowed for taller buildings, but also demanded them, as space was already becoming a valuable commodity. Manhattan was the capitalistic brain center of not just New York, but of the entire volatile nation. The cobbled streets were bustling with financers, politicians, attorneys, tradesmen and salesman of every stripe and color, while horse-drawn carriages carted the elite to and fro. Meanwhile, street sweepers whisked the garbage and horse manure into piles, while on the corners penny-ante merchants peddled their wares and tonics like vendors at a circus.

Huxley's good friend—and financier extraordinaire—John Pierpont Morgan greeted Archibald warmly. The stout young man with a bulbous gnarly nose and bushy mustache slapped Huxley on the back. "Good to see you, Archie! How was your little duck hunting trip?"

Huxley smiled. "Excellent. Long Island has the best duck in the world!"

"You should know," Morgan replied.

He and Huxley shared many things in common, ambition being the primary trait, yet in other matters, they were worlds apart. With a touch of derision, J.P. added, "Christ, Archie, is there anything you don't hunt and kill?"

"Not a thing," Huxley boasted proudly, "including men!"

An uncomfortable shiver ran down Morgan's big spine. It was comments like that, which truly unnerved J.P., having heard of Archie's boastful claim about killing J.E.B Stuart and his alleged 63 kills during the war that earned him four medals. Yet, despite the Stuart discrepancy, Morgan believed every other kill to be fairly accurate. In fact, he knew of several eyewitnesses who corroborated the tally, and knowing of Archie's innate bloodlust, 63 kills seemed disturbingly plausible, if not shy of the true total.

Uncomfortably, Morgan shook his head. "Ah, the Civil War. That bloody game wasn't for me, Archie. I gladly paid my $300 to have some poor slob fight in my place. My game is hunting and killing my competition. It's all about making a profit and living like a king."

"Oh, I enjoy living like a king," Huxley said proudly as he tugged on the glittering lapels of his flashy outfit. "In fact, you must take a ride out to Long Island to see Huxley Manor. There is simply no better palace to be had in all the states!" Archie gazed down at his oversized, bronze belt buckle. It featured an embossed image of a buffalo being hunted by a cowboy on horseback. He grabbed the medallion and twisted it upward to give J.P. a better look. "But, I just can't give up the thrill of killing something, especially a mammoth beast like this." Patting the bronze buffalo, he looked up at Morgan. "You must join me someday. I'd love to see you with a .52-caliber Sharps rifle in your hands, reveling in the kill!"

Morgan waved his hand. "No, no! That's not for me. The only time I ever got involved with rifles was at the start of the Civil War." A devious smile washed over his face as he continued, "I bought up 5,000 Hall's Carbines from the U.S. government. They were looking to unload the defective firearms, and I snatched them up for a measly $3 a piece. A few months later I sold them right back to the boneheads as refurbished and improved weapons for a whopping $22 each!"

Huxley laughed. "What a killing!"

"Indeed it was!" Morgan said with glee—knowing that a swindler like Huxley would appreciate his bountiful transaction. He pulled out a cigar and lit up, and then said smugly, "Now that's the sort of *killing* I revel in!"

As Huxley contemplated J.P's shrewd maneuver, however, his approving smile softened. "Now hold on a second," he said as he squinted. "Tell me, did you really refurbish and improve those carbines?"

Morgan shrugged his shoulders as he blew out a cloud of smoke. "Well, my boys did polish them up. They looked brand spanking new, they did."

Huxley stared deep into his friend's eyes. "I generally don't give a hoot about the common man's plight, J.P, as I believe it's their own shameful sluggishness that makes them the pathetic mediocrities they are. But damn, arming good Union soldiers with defective carbines probably caused a fair number of our men to die unnecessarily."

Morgan's head recoiled. "What's this? Archibald 'Demon' Huxley has an ounce of humanity in that cold, black, anthracitic heart of his! That can't be!"

Huxley stood momentarily emotionless, sizing up his hefty friend. Then with a cold glint in his eye, he suddenly chuckled—the sappy thought being obliterated like the duck he had just vaporized. "Hell, if any fool doesn't learn about his weapon—or at least test it out before heading into battle—it's his own damned fault! Am I right?"

J.P. chuckled. "You're asking the wrong man. No argument here!" he replied as smoke blew out his nostrils.

"So, what's this I hear, you're paying your old war buddy, General Garfield, a visit?"

"That's right," Huxley said with a reflective smile. "It's still quite hard to fathom that my former commander is now our president. Amazing, isn't it, how a simple farm boy could become President of the United States?"

"That's what I love about this country," Morgan said as they began walking, "anything is possible!"

"Very true!" Huxley concurred as his mind began to conjure up memories. "I recall, way back, when the general told me about how he left home at sixteen to embrace the fortunes of the river trade, becoming a canal boy." Archie suddenly chuckled as Morgan queried, "What's so funny?"

Huxley looked at J.P. with laughter in his eyes. "He told me that he fell into the river and almost drowned. He ran back home, just like a lame beaver that was somehow born with an owl's brain!"

Morgan chuckled. "So, I reckon the wise lad learned that swimming and helmsmanship were not his forte?"

Huxley nodded with a reflective grin.

Actually, Garfield's fall into the river was no joke, but rather a serious life-changing event. The young canal boy had never learned how to swim, knowing only the ways of a farm hand. Up to that point, James had lived with his widowed mother and three siblings on a desolate and landlocked farm in Ohio, but had decided it was time to explore the world. Having sought the excitement of the river, as did so many boys of the day, James landed himself a job and an adventure that nearly took his life. That unforgettable night he had been cruising down a river, when the crew fell asleep. James had stood alone on the bow as the ship cut its way through the dark, choppy waters, being lit only by the faint rays of moonlight that diffused through a veil of clouds. Garfield had been trying to untangle a coil of rope when he lost his footing and fell overboard. In horror, he had watched as the gray, blurry image of the boat pulled away from him. Desperately, James flailed his arms and had gasped for air, only managing to swallow lapping waves of murky water. By chance, his hand happened to grab hold of the rope that caused his fall, yet a disturbing recollection had numbed his mind—the rope was not attached to a cleat! Left with no recourse but to pull or sink, he had frantically pulled hand over hand until somehow, quite inexplicably, it became taut. In no position to question the oddity, young James had managed to pull himself through the current and climbed safely onboard.

As he sat drenched and pondering his fortune, James realized that the untied rope had miraculously caught itself into a crack in the ship's wooden hull and knotted itself. It was then that Garfield was struck with a revelation; Providence had looked down upon him, sparing his life for a higher calling. And, indeed, the half-drowned beaver did become a well-educated owl. Devoting his life to intense study, Garfield graduated with honors from Williams College, became president of the Eclectic Institute, and proved to be one of the wisest owls of his day.

As they continued to walk along the busy street, with young boys running to and fro, and one being chased by a fruit vendor for stealing a peach, Huxley contemplated Morgan's response about Garfield's lack of skills at helmsmanship as he said, "Actually, it's rather peculiar. Because one of Garfield's many feats of heroism during the war was when he piloted a steamer through dangerous waters in Sandy Valley. And now, as I ponder it, his delivery of food supplies was an important event, not only for his happy troops, but also for his career, as that's when the colonel became a general."

Morgan appreciated the small tale, and took the opportunity to relay a tidbit of his own philosophy, "I always say: what one learns along the way in life—no matter how insignificant—will always find a way to come in handy later on, *if* one has the clarity of mind to apply it when destiny beckons."

"I reckon that's very true," Huxley agreed. "And Garfield sure did take advantage of every danged opportunity that came his way. After all, who can forget how he unexpectedly became the nominee for the Republican Party last year?"

As a disheveled organ grinder cranked out his music, while his monkey ran to collect coins from spectators, Morgan grabbed Huxley's arm, and with an irritable huff, veered course. "Yes, just like that damned Dago's shrilly music, Garfield's rise to power sure did cause a terrible ruckus. The man wasn't even a candidate, for Christ's sake, yet he somehow managed to win the nomination *and* the presidency. It makes you wonder: was it talent or Providence?"

Huxley smiled. "Well, I'm certainly no man of God, but it sure seems like the Lord shines a path before that man."

As they passed several street vendors, Morgan replied, "Well, that may be true, but one thing is certain: Garfield cannot walk on water. Hell, he can't even swim in it!"

As the two laughed, Morgan's feelings about the president continued to ooze out, "But I must tell you, I had one hell of a time calming Senator Conkling down. He thought for sure Grant was going to secure a third term."

Roscoe Conkling happens to be a feisty New York Senator who is also the tyrannical leader of the Stalwart faction of Republicans. The Stalwarts routinely, and rather heatedly, butt heads with their counterpart, the moderate Half-Breeds, of which Garfield belongs. Conkling and his underlings have a deep, abiding love and loyalty to their precious spoils system; thus Roscoe clamored to get Grant re-elected—knowing that the former president would continue to support their entrenched machine, or at least turn a blind eye.

The spoils system is a corrupt racket where state and city appointments are based on cronyism rather than merit, and kickbacks and embezzlement run rampant. Conkling, meanwhile, is the mastermind who orchestrates this massive machine. Worse yet, employees recruited into the machine are expected to offer up 3 percent of their salaries to feed Conkling's *spoiled* Republican empire. Underlings—like Chester A. Arthur, who served as customs collector for the Port of New York—all rake in enormous salaries for cushy jobs. Therefore, the financial and political implications are enormous, and Conkling was not happy when James Garfield, a righteous Half-Breed, uprooted the Republican convention to become the nominee and ultimately the president.

As these thoughts flashed through Morgan's mind, he continued speaking, almost as if dreaming aloud, "Although Grant's two terms were unsuccessful in some ways it would have been nice to see the Old General reclaim his office."

Huxley walked intrepidly along, cutting a striking and intimidating figure as pedestrians instinctively veered out of the hunter's way. He gazed at Morgan, and retorted, "I'll have to disagree with you J.P."

As Morgan awoke from his reverie, Huxley continued, "I know you boys here in New York love the spoils system, and hell, so do I; but the reality is, all good things come to an end. As much as we try to control our destinies, change is just a natural course of action, J.P. Just like how as children we think we'll live with our parents until the end of time, yet they eventually die, leaving us standing on our own two feet to chart our own course."

"I suppose you're right, Archie. And quite frankly, I'm a tad perplexed. I never took you to be a thinker," Morgan said as he eyed up Huxley's garish outfit. Archie's rawhide hunting jacket was excessively ornate, with colorfully embroidered scrollwork, fancy gold studs that outlined his black velvet lapels, and red tassels on the sleeves.

Huxley smiled as he swaggered along the sidewalk. "Most people don't either, and that has duped many a fool who took me to be just a mean, empty-headed son-of-a-bitch!" As Morgan chuckled, Huxley's face morphed unexpectedly, turning gloomy and introspective. "But, you see, my parents died when I was twelve years old, J.P." Morgan's smile vanished as Huxley continued—his voice somber and dark, "They drowned when a large steamship collided into their wooden riverboat at night, slicing it in two." Archie swallowed hard, then resumed, "They were horrifically mutilated, being chopped up by the steamship's propeller. Their bodies washed ashore the next day. Needless to say, my life changed most dramatically that day." Huxley's sullen, mechanical voice suddenly took on a more harsh tone as he continued, "Yet the nightmare didn't end there. My shit-for-brains Uncle Jack—who enjoyed beating me just as much as he did his half-assed mule—took me in." Huxley stared emptily into space as he snarled, "God, how I hated that man and his stupid ass!"

Darker memories of Huxley's uncle began to emerge out of the deepest recesses of his psychologically damaged mind. As the disturbing scenes flashed chaotically before his mind's eye, one in particular took center stage. It was the dark night his drunken uncle had just come home late from the saloon, his eyes glazed, and his knuckles hacked and stained with dried blood from a nasty brawl. In a fit of rage, he had given little Archie a shellacking for not putting the water bucket back by the well where it belonged. Uncle Jack had beaten Archie many times before with the back of his hand or a broomstick to the head, but this time he used his thick leather belt—knowing that his sore hands wouldn't be punishing enough. The metal buckle had cut deep, permanent gashes in Archie's back and left him with the visible scar he still wears today on his chin. As the child-beating creep staggered towards the well to return the pail, little Archie crept up behind him and split his skull open with a hoe. He then tossed the bloody body headfirst down the 60-foot vault. The next day, the local sheriff accepted young Archie's explanation of the accidental fall, knowing very well that his Uncle Jack enjoyed hitting the bottle, among other things.

Waking Huxley out of his macabre reminiscence, was Morgan's sympathetic voice, "I'm rightly sorry, Archie. I never knew about your tragic youth."

As they were approaching an old street sweeper loading his cart with debris and horse manure, Huxley rubbed his forehead and then gazed up at Morgan. "Well, at least my uncle's inheritance allowed me to sell his farm and begin a new life." Huxley's face had already transformed from victim to victor as he added, "You see, I was determined not to allow those hardships to ever stop me, J.P. And as I look back on it now, I reckon that was the greatest motivation and gift I ever received. Cause I vowed to live my life to the fullest before the Angel of Death arrives to carry *me* away. And no one, I mean no one on earth, will ever stand in my way!"

Morgan offered up his feisty friend an admirable smile, yet had to laugh when the street sweeper stood in Huxley's way. Archie, however, didn't find the symbolic joke funny, that a shit sweeper would stand in *his* way. With a snort like a bull, Huxley pushed the old man backwards, causing him to fall into the dung-filled cart.

Morgan shook his head disapprovingly as two women and a boy helped the old man up. Huxley, however, continued walking as Morgan caught up and resumed their journey.

Meanwhile, Huxley had conveniently failed to mention that besides having killed his uncle he had also forged his will—gaining all his worldly possessions and cheating his cousin Jack Jr. out of his inheritance. That, too, had erupted into an ugly face-off as the two had found themselves standing on a field of honor, surrounded by trees, pointing pistols at each other. It was Archie's first encounter with a firearm and, as soon as he pulled the trigger that day, he knew they clicked as he watched his cousin Jack keel over like a felled tree. The ease at which he was able to kill his second victim and the exhilaration from realizing that *he* had the power to play God was euphoric. Archie had truly believed that his first act of killing his abusive uncle was a noble act, guided by God's judicial hand. However, after killing his cousin, Archie was struck by a second and far more powerful revelation—neither righteousness nor God had any role to play in this epiphany. Basically, good deeds and honor meant nothing. The lesson Archie learned was that life does not play by the manmade rules of religion or law, and his mantra had become the most radical form of the new catchphrase "survival of the fittest."

Huxley had later learned that this powerful phrase, which at the time was deeply ingraining itself into the era's consciousness, was not conceived by Charles Darwin, but was actually coined by Herbert Spencer—the British philosopher and Father of Social Darwinism. Lacking a formal education, Huxley had an affinity for meeting with thinkers of all variations and denominations, yet, unfortunately, he routinely distorted much of what he heard to suit his own primal needs. In fact, several months ago,

Huxley had written a letter to Spencer, requesting that he visit America, since the influential thinker had never crossed the Atlantic. Having heard that Spencer detested pomp and speaking engagements (preferring the solitude of his own thoughts), Archie quite cunningly used his very name "Huxley" to win Spencer over. However, it was not the rich tycoon of Huxley Coal who would win Spencer's approval. It had become common knowledge that Thomas Henry Huxley was Charles Darwin's dear friend and his most fervent publicist, even devising his own sobriquet "Darwin's Bulldog." As such, Archie claimed to be a distant American relative of the famous Brit, thus winning over the reluctant hermit. However, Spencer could not leave England anytime soon; thus Archie scheduled the voyage to take place in August of 1882, on a steamship that also happened to be booked by Archie's friend, Andrew Carnegie, who likewise had an interest in speaking with Spencer. Yet, this particular voyage and meeting was a full year away and was not truly crucial to Huxley's own fiscal survival. However, right now, Huxley did have an important meeting to catch that *would* have financial rewards. And *money* was the true magnet that drew Huxley's attention.

Archie slapped J.P. on the back as the two titans walked toward the harbor and wrapped up their interesting chat. Morgan looked at Huxley, and, with a sense of relief, bid the flamboyant-hunter/homicidal-tycoon farewell.

Boarding the ferry, Archie turned and waved as the huge paddle wheels began to churn up the salty bluish-green water. As the steam boiler belched and hissed, the vessel slowly began to leave the pier. Crossing over the choppy Hudson River, the steamship pulled into port in New Jersey. Archie gazed down at his pocket watch and rushed to the Baltimore & Ohio terminal. As the huge black locomotive came to a stop, Archie hopped onto a new

Pullman passenger car. It was lined with decorative trim and sported a fancy interior, clad in varnished dark woods and pleated window shades with tassels. As he walked down the aisle, looking to locate a seat, his eye caught an old army buddy through the window—he was running alongside the moving train on the wooden platform.

"Archie!—you old rascal," the man bellowed over the din of steam-fired pistons and clattering metal wheels. "I've been meaning to speak to you about a job. I hear you're an industrial bigwig now?"

Huxley leaned rudely across two women as he bent over and opened the window fully. "Bradley, ole boy. Yes, indeed I am. How about you join me? We can talk on the way down to Washington."

Bradley nodded. "Much obliged!"

Meanwhile, the train was gathering speed quickly, and his friend suddenly ran out of platform. Jumping like a gazelle to the ground, Bradley began running on the grass toward the rear entrance of the Pullman car. Meanwhile, Archie had already walked back and exited the passenger car, and he now stood on the metal platform between his car and the one linked behind. As the train rocked and swayed, with its couplings clattering noisily, Huxley leaned out, looking for his friend. As his short gray hair blew in the breeze, he could see that Bradley had fallen behind. Meanwhile, the train continued to gather speed.

"Hurry up! Brad," Archie yelled, "I see you're still a lard ass!"

Bradley laughed just as he clutched onto the railing, but lost his footing. Archie's adrenaline surged and he reached down quickly to grab his friend's hand. Yet, Bradley's eyes were wracked with fear—dreading the gruesome fate that he knew awaited him. Bradley fell face first on the track as the trailing passenger car slammed into his body. The flanged-wheels sliced Bradley in half like a huge pizza cutter as the train bounced and continued chugging along.

Archie gazed at the trembling palm of his adrenaline-pumped hand; it was Bradley's only hope for survival, but now it was barren. But quite chillingly, so too was Archie's conscience as he gazed coldly down at the blurry cascade of moving railroad ties. The shock had passed quickly, and his hand was now calm and steady.

It was only a brief moment, when a conductor rushed out onto the platform. "What in God's name was that terrible thump?"

Archie turned. Nonchalantly, he shrugged his shoulders. "Not sure. I reckon we hit a deer or some stupid animal."

The conductor's worried expression vanished with relief as Archie pulled out his pocket watch and glanced at its two ornately sculpted gold hands. He slipped it back into the inner pocket of his flashy hunting jacket, and inquired, "We *will* arrive in Washington on time, correct?"

Dutifully, the conductor nodded. "Why, yes, sir! The B&O always runs on time!"

Huxley smiled. "Splendid! I have an important meeting with President Garfield, and must not be late."

The conductor was elated to hear that his passenger was a man of importance, and he stepped cordially to the side of the doorway, then thrust his left hand into the entranceway. "Please, sir, we must get off this platform. It is far too dangerous, especially for a man of distinction, such as yourself."

Archie acknowledged the compliment, and entered the car, while the conductor followed, closing the door. Becoming overtly obsequious, the conductor's voice and manner became more debonair, as he stepped in front of him. "Allow me, good sir, to show you to our new Pullman dining car. It's the newest top-of-the-line rail car with the most luxurious interior you've ever seen. People simply love it. It's fantastic!"

"Well, I'm not interested in dining cars for people," Huxley said frigidly, "only in hoppers for commodities."

The conductor gazed apprehensively at Huxley's stone-cold face, waiting for a smile to indicate that he was jesting. But none came. A bit unnerved, but still the gracious host, he replied, "Well, we have several new dishes that I'm sure you'll enjoy, and a full bar—" his voice lowered to a whisper, "and for special clientele, such as yourself, we have the finest brands of liquor and the best cigars, including the new Jose L. Piedra cigars from Cuba!"

Huxley glanced over and winked. "Now *that's* fantastic!"

❦

Back in Pittsburgh, the Wozniaks were just now sitting down to eat dinner—their faces solemn and their minds still in a haze.

Meanwhile, things at Huxley Coal were still in turmoil. Miners were working feverishly to repair damages, while others continued their search-and-rescue missions. Hastings was still frustrated, being unable to contact his fiery boss, as Huxley only utilized telegraphy for business communications. Archie enjoyed his privacy too much to have his houses equipped with a telegraphy room or even the new telephone systems that were beginning to make their way into the businesses and homes of his elite friends. Overall, however, communications in 1881 were painfully slow, and Huxley now continued his journey to Washington D.C., oblivious to the disaster.

A Presidential Visit

June 30, 1881

The cerulean hues of daylight had long since given way to phthalo shades of twilight as the locomotive blew its whistle and pulled into Washington D.C. Archie had a belly-full of roast beef and a nicely numbed head from drinking Walker's Old Highland specially blended whiskey—just enough to bolster his bravado a tad more before meeting the most powerful man in the United States.

Actually, Archie smiled as he thought of that old cliché, knowing it to be just a ludicrous farce. He clearly realized the growing influence that he and his capitalist friends attained since the war's end. The Industrial Revolution changed not only the economic and social structure of the nation, but also the hierarchy of power, putting industrialists in strategic positions of enormous political influence. In fact, his whole reason for meeting with Garfield was to lobby for his own financial self-interest, something Huxley excelled at.

Stepping off the platform of the Baltimore & Potomac Station, Huxley hailed a carriage, and began riding through the dark cobbled streets toward the White House. Lampposts shed their warm, fiery glow over the facades of Victorian and Queen-Anne buildings and the passing bodies of pedestrians—some men wearing top hats, and others bowlers, while women wore bonnets or bows. The night air was rather warm from the recently set June sun, yet the damp marshes all around the city had already begun releasing their foul odors, while mosquitoes looked forward to a summer of good hunting.

Arriving at the White House at around 7:30 p.m., Huxley paid the driver, without giving him a tip, and was greeted by an official at the front entrance. He was escorted into the Reception Room, which, to his surprise, was still filled with a throng of visitors; some wishing just to meet the president, but most seeking favors and job appointments. The prevailing policy allowed the public free access to call upon the president from 10:30 a.m. to 1:30 p.m., Monday through Friday. However, since Garfield was out of town for a week (having taken his wife Lucretia, who had been serious ill, to New Jersey in preparation for his planned vacation in two days), he rescheduled the visitor session for this evening to accommodate the public. Ironically, despite Abraham Lincoln's assassination 16 years ago the government failed to establish a security policy of any kind, believing that a free nation, run by the People, afforded them the right to see their president. Hence complete strangers had free access to the president right in his living quarters without so much as being screened. Nevertheless, despite only being in office for four months, Garfield's personal secretary established a new policy, whereby only permitting access to people he met first. Yet, as time would tell, false first impressions and the inability to verify credentials still plagued this flawed system.

Huxley was guided through the crowd and directly up the stairs to the central Blue Room, which, oddly enough, would be redecorated some years later by Huxley's hired architectural firm: McKim, Mead and White. As Huxley followed the aide through the great big building, he was sadly taken aback by how it had fallen into disrepair. The wooden floorboards squeaked, the wallpaper was faded and peeling, and the paint was cracked, dull and full of scratches. Yet Archie gained a modicum of relief when he spotted two carpenters at the end of the cross hall with hammers and scrapers, and at least beginning to make repairs.

The official knocked on the door of the Blue Room as Garfield's voice resounded promptly, "Enter."

The aide turned the knob and swung the door open. With a nod, he made an about-face and left.

As Huxley entered the oval-shaped room, Garfield rose from his pale-blue chair and placed the recently published biography of his life, *From Canal Boy to President,* down on the end table. The Blue Room, however, was still in excellent shape with its tall ceilings, dental moldings, white fireplace, and a large oval carpet with a busy floral design blanketing most of the floor.

Huxley walked over and shook his hand firmly. "Hello, General Garfield!"

The president smiled, his thick beard and mustache parting as he said, "Greetings Lieutenant Huxley. It has been quite a number of years since the war."

Huxley had two primary sore spots; one being in the presence of intelligent men who attended college and the other was being around men that attained a higher rank than he in the army. As such, he knew this meeting was going to test his patience, for James Garfield happened to be both. Therefore, he went straight on the defensive, "Well, unlike you, General, I lacked the advantage of a college education upon entering the army. Nor were my gallant actions rewarded with promotions—as they should have been."

Garfield, the intellectual gentleman that he was, responded diplomatically, "Military rank has little meaning in regards to one's abilities, Mr. Huxley. I believe General Grant's two abysmal terms as president proves my point most clearly. Not that I don't have the utmost respect for his military career and his place in American history for saving the nation from complete ruin, mind you."

As Huxley gained some comfort from the president's remark, Garfield added, "Besides, you certainly out-gunned me, and many others, with your impressive war record and medals."

Huxley smiled; pleased that the general would remember his citations, yet, being the consummate con man that he was, realized he needed to stroke the newly elected president in kind. "Yes, but in all fairness, I respect your bravery, General. After all, having your horse shot out from under you and seeing your orderly killed at your side while charging through enemy lines is not for the faint of heart!" As Garfield acknowledged his appreciation, Huxley sprinkled another lump of sugar on his tribute. "However, I must be candid. What I admire even more than your courage on the battlefield was your gutsy nerve to lodge a scathing complaint about your commander's inaction. I can just imagine Major General Rosecrans' face upon receiving word of your brash reprimand."

Calmly, Garfield shook his broad shoulders. "Actually, Old Rosy took it better than I ever expected. I suppose deep down he knew that he stuttered at a moment that required a firm and resolute command of action. As for my audacity, Lieutenant, what I've learned since then was that it is not always to one's profit to lambaste one's superior behind their back, as men in positions of power are always surrounded by friends in power. Sometimes poisoned honey is indeed far more prudent than a saber to the gut!"

As Huxley laughed, realizing the president's military play on the cliché to be true, Garfield cracked a smile and motioned for him to sit. As Huxley complied respectfully, the president began pacing the room. "Yes, especially in the arena of politics, diplomacy—or rather duplicity—appears to be the apogee of this sullied art." As he continued pacing back and forth, he rubbed his forehead. "I'll be quite frank, Mr. Huxley. The more I engage the machine of politics the more I loathe it. As you know, my election campaign was marred by false charges trumped up by the Democrats. They had the audacity to forge my signature on phony documents to buttress their pathetic lies. Their wretched deeds have brought our nation to an all-new low. It is most painful and repugnant!"

Huxley peered up at Garfield with a bit of surprise in his eyes. Although being a full-fledged con artist, Archie's tremendous rise to power had bloated his ego and suppressed much of his tact and etiquette, thus allowing his innate lacerating tongue to speak whatever was on his foul mind. "Well, I beg your pardon, Mr. President, but how you handled your predecessor's election was what many Americans found painful and repugnant. As we all know, President Hayes' victory was a fraud by all accounts." Garfield stopped pacing and turned quizzically toward his unexpectedly candid guest, who continued his assault, "It was no secret that Governor Tilden was the front runner in that election, especially considering his role in trying to clean up the Boss Tweed ring at Tammany. By all accounts that I'm aware of, Tilden had the majority of public and electoral votes in the bag, until those voting issues arose in Florida and two other states."

Garfield's tense lips suddenly released an ever so slight smile, both concealing and revealing. "Yes, but that decision was not mine alone, Mr. Huxley. I sat on the commission with fourteen others to determine the final tallies of those disputed states and, yes, the final result of the election." Garfield's face became stern and resolute. "I simply could not allow the exhausting efforts I put into Rutherford's campaign to all be for naught. I'll have you know that I hit the stump all across the northeast for Hayes, even though not being in complete harmony with his convictions." Garfield's demeanor softened as he became more introspective. "Furthermore, that decision behind closed doors was to ensure that the Southern Democrats and their iniquitous slave-owning ways would not take hold of this office. Ever since Lincoln reunited this nation, we Republicans have held the Presidency with the clear understanding that the Southern Democrats are not ready to conduct national affairs from the executive branch. And my role in making sure Hayes took office was most precarious; I'll have you know. My party members were even prompted to supply me with a bodyguard after those deliberations, since my assassination appeared quite imminent."

Huxley chuckled with a sinister twang, changing the mood. "Yes, I can imagine. I know of several men who would have loved to put a bullet in your head. Myself included!"

Garfield didn't find Huxley's dark humor to his liking. "Lieutenant, my war days are far behind me, and seeing fields draped with thousands of young bodies, seemingly in a state of slumber, yet very much dead, has steeled me to the realization of the sanctity of life and the seriousness of death. Hence, I find such crass remarks to be most inappropriate and distasteful."

Huxley ignored the reprimand with a sadistic smile as he ran his finger along the seam of the upholstered chair. He then switched gears, attempting to add another dose of sugar. "Well, General, how you managed to emerge as president yourself four years after your Hayes victory is a testament to your political genius. I like a man with ruthless ambition!"

Garfield gazed down at Huxley with his usual calm exterior, yet his keen mind couldn't stop thinking about why he never really liked Huxley right from the start. It had been during the war when Garfield's 42nd regiment came across the lieutenant, who had gotten separated from his company while chasing down eight Confederates through a thicket of trees. Huxley had proudly boasted about how he hunted them down, killing all eight of them singlehandedly—the last three quite gruesomely, having slit their throats with a knife and then cutting off their ears for mementos. Archie had stayed with Garfield's regiment for two weeks until being reunited with his company, yet Garfield had grown sick of hearing Huxley blowing his own horn, a trait that Garfield loathed intensely. He also recalled quite clearly the lieutenant's deep admiration for his ambitious and reckless commander, General Custer. And looking at Huxley now—standing before him with his garish hunting outfit—the only change he could see, so far, was that Huxley cut his long Custer-like locks short, and they had turned gray. The man, himself, however, still appeared to be the same old deadly mixture of sugar and strychnine. Garfield was well known for never losing his patience and never hating his enemies, for he had once said, "I am a poor hater."

As such, Garfield looked calmly at the wolf in fancy sheep's clothing and simply pulverized Huxley's ruthless philosophy. "Lieutenant Huxley, I hate to shatter your delusion, but it was not my design or political genius that got me into this office. I never once entertained the idea of seizing this lofty seat. In fact, there is a tone of sadness running through this triumph, which I can hardly explain. I'll have you know, it was by a lark that I rose from being a non-candidate to become the party's nominee, and then, to my greatest surprise and dismay, being elected president. So, this honor comes to me unsought. I have never had the

Presidential fever; not even for a day! Nor should any man, in any walk of life, have such a fever of *ruthless* ambition!"

Again, Garfield began to pace as he stroked his beard. He was curious to see if there was more to Huxley than what his memory told him or what Huxley's raw interior and flashy exterior have presented thus far. "It worries me, Lieutenant. This nation of ours began so magnificently with luminous figures like Washington, Adams, Jefferson, Madison and Hamilton—all brilliant in their own unique way—yet here it is we have witnessed a bloody Civil War that claimed the lives of over half a million of our own, then the shocking assassination of President Lincoln, the impeachment of Andrew Johnson, and the rank corruption under Grant's two iniquitous terms." Stopping in his tracks, he gazed at Huxley, "Does any of that concern you?"

Huxley stood up and pulled a cigar out of his hunting jacket's inner pocket and waved it, offering one to the president.

Garfield refused politely, while Huxley lit the stogie and walked over to the huge double-hung window. Lifting it up for ventilation, he turned around and said, "Mr. President, I reckon my eyes see a different nation than yours. I see a land of opportunity." As his eyes caught a glimpse of the book on the end table, he continued, "I see how *you*, a canal boy, rose to be president. I see in the mirror an orphaned boy who lost his parents and endured hardship to become the owner of one of the largest anthracite mines in the country. Everywhere I travel, like New York City this morning, I see great marvels of engineering rising up like cathedrals that praise the human spirit. I see our nation moving into a far more prosperous and industrious time, Mr. President, a time that Mark Twain rightly called a Gilded Age!"

Garfield gazed inquisitively at Huxley with a renewed set of eyes as he returned to his chair to sit down. Pausing a brief moment, he rested his elbow on the arm of the chair, while his fingers rustled through his thick, wiry beard. He then looked up at Huxley with his magnetic eyes. "I appreciate and share much of your enthusiasm and positive perspective, Mr. Huxley. However, you *are* aware of Twain's brilliant sense of wordplay, are you not?"

Huxley hesitated, and then shook his head ever so slightly. He didn't wish to appear ignorant, but he hadn't read Twain's book, nor many others for that matter, having only heard friends and journalists speak of Twain's novel *The Gilded Age: A Tale of Today*.

Garfield crossed his legs as his voice became somewhat professorial—resurrecting his penchant for serious lectures and debates when he was a teacher. "Lieutenant, Mark Twain used the word *gilded* in lieu of *golden* for a specific reason. Yes, he sees our age, superficially, as golden, for those labeled 'Robber Barons'—hence *you* and your rich ilk. Yet gilded, in a literal sense, is a thin veneer; hence our age appears golden and radiant on the outside, yet it is inferior at its core. And it is this shoddy core, which is the byproduct of your abuses, as well as this deceptive veneer of gilt, which concerns me."

Huxley took a deep drag of his cigar, turned his head, and blew the pungent puff of smoke out the window. He gazed down at the smoldering brown cylinder of tobacco and smiled. "Everyone blames us capitalists, Mr. President. Yet Uncle Sam has no problem reaping *one third* of all his collected taxes right from this little roll of tobacco!...sucking the life out of hardworking tobacco companies and taxpayers just like how I'm sucking the life out of this cigar." Huxley turned and looked at Garfield with reproachful eyes. "So, Mr. President, there is certainly enough guilt in this Age of Gilt to go around. Is there not?"

Garfield, whose opinion of the complex man before him was now in flux, offered a conciliatory nod as Huxley stood boldly erect and continued his charge with surprising lucidity, "And I will admit that I lack a college education, and I'm not well read, but I'll be damned if I'm not one hell of a keen observer and listener, General. I've rubbed shoulders with men of all vocations and all levels of education, and one thing I've learned is that even the great Roman Empire had its share of high-minded authors bemoaning how great men achieved great things at the expense of the common man. They, too, had a Golden Age under Augustus; yet there will always be the winners who see it as Golden, and the whiners who will vilify it as Gilded. There will always be the Haves and Have-nots, Mr. President." Huxley's impressive rebuttal, however, was about to take a downturn as a piece of his dark soul escaped in the heat of passion, "And my deepest concern, General, is this new wave of voices from down below, crusading for the equal rights of Negros and women!"

Garfield sat upright; his stance on civil rights happened to be *his* sore spot. Being well noted for championing the cause of the Negroes, Garfield had proudly designated Frederick Douglas to lead his presidential procession on the day of his inauguration, making a powerful statement about the slave-free nation and his vision of tolerance. As such, Garfield's voice became indignant, "Lieutenant Huxley, this nation was almost destroyed in its noble attempt to eradicate the primitive ways of slavery. And, you, sir, are in the distinct minority with such a barbaric viewpoint! You speak of the grandeur of Rome and its great achievements, which I'll certainly agree with, as did our Founders, yet your archaic comment now places you firmly in the ranks of the barbaric Goths!"

Huxley laughed, taking pleasure in finally pricking Garfield's seemingly impenetrable bubble of benevolence. He took another puff and exhaled a cloud of odorous tobacco— this time not out the window, but antagonistically towards the president's face. "Actually, I'm not too concerned about the Negro, Mr. President. Let them have a voice, for what it's worth. After all, they were the archaic animals that started this whole mess by selling their own kind! Not to mention how after half-a-million of our white brothers died to free them, they still resent us. What's more, hardly a single one fled north to earn a better life. No! Most stayed rooted in Southern soil, only to be harassed by their former masters. So let their own lazy and ignorant ways be their downfall."

Irritated, Garfield waved the smoke out of his eyes as he countered assertively, "Mr. Huxley, evidently, you are glaringly unaware of men like Booker T. Washington. For your information, he is soon to be the president of the new Tuskegee Normal and Industrial Institute, which is slated to open its doors next month. This is a brilliant first step toward educating Negro men to learn a trade and gain respectability. And, I assure you, he is not alone in their noble crusade!"

Huxley rolled his eyes. "Sure, there may be a handful, but I have yet to see even a houseful. However, the issue of women, especially the so-called *educated women*, I find to be another matter. They are the ones who will wreak havoc on our nation. Mark my words!"

Garfield shifted uneasily in his seat, not knowing how much longer he could listen to Huxley's rhetoric, as Huxley took another puff and continued, "You see, my wife is an educated woman, Mr. President, and if I gave her a shard of coal, she would eventually demand the whole mine. Women yearn for control, just as much as men, except their minds and dispositions are drastically different from ours. If given a chance, women would strip men of their bravado, our need for competition, innovation and progress. Instead, seeking equality for all, even if that means castrating the bull to make him a cow!" Huxley spit out a small piece of tobacco leaf that was drawn into his mouth as he added with a bit of humor,

"And a United States teaming with herds of docile Guernsey cows is something that should concern every darn one of us ballsy bulls! Wouldn't you agree?"

Garfield actually managed to crack a smile, yet he remained non-committedly mute. Meanwhile, Huxley's voice gained a darker, more sullen tone—his mind slipping into the murky waters of his troubled past. "You see, my mother also happened to be an educated woman, General. Oh, yes," he said as his glazed eyes drifted off into an eerie void, his voice now becoming soft and mechanical, "she was a sweet, loving creature, she was. And boy, how she used to enjoy coddling me. I'll never forget how she used to scurry around doing all my chores to protect me from my father's tirades. Or how she made my bed and laid out all my clothes in the morning for me. God bless her soul," Huxley said as he paused briefly. His eyebrows pinched as a disturbed expression washed over his face. "But although well-meaning, my dear old mom undoubtedly weakened my constitution. Oh, yes, she sure as hell did." Huxley's brief visit with his tender memories abruptly ended as his voice began to rise with angst, "As such, upon reaching the age of fourteen, I was no young bull, General, but rather a neutered cow—one to be continually milked of its vitality. In hindsight, I now see how my mother's death and the subsequent hell I was forced to endure under my uncle's wrath was the true Godsend that transformed my life." Huxley gazed over at Garfield—his eyes now clear, his voice now steady. "Without those hardships, General, I would have been just another soft, slothful mediocrity. But, no, I struggled and learned to endure wave after wave of traumas and suffering. It was by regaining my inner sense of male strength that I managed to brave the storm and emerge a victor, not a victim. And that tale of woe, in essence, is what allowed me to build my own empire! A coal empire that dominates most others in this nation." Huxley took another quick puff as he stood prideful and erect. As he began to speak, his voice visually materialized with dissipating waves of smoke. "So, while you or Mr. Twain may look upon the gilded life I crafted as being shameful, cruel and inferior, what emerged from my dark past, in reality, was a superior stock of man. A man you might very well say became King Midas!"

Garfield glanced at the book on the table beside him, and then back up at Huxley, as he once again took a professorial approach, "Well, I, too, had toiled and risen from poverty to prosperity or, if you like, from pauper to president, Mr. Huxley. However, your zeal for gold and riches is sadly misplaced. If you knew the ancient Greek myth about King Midas, you would understand that he came to the painful realization that having been granted the power to turn anything he touched into gold only left him with a cheap abundance of the shinny metal. It brought Midas no happiness. Therefore, the moral of the story was not his ability to turn anything into gold. Nay! It was his enlightened plea to have that gift—or in reality, curse—rescinded. Yet, rather unfortunately, you seem not to have understood that tale, nor have you reached such an epiphany, Mr. Huxley."

Archie gazed uncomfortably at the floor, more perturbed about not knowing the Midas myth than about its silly and useless moral lesson. Undaunted, he looked back up and resumed his initial, misogynistic charge in one lengthy breath, "The epiphany *I* have reached is that this crusade by women—who are already clamoring for the abolition of liquor, closing of saloons, and, I hear, seeking to side with labor unions to demand higher wages, health benefits, and, dare I say, compensation and welfare for the weak or useless—is a clear sign of the soft, socialistic Guernsey State that would emerge if women get their way!"

Garfield had been listening patiently with an analytical ear, while his furry chin rested on his knuckles. He was not about to debate certain issues that he suspected were too deeply imprinted in Huxley's hard skull; tainted thoughts that were like tattoos, which could never be erased. Opting to respond diplomatically, with a clever touch of subterfuge, Garfield lifted his head. "Well, Lieutenant, I certainly cannot say that I agree with all that you posited or prophesied. However, I do see some aspects of your life and bold perspectives that are quite intriguing, and they'd make splendid material for further examination by psychologists regarding the human condition."

Not fully comprehending Garfield's wordplay, Huxley nodded. "Indeed, I am sure there is much people can learn from me, Mr. President. And that brings me to my reason for this visit."

Garfield rose from his chair and walked over to the small liquor console. Lifting the etched glass decanter filled with bourbon, he asked cordially, "Would you care for a drink?"

Huxley exhaled another stream of smoke, this time out the window, as he turned back. "Sure! There are three things I never refuse; money, a drink, or a woman's charms!"

Garfield was having a hard time maintaining his diplomatic façade, yet he had been dealing with all breeds of the human species long enough to know how to grin and bear it, yet a drink would help him get through the rest of this meeting a little easier.

As Huxley walked over and received his drink, he looked at Garfield and clicked glasses. As they both took a swig, Huxley continued, "As I was saying, my reason for this visit is to inform you that it would be in the best interest of the country if you make sure Congressman William Kelley gets his tariff bill passed. Those tariffs are crucial to protecting our coal and iron industries in Pittsburgh."

Garfield's bushy eyebrows pinched as he took another nip of his bourbon. He savored the potent liquor in his mouth and then swallowed it slowly. Licking his teeth clean, he then said, "I am quite familiar with "Pig Iron" Kelley, and his hot crusade to favor the coal and iron industry. But I do hope this is not some intonation of graft, Mr. Huxley?" Garfield's eyes stayed glued to Huxley's as he patted his moist mustache with a napkin and continued without missing a beat, "As you must know, I just launched an investigation into the Star Route scandal. Postmasters, in collusion with their crony private contractors, have swindled *four million dollars!* Not from a private competitor's pocket, no, it was from the innocent pockets of American taxpayers. And I am wholeheartedly committed to eliminating this rampant corruption that plagues our great nation. Too many hands are being greased between politicians and businessmen. Despite Tilden's noble efforts to eliminate that abomination called Tammany Hall, Conkling's malignant, spoiled system still operates—oozing with cronyism, embezzlements and *graft!* So, I hope for your sake this is not what you mean?"

A devious twitch distorted Huxley's face. "Of course not, Mr. President. This has nothing to do with graft; this is purely good economic sense. Our country cannot continue to be undercut by foreign nations, especially by that industrial powerhouse Britain. You do realize that I employ hundreds of workers, and it is crucial that I and others in my field stay solvent and in business?"

"Why, yes of course, but—"

"So *we need* these tariffs, Mr. President!" Huxley interjected adamantly, "plain and simple. After all, your goal is to make the United States a leader, and without our home-grown ability to manufacture goods we would end up like any other penny-ante nation living off the crumbs of our British overlords."

Garfield paused, and then nodded. "I suppose that is a sound fiscal strategy, Archibald. I have no objection to keeping our industrial enterprises on an upward steady course. As you say, the nation, despite its flaws, *is* exploding with vitality and innovation, and I'll eagerly support any initiative to help bolster that upward trajectory."

Huxley grinned; having won his point, coupled with the fact that the president dropped the formality—addressing him by his first name. Huxley felt a surge of confidence as he extended his glass. "I'll drink to that!"

As Garfield clicked his glass and began to take another sip, Huxley didn't even join him as he continued impulsively, "And, I must say, another problem we face is this growing eagerness to expel the Chinks!" As Garfield peered at Archie's distorted face through the bottom of his glass, Huxley continued, "They may not be citizens, but Chinks have built our railroads for many years. As you know, 80 percent of Union Pacific's workforce is now Oriental. Hell, they work just as hard as the Polish or Irish and cost an awful lot less. That is why I started to hire a few Chinks myself." Huxley finally took a swig of his bourbon, which he barely swallowed, and continued stridently, "It appears my other employees are becoming rather agitated, and for no good reason. It's really quite simple. They either need to work harder or accept less money. After all, capitalism is all about competition."

In his haste, Huxley seemed to forget that the forged letter by the Democrats during Garfield's election, which the president made reference to earlier, happened to deal with this very issue of Chinese immigration. The Morey letter, as it had come to be called, was to have been allegedly written by Garfield, wherein he extolled the rights of industrialists to hire cheap foreign labor, while welcoming an unrestricted influx of Chinese immigrants who were not even U.S. citizens. However, Garfield harbored no such notions, for both parties had rallied behind public sentiment, which clamored for a Chinese Exclusion Act.

Garfield placed his glass back down on the ornate silver tray. "You puzzle me, Mr. Huxley, just like your rich friends who demand an audience with me. In one breath, you fear the government getting involved with unions, welfare, or immigration laws—all, in essence, aimed at helping our poor fellow American—yet, in another breath, you look for tariffs and even subsidies. Why? To eliminate your competition and favor your fat profit margins—that's why! Do you not see the duplicity in these self-serving requests?"

Huxley slammed his glass down on the silver tray harder than he wished, but he didn't appreciate the president's insinuation or his impersonal return to formality. Flagrantly pointing his cigar at Garfield's face, he growled, "Mr. President, I am not seeking special treatment, nor am I a whining, little cheater in the rough and tumble game of capitalism. I am well aware that the government has subsidized Union Pacific, giving it millions of dollars to build railroads across the nation, but I have not asked for a red cent! I have earned every penny my coal mine makes by hard work and the sweat off my brow. I began as a miner myself, so I know the grueling work involved all too well. But just because I seek protection from foreign countries that do not have our best interests at heart, or I look to make my business more profitable by hiring cheaper labor, so I can reinvest that money into buying new tools and machinery to keep my company ahead of my competitors, does not make me a duplicitous cheater or a robber baron!"

Garfield maintained his calm bearing, but raised his voice slightly, "Lieutenant, I advise you to point that flaming torch in another direction, or else it, along with this meeting, will be extinguished!" As the lieutenant intuitively obeyed the general's command, Garfield continued, "I appreciate your sweat and toil, Mr. Huxley, but your investment in new machinery and tools brings to mind two burning issues, which robber barons rarely, if ever, heed. The first being worker safety. Dangerous working conditions have crippled, maimed and killed many workers across the board, and no serious efforts to address these issues have been made. The ability for men like you to examine and honestly correct your errors or make costly improvements has not shown itself. Even a religious man needs weekly sermons to keep him on track, for very few men can truly govern their own actions fairly without oversight. Second: is the gross divide between wages. You earn in three hours what your average worker makes in a whole year! Such disproportionate sums of compensation can never be explained away as being fair or deserved, no matter how brilliant and innovative the entrepreneur or how insignificant the skills of the laborer. And both of these critical issues demand legislative oversight!"

Huxley released a sarcastic chuckle. "And just *where* in the Constitution does it give *you* the authority to meddle in private enterprise, Mr. President?"

Huxley hadn't read the Constitution, but his wealthy friends had, and government intervention into their affairs was widely discussed in private and firmly trounced upon in political forums.

Garfield looked at a framed portrait on the wall, drawing Huxley's attention to the likeness of Thomas Jefferson. With poise, he replied, "Before his passing, Jefferson left instructions that his tombstone was to be inscribed with only three achievements that he was most proud of. Do you know what they were?"

Huxley rolled his eyes; while Garfield glanced at him, then back at the celebrated painting. "The first inscription was for authoring the Declaration of Independence. The second was for his Statute of Virginia for religious freedom. And the third was for being Father of the University of Virginia."

Turning back to face Huxley, he added, "*Nowhere* did Jefferson mention his role as president. Do you know why that is, Mr. Huxley?"

Archie huffed. He was tired of being lectured to and made to look like a fool. Irritably, he smirked and shook his head, no.

"Because Jefferson was an idealist, Mr. Huxley. And his Declaration along with the Constitution were both manmade documents positing *ideals*. They were conceived entirely from the idealistic minds of mortal men, not the indisputable mind of God. Therefore, they were not flawless, nor were they written in stone. That Jefferson and Madison were both forced to disobey their own hallowed words as presidents, by Jefferson's making the Louisiana Purchase or Madison's call for a standing army and a national bank, which were overtly unconstitutional, made each great thinker deeply despondent. That is also why our Bill of Rights became a necessary addendum. In essence, Mr. Huxley, in the real world idealism can never trump realism! So, you and your friends can try to defend your greed and recklessness by standing behind the shield of the Constitution, yet our own Founders have punched so many holes into that armor that, inevitably, you *will* receive our corrective blows."

Before Huxley could respond, the door had opened and an aide stepped in. "I beg your pardon, Mr. President, but we just received a telegram for Mr. Huxley. I was told to bring it here."

As Huxley squinted with curiosity, Garfield waved to the messenger to bring it to his guest. Dutifully, the aide delivered the yellow slip of paper, then pivoted around and exited the room. Garfield mindfully retook his seat as Huxley extinguished his cigar and gazed down at the letter. It was surprisingly brief, yet shockingly blunt. Huxley's eyes suddenly widened as his complexion faded to a pale shade of white.

It was painfully clear to Garfield that the letter contained grim news as he inquired concernedly, "What is it?"

Huxley strolled quasi-dazed over to a chair and fell backward, landing in the pleated upholstery, while his hand draped over the arm—the letter dangling like an unwanted piece of toilet paper.

"Shit!" he blasted as he slammed his fist on the arm of the chair, this time the telegram falling to the floor. "There's been an explosion at the mine this morning. This one appears to be a fiery whopper."

"I'm truly sorry, Archibald," Garfield said with sincerity and compassion.

Huxley, however, sat fixed—smoldering and oblivious to Garfield and the world around him. His pale green eyes oscillated wildly, evaluating the impending damages and fiscal repercussions, when suddenly, he exploded again, "I have three huge orders from Carnegie and dozens more from various railroads that have to be fulfilled. Those damned idiots! Damn them, damn them all! Heads *will* roll!"

Garfield squinted—his mind just now beginning to realize that something was amiss. Huxley's response was odd. Something crucial was missing. His eyes zeroed in on Huxley's face as he queried, "So, how many miners have been injured or killed?"

Huxley gazed up at the president, somewhat dazed, his eyes conveying that he hadn't even given his workers' lives a thought. Mindlessly, he admitted as much as he stuttered, "Uh, well, I...I don't quite know." Archie bent over swiftly to retrieve the telegram and rapidly scanned the initial words he had read *'Mine explosion. Major destruction. Still attempting to assess damages,'* finally landing on the last lethal line, *'Human toll: 42 dead, 16 wounded, still counting.'*

As Huxley relayed the tallies, Garfield shook his head with a jarring mixture of sympathy (for the casualties and their families) and disgust (over the appallingly avaricious and callous man sitting before him). Garfield had been wavering in his estimation of Huxley, but had now seen several glimpses of his dark soul that made it quite easy to pass a final verdict, and it was not good.

Huxley could see clearly by the indignant look on the president's face that his own true and tainted colors were revealed, and he now tried to paint a rosier image. "I reckon I should catch a train immediately, Mr. President. I need to care for my employees and their families, and naturally begin the process of making repairs." With a touch of melodrama, Archie rubbed his forehead, and added, "It's just terrible."

"I'll tell you what's terrible," Garfield fired back, his voice startling Huxley. "What's terrible is that this is the fourth or fifth explosion at your mine in, what?—ten months?"

Huxley barely had a chance to nod as Garfield's voice rose with even more disdain, "The timing of this tragedy is simply uncanny! It underscores my whole displeasure with this rapid growth of industrialization, which I know has many citizens disoriented and distressed. It has taken root so darned quickly that it has not only transformed our landscape with its filthy and dangerous presence, but has shifted families from healthy rural farmlands to squalid city tenements. I am not at all pleased with how these shanty buildings have sprout up like firethorn, Mr. Huxley. Not only are they eyesores, but their cheap construction has also caused disasters, of which the devastating fire in Chicago several years ago attests. And this vertical monopolization by tycoons, whereby owning every facet of their production, from owning the companies that manufacture their raw materials and tools to the core of the trust itself, has now included the building of these cities to incarcerate their captive laborers. This is not what I, or our Founders, would call freedom, Mr. Huxley. It is what I call *frightening!"*

Huxley had enough of being scolded, and stood up forcefully. "Mr. President, you once again are heaping only the faults of progress upon us industrialists. Like it or not, we are the true backbone of America, for without our creative vision, vigor, and innovations the common man would be content to sit on his little parcel of land and feed only himself and his family. I invested a great deal of money to build those tenements to care for my workers. And despite the fact that people are now less self-sufficient and need to buy groceries and clothes from others there are positive tradeoffs, which you fail to recognize, such as the new jobs created to fulfill those needs, and most importantly, how these city tenements bring people together."

Garfield rolled his eyes. "Yes, like cattle being corralled, or as you stated yourself, like cows to be milked dry!" The president had personally seen Huxley's decrepit tenements, which were not even new buildings, but rather old revamped structures from the 1700s that should have been demolished. As such, he knew the gifted conman was lying, and he continued vigorously; "George Pullman is the only tycoon I know of that has done something right! Pullman, Illinois is currently being built with a sense of purpose and pride for his railcar employees. Yet he is the exception rather than the rule! You all could learn something from him about giving back to society, after all, it is not like you don't have the money!"

"You're starting to sound like my coddling mother!" Huxley huffed. "I see you, too, expect the movers and shakers of this country to be wet nurses. Every man, Mr. President, has the freedom to choose a static or kinetic life—just as you gave up being a canal boy to get an education and become a general, congressman, and now President of the United States!"

Just then the door swung open as a rather lanky man, with short hair and a mustache, stepped in. "Oh! Excuse me, Mr. President. I wasn't aware that you were conducting a meeting."

Garfield's tense face gave way to a mellow smile. "No, no. Please. Come in."

As the man entered, Garfield purged his angst and looked at Huxley, once again, with diplomatic poise. "I would like to introduce you to my secretary of war, Robert Lincoln."

As Lincoln stretched out his arm to shake hands, Huxley bowed his head slightly. "It's an honor to meet you, Secretary. Your father was a great man."

"Thank you," Lincoln replied, "and you are Lieutenant Huxley, correct?"

"Yes, very good, Secretary," Huxley said, his ego enjoying the recognition. "I'm surprised a young man like you would know me, especially since you were studying at Harvard while old men like us were fighting."

"Well, I did witness the surrender at Appomattox, sir. But as secretary of war, I reckon it's my business to know," Lincoln said officially. Then with a touch of humor, he added, "Even if it is *ancient* history!"

As the two smiled, Garfield stepped closer, concerned. "So, Robert, how is your mother holding up in France?"

Lincoln smirked as he turned toward the president. "Odd you ask. She has finally returned after four-years absence. I need not tell you how difficult it has been since my father's death. It only saddled her with greater depression after suffering the loss of my three brothers." As the president and Huxley bowed their heads, speechless, Lincoln continued, "I do apologize. I came to speak with you about my recent appointment, not personal matters."

Garfield looked up. "Nonsense. By all means, speak freely. We here all know the tribulations you and your family have suffered, and I am most curious to know what ails you regarding your position?"

Lincoln cracked his neck, and stood erect. "As you are well aware, my mother's erratic behavior had concerned me greatly, and our relationship has been strained ever since I was forced to commit her to an asylum. But since her release, and subsequent stay in France, I had hoped for a rejuvenated woman, sound of mind, to return home. But such is not the case. Although somewhat more stable she still is overwrought with phobias, one being that she fears I, like my father, will be assassinated by taking this position."

Garfield gazed into space. "Ah, yes, of course. Secretary of War does have an ominous ring to it." He looked up into young Lincoln's eyes. "Have no concerns on my behalf, Robert—the choice is yours. Whatever your decision, I'll abide by it without passing judgment."

"Thank you, Mr. President," Lincoln replied, his eyes now distant and lethargic. "Everything seems topsy-turvy with my mother back home. It has not been easy."

An uncomfortable silence held the room in limbo for an odd moment, when Huxley suddenly took a bold step closer. "Excuse me, Mr. Secretary, but life is not easy. I, too, have suffered similar pains, but as I tried to explain to the president, you must chart your own course. The *fears* of a mother must not inter*fere* with your destiny! Choose the path that *you* want for *your* life, not *hers!*"

Lincoln gazed over at Huxley, at first a bit startled by his candor, yet now seriously digesting his stimulating advice. His eyes then glanced over at the president—whose eyebrows rose in anticipation—and then back to Huxley's. After another moment or two, he cracked his neck, once again, and nodded affirmatively. "Yes, you are absolutely right." His eyes darted back to Garfield. "Forgive my fleeting bout of indecision, Mr. President, but the Secretary of War has important matters to attend to. I do apologize for the intrusion. Please excuse me."

Garfield nodded happily and waved his hand as Huxley looked at the young secretary and winked. Lincoln pivoted around with a renewed sense of vigor and exited promptly.

Garfield turned and looked at Huxley. "I suppose some of your hard-skinned ways have their merits, Lieutenant!" As Huxley cracked a smile, Garfield added, "Well, I, too, must get back to work. Allow me to escort you downstairs."

Exiting the Blue Room, they began walking through the cross hall, which was partially covered with drop cloths, strewn planks of lumber and pails of plaster. The carpenters had left for the day, yet the renovations had been making even more of a mess, and Garfield apologized. He explained that Lucretia had been concerned about their five children and his mother, who were all expected to make the White House their home. Since the end of the Civil War, little had been done to maintain the huge building, and Garfield had made himself available to aid his wife in picking out paint, wallpaper and other furnishings. However, with Lucretia's recent illness, things became a bit more chaotic around the house, as Garfield's every waking moment had been filled with concern for her survival. However, that Lucretia seemed to escape the clutches of death, and was on the road to recovery, Garfield and his children were beginning to regain their typically upbeat and jovial sense of warmth.

As they strolled along, Garfield pointed to some of the remnant artifacts of past presidents—explaining to Huxley some of their ordeals, and then revealing some of his own. He elucidated how his troubles came not only from the Democrats, but also from his fellow Republicans. The tug-of-war between the Stalwarts and Half-Breeds had Garfield at his wits' end with their flagrant jockeying for power and self-interest. Even before his inauguration four months ago, his Half-Breed companions had moved swiftly ahead without his knowledge and nominated Chester Arthur as his vice president. Chester was not only a Stalwart, but was Conkling's number one man in New York, who also happened to lose his coveted seat as customs collector when President Hayes fired him on charges of cronyism and corruption. Since the Half-Breeds had thwarted the Stalwarts attempts to reinstate Grant, by handing Garfield the nomination, they felt a bone had to be thrown to the Stalwarts, and Arthur seemed like a fair tradeoff. However, as their fellow Half-Breed, John Sherman, opined, "The nomination of Arthur is a ridiculous burlesque. He never held an office except the one he was removed from!"

Huxley looked at the president as they descended the stairs. "I can appreciate your situation. Even you, as president, must make concessions with your team of power-hungry wolves. Whereas I, on the other hand, rule the roost!"

Garfield chuckled. "Indeed you do! And, at times, I do envy your unfettered tyrannical power. However, I could never acknowledge such a system as being the best mankind can craft."

Huxley shook his head. "From my position, there's certainly no better system—I assure you! And I never have to fret about my head supervisor causing me grief or ever taking my place."

"Well, the chances are slim to none that I'll be handing over my presidency to Chester. After all, such a transfer of power has only occurred twice in our nation's history, and I am as fit as an ox."

As Garfield slapped the sides of his sturdy, broad chest, Huxley smiled. "That's very true, General."

Garfield grabbed Huxley's arm and came to a halt half way down the stairs. He brought his attention to a small photo of President Grant hanging on the wall. "It's a shame. The man was perhaps this country's greatest general, yet such a failure as president."

Huxley gazed at the resilient warrior who was captured in a few seconds of elapsed time, leaning against a tree—unassuming, yet unassailable. As his thoughts contemplated Grant in his role as president, a disturbing burning sensation began to well deep in his heart. Grant and Custer were his two idols, particularly due to the fact that Custer finished last in his class at West Point, while Grant proved only average. Huxley always believed in the underdog, being one himself, and it galled him to speak poorly of Grant. "I'll have to admit," Huxley replied tactically, "he sure did let his *administration* get away with murder." Content at having shifted the blame away from his hero, Huxley now drew attention to this broader body of corruption. "It's funny how you enjoy scolding us tycoons, while your precious Congress is infested with rats!"

Garfield actually smiled. "It grieves me to no end to agree with you, Huxley. But, yes, there was, and still is, a great deal of corruption in Washington. But as I had stated some years back, the people are responsible for the character of their Congress. If that body be ignorant, reckless, and corrupt, it is because the people tolerate ignorance, recklessness, and corruption. If it be intelligent, brave, and pure, it is because the people demand these high qualities to represent them in the national legislature."

"Well, you do have a point," Huxley replied, "as no one can vote *me* out of office. However, what disturbs me is that our Founders established a system where it was supposed to be a temporary and noble calling to serve our country. But nowadays statesmen have permanently implanted themselves in office—like deep-seated weeds that mingle with lobbying networks of ivy. And the entire House is now overgrown. I'd say that some serious pruning is needed!"

Before Garfield could respond, Huxley glanced back at the photo of Grant and quickly back at him as he dished out a final and direct punch. "And speaking of the corruption within your own House; don't you find it odd that our country has been suffering the economic pains of Reconstruction, yet you never lodged a complaint about how Grant's administration doubled your princely salary from $25,000 to 50,000!"

Garfield gazed uneasily into Huxley's eyes. "Well, I have only been in office for four months, so I will take that suggestion under consideration. However, the rapid expansion of this country did necessitate some sort of salary increase. Just what the proper ratio is perhaps needs closer scrutiny." With a look of sincerity, he added, "I believe we both made some injurious yet healthy comments here today. Let's pray to God that we all shall see our way through this ugly mess!"

Despite Huxley's sound critiques, Garfield still knew he was a deceitful viper, never to be trusted. Nevertheless, Garfield nodded cordially and extended his hand downward, thus resuming their descent.

No sooner did they take a step, than the youthful voice of Garfield's ten-year-old son Irvin sound out behind them, "Clear the way! I'm coming through!"

The two men turned and immediately pressed themselves against the railing as little Irvin came barreling down the staircase riding his bicycle. As Huxley looked on, astonished, little Irvin bobbed and rattled as the wheels banged each step. As he swerved to avoid hitting his father and guest, Irvin's handlebars scratched the wainscoting as he continued his descent, giggling the whole way down.

Huxley looked at Garfield, awaiting a reprimand, yet none came. He shook his head. "General, are you telling me that you permit such wayward behavior…in *this* house, no less?"

Garfield smiled. "Lieutenant, this is not the army. Nor do I run my house like a military unit. These are children, and believe me when I say that I press my children's noses to the grindstone each and every day—quizzing them on Homer, Cicero, Adam Smith, Dickens, history, art, and much more. But, children, Mr. Huxley, are just that—*children*, and they need to have fun, for youth surely is fleeting."

Huxley's face twisted, his eyes reproachful and piercing. "If *my* children ever dared to have such *fun* they'd get themselves a swift beating!" He then looked at the scratched wainscoting. "And you say renovations must be made. For what? This abuse!"

"That sort of abuse, Mr. Huxley, is what I consider acceptable, being that they are material items and can be easily repaired. However, physical abuse of a child, which also causes mental abuse somewhere down the line, is what I consider unacceptable abuse."

Just then Joseph Brown, Garfield's personal secretary, scurried up the stairs. Cupping his hand along the edge of his mouth, he leaned toward Garfield's ear and whispered, "Mr. President, the throng of irritating job seekers are growing restless!" As Garfield rolled his eyes, Brown continued, only this time his voice was well above a whisper, "As you instructed, I told them to be patient. Yet some are becoming rather indignant."

Garfield turned toward Huxley—knowing very well that he heard the aggravated secretary's message—and he huffed, "My God! Do you see what I mean? It never ends. My day is frittered away by these desperate job seekers, when it ought to be given to the great problems which concern the whole country. Just think of what a president could accomplish without having to waste precious time with such utter nonsense!"

"I don't know how you manage it," Huxley concurred.

Garfield turned back toward Brown. "Joseph, please go down and tell them to come back tomorrow at the usual afternoon time slot. Between tending to matters of state and preparing to leave in two days to meet Lucretia, I simply have too much to do, and it already is quite late."

Dutifully, the secretary descended the steps, as Garfield gazed back at Huxley. "I cannot wait to go on vacation! Some of these opportunity seekers are so unscrupulous and ravenous in their zeal that I image they would consume my brain, flesh and blood!" As Huxley laughed, Garfield continued, "This one man, Charles, for instance, has no qualifications, yet lauds the fact that he is a fervent supporter of the Stalwarts, as if I, a Half-Breed, endorse cronyism. And if that is not bad enough, his first request, quite brazenly, was to be named minister to Austria." Huxley's eyebrows rose with astonishment and amusement, as Garfield added, "Then, just recently, on a whim, he changed his plea. Charles now wishes to be council-general to France. Is that not the most perfect illustration of unparalleled audacity and impudence!?"

Huxley laughed. "Either that, or a perfect illustration of a colossal set of balls!"

Garfield didn't appreciate crude humor, yet being a jovial man by nature, he had to chuckle.

"Take a look down there!" Garfield said as he pointed to the crowded foyer, some 12 steps below. "This routine of allowing the public free access to the executive branch has been a staple of our libertarian system, yet my administration has taken steps to decrease this nuisance, cutting the three hours standard down to one. That is more than enough time to waste speaking to Stalwart leeches like Charles Guiteau or whatever else wriggles down there."

Huxley's eyes widened as he gazed at the president with a half-cracked smile. "Did you say Charles Guiteau?"

Garfield looked at Huxley, surprised. "Don't tell me you know that little weasel with his threadbare suit and mangy appearance?"

Huxley's head recoiled. "Mangy? Odd, the Charles Guiteau I knew was always decked out in the finest linens and wool. But, he *was* petite of frame." Huxley leaned toward Garfield, inquisitive. "Very short hair, large penetrating eyes, beard and mustache?"

"That's the man alright," Garfield confirmed. "And to the utter dismay of my staff, he kept returning like a bad penny!"

Huxley laughed. "Ah, yes, that's Charles alright. He was a very persistent little devil. He really didn't have any friends, being a bit of an odd duck, but whatever he set his little mind upon became an obsession. I imagine the lonely drifter fell upon hard times."

"By his shabby appearance and lack of substance, I should think so!" Garfield replied. "And an odd duck indeed! He has written me several letters, making all sorts of outlandish claims, and for a long while, as I said, made daily visits. He had become a recurring nuisance to my staff here as well as at the State Department. Yet, from what I've been told, I believe my secretary of state, James Blaine, gave him a good tongue-lashing. I imagine Blaine did a fine job of plucking his mangy feathers, since Guiteau has not been seen nesting around here for the past few weeks." Garfield rubbed his hairy chin as he added, "So, you say you actually know this peculiar bird?"

Huxley chuckled. "I'm afraid so. It was right before the war when, by chance, I had run into him. Our discussion soon landed upon what we did for a living, and I had mentioned I was making a start in the coal business. As for Charles, well, he told me that he was in the employ of Jesus Christ & Co., the very ablest and strongest firm in the universe!"

As Huxley chuckled once again, only louder, Garfield shook his head, only quasi amused. "Well, it doesn't surprise me that he claimed to hold a position in the Lord's administration, for he had also claimed that his one brief speech in New York is what made me president."

Evidently Chester Arthur—the Stalwart who had been latched onto Garfield's Half-Breed hip as his vice president—had given Charles Guiteau the chance to make the stump speech. That was because Guiteau had also made a nuisance of himself to Arthur, even appearing at his front door one day, professing his Stalwart allegiance and begging to say a few words on behalf of the presidential candidate and their beloved Republican Party. However, Guiteau's speech had been only a few minutes in duration. Moreover, it was so inconsequential that its duration in the minds of the attendees was even shorter; to the point that one could say it was fleeting and soon forgotten.

However, unbeknownst to all was that this zealous Stalwart—who had obsessively knocked on their doors for months—had an epiphany three weeks ago. Being rejected a position, and coldly rebuffed by Secretary of State Blaine, Guiteau was miraculously struck with a directive from the heavens above as if by lightning. It had all become abundantly clear to him that, for the benefit of the nation, President Garfield had to be removed. Charles did not like the words kill or assassinate, for this divine mission was indeed one of cleansing, namely cleansing the Republican Party of its Half-Breed leader so that the Stalwart Chester Arthur could take office. Hence, Guiteau preferred the term removal.

Three weeks ago, Charles had stepped into John O'Meara's firearms shop and—despite his total ignorance of guns—spotted his cleansing tool of choice. It was a .44 caliber British Bulldog with an ivory handle—the largest and most powerful handgun in O'Meara's display. Oddly enough, O'Meara had a bad feeling about this particular customer, who had "a peculiar manner, a peculiar attitude, and a peculiar walk," but, hey, the quirky little man had the right to bear arms, and it wasn't O'Meara's business to ask questions. So, the ten-dollar sale was made, and the peculiar little man took his new little bundle of death—along with a box of cartridges—and headed to the Potomac River to shoot some trees and aquatic birds to get better acquainted.

A week later, on June 12th, Guiteau had felt ready to fulfill his mission and even made his first attempt. He had stalked Garfield, who, after missing church for several weeks due to Lucretia's sickness, had decided to resume attending services. As Guiteau stepped into the church that day, he easily spotted the tall, broad-shouldered president, who dwarfed the others in his pew. However, the religious fanatic found himself sidetracked by the sermon and, unable to restrain himself, he heckled the pastor. Oddly enough, that outburst had even prompted Garfield to log in his diary that night the incident of "a dull young man, with a loud voice, trying to pound noise into the question."

Needless to say, Charles had been sidetracked that day, and the irritated would-be assassin had marched out of the church. Guiteau had failed to complete his mission, but his disappointment had soon been replaced with delight when he read an exciting bulletin in the paper. Garfield was scheduled to take a vacation, and would be at the Baltimore & Potomac rail station the following Saturday. Upon reading that tidbit of news, Guiteau's weaselly face had twisted with a sinister grin.

However, when Saturday arrived, Charles had been confronted by yet another interruption. Upon seeing Garfield escort his frail and recuperating wife through the station, Charles had a change of heart—he did not wish to upset Lucretia. So, the removal was postponed, once again. However, Garfield had only taken Lucretia to New Jersey that day and returned promptly. His plan was to spend several more days in Washington before taking the train to meet her for their official vacation.

Now that Garfield was back in town, and preparing to leave in two days, Guiteau recognized his chance, and was now impatiently lying in wait to make his saintly strike. Filled with anticipation, Guiteau looked forward to fulfilling his divine mission and then basking in the embrace of his fellow Stalwarts, reveling in the glorification of fame, and earning his illustrious place in history.

Meanwhile, as Garfield stood on the stairs with Huxley, he was still contemplating Guiteau's wild claim that his stump speech had made him president. He was equally dumbfounded by the fact that Huxley knew this disturbing little man who claimed to work for Jesus & Co. "What more can I say, Lieutenant, the man is a flimflamming lunatic!"

Huxley laughed. "Yes, but I found his eccentric nature to be rather intriguing. In fact, about three months before I signed up with my regiment, Charles invited me to the Oneida Community in New York."

Garfield squinted. "What exactly is that?"

A devilish smile wrinkled Huxley's face. "Well, let me put it this way; it certainly wasn't a community that Jesus would condone, it was more like a cult from Sodom or Gomorra. But we did have one hell of a good time there."

Intrigued, Garfield prodded Huxley to continue, which he did. He explained how the cult was led by the spiritual grand master John Humphrey Noyes, who claimed he had reached a state of divine perfection, and thus was anointed by God to guide others. One of Noyes' divine directives to his 300 plus members was his unique concept of complex marriage, or free love. His provocative edict declared that it was unhealthy and pernicious, not to mention selfish, to give oneself only to one other person, and so multiplicity in lieu of monogamy was their sworn duty. However, while Oneida's utopian sex-community engaged in these perpetually rotating couplings, of which Huxley took part of for two lustful months, there was one very odd young man whom most women roundly rejected—Charles Guiteau.

Garfield gazed at Huxley without so much as a quiver. At this point, there wasn't much Huxley could say anymore to astonish him. In fact, the more he thought about it the more natural it seemed that Guiteau and Huxley had crossed paths, and engaged in lewd sexual activities.

As they resumed descending the stairs, Garfield's personal secretary took several steps up to meet them. "Mr. President," Brown said, "I'm pleased to report that I managed to shoo away the pestering flock of office seekers, all, that is, save for one ornery man in a white suit."

Garfield looked at Brown, and said adamantly, "Well, tell the pesky dove to fly away!"

As they reached the foyer, a Southern voice boomed, "Have no fear, this beautiful bird won't be nesting in a dump like this!"

The three men laughed as Garfield's face lit up. Eagerly, he extended his hand. "Why, Mr. Twain, how good to see you. In fact, your name had recently come up in conversation."

As the two shook hands, Twain replied, "Well, I hope it didn't come up like indigestion!"

"Not at all!" Garfield said with a giggle. He then turned toward Huxley. "Have you ever met Mr. Twain?"

Huxley extended his hand. "No, I can't say I have."

Twain smiled as he shook his hand. "Actually, *you can say*. You can say whatever you want. This is a free country."

As they all chuckled, Garfield added jovially, "And it shall remain free as long as *I* am president!"

Just then the peculiar ring of the new device called a telephone could be heard; it had been installed under the previous administration by President Hayes.

Joseph Brown glanced at the president. "I reckon I should get that!"

Garfield nodded. Brown politely excused himself and ran down the hall. Garfield then turned toward his two guests. "That is one interesting device Mr. Bell invented."

Twain smiled and responded with his typical brand of humor, "As far as I'm concerned, the voice already carries entirely too far as it is. If Bell had invented a muffler or a gag he would have done a real service!"

Garfield laughed, while Huxley took the joke seriously. "I could not agree more. I can just imagine my wife getting her hands on this contraption and chewing my ear off while I'm at work."

Twain's smile mellowed. "Well, sir, I imagine there will be some that will abuse this newfangled device, but its gargantuan potential seems self evident. I've already signed up to have two installed in my home; one downstairs for the family and one for myself in my billiards room."

Huxley smirked. "Well, you better have a ball in your billiards room while you still can, Mr. Twain, because once your lair is tapped by a conduit, like my mines are by drillers, I can assure you—all that you cherish in that room will be extracted! Your privacy, your recreation, your very freedom!"

Twain gazed over at Garfield and raised his bushy eyebrows. "I believe your friend, here, has an aversion to progress and people, Mr. President."

Huxley couldn't care less what Twain thought of him. As far as he was concerned, Twain was a mere loafer who no longer held a real job, but just sat around scribbling silly stories with his soft, clean hands. Such a person served no purpose in Huxley's world. If Huxley couldn't use a person in some fashion to bolster his bottom-line they were as good as useless. And the fact that Huxley hadn't understood Twain's *gilded* play on words, nor much else that radiated out of the bard's quicksilver mind, only reinforced his belief that understanding such things was of little practical use, since it never held him back. After all, he was one of the richest men in the United States, so he had neither the need nor desire to waste his precious time with high-minded nonsense, especially with a man who had wittily criticized men like Huxley, calling them Robber Barons.

"Mr. Twain, I happen to be Archibald Desmond Huxley, owner of Huxley Coal. And I have no aversion, as you say, to progress, because I am *actively engaged* in *making progress,* and not simply sitting on my ass with a white suit and feather quill deriding it!"

Twain glanced at Garfield (who uncomfortably shrugged his shoulders) and then back at Huxley. "Well, it appears my feathery quill has just as much power, influence, and value as any robber baron, for it evidently pricked *your* boorish skin!"

Naturally, Twain's boorish play on words also referred to a boar, in light of Huxley's garish hunting jacket, yet Archie only knew of the wild smelly animal, not the crass insensitive boor, which he also was.

Huxley huffed, "You can stick that feathery little quill up your ass! You may think you're superior just because you write lofty words in your white suit with a feather plucked from your self-righteous, angelic wings, but it's men like me who grapple in the pits of hell on this earth that make progress and who truly deserve acclaim. And as for me being a boar, I'll tell you this: I've shot and killed more boars than you could ever record with that flimsy little feather of yours!"

Garfield's face turned red. "Lieutenant! Watch your foul tongue, especially towards such an esteemed guest as Mr. Twain. Is that understood?"

The steely glint in Huxley's eye was unnerving, even to the seasoned general, as he seethed through his teeth, "I've wasted enough time here anyhow. I have a mine that has just been destroyed by an explosion to attend to!"

Twain tried not to smile, knowing that lives were certainly lost, but the validation of his comment was just too much for him to keep silent. "Ah! So I see! And just how many explosions should my feathery quill record for Huxley Coal now? Is it five? Seven? Or ten this year?"

As Huxley's patience withered and his nostrils flared, Twain added, "And how many lives have you trampled on in your stampeding zeal to extract gold from coal? And for that matter, how much gold falls into your bank-sized vault as compared to the tattered pockets of your browbeaten moles?"

Huxley gazed at both men and simply huffed. "I have a train to catch! So to avoid bloodshed, I'll say good night, gentlemen." With that, Archie paced heatedly to the front door and saw himself out—slamming the door behind him.

Garfield looked at Twain. "I do apologize. That man, I must make clear, is not, nor was he ever, a friend of mine. Unfortunately, becoming president has only added another measure of aggravation to my life. It seems the greater power and influence a man attains in life the greater the barrage of leeches and lunatics that come out of the woodwork to accost him. Or in Huxley's case, slither out of dirty mine holes!"

Twain smiled. "Yes, I envy you not. I never met the man before, but I should have guessed with that garish costume. I have read a great deal about Huxley in the news, and from what I have read and recorded myself, he did not disappoint me. He is a most colorful character!"

Garfield shook his head. "No, Mr. Twain. Huxley is the absence of color—namely black. And that man's soul is as black as the coal he unearths."

"I stand corrected," Twain said. "It's gratifying to be in the company of a man smarter than I—" then in jest, he added, "it doesn't happen often!"

Garfield laughed and patted Twain on the back, knowing very well that Twain was the nation's greatest humorist and self-educated. "Well, I had the good fortune of going to school and college, Mark, but I dare say you are smarter than most of the educated men I know!" Looking into his eyes, he queried, "So, what brings you here?"

"Actually, I was just passing through, and read in the paper that you plan on taking a vacation in two days. So, I just wanted to say hello and extend my best wishes that the First Lady has a full recovery." As Garfield thanked him for his sympathies, Twain checked his watch. "In fact, I have to catch a train myself. I just hope it's not the same one that viper will be slithering on!"

Garfield chuckled and cordially grabbed Twain's elbow. "Well, thank God there are plenty of Pullman cars you can choose from. But, please, allow me to escort you to the front porch. I'll have my personal carriage take you."

As they stepped out the door, they could see Huxley's carriage receding slowly into the blackness of night.

Twain gazed at the president. "As much as that man repulses me, I reckon the country needs crude men like Huxley. Certainly no Harvard professor would dare to rape the earth for the crude commodities our country needs to prosper."

"Perhaps," Garfield replied as his eyes watched the carriage vanish into the dark haze. "That man is a mystery,

Mr. Twain. At times, he appeared philosophically sound, and at other times…well, just as dense, cold and dangerous as dynamite."

Twain smiled. "Yes, after what I've read, and have now witnessed, one thing seems quite evident. Archibald Desmond Huxley has no desire to rethink anything that has been etched into his anthracitic head. And I reckon a jackhammer is about the only thing that would rattle some sense into him!"

Garfield laughed as he summoned for his carriage. Meanwhile, Twain's eyes caught the odd vision of the unfinished Washington Monument in the distance. Bathed in the bluish-gray glow of moonlight it evoked a somber impression.

Garfield turned and noticed Twain's line of vision. "Ah, yes, *that* is another mystery. Why that monument has never been completed is a national disgrace. For thirty-three years, it has been a constant reminder of how unfinished and unpolished this nation truly is."

Twain's eyes remained fixed on the truncated obelisk. "Well, then perhaps it's most fitting that it remains just as it is," he giggled. "Actually, it looks like a factory chimney with the top broken off."

Garfield glanced at Twain and chuckled. "It does at that." His face became solemn. "I must admit, after hearing about Huxley's explosion and so many other disasters that plague our factories, I suppose you're right. This nation is far from complete." As he gazed back at the pathetic monument—dedicated to the valiant Father of the nation, who selflessly refused kingship to help create the freedom-loving republic that would influence the entire world—Garfield was overcome with emotion.

As the carriage pulled up, Garfield looked at Twain. "Well, although the monument captures the reality of our nation, Mr. Twain, I must disagree—it *must* be completed. We are a nation with high ideals. And despite our flaws, it is the eternal striving for that ideal that makes us the greatest nation on earth. We can never allow that noble vision to fade."

Twain smiled as he shook the president's hand. "We are a fortunate nation to have such a wise and noble man at the helm. I thank you, the nation thanks you—" as Twain stepped up into the coach, he turned and added with a giggle, "and I thank you, once again, for this presidential transportation!"

Garfield smiled. "My pleasure, Mr. Twain. Especially since I borrowed that carriage from Rutherford Hayes. The truth is, I cannot afford one!"

Twain laughed heartily. "Well, then I thank you both; Rutherford for the carriage, and you for offering it!"

With a crack of the whip, the horses bucked and the carriage took off down the gravely driveway, receding into the dark dewy drapes of night.

Back at Pittsburgh

July 1, 1881

The amber glow of dawn illuminated the threadbare curtains covering the Wozniaks' kitchen window. Marc and Stan were eating breakfast and playing a quick game of poker, while their mother began scrubbing the crispy ring of egg remains off the skillet.

Stan closed his trusty Bible, which he read religiously every morning, and then looked at Marc. "So, what in God's name are we going to do now? How can we possibly survive without pa and Tasso?"

Marc stopped shuffling the deck, and swallowed a lump of scrambled eggs. He looked at his older brother with a mature gaze that was well beyond his years. "I know you may not like to hear this Stan, but pa, right before he…well, he told me to handle things. So, please, don't worry. I'll take care of you and momma."

As Marc began to deal out another round of cards, Stan looked helplessly down at the table. He put his hand on the Bible and closed his glazed eyes. "God help us!"

Ever since his own crippling disaster at the mine, Stan's absorption of the healing words of the Bible aided his day-to-day existence. He had found comfort and some degree of acceptance for his misfortune, which was reinforced primarily by his devout father, but now all seemed lost.

Sophia dried her wet hands and walked up behind Stan. She wrapped her arms around him, offering comfort and strength, but soon found herself slowly descending— her legs giving way as she began crying. Landing on her knees, she clutched firmly onto Stan as she sobbed on the back of his shoulder.

Marc sprang to his feet, and then knelt beside his brother—placing his hand over his (both caressing the Bible), while his other hand touched his weeping mother's shoulder. "I swear to God, I *will* get us through this. I promise!"

Sophia had a sleepless night, hoping to awake as the stone pillar to support them through this dreadful nightmare. However, upon hearing Stan's tremulous question about their survival, reality struck hard, and she crumbled. She couldn't fathom how Marc could ever carry the load all by himself, especially since Ted—with his cursed gift for bad decisions—chose the most inopportune time to run off.

Sophia's once solid foundation of Catholicism had likewise started to crumble years earlier when she started reading Darwin's startling theory of evolution. Academia had first lauded the theory, yet over the ensuing years it had been greatly publicized and was now gaining a strong foothold in America. Adding to Sophia's loss of faith was her pragmatic view of human nature and the events of her life, which also had been her teacher. Having prayed in vain countless times for God to help her rectify Ted's perpetual transgressions, coupled with Stan's crippling disaster, and now Jedrek's brutal and senseless death, it seemed that Ted's abandonment of his family in this time of great peril further confirmed what she had suspected all along; namely, a truly loving God could *never* be so cruel and merciless.

Sophia prided herself on being different from the seemingly helpless lot that Jedrek and her were forced to live among, who, in her eyes, all listlessly suffered the abuses of Huxley's slave machine along with a reticent government in pathetic silence. Sophia also found it humiliating how these people all looked to passages in the Bible for strength, such as the often-quoted trials of Job, which Sophia believed any rational person could see were heartless torments, bordering on sadistic murders. Yet such beliefs only acted like ether to pacify these sufferers, rather than spur them on to fight with their own will to better their lot in life.

Nevertheless, Sophia was well aware that it was at moments like this (when death and loss offered nothing but pain) that religion offered one of its truly magnificent benefits—it acted like a potent tonic, soothing the pain and strengthening resolve. The key, however, was to remain religiously drunk—never to be cognizant of its false, delusional nature. Yet Sophia was finding that harder to do with each sobering day of her dreary life and with each new disaster that tore away another chunk of her very heart and soul. Now gutted and worn out, Sophia suddenly found comfort in little Marc's seemingly believable promise to get them through this disaster. After all, she thought, what was left to cling on to?

She looked up at her angelic little ray of hope and smiled. Rising to her feet, she leaned over and lifted Stan's chin. She could feel the stronger side of her Gemini spirit also rising to the fore as she said, "Stan, we must give Marc all of our support and trust." As Stan sniffled and gazed up, she turned toward Marc—her eyes deep and passionate. "Honey, if there is a God who is offering us a shred of hope, that shred is *you!*"

The corner of Marc's lips lifted along with his confidence as he said, "Thank you, Momma." His eyes veered toward the floor and back up, while his face turned austere. "But, please, do not call me Honey anymore. I'm *not* a baby!"

Sophia smiled and nodded affectionately. "Very well, if it means that much to you, then I shall try not to say it ever again. But, Marc, it was not meant to address you as a toddler, but rather as my loving son."

Marc's face mellowed as he began to rethink his request. His lips twisted ever so slightly. "Well, I reckon if you meant it like that it's fine. But, I just think Honey sounds too gooey and sweet!"

As Sophia giggled and drew her sons in for a hug, Stan suddenly noticed the three Aces he had just been dealt. Excited, he placed them down, face up. "Wow! Would you look at that?"

Oddly enough, the trio's embraces and Stan's three Aces were simultaneously accompanied by three knocks on the door.

As the three turned, Stan's eyes widened. "Oh, my God!" he said, clearly recognizing the three sets of triplets. "That *must* be good news; perhaps it's a spiritual blessing by the Trinity."

Sophia squinted, believing it to be some odd astrological convergence of three signs foretelling good luck.

Meanwhile, Marc sprang up and ran to the door. Swinging it open, he said, "No, it's just R-R-Rusty!"

As Sophia and Stan chuckled, Mulvaney looked at them, dumbfounded. "What's so blamin' funny?"

Sophia waved him in. "Oh, nothing, please come in. We three are simply glad to see you. That's all."

As Mulvaney stepped in, he scratched his furry red beard. "You're one hell of a strong family. I expected to be greeted with a round of sad faces and tears."

No sooner had he spoken those words, had the three faces before him already returned to their serene form—or in Stan's case, a sullen portrait of despair.

Sophia solemnly glanced down at her apron and brushed off the breadcrumbs. "I suppose it was just an odd occurrence, Rusty. A little bit of levity helps people cope, you know. But we sure have our work cut out for us."

"Indeed, we all do," Rusty replied, dejectedly. "Mr. Huxley will have my head today when he finds out about Tass—I mean Ted, stealing his stallion."

"Oh, my," Sophia said, "I didn't even think of that. I'm sorry to have put you in this position. I'll accept full responsibility for Ted's actions, Rusty."

"Now, now! Please," Mulvaney said emphatically, "I'm a danged fool for even mentioning it. I do apologize. Don't you worry none, Sophia. You have far greater things to worry about than this silly old horse business."

Marc's right foot was tapping the floorboards heatedly, while his left hand gripped his suspenders firmly. "Mom! I said I would take care of things! You just worry about Stan and the house. I'll handle this."

Sophia glanced uncomfortably up at Rusty and then down at Marc. "Yes, yes. I know, Hon—uh, Marc. But know this, I do not want you getting in over your head. I am here for you as is your brother. So, while you are the man of the house, we still are a family that pulls together. Remember what I told you about the Roman fasces. *Capisce?*"

"Yes, yes, fine," Marc huffed, "but don't bother staying up tonight to cook my dinner. I have a busy day. I reckon I'll be at the mine all day, and after work, I'll be going to Pendleton's iron shop."

As he kissed his mother, he gazed over at Stan. "Great hand, Ace! You win. I'll see you tonight or in the morning."

As Marc walked out the door, he gazed up at Rusty. His face mellowed. Although he was happy to be the little man in charge, he wasn't looking forward to going back to the mine that killed his father. The incomprehensible loss of his father, once again, came rushing back and struck him hard; as his heart dropped with each tepid step he took toward the street. But somehow Marc knew his father's last words would guide him through this difficult nightmare, and he raised his head and marched up to Huxley's roan horse.

Rusty was already in the saddle, and Marc hopped up behind him. With a firm kick, they began to canter down the street. Passing a variety of shops, whose owners were just beginning to open up their doors, and mothers emptying dirty washbasins into the cobbled streets, they exited the city. Riding over hills and through the peaceful valleys of Westmoreland County, Rusty impulsively decided to veer off the main path and began galloping alongside the railroad tracks. However, on this morning there were no trains loaded with coal beating up the rails. All was quiet and disturbingly odd; a primer for what they were about to face as the faint visage of Huxley Coal's main plant appeared in the distance. As Rusty ratcheted down from a gallop to a canter, the mare snorted. It was oddly the only sound they heard, other than the clatter of hooves hitting the dirt. The humming and clanking of motors and whooshing blades in the Fan House were silent, no steam engines or mules were carting coal, and not even the harsh sounds of jackhammers could be heard. The silence was unnerving and unnatural. No sooner did they take another step, did a loud explosion shatter the still morning air—nearly knocking them off their horse as the animal reared up. The power of the shockwave was so strong that their bodies felt the physical punch, as did the horse, which now turned in panic and began to run.

Rusty yelled back to Marc, "Hold on! I'm going to try one of your pa's moves." With that, Rusty held the rein in his left hand and gave the horse a solid punch with his right to its thick, meaty neck.

Pulling the reins evenly downward, Rusty got the mare's attention, and it slowly complied.

"What, in God's name, was that?" Marc exclaimed, "I thought the firedamp explosions ended yesterday?"

Rusty looked up at the billowing black smoke that rose some 200 yards away. "I'll be danged if I know? But we best get over there right quick. They'll need our help!"

As the echo of the blast ricocheted off the surrounding cliffs and slowly dissipated, they galloped to the central depot of the mine. It was curiously vacant. Slowing the horse down to a balls-crunching trot, Rusty pushed himself off the saddle with his long legs.

Meanwhile, Marc grabbed his crotch and cried, "Rusty! Slow down, please!"

Rusty turned. "Sorry, little one. But things are awfully peculiar around here. Where the hell is everybody?"

As the horse came to a soft and slow saunter, Rusty and Marc's head swiveled around, attempting to spot any signs of life. But all they heard was the horse's shoes clopping the hard, rocky ground, while smoke continued to billow upward out of the mine's airshaft.

A voice suddenly rang out, "Hey, Mulvaney, you have a death wish or something?"

As they turned toward the voice, they saw Supervisor Jack Hastings walking toward them.

"What's that?" Rusty replied, not hearing what he said.

As Hastings approached, other workers began to emerge from around the perimeter, converging on the open lot.

"Didn't you see the sign we posted about a mile back?" Hastings barked.

Rusty spun around and looked at Marc. "Did you see any sign?"

Marc shook his head and turned toward Hastings. "Well, actually we rode along the tracks today, instead of the main path."

Hastings huffed. "Well, the sign said 'BLAST AREA! Do Not Enter until 9:00 a.m.'" He gazed down at his watch. "And it is now 8:45. You're awfully lucky you didn't arrive one minute sooner. You two would have been pelted into Swiss cheese!"

Rusty scratched his head, still not comprehending what was going on.

Meanwhile, Marc hopped off the horse and looked quizzically up at Hastings. "But, I don't get it. Why are you blasting?"

As Hastings began to reply, a deep, booming voice drowned him out, "Because this leg of the mine is shot! That's why!"

As they all turned, there was Archibald Huxley walking toward them slapping his riding whip against his leg. All eyes watched as he stepped right in front of little Marc and gazed down at him.

"Now, I know you lost your pa, son, and I'm awfully sorry to hear about that. But I have a business to run." Looking up at Rusty, he added, "So, get my horse in the stable and haul that big cloddy ass of yours down to tunnel 13. You'll be doing a hell of a lot of drilling today."

Rusty's eyes widened. "You want me to start drilling in *tunnel 13!?*"

"Are you deaf?" Huxley snapped.

Archie's patience and any ounce of compassion he had for the dead was being quickly obliterated as an avalanche of projected repair bills and cancelled sales slips cluttered his mind. He didn't have time to explain every detail to a numbskull like Rusty, but decided to offer another dose of information to clarify his intentions, "Look, Mulvaney, the largest vein of anthracite had recently been found there, so, guess what? That's where we drill. I know that may come as a big surprise to you, but get your gear and start drilling!"

Rusty's dilated pupils betrayed his trepidation. Knowing that yesterday's explosion was due to a methane build up in that artery, he considered it a death sentence. "B-but, Mr. Huxley, w-what about all the firedamp?"

Huxley's face flashed with rage as he blasted, "Do you want a job, you dumb, cowering Mick!? If not, there are dozens of Chinks who will jump at the offer!"

Rusty's lips twisted at the insult, but he was painfully aware of the cheap Chinese laborers that had put a few of his friends out of work, one being Ying. Rusty steadied his horse and nodded meekly. "Yes, sir! I'll get there faster than a jackrabbit."

"You damned well better!" Huxley blasted.

Rusty pulled the reins, spun the horse around, and bolted.

Marc realized this wasn't the best time to voice his grievances, but after losing his father, he was beginning to feel that nothing seemed too darned important at Huxley's hellhole. After all, he still had an invitation by Pendleton to do ironwork, and Cal was a good, honest man that besides knowing how to *temper* iron, never lost his own.

"Pardon me—" Marc said, just as Huxley was beginning to march away, "I still don't understand."

Huxley stopped and spun around. "Understand what?"

"Why you blasted the main leg of the mine?"

Huxley rolled his eyes as he slapped the side of his leg with his riding whip. "Look, son. I really don't have time to give *you* an education about *my* business. You just report to your supervisor like a good little boy and do whatever they tell you. Be that feeding the mules, collecting debris or whatever it is they have a little tyke, like you, do. *Now* do you understand?"

As Huxley pivoted around and began walking away, Marc yelled out, "No! *I do not.* The main leg contains the airshaft. How will we get air down there?"

Huxley stopped so suddenly that his flashy boots kicked up a puff-cloud of dust. His head spun around like an owl's, while his eyes shed a steely glint that was razor sharp. "Listen, son, it is none of your damned business how I run my mine! And if you keep it up, you may just have to find yourself another job."

"Fine!" Marc retorted. "Go ahead! Fire me." He gazed at all the stunned workers who were now glued to their rousing conversation, and added, "That would look real swell in the *Pittsburgh Gazette.* 'Huxley's Mine Kills Boy's Father, then Huxley Fires Son!'"

Once again, Huxley whipped the side of his leg, only this time harder. He gazed at the mob and tried awfully hard to douse his blazing anger. At this point, he had visions of picking this little dwarf up and tossing his ass down the airshaft. But that very image made him realize that the blabbering midget had hit a sore spot. The main airshaft was indeed blasted shut, and oxygen would be extremely limited, especially in the newest and most distant arteries where he had just sent Rusty and 60 others. He had many pressing issues to attend to, too many for even his calculating mind to handle, but this rousing little thorn, which evidently was pretty sharp, had to be extracted, and it had to be done delicately. "Very well. It is Marcus, isn't it?"

Marc shook his head. "No, just Marc."

Huxley's smile clearly indicated that he wanted to slap the little pest, yet he said quite calmly, "Very, well, *Marc*. Why don't you step into my office, so we can discuss your situation man to man." He then lowered his head, and added, "Okay, little fella?"

Marc grabbed both of his suspenders and cockily tilted his head. "Well, what is it? Man or little fella?"

Huxley's face twisted as he stood erect. "Listen, son, your petty annoyances are worse than having to burn ticks off my ass while hunting buffalo! Now stop ticking me off, and get your little ass in my office. *Now!*"

Marc realized he had done more than enough pricking and grandstanding among his fellow workers and decided not to pursue it further.

Meanwhile, Huxley gazed at the crowd. "Well, what the hell are you all standing around for? Do you want your severance checks?"

The scruffy looking mass of laborers began to scatter like mice as Huxley looked back at Marc and pointed with his riding stick. "That way. Move it!"

As Marc began walking, Huxley looked stormily at Hastings. "Get tunnel 13 back up and running, and I mean pronto!"

Hastings nodded nervously and scurried off, barking out orders with each double-step he took toward the cage.

Huxley marched behind Marc, reaching the dusty wooden door to his office at the same time. He looked down and demanded, "Show me your boots."

Marc lifted his boots one at a time to display their soles. "They're clean, sir."

Huxley looked them over and then turned the door handle. He pushed the door open and swung his riding whip into the doorway. "Enter. And don't touch a thing!"

As Marc stepped into the office, Huxley brushed his boots on the cast iron boot scraper—meticulously removing every particle of dirt off them.

Meanwhile, little Marc had taken only two steps inward and stopped. He was utterly taken aback. He had never been in Huxley's office, and from the dusty and unassuming exterior he never expected to see such an immaculate and well-decorated interior. It looked like an upscale hunting lodge, sporting a fine collection of buffalo and elk heads, stuffed raccoons, mounted rifles and swords, western sculptures and two large canvases, one by Albert Bierstadt and the other by Frederic Church.

Huxley entered and closed the door behind him. Intently, he watched Marc walk over to one of his prized paintings—it was 10 feet high and 15 feet wide. Marc gazed up at the huge canvas entitled "The Domes of the Yosemite". His eyes scanned the scene with its towering, majestic peaks, scattered array of trees, and tall gushing waterfall. "My, oh, my," he said in awe, "I feel like I'm standing right there!"

"Yes," Huxley said, "there is nothing like the raw beauty of the Wild West, and no one captures its soul and grandeur like Bierstadt."

Marc felt consumed and momentarily lost in another world. He was utterly enthralled by the magnificent handiwork of Mother Nature—unaware that just as spectacular as those actual chiseled peaks and lush valleys, was Bierstadt's miraculously deft hand, which created this two dimensional masterpiece of pure illusion.

Marc then walked over to Huxley's other large painting, which featured a dramatic scene of Niagara Falls.

Marc's eyes widened. "Wow! This one is exciting!...and a bit scary. I feel like I'm going to fall over the edge!"

Huxley gazed admiringly at the painting. "Yes, that's what I like about that one. Church captured something no one else has; he positioned himself very close to his subject, showing only the turbulent rush of water." Huxley stepped closer to the painting, gazed at the deadly rapids, and then penetratingly back at Marc. "Do you notice how there isn't a single piece of land or rock to stand on? It kind of tells you that there are times when you have to step back in life—as getting too close to a volatile force of nature *can* be very dangerous."

Marc was young, but he sure as hell wasn't stupid. He was well accustomed to the parables that his father and brother Stan quoted from the Bible, not to mention, able to sense the intimidating inflection in Huxley's voice. As such, he had gotten Huxley's innuendo loud and clear. "Well, perhaps that's why I love this painting, Mr. Huxley. Because I intend to face challenges and live my life to the fullest!"

Huxley was briefly taken aback, but then smiled at the brazen youth as he slapped the side of his leg with his riding whip. He pivoted around and walked over to his massive, hand-carved desk and took a seat in his wildly unique chair, which looked more like a bestial throne. Standing at almost six-feet tall, with buffalo horns for armrests, elk skin upholstering, and twisted ram's horns perched at the top, it made Huxley look like a tribal warrior chief. "Have a seat, Marc."

As he complied, Huxley placed his riding whip on the desk. "Well, it's great to be adventurous, Marc, but being reckless is another matter. I see you are a bright boy, so I know you have things on your mind."

Marc sat upright as he looked up at the wall-mounted buffalo head sitting directly above Huxley, and then back down at its killer. "And I see you don't mind killing things, Mr. Huxley; either for sport or in order to make money."

Huxley grimaced, but then laughed as he leaned back. "Damn! You really are a gutsy little whippersnapper, aren't you?"

As Marc sat mute, scrutinizing the carved cougars and elk on the desk, Huxley leaned forward. "Now, listen here, Marc. I'm really going to try to keep my cool, because you are not a man just yet, little fella. You have grit, but you have a long way to go before you can start dueling with a man of my caliber." Huxley lowered his head trying to make eye contact. "Am I making myself clear?"

Marc leaned backward and crossed his legs—finally resuming eye contact. "Sure, Mr. Huxley. Perfectly clear. But, I need to make a few things clear myself," he said. Then diplomatically, he added, "If, of course, you don't mind?"

"Go on!"

"First of all, my father d-died yesterday," Marc said, struggling to keep his voice from quivering. "Not only is his b-body still down there, which I m-must find, but I now have to support my family."

Huxley leaned back, placing his elbows on the horny arms of his chair and resting his chin on his interlocked knuckles. "I'm aware of that, Marc. We will attempt to recover all the bodies, and we—"

"But how can you do that—" Marc interjected as he irritably uncrossed his legs, "—if you're blasting it shut with dynamite!?"

Huxley closed his eyes briefly to regain his patience, and then continued calmly, "As I was saying. We will try to recover every dead body down there. That part of the mine had already been inspected and was clear to blast. You are too young to realize that leaving that section of the mine semi-operational would have only caused more deaths, because some of the idiots around here would have been messing around down there, causing more cave-ins and even more deaths."

Marc's face tensed up. "They would be *messing around*, sir, looking for the dead bodies of loved ones! And that's something I reckon you don't care about," Marc said, his voice reeking with emotion.

Huxley clenched his teeth, and spat, "You're starting to sound like my wife, young man." Gravely, he added, "And let me assure you...neither of your frail constitutions exempt you from serious repercussions. So tread carefully!" Huxley then gazed at the photo of his Uncle Jack on his desk. He spun it around for Marc to see. "Do you see this fellow? He was my dear Uncle Jack. And he raised me for a time. You see, Marc, I lost *both* of my parents when I was about your age. So, I know darn well where you are coming from."

Marc scanned the top of Huxley's desk, but the only photos he had were of himself holding a variety of dead hunting trophies and this haggard-looking specimen of a man called Uncle Jack. "I don't get it," he inquired, "why don't you have photos of your wife, children and parents?"

"Never mind that," Huxley snapped impatiently, "I keep this photo of my uncle up here for a special reason. You see, he was the first person to make me realize a very important lesson. That being, I had to do what any real man must do to survive." Spinning the photo around, he gazed at the blurry print. As his eyes connected with those of his dead uncle's, the gory vision of his homicidal rite of empowerment that night by the well stimulated his senses. Then gazing up at the young cherubic face before him, he said, "So, Marc, it is time for *you* to become a man. And from what I see, you will do just fine." He spun around on his swivel throne and leaned down. Sliding a cabinet door open, he revealed a stash of liquor. He grabbed a bottle of gin and spun back. "I think you need to re-gear your thinking, son. Rather than worrying about your loss and problems, you need to think about *Marc!*" As he poured two glasses of gin and squirted each with a shot of seltzer water, he said, "This calls for a drink. A drink to the Sacred Ritual of Manhood!" He pushed the glass across his desk and lifted his. "Cheers!"

Marc grabbed the glass and took a sniff. His nose wrinkled and eyes watered as he lost his breath. "Woo! You drink this stuff?"

Huxley laughed and then mischievously prodded the boy. "Go on, drink up!"

Marc brought the potent tonic up to his mouth. Then closing his eyes he took a sip. As the fiery liquid burned its way down his esophagus, Marc gagged and choked. Tears dripped down his innocent face as he coughed out a flammable sentence, "This...s-stuff tastes like...k-kerosene!"

"Welcome to manhood, Marc! As I told you, you have a lot to learn and much to experience if you want to live your life to the fullest. So, go on—finish it up!"

Huxley's cattle prods were making Marc very uneasy as he watched Huxley lift his glass and down it in one shot. He couldn't fathom how Huxley didn't even flinch—not a gag, nor the slightest sign of a burning tear. After his horrible first encounter, Marc knew this tonic was deadly, yet as he looked at Huxley's goading smile, he just had to prove himself a man. He lifted the glass and took a larger sip. This time he gagged only once and felt encouraged. Yet through his glazed eyes he could see the gray-haired hunter's penetrating stare fixated on him as if waiting to make the kill. The unsettling moment gave Marc pause to heed his gut instinct and rethink Huxley's intentions. He put the glass down, more than half full. "I won't drink this anymore, Mr. Huxley. This is *not* what makes a man. I've seen Rusty and many other men drinking this kind of stuff, and my father had often warned me to steer clear of it. He told me, it wasn't the *Joyful Spirits of the Lord,* but rather the *Deceptive Nectar of the Devil.* So if you please, I'd like to tell you about another problem."

Huxley leaned back, foiled and disappointed. "There you go again, Marc, fixating on your problems!" he huffed, while irritably grabbing the bottle of gin. He loaded his glass, this time straight up, and downed the alcohol in one gulp. He slammed the glass down and looked at Marc with a petulant grin. "Go on, little fella. Let's hear your problem."

Marc stood up and walked to the window. Peering out briefly—as if looking for someone or some miracle—he then turned and looked back at Huxley. "I don't know how else to say this, but my brother took off with your Arabian stallion."

"Yes, I know," Huxley replied nonchalantly, "Hastings told me, he borrowed it yesterday. So—" he just realized what Marc said, and his blood pressure began to rise. "Ah! So, you're saying he *stole* my horse!" With that, Huxley sprang up and grabbed his riding whip. Meting out two hammering swats to his desktop, he erupted, "Damn it! That young stallion is one of my prize possessions. Do you have any idea how much I paid for that animal? It's a purebred!"

Marc anxiously shook his head. "No, sir. But I plan on paying you back."

Huxley snickered, "Paying me back!? Ha! With *your* salary? It would take you three years!" Archie sat down—fuming in his bestial throne as he swiveled tersely back and forth. "So where did this little rascal brother of yours go?"

"That's just it, I don't know, sir. And I reckon this time he's not coming back."

Huxley grit his teeth and whipped the desktop, once again, as papers flew up into the air. "That little son-of-a-bitch! This is just what I needed; more bull shit! As if I don't have enough on my plate already. Believe me, I'll find the little bastard, and when I do, I'll—" catching himself, Huxley took a deep breath and continued, "yes, you will indeed start paying me off. I shall begin by deducting half your salary. But don't worry; I'll gladly upgrade you to a driller. I'll have them instruct you immediately."

Marc walked back toward the desk. "Mr. Huxley, your mine killed my father and crippled my oldest brother. And now my other brother Ted ran off. I am the sole means of support for my family. You cannot expect me to give you half of my salary, even as a driller. I must make more money than that for us to survive."

Huxley twitched as he swiveled to a dead stop. Wildly tapping the buffalo-horned arm of his chair with his rhythmic fingers, which made an odd galloping sound, he said with a frustrated cackle, "So, what exactly are you saying, young fella? That you deserve to be promoted above a driller? To what exactly? A mechanic? A foreman?" Huxley laughed, "An engineer?"

Marc looked deep into Huxley's eyes. "No, none of those positions, sir. I'm through working down below. It is far too dangerous, and my family cannot afford another death. I happen to be excellent at arithmetic, Mr. Huxley, and I've seen how Paul Jackson handles your manifests, and I can tell you this—he's no Sir Isaac Newton!"

Huxley's condescending smile withered to a thoughtful stare. "Arithmetic, huh? And how do *you* know so much about mathematics and Newton?"

"My mom is a very smart woman, Mr. Huxley, that's how. She also taught me how speak Italian, French and Latin, while my father taught me Polish and German. So, I can help you with any dealings you have with foreigners. And I do learn quickly!"

Huxley leaned back and chuckled. "Yes, I see you do!" He pulled open his desk drawer and pulled out one of his manifests, along with several spreadsheets. He threw them on the desk. "Look at those, and explain to me what you see?"

Marc stepped over and gazed down at the mathematical matrix. As his little finger ran across the multi-columned sheets, he sounded off; demonstrating a firm grasp of mathematics, which was remarkably advanced for his age. And, for good measure, he even rattled off a few industry terms that he had heard Jackson say while doing physical inspections.

Huxley looked at the dazzling youth and smiled. "Well I'll be damned! I reckon you're one of those prodigies. And you know something; lately I've been mighty suspicious of Jackson. That fat little gnome just might be screwing me. I caught him in one discrepancy already, so I don't know if he's stealing from me, or just plain stupid, but I think you would make a good assistant. Fine, young fella, you got the job!"

Marc grinned. "That's just swell! Thank you, Mr. Huxley. So, how much will I make?"

Huxley shook his head. "You really are a whip! Well, let me say this, your salary could be five times what you make now, but *only* if you prove yourself worthy."

"No problem, sir!" Marc exclaimed. "But if I find mistakes that save you a lot of money, I'd like to get a percentage of those savings, say like 2 percent."

Huxley laughed. "You never cease to amaze me, son. I can honestly say that I've never seen such a young, calculating whippersnapper like you in all my days!"

"So, does that mean yes?"

"That means you drive a hard bargain, and you're sharper than many of the college-grown bananas I have around here. And I like that! You got brains and balls, kid. So, that's a yes. But, you had better sharpen your pencil, too! I *will* expect you to save me money."

As Marc clenched his fists with glee, Huxley added, "But let's not forget—you owe me for the precious Arabian stallion that your stupid brother stole. So, let's see...I'll withhold one quarter of your salary. Got it?"

"Got it!"

Ted's Ride to Freedom

July 1, 1881

Meanwhile, Ted had ridden Huxley's young stallion over 120 miles, up along the winding Cuyahoga River, finally arriving in the city of Cleveland, Ohio. His trip had taken some unexpected turns, since he had earlier stopped in Akron by mistake. He had originally been heading to Chicago to catch a performance by Bill Cody and Texas Jack—but he was told the traveling show had already moved on and was headed for Cleveland.

As Ted rode straight through the bustling city, he unwittingly came upon Lake Erie. It was the first time he had ever seen such a huge expanse of water, and it was simply breathtaking. Nearby, barges loaded with iron ore were arriving from Minnesota, while hopper cars filled with coal arrived by rail. Ted was keen to notice, with a bit of disgust, that most of the hoppers had the Huxley Coal insignia on them.

Not far away was John D. Rockefeller's main office for Standard Oil, while not too much further stood one of his many plants—busily producing his precious kerosene. His savvy dealings with his railroad tycoon buddies allowed him to transport his kerosene cheaper and quicker than his competitors and his prices dropped almost in half. Rockefeller's sales boomed, burning up his competition, much like a match tossed on his volatile commodity.

Turning his horse around, Ted galloped along the coastline, breathing in the hot, humid air, which his lungs found strange. But Ted didn't mind, he felt liberated and in full control of his life, for once!

As he rode along, he came upon an elegant couple strolling along the lake. The man sported a fine linen vest, and had his jacket folded over his arm, and his partner was wearing a long white dress, and holding a fancy parasol with tassels. Ted wiped the sweat off his brow with his soot-stained sleeve as he inquired where the theater was located. As the gentleman pointed and politely began giving him directions, a farmer's wagon loaded with vegetables and fruit passed by them, while two factory workers, late for work, scurried past; one still buttoning his shirt. Ted listened and thanked the gentleman. With a grin, he then lifted his dirty cap to signal the same to the woman.

Ted was finally two miles away from realizing his life's dream, and the exhilaration shot from his head down to his toes as he kicked the loins of the Arabian stud, which bolted forward. As he took off down the dirt path, he veered toward the farmer's cart and swiped an apple. The farmer cussed and shook his fist, yet Ted turned and laughed as he broke into a wild gallop. Breezing past a row of trees, Ted soon came upon a row of buildings as he finally entered the city. He slowed his stallion down to a trot, as he threw the core of the apple away—his belly somewhat contented. Clopping his way through the city streets, he finally arrived at the Carter Playhouse.

Ted eagerly dismounted and tethered the horse to a post. Stroking its beautiful, shiny brown coat, Ted said, "You stay here, Mazeppa. I'll be right back."

Ted decided to name the horse after Franz Liszt's famous symphonic poem *Mazeppa*, which musically depicted the stormy horse ride of a Lithuanian man, who was tied naked to the animal as punishment for having seduced a Polish nobleman's wife. That Ted's mother had told him how Liszt composed symphonic poems about Mazeppa and Tasso, his namesake, many times, the intriguing stories stuck. And that the trusty young stallion was now his best friend, Ted figured why not?

It was only nine o'clock and the theater was closed; yet, to his delight, Ted saw that the door was ajar. Better yet, he could hear voices inside, squabbling. Slipping through the door, Ted stepped into the rear of the orchestra, and saw two men on stage arguing with a leathery-faced, rugged-looking fellow standing down below in the aisle.

One man on stage noticed Ted and called out, "Who are you?"

As the two other men turned and looked, Ted replied, "My name is Ted Wozniak and I'm looking for Bill Cody and Texas Jack."

The man rolled his eyes. "Well, you've found us, I'm Texas Jack," then pointing to his stage partner, he added dryly, "And here's your Bill Cody."

The man in the aisle now wore a look of disgust as he blustered, "Go on and scram, son! You can get their autograph after the show tonight, *if* you buy a ticket!"

Ted marched forward, uninhibited, as he removed his cap. "I'm not here for an autograph, sir, I'm here for a job."

As Cody and Texas laughed, the stout man in the aisle, with his leathery face and thick mustache, grunted. He was Ned Buntline, the self-appointed director, co-actor, and author of their popular show *Scouts of the Prairie*. It was now in its ninth year of touring and was just one of Buntline's many fanciful literary works. However, Ned was a colorful character in his own right. Having a fondness for stardom, alcohol and women, Ned had an affair with a man's wife in Tennessee, some 30 years back, and found himself in a duel with the husband. Buntline discharged his flintlock and shot the disgruntled man dead. Interestingly enough, while Buntline was on trial for murder, the victim's brother had pulled out a pistol and shot Ned, who fled the courtroom with a flesh wound. A few blocks away Buntline was caught by a lynch mob and strung up by his neck on an awning, doubling as gallows. Feisty ole Ned had kicked wildly as his eyes bulged and saliva gurgled as he choked, but friends came to his rescue and Ned survived the ordeal; even being set free by a Grand Jury that refused to indict him.

Ned looked at the scrawny youth and inquired, "And just what the hell is it that you do, son?"

Ted walked down the aisle toward Buntline, yet gazed up at Cody. "I ride a horse pretty darn well, and word has it that you, Mr. Buffalo Bill, intend to create a *real* Wild West show. Not some frilly stage show like this, but one that's out in the open air. You know—a live action-packed festival!"

Buntline snickered. "Listen son, how dare you strut in here and belittle my work! I wrote this stage play and even invented Cody's Buffalo Bill stage name! Why, aren't you familiar with my book *Buffalo Bill, the King of the Border Men?*"

Ted turned and looked up into Buntline's piercing eyes, which had leathery bags underneath. "No. I'm not. And who gives a smelly cow plop about your stupid buffalo book!?"

Ned snorted as he blasted, "Listen, you little snot-nose, I invented that character back in 1869! It was my original intention to have Wild Bill Hickok play that role, but Hickok was a, well, he was a tough son-of-a-bitch who even scared me! Anyhow, Buffalo Bill, here, is set to continue this *wildly* famous show of mine. So, scram, kid!"

As Ted's hopes began to wither, Buffalo Bill called out from the stage, "Listen, son, the fact is I do have intentions of devising a live show, but that may not be for quite some time." As Ted and Ned both looked up at Cody, each with a polar expression on their face, he continued, "This show, despite some poor reviews by critics, is a national success with the public. And we'd be pretty foolhardy if we tossed in our hats just yet."

Ted stared at his idol as his heart choked and skipped a few beats. "Well, is there anything I can do here? Anything at all? I'll move props, build anything you need, and hell, I'll even tend to your horses!"

Ned was certainly not happy to hear about Cody's plans, which had indeed been fueling the rumor mills lately, but this kid was simply getting on his nerves. "We have no need for prop handlers, son. Every playhouse provides that service wherever we perform. And as for our horses, local stables take care of that, too!" Then came the final deathblow, "So, *get lost!* And don't show your scrawny little face around here again, unless you have a ticket in your hand. We have a show to rehearse. So, *scram!*"

Ted cowered from the menacing blast as his aspirations died. Amplifying the grim news was the toxic wave of fumes from Buntline's blunt line. The mixture of whiskey and bad breath made Ted's nose wriggle and his eyes water. He pivoted around, and began to walk slowly towards the exit as a tear streamed down his cheek.

As Ted placed his cap back on his head, a voice rang out. "Hold on, son—"

Ted stopped short and eagerly spun around as Cody continued, "My suggestion is that you get some real experience first before you jump into this business with both feet. I think it would be mighty helpful if you joined up with P.T. Barnum for a while."

Ted grimaced. He was hoping that Buffalo Bill would offer him some sort of menial job, and take him under his wing, but this was a cruel punch to the gut, and an insult to his pride. Heatedly, Ted wiped the tear off his face as he blurted, "I ain't no *freak!*—Mr. Buffalo Bill. The circus is just a stupid traveling show of weird and ugly oddballs!"

Cody gazed down at Ted with an experienced set of eyes that radiated good intentions. "Listen, son, Phineas Taylor Barnum is a brilliant businessman and a promotional wizard. He does advertising like no one else, and has made the world stop to come see his shows no matter where he travels. And now that he merged with James Bailey he's going to be an even bigger success. That is why it's called *The Greatest Show on Earth!* It has grown to be far more than just a freak show. Granted, Mr. Barnum still has little Tom Thumb and a host of other misfits, but his show has expanded quite dramatically. It now features some very talented acts, including dazzling horse shows."

Ted's watery eyes began to clear. "Horse shows!?"

"Yes," Buffalo Bill said with a smile, "I think it would be awfully wise of you to gather some good experience, and gain some exposure, by investing a little of your time with Mr. Barnum. In fact, his show is scheduled to appear in Detroit in just a few days."

Ted squinted. "Detroit? Where is that?"

Cody smiled. "It's in Michigan. Just start heading west and follow the coastline of Lake Erie and you'll run right into it. It's about 170 miles northwest. So make sure to feed and water your horse plenty!"

Ted's face beamed. "I sure will, Mr. Buffalo Bill! Much obliged!"

Running out to the street, Ted unloosed Mazeppa, kissed him on the snout, and began his wild ride up the coast toward Detroit.

7

Marc's First Day at a New Job

July 1, 1881

Marc had put in a long and eventful day, sitting in one of Huxley's office cabins behind a small makeshift desk. He had carefully observed Paul Jackson writing up his manifests, and took personal notes. Jackson seemed a bit on edge most of the day, having the little tyke peering over his shoulder and asking too many damned questions. Paul liked three things, in this order: sales, silence and slothfulness—the last two in order to read literature. Actually, he would have loved to include sex on his sensational list of S's, but the dull and unsightly little bachelor never seemed too appealing to women. However, with Marc hovering and buzzing about all day, his yearning for silence had risen to first place.

Meanwhile, Marc was so taken in by all the new experiences that he hardly had time to mourn. It was only earlier in the day at lunchtime when he had received word that the tunnel his father and 10 others had been in totally collapsed. Marc had descended into the mine, anxious to view the situation. But to his chagrin, Hastings had ordered all body retrievals in that vicinity to be terminated. A priest had been summed to give a blanket prayer, and plans were made to mount a bronze plaque listing all the names of the dead. No sooner did Marc weep and say his own prayer, when he was called back into the office, and the hustle and bustle consumed him once again.

Despite that sullen interlude, Marc couldn't believe he managed to pull off such a great promotion, and, better yet, he was now sitting in a clean office, breathing fresh air, and enjoying the food and drinks that a few of his fellow office workers offered him. It all seemed unreal, not getting his hands dirty or not breaking his back lifting heavy loads of coal. Yet, despite not being accustomed to sunlight for such long spells, and getting strange looks and derogatory slurs from a few jealous coworkers strolling in and out of the office, he knew one thing already—he loved this job.

He reached down into his pocket, pulled out his handkerchief, and smiled—it was pure white. Usually by this late hour of the day, it was black and gritty from all the soot he blew out of his nose every 30 minutes or so. But as Marc gazed at his trusty old cloth, his smile withered. He suddenly recalled that his father had given him the handkerchief to protect his lungs, and in a most disturbing way, the sparkling white cloth did not appropriately reflect the dark black tomb that his father now lie buried in. Marc gazed up at the clock on the wall. It was almost 9:00 p.m., time for him to quit.

He looked at Jackson. "Pardon me, Paul, but do you mind if I look for Bill Mulvaney?"

Jackson looked up from his desk, somewhat befuddled. "Huh, what? Oh, yeah, you two ride together, right?"

"Yes, sir," Marc replied politely.

"Sure, run along," Jackson huffed as he buried his head, once again, into the concealed book on his lap.

Paul was reading Mark Twain's newest release, *The Prince and the Pauper*, which currently was only published in Canada. He couldn't wait for its U.S. release next year, so he had one of his contacts in Canada send him a copy by post. Paul was fascinated how the two main characters switched identities. As he thought about the pauper being mistaken for a royal prince, he was having fanciful illusions of himself switching roles with Huxley, thus living happily like a king. However, that Archibald was ruggedly handsome, while Paul was short, fat and bald, with crooked, yellow teeth and bushy sideburns that looked like two bushels of tumbleweed, seemed to elude him.

Meanwhile, Marc scurried out the door and managed to make his way to one of the two remaining cages that were still operational. As he descended into the blackness of the shaft, Marc's heart likewise dropped—knowing that his father's body would be entombed down below forever. Moreover, that his former fellow workers were still relegated to this infernal hellhole, while he had a clean job up above, now began to eat away at his conscience. Marc now felt like he betrayed his old friends for his own selfish needs.

As the cage reached the bottom, Homer slid the door open. "Is that you, Marcus?"

Marc mustered up a smile, yet it was marred with empathy for the old man who spent his entire life in this dismal catacomb. The only consolation Marc had was that Homer could not see the anguish and compassion on his face. He knew the old sage accepted his fate (for some odd reason that eluded him), and sympathetic whimpers were not only futile, but unwanted. "Yes, Homer. It is I."

"Glad you made it out alive yesterday," Homer said with a smile. Yet his puffy wrinkled checks soon wilted. "But I'm awfully sorry about your pa."

Marc's face mellowed. "Thank you, sir."

Homer's lips tensed up. "The team dug out several bodies today, but I'm sad to say, Jedrek was not one of them."

Marc's voice buckled, "Yes, I k-know. I've been t-told that section is too badly damaged. But, Hastings is having a plaque made to list all those who lost their lives."

Homer could sense the anguish in Marc's voice and quickly changed the subject. "I heard your brother Tasso ran off with Huxley's prized Arabian." Unexpectedly, Homer laughed. "What a hoot! Good for him. I hope he makes a better life for himself out there."

"So do I," Marc said, gaining some relief from the new topic. He knew his brother had issues, but he also had faith that Ted would somehow make it. However, the thought of having to pay for Ted's stolen stallion didn't help matters.

Homer pointed toward the entrance of one of the tunnels. "Come along, I'd like to show you something."

As Marc followed the old timer, a deep rumbling noise grew louder and louder—vibrating his small frame. As they reached the entrance of the tunnel, he saw a small steam engine—its flywheel spinning furiously as it generated electricity to power a string of light bulbs. Marc's eyelids parted in wonder, while his pupils contracted to the bright glow.

Homer smiled. "They just installed this beast today!" he said. "Even *I* can see things with this new marvel."

"This is fantastic!" Marc said as his eyes surveyed the receding row of incandescent bulbs. A long, thick black electrical wire was tacked along one side of the rocky wall, with bulbs every 10 feet—their luminance flickering slightly to the uneven pulse of the steam engine. "This should also protect us from firedamp explosions. Right, Homer?"

Homer turned toward the blurry vision of Marc's body. "Yes. Well, at least for the most part. Electricity, Marc, can be just as deadly as a flame if it is unleashed from its casing, be that the tar-like coating on the wire or the brittle glass of the bulbs themselves."

Marc squinted as he looked at the bulbs. "My, the glass is so thin."

"Exactly. So they must be treated with great care," Homer advised.

Marc gazed back at Homer. "But what about tunnel 13, do they have this new lighting system?"

Homer pointed to the churning steam engine. "We only have this one, and it's only capable of powering about 100 yards of light bulbs. So even the rest of this tunnel is left to the Davy's and head torches."

"That's stupid!" Marc blurted. "When is Huxley getting more generators down here?"

"So, *I'm stupid!*" Huxley blustered as he emerged out of the abyss of an adjacent tunnel, marching angrily. Anxiously following Huxley, were Supervisor Hastings and a small entourage of engineers and carpenters.

Marc spun around, startled. Taking a step back, he stammered, "I, I didn't m-mean it in a bad way, Mr. Huxley. I was just—"

"Shush!" Huxley blasted as he waved his hand irritably. "The reason for one generator is very simple, Marc. I sure hope you're not blind, like this old fool," Huxley snapped as he glanced disgustedly at Homer. "My business is in utter turmoil because of this damned explosion! If you paid attention to Jackson's manifests today, Marc, you should have noticed that they were dreadfully sparse. Even someone your age should have picked up on that!"

"Well, sir, I had no way of knowing how many invoices you process normally," Marc said defensively, "so, I had no way of—"

"Whatever!" Huxley grumbled impatiently. "But the situation is this: production has come to a complete and utter standstill, and I was forced to cancel several huge orders today. Carnegie needs coal for his steel factory in town, Rockefeller for his factories in Cleveland, and several railroad and steamship companies for their numerous coal stations. However, I was only able to deliver what we extracted before the explosion, which amounted to a measly 10 tons per client. We're talking about hundreds of thousands of dollars, lost! Down the drain! Worse yet, not a single dram of anthracite has been extracted today. So, never mind a lighting system, I cannot even afford to buy a single pickaxe!"

As Marc and Homer were stunned into silence by the economic devastation and astronomical dollar figures, Huxley turned and looked at the generator. "As it is, Mr. Edison was nice enough to loan me this contraption for two weeks. However, I know it was with the foolish hopes that I would somehow be enamored with his toy, and then buy it in bulk." He gazed at the Davy lamp nearby, "But wasting money on something I already possess, which is also much cheaper to operate, is what I deem *truly stupid!*"

Marc naively offered his enraged boss a logical rebuttal, "But, Mr. Huxley, Davy lamps and head torches are dangerous. They caused your grief in the first place."

Huxley's entourage looked anxiously at one another, afraid to speak their minds, but silently concurring with the boy's astute assessment.

Meanwhile, Huxley impatiently waved his hand. "Nonsense!" he blasted, "a Davy lamp does not cause fires or explosions, Marc—careless or just plain stupid people do! And it seems we have no shortage of them around here."

The entourage remained painfully mute as Huxley's head snapped back toward Hastings. "And I must tell you, Jack. The inspection of tunnel 13 has come as a colossal disappointment! Their lack of progress is appalling. We *must* reach that new vein of anthracite again, or, God knows, I'll have to shut down this entire operation!"

Huxley gazed menacingly at his staff and shook his head. "Well, don't just stand there—*get busy!*" As they nervously began to scatter like roaches subjected to light, Huxley turned and looked at Homer with searing eyes and then over at Marc. "And just what are you two up to?"

Homer rubbed his chin. "Well, I was just showing Marc the generator and helping him find tunnel 13. He is—"

"I'm looking for Bill Mulvaney," Marc interjected. "He's a lead driller down there, and—"

"Yes," Huxley cut in, impatiently, "I know, I sent that big red-headed buffoon down here this morning! I may not know everyone's name, but I sure as hell can remember this wretched morning, and you two riding into our blasting area. It's a day I'll never forget! But as for you going to see Mulvaney, you can forget it! He's *not* going anywhere. His entire crew will be staying here, day and night, until we break back into that vein. So, I don't want you, or anyone else, to interrupt their work. Is that understood?"

Marc nodded hesitantly as Huxley pulled out his pocket watch and then furiously snapped it shut. "Time is wasting, and not a single shard of coal has been extracted. Yet, bills keep rolling in, along with complaints about the lack of shipments." He gazed heatedly at Homer. "And as for *you!* My days of putting up with your sorry ass are over. Pack you gear! I can't afford a useless old piece of shit like you anymore. You can collect your final paycheck in two weeks."

With that, Huxley paced angrily toward the cage.

Homer was stunned and lost his balance. Marc reached over and grabbed his arm to steady him. He had never seen the old man so shaken and mentally lost. Marc tried to console him, but Homer gazed emptily at the ground, hardly hearing a word Marc said. Finally, Homer looked towards his voice. "Marc, I have nothing. No family and now no job. I've spent the better part of my life down here, and now what do I have to show for it? Nothing! Absolutely nothing!"

Marc didn't know what to say, but tried to offer up words of encouragement, "Well, you can't say you have nothing to show for it, Homer. I learned many things from you, as did many others, things that will help us for the rest of our lives. You're a very smart man. So, that's a darn good thing, you know, to help and teach others."

Homer cracked a brief smile, and reached down feeling for Marc's shoulder. Making contact, he grabbed Marc and patted him affectionately. "You're a special boy, Marc. And I, too, have learned things from you; so don't ever think that only a child learns from an adult. You're a young boy, but I hear you already have a position in the office up above. That's fantastic. Good for you!" As Marc smiled, Homer continued, "But heed what I say, Marc. Get out of Huxley's dark domain as soon as you can. Learn what you can up there and then seek new and brighter pastures."

"I intend to, Homer, but that just might take a while. I have a lot of debts to pay and my family to support."

Homer grabbed Marc's arm with his gnarly hand and squeezed it. "Please! Listen to me. I need to tell you something. But first, is there anyone nearby?"

Marc spun his head around. "No, it is all clear, but what—"

"Shh!" Homer said, "it is very important that you listen to me. You must get away from here as soon as an opportunity presents itself. I must tell you why I consigned myself to this hellhole. Surely you must know that my mind was suited for a higher calling than this?"

Marc gazed up at the old man. "Well, sure, I always thought it quite odd that such a smart man like you would be shoveling dirt."

"Exactly. You see, I'm the man who discovered the anthracite in these hills."

Marc squinted. *"You!* You found it?"

"Yes, Marc, some thirty years ago."

"But this is Huxley's mine," Marc said, confused.

"Now it is," Homer said, "but he stole it from me along with something else, something far more precious."

Now Marc was really baffled. "More precious than Huxley's mine!? What on earth could possibly be worth more than this mine?"

Homer choked up as he struggled to form his words, "He s-stole m-my daughter Jenifer from me."

"What? How could he do that?"

Homer took a deep breath and exhaled. "Huxley is a cold and ruthless man, Marc. My daughter had fallen in love with him at a very young age, just about the same time I had discovered the anthracite here and began excavating. An awful lot happened back then. Anyhow, I wish I knew then what I found out a year later." Homer paused as memories of those dark, distant years flooded his mind. He then uttered, with a disdainful tinge, "What a player."

Marc turned his ear toward Homer. "A what?"

"A *player*, a scam artist, a conman!" Homer said as he regained clarity. "You see, as soon as Archie found out about my mine, well, he immediately asked me for a job. He did manual labor for only a month or so, and then shrewdly married my daughter. That was when my dear son-in-law used his charm and savvy business sense to become my partner. And that's the thing, Marc. Huxley has the ability to sway people, making them believe he's a good man, but I assure you, the man is evil—lock, stock and barrel!"

Marc gazed at Homer, still unsure. "Well, it's clear to see that Mr. Huxley has a rotten temper, but he did give me a great job today, and he—"

"Marc, my dear boy," Homer interrupted, "Huxley's bad temper is indeed more prevalent with each passing year that he accumulates greater wealth and power, yet he still knows how to win people over. Just like how he won you over with money. That has become his ultimate tool to manipulate people as well as his deadly weapon to destroy anyone who gets in his way."

Marc's little mind was soaking in all of Homer's shocking news and trying to make sense of it as he asked curiously, "So, what happened to your daughter?"

"Well, as I said," Homer replied, his voice sullen, "Archie married my darling little Jenifer, and then after accumulating a large sum of money, he bought hundreds of acres of prime real estate in the Sierra Nevada. That is where he had a large ranch built, and then brainwashed my daughter to live there."

Marc's head tilted. "Where is the Sierra Nevada?"

"Oh, it's very far from here, in the Wild West. In fact, a few years ago, the Wawona Hotel was built for adventurous tourists, and, I hear, they even have a huge sequoia that they bored a large hole through, so horses and carriages can ride through it. It's not far from Yosemite Valley."

Marc's eyes lit up. "Yosemite! You mean like Huxley's huge painting in his office?"

Homer nodded. "Yep! That's why he commissioned Bierstadt to paint that scene. He loves the West, not to mention hunting buffalo, elk and any other creature that walks. That's what drew him out there in the first place."

Marc's little mind was reeling as pieces of the scattered puzzle were coming together.

As the generator still labored and the lights softly flickered, Homer nervously wiped his forehead, and continued, "But here's where the story gets ugly, Marc. You see, Archie really moved my daughter and their children out there because he was seeing another woman, his present wife Penelope."

Marc's head snapped back—surprised, and now totally confused. "Hold on a minute! How can Huxley be married to your daughter, if he's...I guess he got that thing, what is it? A deforce, or something?"

"A divorce," Homer corrected. "*No*, he did *not* get a divorce. You see, the filthy bastard is married to two women and has two families, neither of them knowing about the other, or the dual lives he leads!"

Marc was flabbergasted as he choked, "What? Two wives and two families? How? I mean, that's not allowed. God said...wait, isn't that against the law, too?"

Homer nodded. "Yes, Marc. It breaks all those laws. But the worst part is that when I tried to tell my daughter the truth, so many years ago, she was too infatuated with that two-faced liar to believe me. It erupted into a nasty fight, and she swore never to speak to me again. So, moving far away suited her just fine. Meanwhile, I was left behind with this dirty snake that also managed to steal my mine right out from under my nose."

"How ever did he do that?"

Homer looked at the ground as his mind unhappily resurrected the dark, old tale. "He had come over one night claiming to make amends. Archie broke out a bottle of gin and, well, I'm no drinker, so before I knew it, he had me awfully dazed and confused." Marc squinted, realizing how Huxley tried the same stunt on him, as Homer continued, "He then lured me to sign what I thought was a formal partnership agreement—to legalize our verbal pact and win back my daughter—but it was a con! I signed it all away."

Anger welled in Marc's little face. "So, couldn't you do something to get it back?"

Homer shrugged his shoulders. "Nope, not really. I couldn't afford to confront his highfalutin team of lawyers or the judicial jackals he greased. You see, I had focused only on conducting a legitimate business, while Archie, from day one, had shrewdly befriended these men in power, knowing he could use them to his advantage. And Huxley owns them all. Therefore, my efforts were useless. It's just a very sad and broken part of this great system of ours. Justice is served to the man with the most money and best connections, Marc. And don't let anyone tell you otherwise!"

Marc shook his head. "I don't know, Homer, I would do anything to keep fighting him. As a matter of fact, I know a good lawyer in Pittsburgh. I could ask him to speak with you. I'm sure there must be something he can do."

Homer shook his head. "That is very kind, Marc. But it's too late. That was too many years ago, and I'm too old and tired to fight anymore. And besides, after he stole my one and only child, I had nothing left. My wife had died years earlier, so, you see, there's nothing left to fight for." As Marc's heart dropped with each new layer of depressing news, Homer continued, "Maybe when you get older you'll understand. But, you see, I had always been motivated by my wife or daughter to at least strive to achieve great things. They were my fuel, my reason for living. But once Archie took that last flame of love and inspiration away from me, my internal flame died." Homer placed his hand on Marc's shoulder. "What use are all the riches Huxley acquired if you don't have people you love to share it with?"

Marc was trembling with sympathy and sorrow for his dear old friend as he gazed up at his cataract-clad eyes, which were now glazed and on the verge of overflowing with tears. Marc hugged Homer tight and, as he did, the optical dam broke loose as tears began to flow down Homer's weathered face.

He gently pushed Marc away, and said, "You better go now. And remember what I said. Get away from Huxley as soon as you can."

Marc looked up at Homer, concerned. "But what will you do now? You have no job."

Homer smiled. "Don't worry about me. I already have another job in mind. I'll be just fine. Now you run along. I need to collect my things, and I'll be on my way."

Marc leaned in for another hug, then turned and head for the cage. Homer listened as Marc's footsteps began to fade. He heard the rattling of the cage door as it slid open and then shut, and the motor kicking in as it began its ascent. Homer listened as the cage came to a stop. It was dead quiet.

He called out, "Marc, are you there?"

No response came.

He paused a moment, and then turned and began walking along the string of light bulbs towards the furthest point of the tunnel. After 100 yards, he sensed the glow dissipating. He had reached the end of the electrical line, and now called out, "Is anybody down here!"

Again, silence.

Homer was well aware that all the workers were far away, working laboriously down tunnel 13. And now with the main airshaft still closed, and the ventilation system temporarily down, Homer could smell the accumulation of methane that now collected in the entire length of tunnel 9. It was where Huxley intended to start drilling tomorrow, being that it contained the second largest vein of anthracite. Miners had worked on the new airshaft that would tap into the tunnel before dawn, yet they had all left. Homer picked up a chunk of shale and looked up at the thin, brittle glass of the nearest light bulb. He cried out, "Forgive me, Lord!"

Homer threw the jagged chunk of shale, smashing the bulb. The filament flared up and instantaneously ignited the flammable gas. A huge fireball engulfed Homer's body, vaporizing it in an instant, as the explosive firestorm raged through the tunnel. The string of light bulbs burst as the thick tar-like coating on the wire melted, dripping like black paint. As the fireball reached the generator, the intense heat turned the iron red, seizing all the moving parts, and continued toward the cage. Seeking its escape, the fire surged up the elevator shaft and blew out the top.

Marc had already been 60 feet away from the cage, when he spun around. Instantaneously, his little body was blasted to the ground by the 300-foot-tall torch that lit up the night sky. As workers scattered to gain cover, Huxley stormed out of his office and began running toward the fire.

"Son-of-a-bitch! This can't be. What the hell happened now!?"

As two workers held up their lanterns and attempted to explain the possible causes, Hastings, two foremen, and three engineers all scuttled to take action. Marc glanced back and saw Huxley standing in quasi shock and smoldering as he briefly lowered his head and tugged on his short gray hair. Marc immediately sprang to his feet and made a dash for the one last operating cage. He somehow had to alert Rusty and the crew in tunnel 13 to get out. As he swerved around the blazing torch, his mind suddenly realized what possibly caused the blast. He stopped and just gazed at the flaming column. As the intense heat began to roast the front of his little body, Marc recollected that he had just left Homer down in tunnel 9, and there wasn't any activity in that section all day. Recalling Homer's harrowing last words —of having nothing left to live for and telling him to run along—it finally struck Marc (with the same force that the fiery blast had when it knocked him to the ground) as to what really happened. Marc fell to his knees, and then covered his face and began weeping. He now knew that Homer took his own life and had purposely set tunnel 9 on flames. It was the only way Homer could fight the colossal might of Archibald Desmond Huxley, and it was a valiant, yet devastatingly tragic, last attempt.

As the burning heat dried Marc's tears almost as quickly as they trickled down his cheeks, he suddenly felt a firm kick to his boot. Looking up, he saw Huxley gazing down—his piercing eyes glowing from the red flames.

"Get up, Marc!" Huxley said, extending his hand down.

Marc couldn't tell which Huxley he was looking at anymore. Was it the man who just gave him a wonderful new job and raise that would finally allow the Wozniak family to get on its feet and prosper? Or was it the power-mongering despot who cheated Homer of his mine, stole his daughter, and lives two disparate lives?

Huxley cracked a smile as he grabbed Marc's little hand and hoisted him up. Gazing at Marc with his penetrating pale green eyes, he said calmly, "I was told you were the last one to come up from the cage. Is that right?"

Marc nodded nervously, while Huxley continued, "So, tell me, what or who do *you* think set this explosion off?"

Marc was still half paralyzed with shock, grief and confusion, but he was not about to reveal what he knew, and simply shrugged his shoulders.

Huxley looked back at the raging flames. "I reckon it may have been sabotage." Then looking back down at Marc, he added, "Do you know what sabotage is?"

Marc shook his head, preferring to remain mute. His little heart and mind were still throbbing from being bludgeoned by the traumatic chain of events that stole his father and now Homer.

"Well, I'll tell you," Huxley said, "*sabotage,* means when someone deliberately destroys the property or machinery of someone they hate. So, do you know of anyone who might hate me, Marc?"

Marc looked up into Huxley's flickering orbs as the raging fire nearby continued to reflect its reddish-yellow waves in them, evoking a most sinister specter. Yet Marc was beginning to at least regain mental control over his rattled emotions, and he answered convincingly, "No, sir, I do not."

Huxley lowered his head to gaze deeper into Marc's eyes. Meanwhile, Marc stood incredibly emotionless as a tempest of mixed emotions roared inside his little head and heart. Evidently playing poker with his brother Stan for many years had honed his skills at facial control, and it was now being put to great practical use. Huxley attempted to scan for the motive behind his eyes, but couldn't discern a thing. A bit baffled, Huxley lifted his head, apparently convinced, but still harboring doubt.

Huxley knew he had effectively neutered Homer many years ago, for the old man knew that if he uttered a word about anything to anyone, Huxley would have battered or even killed his daughter as easily as he would a cockroach. Yet, Huxley realized that, in his anger and haste, he had fired Homer without giving the matter much forethought. Under normal circumstances, he would have made sure Homer had an accident or just eliminated the old oaf. But between the previous explosion and devastating loss in business, Huxley was out of sorts.

However, Archie felt quite sure that this was the handiwork of Homer. The old bugger finally gave him a solid blow—literally to his mine and figuratively to his pocket—and this fiery attack truly put Huxley on the precipice of disaster. Still unable to recover from the first blast, this second explosion would now halt work on extracting the second largest vein of anthracite. Considering these devastating chain of events, Archie was amazingly calm, yet he had been blowing his stack all day, and was now spent, not to mention quasi numb. Furthermore, he had taken sadistic pleasure in keeping Homer alive for some 30 years as his slave, and he now conceded to reaping Homer's one and only retaliatory strike. In fact, he even had a tinge of respect for the spineless old slug that had buckled and lived like a mole for so long, for at least now Homer showed that he *did* have a pair of balls, even if it took him over 30 years to realize he had them.

Huxley once more gazed down at Marc, only to see his sullen face suddenly light up as he exclaimed, "Rusty! You're alive."

Marc ran over and gave Rusty a bear hug as the brawny Irishman smiled. "Yep. We managed to get out, thank God. It appears only tunnel 9 caved in along with the cage and new airshaft."

Huxley grit his teeth and briefly closed his eyes. Not only was his second largest vein of anthracite now unreachable, but, for weeks, his crew had been drilling a new airshaft to feed tunnel 9 and several others and now that, too, was destroyed. He was well aware that he operated with insufficient airshafts for the large maze of tunnels he had, which jeopardized his workers' ability to breathe, but it was too costly and time consuming to build more. However, this new airshaft was indeed crucial, since fewer airshafts didn't allow the deadly firedamp to escape. As such, the probability of more explosions would now be amplified, and this Archie was keenly aware of, despite his workers being in the dark, all, that is, except for Hastings and the six engineers on his staff who had all been warned to keep their mouths shut. Huxley shivered at the thought of all the weeks of hard labor, materials and salaries that he would have to shell out just to get back what he lost.

As workers still scurried to and fro to combat the flames, Huxley looked up at the night sky; it was filled with dark gray clouds and billowing black smoke that partially obscured the shinny sliver of the moon. He gazed down at Marc and then Rusty. "Take the boy home, Mulvaney. You both can use some rest. Tomorrow and the next month are going to be *very busy*."

Just then Hastings emerged out of the darkness of night, his body now glowing from the burning torch that was slowly being snuffed by nearly 100 workers. Hastings lifted his clipboard and began to give Huxley his latest report.

Archie attempted to listen, but then shook his head, and waved his hand. "Not now! I'll deal with this in the morning, Jack. But know this, there will be some significant changes made tomorrow. Forty workers will be fired. It is quite clear that we have a tired and clumsy crew, and it is time to clean house. We will hire forty Chinks tomorrow and get this house back in order! Is that understood?"

Marc and Rusty stood numb as Hastings replied, "Forty!? Archie, that's an awful lot of good, loyal families that you're turning out to the streets."

Huxley remained cold and unflinching. "This company has no room for slackers or imbeciles, Hastings. We just had two debilitating explosions caused by carelessness or..." Huxley didn't wish to divulge Homer's sabotage, and continued, "stupidity, and this crew failed to clear tunnel 13. I had expected to retap that vein today, but not only did they fail in that task, but our second largest vein and the new airshaft have just been destroyed. This is a time of do or die, Hastings. And I, Archibald Huxley, will *not* die! Is *that* understood?"

Hastings nodded obediently as Huxley added, "And in a further effort to cut costs we will start using support beams more sparingly. So, space them further apart. That also eliminates the need for so many carpenters. So, as you see, Hastings, Huxley Coal *will* prevail!"

Hastings' hand with the clipboard fell to his side, his face deeply etched with anxiety. "Did you run this by our engineers? As it is these tunnels could use more support beams, not less."

Huxley didn't appreciate being questioned, especially in front of mere laborers who had no right to hear such safety matters, and his face stiffened. "The tunnels simply need more diligent workers, *not* more supports. The tunnels would not collapse if these numbskulls didn't cause all these damned explosions!" Huxley's voice and temper began to rise as he added, "And we don't need so many high-salaried engineers either. Edmonton and Healy will also meet the axe tomorrow."

Hastings face was getting paler with each new chop as he replied anxiously, "Archie, this may cause a riot! You may find yourself in the throws of a deadly revolt, just like the great railroad strike four years ago!"

Hastings was referring to America's first major strike, when during the recession of 1877 rail tycoons laid off workers, cut salaries and increased their workday. Workers began derailing trains and causing havoc, thus prompting the owners to request that their respective states should supply militias to put down the revolts. The worst atrocity occurred right in Pittsburgh when the militia fired upon and killed 10 rock throwers and wounded many others. Finally, President Hayes had to send federal troops to effectively quash the strike.

Huxley sniggered, "Believe me, Hastings, if my workers, or fired deadbeats, ever dared to cause a revolt, I would not waste my time calling the state for help. Oh, no! Not I! I would gladly show them just how good a marksman I really am!"

As Hastings swallowed hard, Huxley turned and looked at Rusty. "And didn't I say you need rest!?" Then gazing down at Marc, he added, "That goes for you, too! And don't forget, little fella, I expect you to save me even more money!" Huxley turned and pointed to the main depot. "There, you see? The transport wagon is up and running again. So, *get going!*"

Marc and Rusty looked at one another and eagerly complied. They walked 30 yards away to where the large farm-wagon was parked and hopped on, along with 16 other workers, including Ying and Rusty's buddy Jack O'Malley. The miners were all exhausted, and they quietly took their seats in the stacks of hay, while Rusty sat between Marc and Jack. Two lanterns—one mounted on each side of the driver's bench—gave off a warm glow in the darkness of night. With a crack of the whip, the two horses bucked and began hauling the large, wooden wagon over the rutted path.

Jack O'Malley pulled out his bottle of moonshine, took a swig, and then passed it over to Mulvaney. Leaning back against the low side rails, Rusty lifted the bottle and guzzled a healthy dose.

Jack laughed, revealing his huge rotted horse teeth. "Hell, Billy Bourbon, take the damned bottle, I got me another one anyhows."

Rusty gazed over and nodded. "Thanks, Jack. I need it. It's been an awfully rough day. That damn drill has numbed my bloomin' ears and rattled my brain."

O'Malley chuckled. "Yeah, I know whatcha mean, BB. But haulin' all that damned debris you make ain't no fun neither. So, drink up, me boy!"

Rusty began chugging down the potent moonshine like water, while Marc looked up at his old friend. "Rusty, you really shouldn't drink so much of that stuff."

Rusty lowered the bottle from his parched lips. "Look Marc, you're still but a young lad. When you've slaved here as long as me and Jack, then you'll understand—booze is a man's salvation. It's how we cope."

"Yeah, in a fog," Marc replied. "Huxley gave me a shot of gin this morning, and it nearly melted my innards."

Rusty laughed, and without much thought, he took another slug, and then said, "Yeah, it takes some getting used to. But after a while, you crave this damn stuff."

"Well, my pa never did."

Rusty gazed down at Marc. "Well, your pa was a strong man. He was—" suddenly, his sluggish mind finally processed what Marc had said earlier, and he blurted, "Wait! What's this? Did you say Huxley gave *you* a drink?"

"Yeah, I think he was trying to get me all foggy headed on purpose."

Rusty frowned. "Gees, that devilish son-of-a-bitch really does have a red, pointy tail stuffed in his trousers!"

As they chuckled, Jack peered over and said, "*Hell*, I'll drink to that!"

As the three laughed, Marc looked up at Rusty, and whispered, "But I still can't believe Huxley is going to fire forty people tomorrow."

Rusty turned abruptly. "Shh! Don't stir everybody up."

However, Jack overheard the exchange, and bellowed, "Forty people fired!?"

As all eyes converged on O'Malley, he swiveled his head, gazing at all of them, and added, "Huxley is firing forty of us tomorrow!"

Panic struck the miners, and they sprang upright—pressing O'Malley to know who were going to be fired.

Jack pointed to Marc and Rusty. "Ask them, they're the ones I heard say it."

As all eyes zeroed in on Rusty, he turned and looked irritably at Marc, who then turned and scanned the anxious group. Marc shrugged and said, "We only heard that forty would be let go. We don't know who they are."

Another man yelled, "Well, if Huxley said this to you then you must know if you still have *your* jobs?"

"Yes, we do," Rusty said as he shifted to a defensive posture. "Now I don't want any of you picking on Marc here just because he has a job and some of you won't. The fact of the matter is this little guy has been promoted to an office job, cause he's got himself a keen little mind."

Some of the men glared at Marc, not happy that a child would be granted a promotion, while they, with families to support, might be let go. Yet Rusty simmered the situation down a notch when he explained Marc's loss and harsh family situation. Still, one or two men frowned that a mere boy had a high-paying office job, while they toiled for years down a dark and dangerous hole earning only penny-sized raises.

Marc quickly leaned forward, and began to allay some of their fears by stating that his new position allowed him the opportunity to save Huxley money, and if his business became profitable again, those who were fired could possibly be hired back.

One man was not satisfied. "So, big deal! Huxley *might* start making money again, and hiring again, but that doesn't help those of us who will suffer weeks or months without jobs! How the hell will we survive?"

"That's right!" several men blustered.

Another man leaned forward to catch Marc's eyes. "But it doesn't make any sense. If Huxley fires forty workers, how will he ever get the mine operational again?"

Rusty anxiously looked down at Marc, who looked up at him, and said, "They'll find out soon enough, so I might as well tell them."

At that, the man replied, "Tell us what? What didn't you tell us?"

As the wagon continued to rock and sway over the dark and bumpy path, Rusty instinctively looked over at Ying, sensing the ugly brawl that was bound to erupt. Meanwhile, Marc, unaware of the implications of what he was about to say, rattled off the damning news, "Huxley will be hiring forty Chinese workers tomorrow."

No sooner did he speak those words, than 12 miners' heads snapped toward Ying, with one man carping, "I knew you were just the start of our downfall! You damned Chinks are just work mules. Animals—that don't mind working for spit and living in shit!"

Another man chimed in, "That's right! And now you're gonna force *us* to live in shit! We bust our balls to make our lives better, yet you live like rats in filthy shacks and smoke that danged opium!"

A hefty man rose up, trying to maintain his balance as the wagon rolled over uneven ground, and barked, "You slanty-eyed son-of-a-bitch, you Chinks are not even citizens, yet you have the gall to steal our jobs! Go home!"

"Yeah, get the hell out!" another man yelled.

The hefty man drew his fists and blasted, "Yeah! Get the fuck off this wagon!" With that, he grabbed Ying by the collar, pulled him up, and then smashed him in the mouth, knocking his lanky body to the hay.

Meanwhile, Rusty lunged forward to stop the man from throwing another punch. However, as he managed to restrain the riled man, two other men grabbed Ying (who tried desperately to resist), and they threw him off the speeding wagon. The driver tried to slow down the horses, but he was threatened by the angry mob to keep going.

Marc yelled out, "Stop the wagon! This is madness!"

Rusty leaned over the driver and pulled back on the reins, yet three men grabbed Mulvaney from behind and wrestled him to the straw-covered floorboards. Jack tried to rip one of the men off Rusty, but received a solid right to the chin, knocking the drunken man into a small pile of hay.

Marc noticed a pitchfork lying against the back of the wagon and quickly picked it up. Pointing it at the backs of the three thugs on top of Rusty, he yelled, "Leave him alone, *now!*"

Several other men looked at the brave boy and suddenly had reservations about their lynching of Ying as well as their internal strife. Several men grabbed the three protagonists and ripped them off Rusty, who sluggishly sat upright—bloody faced and angry.

Marc yelled out to the driver, "I said STOP this wagon!"

The driver spun around and gazed at the boy wielding the pointed weapon and then at the faces of those around him. Seeing that the consensus had changed, he turned and pulled back on the reins. As the wagon jolted and came to a gradual stop, Rusty wiped his bushy mustache, which was now even redder, being soaked with blood dripping from his nose. Heatedly, he grabbed the pitchfork from Marc's hands and looked at the three troublemakers. "I hope I don't have to use this, but you three had better go back and fetch Ying, or I swear, I *will* ram this in your gutless guts!"

Seeing that everyone turned against them—save for two shifty-eyed, yet mute, sympathizers—the three ruffians gazed at each other and angrily shook their heads. With grunts and moans, the threesome hopped off the wagon. One grabbed a spare lantern that was entangled in a spare set of reins, and lit it. Grumbling and cussing under their breaths, the three thugs headed back along the dark path.

As Marc watched the men's lantern grow smaller and smaller, Rusty leaned back and began patting his bloody nose with a handful of hay.

Several minutes later, the men returned. Yet with a pathetic and beat-up-looking Ying in tow—the reins used as a noose to further humiliate their hostage.

One thug called out, "We caught us your damned Chink. So all you Chink-loving pansies hop off the damn wagon, or else Ying, here, gets strung up on a tree."

Rusty angrily stood up with the pitchfork in his hands and the moonshine still flowing in his veins, and bellowed, "Just you try to hang him, and I'll fill you three saps with so many holes, you'll look like a colander spewing blood!"

The man holding Ying, yanked the reins and took several steps toward a tree as he barked, "Come on, try it, you big drunken Mick, and Ying will be dead before you reach him!"

A man, named Abe, stood up in the wagon and looked at Mulvaney. "Rusty, just do what they say. I know those dirty hooligans, and they *will* kill him if you try anything. So, let's just give them the wagon, and get Ying safely back."

All but the two sympathizers agreed with Abe, and they began to hop off the wagon, landing in the dark dirt road. Up above, a thick veil of gray clouds slipped in front of the crescent moon, making the dreary night even darker. Meanwhile, the two lanterns mounted on the front of the wagon shed a limited and eerie glow as miners continued to dismount. As Marc hopped off, his eye caught a glimpse of the linchpin that kept the rear wheel mounted to the axle. He tapped Abe on the shoulder and rolled his eyes toward the pin. As the group of men received whispers of the plan they discreetly huddled around them to block the view of the antagonists. Abe took off his belt buckle and used it to pry the linchpin out, and then slipped it in his pocket.

Meanwhile, the alcohol was still firing up Rusty, who didn't like having his nose bloodied, and he continued to have a war of words with the three rebels. "I don't give a shit if you jackasses hang Ying before I get to you, but know this, once I do reach you, your ugly asses will have more than just one hole in them!"

As the two sympathizers on the wagon started to approach Mulvaney from behind, Marc yelled out, "Rusty! Look out behind you!"

Abe gazed up and added, "For Christ's sake, get down! We don't want Ying or anyone else getting hurt."

Rusty looked back at the two approaching men, and then swung around—pointing the pitchfork at their faces. The two men stopped as Rusty shook his head and complied. "Fine. Back off, and I'll let you danged fools have the wagon."

Meanwhile, the three men walked closer, dragging Ying, as one yelled, "Shut your stupid trap, you drunken sod, and get off the wagon. *Now!*"

"Not until you let Ying loose," Rusty countered.

"No way. You hop off first. Once we get onboard, then we'll let your little *yin-yang* loose."

Marc yelled, "Come on Rusty, *please!* Just give them the wagon, so we can get Ying back."

Rusty's face twisted in disgust as he shook his head and hopped off. Simultaneously, the three men jumped up—still leaving the reins around Ying's neck. One immediately jumped up by the driver, grabbed his whip, and cracked it. As the wagon bolted forward, Ying's neck jolted as he fell helplessly to the ground and was dragged. In horror, the group of men watched as Ying choked and tried desperately to grab onto the reins. His attempt to relieve the excruciating pain, however, was futile. His larynx had already snapped, and the bumpy dirt road only exacerbated the thrashing movements that battered and wrenched his now limp body.

As the wagon sped into the darkness, Marc covered his eyes in horror and utter humiliation; he never anticipated such a gruesome outcome.

But then a voice rang out, "And here it is!"

Marc removed his hands to see Abe holding the linchpin above his head. All eyes were glued on Abe's trophy, and then excitedly turned toward the speeding wagon. With anticipation, they watched and waited, until the wagon's wheel began to wobble wildly. Hitting a bump, the wagon's wheel flew off, while the driver lost control and the wagon flipped over. The throng of spectators cheered and then charged toward the crashed vehicle, while two men ran and knelt over Ying's dead body.

Marc sprinted to catch up, and the entourage arrived at the scene almost in unison. The driver had been tossed clear into the nearby brush, maintaining only bad bruises, and the horses had already righted themselves as they snorted and tried to free themselves from the entangled straps. Meanwhile, of the five thugs, three were fatally crushed under the flipped wagon and the two ringleaders lay bleeding and moaning on the rocky road.

Rusty walked up to the two thugs and pointed the pitchfork at their faces. In a voice wracked with rage, booze and revenge, he bellowed, "Give me one good reason why I shouldn't kill you two right now?"

Chants of "Kill them! Kill them!..." rang out, along with one soaring voice that demanded, "they need no judge nor jury. We saw it all. *Death* to them both!"

While one man went to rescue the driver, and two others repaired and fired up both lanterns, the chants grew louder. The nighttime spectacle looked like a Salem witch-hunt as the enraged mob encircled the two fallen sinners, while their lanterns' flickering glow lit up their captives' frightened faces.

Rusty raised the pitchfork and prepared to thrust it down into their throats, when he could hear Marc's distinct, youthful voice amid the din of deadly chants. "Don't! If you do, we'll all be outlaws, just like them!"

Suddenly, another voice added a layer of weight to Marc's plea, then another, and another; until it appeared that half the mob was opting for mercy.

Abe stood alongside Marc, and demanded, "I say we turn these two criminals over to the state for a proper trial. Justice will be served, especially with so many of us bearing witness."

Another stepped forward and barked, "As far as I'm concerned, I have no problem with them killing that damned Chink. Hell, we should get rid of all those filthy immigrants. Did you fools all forget about the forty Chinks who will be stealing our jobs tomorrow!?"

Another man pushed his way to the fore. "Yeah, when forty of us are out of work tomorrow, what then? Will you have sympathy for Ying, or will you rejoice that one of these pests has been eliminated!"

As the crowd swayed with agitation, another voice rang out. It was one of the men who had run over to Ying's dead body. "I don't like Chinks stealing our jobs neither, but what they did is inexcusable. Murder is murder. And these two bastards killed Ying in cold blood. I say a life for a life!"

Abe stepped forward and raised his hand. "Hold on! If we are to be civilized human beings we need to follow the law, or else we'll suffer the fate of becoming a land of anarchists and outlaws. Is that what our republic was built upon—a system of taking matters into your own hands? I think not! Let's not descend into the dark valley to become ruthless scavengers. But rather, rise up to the shinning mountaintop to become righteous bald eagles."

Abe's poetically patriotic words moved many, and even Rusty now found himself confused and frustrated as he lowered the pitchfork.

As the mob continued to haggle, Marc pushed his way to the center, and yelled, "Let's at least honor our republic by taking a vote."

The throng of discordant miners looked at one another and then conceded to the young lad's logical request. As a series of hands shot up for the death sentence, the two culprits looked on, pale and petrified. To them the count appeared to be a verdict, while unnerving chants of "death" rang out. However, as an equal number of hands sprang up to spare them for trial, the thugs breathed a sigh of relief. The juried mob realized that one uncounted voted remained, and the thugs now believed that their fellow miner, whomever it might be, would tip the scale in their favor. However, the last remaining juror happened to be Rusty (who had been standing idly by), and to their horror, Rusty broke the tie, opting for the death sentence.

Marc's shoulders dropped as he gazed up at his father's old friend with disappointment in his eyes and another lump of grief added to his heavy heart. He had thought Rusty would fill the void, if not as a father figure, at least as an uncle. Yet he now felt an uncomfortable gulf between them. The estrangement was all the more potent due to the fact that their difference of opinion rested not upon just an idea, but literally upon the lives of two men. Marc was dumbfounded. "Rusty, why?"

Rusty grabbed the pitchfork firmly. "Because we all saw with our own eyes what happened here, Marc. Besides, these two bastards hammered me pretty good back there, and they're gonna get what I promised them. So there ain't no need to waste a court's time with a case like this. They're guilty—guilty by their peers, I believe the saying goes. So, anyone not pleased with our majority vote can turn their heads or walk away."

As Marc, Abe, and six others turned and stepped away, Rusty approached the two cowering criminals with his raised pitchfork and swiftly impaled them—fulfilling his final role as executioner.

With the loose end of the nightmare brutally put to rest, the mob dutifully joined together to flip the wagon and re-harness the horses. Twenty minutes later, after replacing the wheel and reinserting the linchpin, they set off once again.

The remainder of the ride was plagued by an eerie silence, which only gave each participant more time to reflect upon the horrific chain of events. Worse yet, the corpses had all been neatly piled up on the back of the wagon, adding to the gloomy mood. As the wagon came upon the cobbled streets of Pittsburgh, lined by shimmering rows of lamplights, Marc broke the silence, "Please, let me off here."

The wagon rolled to a stop as Marc hopped off without even looking at Rusty. With a face as ridged and cold as iron, Marc walked towards Pendleton's iron shop.

Rusty called out, "Try and get some rest, Marc. You hear? Like Huxley said, you'll need it."

Marc continued walking without acknowledging him, while the driver cracked the whip. As Marc placed his hand on the ornately embossed doorknob, he could hear the wagon's noisy wheels and horses' clopping hooves slowly fading, along with his feelings for his dear old friend. He turned and looked back; only to see the wagon slip into the night as it turned the corner. With a heavy heart, he took a deep breath and looked back at the door. With a twist of the iron knob, he unlocked the bolt and entered.

Pendleton Iron Works was an enormous brick building with a small front office to one side, while the rest of the interior was a voluminous workspace. Various foundries were scattered about, with blacksmiths pounding smelted iron into various shapes or pouring molten iron into casts.

The wall of heat stifled Marc as he walked toward Pendleton's office. Yet before he could reach his destination, he could hear Calvin's jovial voice booming from somewhere else, "Ah, Mr. Wozniak. I'm over here!"

Marc was unaccustomed to being addressed in such a fashion, which, up until now, had solely been used to address his father. Yet, he liked the sound of it. It somehow breathed the life of his father into his lungs as his little chest expanded with a modicum of pride.

Meanwhile, Pendleton was a compassionate soul who had realized from Marc's brief visit last night that, besides his profound grief, the boy was looking forward to fulfilling his father's wishes. And what better way to make little Marc feel like the man of the house than to call him Mr. Wozniak.

Marc spun around, looking to spot the adventurous and unpredictable man, when his eyes caught Calvin riding on an odd-looking contraption with four wheels. It appeared to look like some sort of cart, yet it was made entirely of iron piping, and was not being pulled by horses. It had two seats mounted on it, along with two sets of pedals, which were connected to gears and chains that powered the rear wheels. Mounted above Pendleton—whose legs were pumping the machine—was an awning covered with bright red and white striped fabric.

With a gregarious grin, Pendleton pedaled the vehicle right in front of Marc and came to a halt. "Hop in!"

Marc gaped at the odd machine. "What is this thing?"

"Actually, I don't quite know. I haven't given the blasted thing a name yet. But no matter, that will come in due time. So hurry up!"

Marc didn't quite hear Pendleton's slurred last sentence, and he inquired, "Did you say surry up?"

Calvin chuckled, "No, no! I said *hurry* up. But I must say, I do like the sound of *surry*." He rubbed his dimpled chin. "Especially since I was born in Surrey, England. It appears you struck a mighty fine chord there, Marc. Surrey would make an absolutely splendid name for this new pedal-cart of mine. Yes, yes, indeed. Surrey it is!"

Marc eagerly hopped in, and the two began pedaling, while Pendleton steered. Taking him for a tour of the large foundry, Calvin explained all the different processes they utilized and all the different parts they fabricated for steam ships, locomotives, construction, merchandise and just about everything imaginable. Marc was awestruck. His life, thus far, had been committed to digging black rocks out of the ground, and for the first time, he could see the shaping of that raw material into practical items.

Pendleton stopped at one station as men ejected intricately fashioned steam engine parts out of their casts. "You see, Marc, for centuries, mankind has marveled over the fantastic job God did in creating nature. Yet his handiwork, I dare say, only gave us raw chunks of anthracite and useless seams of iron ore." Calvin pointed as he pedaled. "Now feast your eyes upon what man is capable of doing! The possibilities, my dear fellow, are as limitless as our imaginations."

Marc looked up at Pendleton. "Are you saying that man is superior to God?"

Calvin chuckled as they continued to ride through the plant. Taking one hand off the steering wheel, he said, "Hell no! Take a look at this." He wriggled his fingers and then pointed to his eye. "No paltry little man could ever design something this fabulous and complex." With an electrifying grin, he continued, "But it sure does fire the imagination when I see mankind shaping seemingly useless elements into magnificently crafted and highly useful items. And these gadgets, my little friend, are enhancing our world at a most alarming rate, the likes of which has never been seen before on this planet." As Calvin cut the wheel and turned down another aisle, he continued, "This, I believe, is because man has foolishly shackled himself with false doctrines of religion, which, rather regrettably, have stymied mankind from attaining its true potential."

Pendleton pointed to five portraits hanging on the wall as they pedaled, one was of Galileo, another was of David Hume, two others were of his friends Carnegie and Edison, and the last one was of Charles Darwin. "You see, Marc, it is no coincidence that the great thinkers of the Enlightenment along with our current industrialists, inventors and scientific geniuses have broken those chains, thus affording us the mental freedom and ability to create these tremendous strides in progress. Therefore, my dear fellow, we must rethink just what our ancient scrolls truly were." As Marc listened intently, Calvin continued, "Were they the Word of God, as dictated by God? Or were they the words of simple mortal men—vague words that have been shrewdly manipulated by countless other men over many centuries?"

As Marc squinted, deep in thought and unable to reach a conclusion, Pendleton said, "Well, I must tell you, judging by all indications of our bloody past and current progress, I believe the latter. You see, the flawed hand of mankind has flawed our religion and has not represented God properly. That is why my British Protestant relatives continue to shun and even kill Irish Catholics, and vice versa. And that foolish loathing continued right here when the Virginia Puritans burned or brutally killed Christians of other denominations. Quite unfortunately, my dear little fellow, too many sects claim to be the only true pathway to God. Hence, may I conclude, that such shameful behavior only validates that mankind does not have the slightest clue as to who is our one and only true God."

"My mother has sort of come to believe the same thing," Marc said. "Yet, she has never explained it quite that way before." Marc's face suddenly became heavy, his voice sullen, "I have often wondered why God does strange things, Mr. Pendleton, like taking my father's life, since he *was* a good man. But I still believe God gives us strength to do great things that we never could have done without his support."

Pendleton's eyebrows shot skyward. "Ah, yes! That reminds me! I must show you something." Turning the steering wheel, he began to pedal as they weaved in and out of ironworkers wielding torches, with a flurry of sparks hitting the floor all around them. Marc ducked from a flying spark as he looked on with awe at all the fabulous parts and gadgets being crafted. Calvin then pulled the brake lever, and they stopped at the rear of the building. Standing before them was a set of large double sliding doors, sealed with a padlock. Pendleton hopped out of the surrey and pulled a set of keys out of his vest pocket. He turned and prodded with a smile, "Well, you silly ninny, don't just sit there!"

Marc chuckled and hopped out to join him, while Pendleton unlocked the doors and slid them open. Standing before them was a huge black carriage, yet its design was unlike anything Marc, or anyone, had ever seen. Rather than tall and boxy, it had sleek graceful lines; all shaped out of thin sheets of iron. It also sported large, metal spoke-wheels capped with a two-inch layer of soft, vulcanized rubber, and four doors with decorative, round glass windows. Meanwhile, the interior was beautifully upholstered and large enough to sit eight people.

Marc walked around the entire carriage marveling at the detail and elaborate workmanship.

Calvin smiled. "It's fit for a king, is it not?"

"For sure!" Marc exclaimed. "It's magnificent."

"Oh, yes," Pendleton said, "and inside it features a pullout bookcase for the thinker, and a pullout bar for the drinker."

Marc chuckled. "My, you thought of everything."

"Oh, no!" Calvin replied, "I—"

"Why, what did you forget?"

"Oh, no, I didn't mean to insinuate that anything was forgotten, Marc. I meant oh, no, I did not plan any of this. This wonderful carriage was your father's creation. He had been working on it for the past year or so, almost every night. That is, after he finished building items for my clients, of course."

Marc's jaw dropped. *"My papa designed and built this?"*

"Oh, yes. Jedrek had a gift for design and very gifted hands. He shaped metal better than almost anyone I know."

Marc still could not believe what he was hearing or seeing. He knew his father crafted little things around the apartment, but nothing like this. Marc was baffled. "But how come he never told us about this?"

Calvin's face mellowed as he said poignantly, "It was to be a surprise. Your father wanted to keep it a secret until it was finished." He then pointed to the rear of the carriage. "You see, he had plans for fabricating a large storage trunk, right back here."

Marc was still puzzled. "But, I don't get it. This must have cost him a fortune to build. Where did he get the money to do this?"

"Well, Marc. Some men spend their money on booze, others on horses or playing cards, and others on fancy clothes or furniture or whatever strikes their fancy. But, your pa put his life's savings into this carriage with the hopes of selling it at a substantial profit. And I dare say that this baby will easily bring in $1,000 or more."

Marc couldn't believe his ears. "A thousand dollars! Oh my God!" Marc gazed at the ground and then back at the sparkling black beauty before his astounded eyes. "I can't believe that one of the last things my pa told me was that he was sorry for not succeeding in America the way he wanted. He said that I would be the one to lift our family out of poverty. My, oh, my, was *he* wrong! I could never build something like this."

Pendleton lowered his head in thought and then gazed over at Marc. "Well, my dear boy, you simply have different talents than your father. And, in one sense, your pa was right. He did not live to see your family's success, but, by golly, he certainly gave you a great start to do what he was unable to fulfill." Pendleton pointed to the carriage. "So, all you need to do, Marc, is finish this trunk and then sell this baby. I'm positive my friends Carnegie or Frick would jump at the chance to buy something this spectacular."

Marc was still somewhat in shock as he rubbed his head. It now became abundantly clear to him why his father's last unfinished sentence was to visit Cal. After a brief moment, he said, "*A thousand dollars.* Gee whiz, I could buy a house for my mother, or a horse for Ted, or a special surrey contraption that my brother Stan could pedal by hand."

Pendleton gently shook his head as he smiled at Marc with admiration. "I noticed you did not mention one single thing for yourself."

Marc looked up as if awakened from a fanciful dream. "Oh, yes. I reckon I forgot."

Calvin walked over and affectionately patted Marc on the head. "Now I know why your father entrusted you with being the man of the Wozniak house." As Marc looked up, Pendleton asked, "But what would make *you* happy?"

Marc gazed back down at the ground. "Well, besides getting my pa back, or Stan's leg back, or my brother Ted back, I'm really not sure." Then looking back up, he added, "Actually, I'd love to see the miners at Huxley Coal have electrical lighting, better air vents, more support beams, and better wages. But I guess that's impossible."

"Not necessarily," Pendleton said, "you could buy Huxley Coal."

Marc laughed. "Well, even I know that you can't buy a coal mine for $1,000, Mr. Pendleton."

Calvin wrapped his arm around Marc. "Indeed. I'm not suggesting that you buy it right now, Marc. But do realize that you are still a young lad, and you *are* very bright. So, if you put your mind to it, I'd be willing to bet my entire shop that you would indeed find a way."

Marc grinned; touched and delighted to hear Pendleton's vote of confidence, yet deep down knowing the old man was just being kind or a bit loopy.

Calvin pointed to a heap of metal. "That, my dear boy, is all yours. So, I suggest you start by drawing up a design for the trunk. Once that is done, one of my men will show you how to transform that idea into a tangible bit of reality. Do you think you can handle that?"

Marc's poker face was off duty, revealing his trepidation. "I think so, sir."

Pendleton laughed. "Well, it appears your face says one thing and your mouth another. Just jump into it, Marc, and let's see what happens. And if you need assistance, then one of my draftsmen will help you. Fair enough?"

Marc's face suddenly beamed with confidence. "That sounds swell. And my face does match my words this time, right Mr. Pendleton?"

Calvin laughed. "Yes, you seem to have mastered that, Marc, now grab a pencil and master the design for a spectacular trunk!"

Marc eagerly ran to the drafting table and grabbed a pencil and some paper. Some 20 minutes later, Marc had a clever idea in mind, but getting that down on a flat piece of paper posed a problem. With the aid of a draftsman, Marc dictated his ideas and 32 minutes later the plans were completed. The stylish trunk contained eight collapsible compartments to accommodate either eight passengers or one, when folded down. When Calvin finally looked at Marc's plans, he was impressed. Rather than featuring just a pretty exterior, Marc's adjustable compartment scheme demonstrated creative thinking.

Yet it was clear that Marc was exhausted. It had been a long and stressful day, and Calvin knew the young lad needed to get rest. Especially since Marc told him about his new position at Huxley Coal, which was going to demand a great deal more of his time.

Pendleton looked at his watch; it was 11:04 p.m. "You did an absolutely splendid job, Marc. Now do go home and get some rest. I know you have a busy schedule. But, please, feel free to work on this anytime—at your leisure."

As Calvin escorted Marc to the door, he mentioned that he had spoken to his attorney, Mr. Donnellson, who reconfirmed the grim news that widows must, indeed, surrender two-thirds of the estate and one-half their personal property to the government. Marc's shoulders dropped, unable to fathom how the government could have such a death-grip on death itself. However, Pendleton also stated that, unbeknownst to him, Donnellson had spoken to Jedrek on several occasions in regards to mining regulations and worker safety issues.

Evidently, a former miner from Ohio, named Andrew Roy, was currently in the process of founding the Ohio Institute of Mining Engineers. Years earlier, Roy had even been appointed by then Governor Rutherford B. Hayes to inspect mines and was now making a pioneering effort to combat ignorance and outright abuses by mining tycoons. As such, Donnellson had picked Jedrek's brain about what he had seen in Huxley's coalmines, and the reports were damning. Pendleton told Marc that Huxley's reckless disregard for having an insufficient number of airshafts not only deprives miners of oxygen but also is the primary reason why there have been so many explosions. Additionally, Jedrek realized that Huxley was using inferior grade lumber for beams, which also accounted for numerous cave-ins and only added to Huxley's egregious death toll. To Marc's disappointment, Calvin ended on a grim note, stating that 98 percent of the people who tried to sue owners for negligence have not won. Yet he urged Marc to maintain hope.

Marc was humiliated, he knew they needed airshafts for oxygen, yet had no idea Huxley knowingly used less. With today's blast destroying the few airshafts they do have, he now knew even greater danger looms. With a sullen face, Marc thanked Pendleton for his advice and generosity. With a firm handshake, he turned and exited the shop.

As Calvin watched the fatherless youth step out into the dark night and begin to walk home alone, his heart dropped. Yet Calvin could see that the boy, like his father, had a certain gift, and he fully believed that he would indeed achieve great things.

As Marc walked down the cobbled street, he could see his tenement several blocks ahead. The dark streets were vacant, and most of the lamps in the surrounding apartments had been turned off as the city entered its nocturnal mode of slumber. His body was exhausted, yet his mind couldn't stop thinking about everything that transpired in this long eventful day. As his eyes looked down at the softly lit stones, he noticed his shadow in front of him. He stretched out his arms and then spun them around, entertaining his troubled little mind with whimsical animations. But then another shadow appeared, and quite unsettlingly, it grew rapidly in size, eventually dwarfing his own. Marc turned, only to see an ominous sight—a beastly-looking man with large, black eyes, and wild, black hair was bearing down on him! Marc's heart skipped a beat as the pug-faced thug grabbed him. "Come with me. And shut your mouth!" he growled as he dragged Marc into a dark alley.

Lifting Marc off the ground, he rammed his little body into the brick wall.

Marc was trembling. "W-what do you w-want?"

Pressing his gnarled, bearded face within inches of Marc's, he inquired with rank breath, "Tell me what you know about Edwin Harrelson?"

Marc's face twitched and his nose wriggled as he stuttered, "I d-don't even know w-who Edwin Harrelson is!"

The thug snorted angrily as he banged Marc against the wall, his head hitting the brick.

"Ouch!" Marc cried, "I'm telling you the t-truth! I don't know w-who you're talking about."

"Don't bullshit me, boy!" the ruffian snarled. "I ain't got no patience for little smart-ass liars. So, one more time; what do you know about Harrelson?"

"I s-swear," Marc stammered, "I don't k-know who—"

Whack! The ferocious beast slapped Marc in the face, still holding him up against the wall with his other paw.

Marc's nose began to swell as the pug-faced brute leaned in and stared at Marc with his large, canine eyes. A tear ran down Marc's innocent little cheek as the thug growled, "I ain't gonna tolerate lies! You *will* tell me what you know, or you *will* suffer, boy!"

Marc turned his head, trying to avoid the brute's wrath and malodorous breath. Looking at the scary beast out of the corner of his eye, Marc said, "But I r-really don't know—"

Thwack! This time, he pummeled Marc with a solid fist as blood spurt out of Marc's ripped upper lip, while red rivulets ran down his chin. A creepy smile etched itself in the barbarian's face—gaining pleasure from the sight of his bloody handiwork. "Do you expect me to believe that you don't know Edwin Harrelson—that blind old dirt bag who worked at Huxley Coal for thirty years?"

Marc choked on the blood in his mouth as he uttered, "Oh, you m-mean Homer?"

The brute squinted as his sluggish brain searched his dull memory. "I reckon some people called him that." He pushed his two large, meaty fists into Marc's chest, crushing his little body against the hard brick wall as he added, "So, you *do* know Harrelson?"

"Y-yes, sir. I didn't know his real name."

"Fine," he grumbled impatiently, "so tell me what you know about this Homer fellow?"

Marc squinted. "I don't understand? What is there to tell?"

The thug snorted as his face twisted with rage. "You've seen what happens when you get me mad, boy. So, tell me! Did that blind old piece of shit say anything to you before he died? Anything at all that seemed odd?"

Marc turned his head and spit out a glob of coagulated blood, and then looked back at the dumb sarcastic thug. Maintaining his skillful poker face, he said calmly, "No."

The dimwitted animal squinted as he once again scrutinized the young cherubic face before him. All looked plain and innocent, and he lowered Marc to the ground. Marc gazed up at the brute, registering his face into his memory: from his wild black beard and large black eyes to the crescent shaped scar on his smashed pug nose. It was a mean and ugly face, hard to forget.

The beast gazed down and growled in a low, threatening voice, "This little meeting never happened. You hear me?" As Marc nodded, he continued, "Cause if you say a word to anyone, I mean anyone, I will not only smash you into pulp and toss your dead body in the river, but I'll also have me a good time torturing and killing your mother and useless crippled brother. You see, I know where you live, Marc!" The brute gave Marc a push to get moving, yet with enough force to almost send him face-first to the ground. Marc stumbled and began to run as the beast cackled, "Have a good night, Marky boy!"

Sprinting down the street as fast as he could, while holding his bloody lip, Marc made it to his front door and pushed his way through. Spinning around, he looked to see if the deranged beast followed him, but the streets were vacant and quiet. Breathing out a sigh of relief, Marc pushed the door closed and locked it. As he spun around, his mother looked up from the couch and yelped, "Oh, my God! What happened?"

Marc turned his head away, covering his swollen nose and bloody mouth with both hands. "It's nothing! Don't worry about it."

Sophia dropped her book and darted over. Nervously, she grabbed his hands and peeled them away. "Oh, my! You need a doctor. This may need stitches!"

Marc pushed his way past her, heading toward the kitchen. "No I don't. I'll be fine."

As he began washing his face in the washbasin, Sophia came up behind him with a towel. "Come here, let me take another look at that lip."

Marc extended his arm back, grabbed the towel, and placed it on his aching face. Applying pressure, he walked over to the kitchen table and took a seat. "Where is Stan?"

"He's asleep," she said. "Never mind Stan. What happened?"

"I can't say."

"Why not?"

"I just can't. That's why!"

Sophia rushed over and sat next to him. "Don't you dare say *that's why* to *me!* I'm you mother! You must be able to tell me everything that happens in your life."

Marc's blue eyes gazed up at his mother as his eyebrows pinched. "Do you really tell me everything that happens in *your* life?"

"I'm your mother! That's different."

"How so?"

"It just is!"

"Oh, *it just is,* kind of like, *that's why!*" Marc retorted.

Sophia looked down at the floor for a moment, lost in thought, and now visibly hurt. Gazing back up, she whimpered, "Very well, young *man*. You don't need to tell me."

She rose up from the chair with a crushed look on her face and walked over to the washbasin. As she picked it up and emptied the red water outside the rear door, she then paused a moment. In a voice deep with emotion, she uttered, "But just know this—as your mother, you can never stop me from loving and caring about you. *Never!*"

Marc's heart took a wallop with that remark as a tear welled in his eye. He pulled the bloody towel away from his face and quickly reapplied it to the oozing wound. He looked back at his mother. "Fine. Some man beat me up in the alley."

Sophia spun around, dropped the basin, and marched back over. "*A man!* I suspected a brawl with some boy at work. Who was this man?"

"I don't know."

"Well, what did he want?"

Marc shook his head. "It was actually rather bizarre. He just wanted to know if I knew Homer. You know, that old blind man at work."

Sophia nodded. "Of course."

"Well, first of all, mom, Homer died today."

Sophia recoiled. "Oh, my Lord! What happened?"

As Marc began to relay the whole story it suddenly became clear to him why the dimwitted thug attacked him. He had not acted alone, and Marc now saw the connection. He recalled how Huxley interrogated him about Homer, trying to see if the blind man said anything about his dark past, and indeed he had. Marc now realized the gravity of knowing this information, which put him at serious risk. Worse yet, Marc mentioned how Huxley's thug told him not to say a word to anyone, and threatened to kill their entire family if he did.

Sophia had listened patiently, but now the aggressive side of her Gemini spirit rose to the fore to allay her son's fears. "Listen, Marc, don't you worry about that hoodlum coming here. And you did well by not admitting anything. As long as Huxley believes you know nothing about his fraudulent past and illegal marriages, you'll be fine."

Still having more to unload off his chest, Marc then revealed that, besides those transgressions, Huxley's lack of proper ventilation requirements and inferior bracing have been the major causes of all the deaths that have devastated Pittsburgh for years. And that naturally included Jedrek.

Sophia had all to do to control her rage, yet she focused on a solution that, she believed, was realistic, considering the power, wealth and influence of their deadly foe. "Listen, Marc, now that you have a higher paying, office job, just play along and make every penny and dollar you can from that dirty crook, but at the same time, you must find a way to crumble his wicked empire." Sophia's face tensed up as she added, "Huxley has killed more people in that mine than the plague, and the virus must be stopped!"

"Momma, I agree that Huxley is a dangerous man and is responsible for papa's death and many others, but I don't see how I could possibly destroy his huge empire without us crumbling with him. Besides, if we go about this legally, you must remember what Mr. Pendleton said; the majority of legal cases against these big tycoons never win. After all, look what happened to Homer." Marc paused, and then added, "But today I have seen ways to improve his company, and if I do, well, then maybe he'll make improvements and make life better for everyone."

Sophia looked at Marc with fire in her eyes. "Marc, back home in Italy we understood the meaning of, and necessity for, *vendetta!* People that are reasonable can be dealt with, but an unscrupulous maggot like Huxley will never change. You are too young and optimistic to realize that sad fact, my dear, but believe me; I know what I'm saying. It may seem harsh and cruel, but that man is evil, and he must be destroyed!"

As Marc patted his bloody face, Sophia leaned over and pulled the towel away. "And there are times that you *must* listen to your mother. So, heed what I just said about Huxley, and get this face stitched up! Your lip is split."

Marc looked up. "Is it really that bad?"

Sophia walked toward the door. "Yes! I'm getting Doctor Galton to come over right now. So keep that towel on your face and stay put."

Fifteen minutes later, the doctor arrived with his black leather bag and began threading his needle. As Marc sat patiently waiting for his torn flesh to be mended with six stitches, Sophia kissed him on the head, and then headed for the door.

As she swung it open, she glanced back. "Doctor Galton always does a fine job, so don't worry. And I've already paid him. I'm going out for a while, so get to bed as soon as he leaves."

Before Marc could question where she was going, the door slammed shut.

Doctor Galton looked down at his patient with a slight smile. "She's a feisty woman, your mother."

"Indeed, she is!" Marc replied.

"Now, would you care for a shot of alcohol, or do I just dig in?"

Marc closed his eyes and leaned back. "Dig in, Doc!"

8

Sophia's Vendetta & Vexation

July 1, 1881

Sophia had asked Doctor Galton to borrow his horse, and she now thrust her foot into the stirrup and hauled herself onto the animal's back. She adjusted the 10-inch carving knife in her apron pocket as she kicked the horse's flanks and took off.

Riding through the dark city streets, the horse's metal shoes clattered against the cobblestones—breaking the silence of night—but suddenly hushed to a soft thump as they finally hit grass and dirt. Sophia's face was stiff and determined as she steered the horse up into the mountains towards Huxley Hills.

The dense clouds parted slightly, while the rays of the silvery moon illuminated the leaves on the trees and the pebbles below along the rutted path. Up ahead she spotted the opulent mansion sitting majestically on the highest peak of Huxley Hills. The 1,200-acre estate was mostly raw and barren, much like the owner's character and soul, yet the grounds surrounding the beautiful mansion were posh and manicured, reflecting Penelope's refined European tastes.

Sophia veered off the path and rode into the dark recesses of trees towards the left wing of the mansion. She had spotted the only light on in the entire complex and figured Huxley would surely be there, awake and calculating how best to profit from the disaster. She tied the horse to a branch and walked slowly toward the huge bay window of the Victorian mansion. Peering in, she saw Huxley sitting on a massive couch in the den, decorated in his typical animal-slaughtered, rugged style. The walls were fashioned entirely out of exotic dark woods, while huge, roughly cut cross beams and rafters networked the cathedral ceiling. The heads of deer, elk, buffalo, mountain lions, and boars decorated the walls, and a huge bear rug lay on the floor with its large grizzly face staring at the mammoth fireplace. One entire wall was fashioned with gun racks, proudly displaying Huxley's vast assortment of hunting rifles, service carbines and pistols.

Sophia crept onto the nearby patio and placed her hand on the doorknob. It was locked. She peered through the pane of beveled glass at the center of the door, still able to make out his fractured shape. She thought for a moment, and then picked up a small rock. Leaning over the patio railing, she threw the pebble lightly at the bay window and stepped quickly back by the door. Within seconds, Huxley appeared at the window—peering curiously into the black night for the source of the sound.

Sophia watched as Huxley stepped away from the window. Her heart began to race as she slipped the carving knife out of her apron, and waited anxiously for the door to open. The seconds seemed like minutes as her mind now wandered back to the vision of Huxley's arsenal. A rush of fear struck her as she envisioned Huxley loading a rifle or pistol with cartridges. She began to sweat as second thoughts began to erode her nerve. Then suddenly Huxley's silhouette appeared at the door window. At first startled, Sophia now realized there was no turning back, and her eyes veered down at the doorknob. It started to turn! Her heart beat even faster as the wooden door opened—the light from within fanning out over the patio, fading into darkness. Sophia remained hidden behind the opened door as Huxley stepped out onto the patio, his back a mere three feet away. Sophia was relieved—Huxley didn't have a weapon. Quickly, she snuck up behind him and stuck the tip of her cutlery into his back. Huxley jolted, but, instinctively, his head spun around, his eyes connecting with her's.

"Don't move!" Sophia snarled, "or I *will* carve you up, you son-of-a-bitch!"

To her surprise, Huxley smiled. "You're a very attractive woman, *and* feisty. I like that. So, my dear, what can I do for you?"

"First of all," she hissed, "you can quit the charm, you don't have any! Second, you can stop sending your big thug over to beat up my son!"

"Ah! So, you're Mrs. Wozniak."

"Yes, and how dare you threaten all of us that way? Who the hell do you think you are? And do you think I'm afraid of you? Well, I'm not!"

Huxley chuckled. "I do love a woman with spirit, but—"

"Enough!" Sophia barked as she drove the tip of her knife into his back, just far enough to prick his skin.

Huxley yelped, but pivoted around and grabbed her hand. Quickly, he whipped her around and, now standing behind her, guided her hand toward her own neck, with the blade pressing into her skin. Having seized complete control, Huxley lowered his head and whispered in her ear. "That actually aroused me, my dear!"

Just then Huxley's boxer, Rex, came running out onto the porch and began barking. Huxley looked at Rex with commanding eyes. "Heel, boy!"

Rex obediently stopped barking, but was curious about the stranger. With mistrusting eyes, Rex began sniffing Sophia's dress.

Sophia stood utterly stunned and humiliated as Huxley pressed his enlarged member against her buttocks, and again whispered in her ear, "Like I said, you're an attractive woman, and I'm sure we can settle this matter."

Sophia struggled and kneed Rex in the stomach when his fresh, wet nose began sniffing her crotch. "Your damned dog is as vile as you are!" she bellowed. "Now, let me go!"

Huxley chuckled. "Oh, no, my dear. It doesn't end that simply. You came here to make a point, which my bloody back attests, and I have a point to make myself." With that, he lustfully grinded her rear with his excited shank as she squirmed and snarled, "Let me go, or, I swear, I'll scream and wake up your wife and children!"

Huxley kicked the door shut with his foot, and began to drag Sophia towards the guesthouse some 800 feet away, while covering her mouth.

Sophia struggled to no avail as they reached the dark, vacant building. Reaching down, he quickly opened the door and pushed their bodies into the foyer.

"Now, my dear, you can scream if you wish, but no one will hear you. I will not have you waking my family." Turning toward Rex—who was now standing on the front porch with his panting tongue hanging from his mouth—he commanded, "Sit, and be a good boy."

As Rex obediently sat down, Huxley closed the door with his foot.

Softly, he said, "I apologize for handling you this way, but you did stick a knife in my back. And as for my playfulness, yes, I do find you attractive, but you can relax. I have never taken a woman without her consent, so, please, have no fear. Let's just talk."

Removing his hand from her mouth, she snarled, "Then get this knife away from my neck, and let me go!"

"Sure, but only if you promise to behave."

"Fine," she said quasi calmly. "Please, let me go."

"Ah, now that's more like it," he said politely as he released her.

Sophia spun around and gazed at the dark figure before her. "So, let's settle this mess."

Huxley lit up two candelabras as a warm glow slowly lit up the foyer, revealing a modest but pleasant décor. Holding one fixture in his hand, he said, "Please, follow me."

Sophia cautiously followed as they entered the parlor. It was handsomely decorated with two couches, four chairs, and several pieces of contemporary American furniture. Placing the candelabra and knife on a cabinet near the door, he turned and said, "Would you mind checking my back to see how bad the wound is?"

With a smirk, Sophia nodded tersely as he lifted his white linen shirt, revealing his muscular abdomen. Sophia tried not to look as Archie spun around, revealing the small oozing puncture and his bloodstained shirt.

Sophia barely looked, and hardly cared as she uttered, "It stopped bleeding. It's fine."

Lowering his shirt, Archie spun around. "Very well then. Can I get you a drink?"

Sophia took several steps further into the room and then stopped, her body uncomfortably stiff. "No thank you. Let's just discuss this and have it over with."

Huxley smiled as he opened a liquor cabinet and poured two glasses of whiskey. He turned and extended one of the glasses. "Please, it will calm your nerves."

Sophia shook her head, no.

Huxley walked over and placed it on the coffee table, which stood between the two sofas, and then sat down. He took a swig, and gazed up at her. "So, Mrs. Wozniak, what is your first name?"

"Sophia," she said dryly. "And you best remember it, because I will not tolerate having my family terrorized by anyone. Not even *you!*"

Huxley chuckled. "Please, Sophia. Sit. I have no intentions of terrorizing anyone. It's just that a man in my position cannot afford to let anyone get away with creating an embarrassing situation for him."

"What embarrassing situation are you referring to?" Sophia said. "That you had a big brute beat up a young boy, or that you run a dangerous business that consistently kills scores of miners every few months, including my husband?"

Huxley squinted, he expected to be chided for his bigamy or how he fraudulently stole Homer's mine, but now Sophia confirmed what his ruffian, Blaggo, had told him: Homer hadn't squealed to Marc. Huxley smiled and took another gulp of whiskey—knowing that his secrets were still secure. Gazing harmlessly into her eyes, he said, "Please, Sophia, I know we can settle this. Have a seat. I assure you, I'm not a monster."

Sophia gazed at Huxley with suspicious eyes.

Huxley smiled and casually leaned back into the sofa. "Okay, I know I have a reputation for being a ruthless businessman, but underneath that public image, which the newspapers have maliciously created, I *am* a good man. Do you realize, Sophia, how crucial Huxley Coal is to our great nation? The railroads would halt and their locomotives would rust without *my coal!* Steamships would sit idle and grow barnacles without *my coal!* Buildings and bridges that need iron and steel would not be built without *my coal!* So, you see, Sophia, I am a very important man, and the newspapers only fixate on the setbacks I face. They have no idea how difficult it is to run an operation like this. Therefore, I can understand your loathing me. But without Huxley Coal, this country would literally stop running. And I cannot afford to let *anything* or *anyone* get in the way of that far larger vision."

Sophia's face and posture had already begun to soften as her gaze veered down at the fancy carpet and back up at Huxley's charismatic eyes. His handsome features and now humble smile seemed sincere, and she thought, maybe the papers did blow things out of proportion. Perhaps he just needs to be informed about the latest safety regulations. Moreover, this man was indeed supplying only what the growing country demanded.

Despite still harboring reservations, Sophia walked to the sofa opposite him and sat down. "I reckon the nation does need your services, Mr. Huxley, but that still does not explain why you had my son beat up. The poor angel is getting stitches on his lip right now, because of you!"

Huxley's amiable face contorted with sympathy. "I never gave Blaggo instructions to beat up your son, I promise. I only said he could shake him, *if* need be. But, these strong-arms I hire sometimes get carried away. I'm truly sorry about that, because I do like your son. He's a smart lad with a lot of spirit, and I'll gladly pay for the stitches."

"That's kind of you," Sophia said, "but that still does not answer my question. Why? Why did you bully him? For what?"

Huxley took another sip of whiskey. "Well, you see, there was this old man named Edwin Harrelson who worked for me for many years. You probably know him by his nickname, Homer." Sophia nodded. She was beginning to believe Huxley. He was making good sense and generously answering her questions, and she decided to pick up her glass of whiskey.

Archie felt a surge of confidence by that gesture as he continued, "And this fellow Homer knew of some confidential information, which I could not afford to have leaked out."

Sophia was almost going to take a sip, but stopped. She still wasn't sure just how honest Huxley really was. Her next question, she knew, would decide that once and for all. Sophia squinted. "What kind of information?"

Huxley smiled. "As I said, confidential information. Nothing personal, it was business related. You know—trade secrets that we at Huxley Coal use to keep ahead of our competitors."

Sophia nodded politely and placed the glass down. "I see. Fine. I guess that clears things up." Now knowing that Huxley was a dirty, lecherous liar, she stood up. "I thank you for offering to pay for the stitches, but that won't be necessary. I just want you to promise that Marc and my family will never be threatened or harmed by you, or your bully, ever again."

"Why, of course not," Huxley said as he leaned forward, suspicious. "But you didn't take a sip of your drink. Is something wrong?"

Sophia felt that her purpose was fulfilled; namely, making sure her sons would not be threatened or killed. That she initially intended to accomplish this feat by confronting might with might, she had now done so as amicably as possible, especially with a snake like Huxley.

Therefore, all Sophia wanted now was to get out as quickly as possible.

"No," she said in a soft, yet nervous voice, "nothing is wrong. But I would appreciate if you didn't mention this meeting to Marc. He is a proud young man, and he'd be mortified if he knew I came here on his behalf."

Huxley reached over to the end table and slid open the drawer. Pulling out something undecipherable, he sat upright and took another swig of whiskey. Then gazing up at Sophia, he said, "Oh, have no fear. Marc shall hear nothing of what happened here tonight, this I assure you." Unfolding the odd rubbery object in his hand, he held it up. "Do you, by chance, know what this is?"

Sophia looked at the long, thin, rubbery tube and shook her head, no.

Huxley pulled and snapped it. "They call it a condom," he said with a lecherous smile. "It is made of vulcanized rubber. It is truly amazing what new inventions mankind keeps coming up with, isn't it?"

Sophia squinted. "What is it for?"

Huxley chuckled. "It's for protection. And men like myself always need protection. You know, to keep me and my family safe."

"Well, I don't see how a silly little piece of rubber can protect you or your family."

"Oh, but it can, Sophia, as well as protect *you*," he said with lustful eyes. "You see, I'm far smarter than you think, my dear. I sense a sudden change in your disposition, and I really would like to change that. Do you not find me handsome?"

Sophia cringed. Huxley's remark was unexpected. Nervously, she glanced at the carving knife sitting on the cabinet by the door. A chill ran down her spine, sensing that the conversation was heading in an ugly direction. She stepped slightly toward the door, not fully sure of Huxley's motives, or what that little rubbery thing in his hand was for. Yet, she wanted to get out of there, and would now say whatever Huxley wished to hear. "Yes, you are a handsome man, Mr. Huxley. But, again, I don't see what that has to do with anything regarding me or my son."

Huxley leaned forward, emboldened and enlarged by the compliment. "I'm glad you find me attractive, Sophia. You see, when I was a young man, I joined this community in Oneida. They preached the Word of the Lord and practiced open love, which I firmly believe in, as no man or woman should selfishly give themselves to only one person."

Sophia took another step toward the door. "Well, I don't agree with that liberal interpretation of the Bible, Mr. Huxley. Although I'm no longer a practicing Catholic, I do believe in the sacred vows of my faith, and agree with the laws of this nation."

"Well, I was truly hoping you'd see things my way, Sophia, but as I've said, I'm a very powerful man, and I *always* get what I want." Huxley unbuttoned his pants and began to pull them down, all the while looking at Sophia with his penetrating pale green eyes.

"What are you doing?" Sophia said nervously as she glanced at the knife, and took another small step toward the door.

Huxley smiled. "I'm going to show you, Sophia, how this rubbery piece of protection works." With that, Archie stood up, completely removed his trousers and underpants, and then slid the condom over his excited member.

Sophia was mortified. "Oh, my God! That's sick!"

"No, no, that's protection," Huxley said, "it is how I'll protect *you* from becoming pregnant, and *my family* from scandal."

Sophia made a dash toward the knife, but Huxley ran up behind her and firmly grabbed both her arms. Once again, he held her tight and rubbed up against her. "I really did not want it to go down this way, Sophia, but now you put me in a very awkward position. You see, you must learn that you and your family are totally powerless. You *will* do what I want! Is that understood?"

A tear welled in Sophia's eye as she squiggled bravely to break free, yet Huxley's boa-like biceps kept her constricted. He leaned over and began nibbling on her ear, gaining pleasure from her whimpers. In a low gravelly voice, riddled with lust, he uttered, "Women need to be put in their place, Sophia, especially a woman like you!" His voice rose with venom as he hissed, "And *how dare you* think that you could ever *tell me* what to do! You and your pathetic little family are nothing. Do you hear me? *Nothing!*"

Sophia closed her tear-filled eyes. The next 15 minutes were the darkest, most heinous moments in her life.

Shortly after 1:00 a.m. Sophia quietly entered her apartment, trembling, as she closed the door. Her eyes were bloodshot from crying the entire ride home, and as she leaned back against the front door she slid down to the floor, weeping. She was defiled, humiliated and utterly broken.

Sitting in total darkness, with her elbows on her raised knees and her hands covering her face, Sophia sobbed uncontrollably. Her mind was torn with disbelief and disgust, when suddenly she heard the floorboards begin to creak. Looking up, she saw the dark silhouette of a figure rolling toward her. As Stan's face became somewhat decipherable, she re-covered her face and buried her head into her knees.

"Momma, what's wrong!" Stan inquired worriedly.

Sophia shook her head. "Nothing. Just go to bed, and do *not* wake up Marc."

"I can't do that," Stan uttered, "I have never seen you cry like this. Obviously, something is *very* wrong. What is it?"

Sophia kept her hands tightly over her disgraced face, never wishing to see, or be seen by, the world again. "Please, go away. This is something that I will have to deal with, and doesn't concern you."

"Momma," Stan said defiantly, "I will *not* go away. And anything that grieves you this much *does* concern me!"

Sophia uncovered her face, which was clearly wracked with pain and saturated with tears. "You are such a good son, Stan. You have endured much pain, and now I join you in being crippled."

Stan's eyes widened as he rolled closer, concerned. "What do you mean? What happened to your legs?"

Sophia actually managed to chuckle. "No, no," she whimpered as her face resorted back to utter grief. "I can walk fine. I mean mentally and emotionally crippled."

"What in God's name could possibly do that to someone as strong as you!?"

"Oh, Stan. I, too, have always believed myself to be a strong woman. But tonight I learned differently and in the most horrendous and humiliating fashion possible." Again, she covered her face and began to cry.

Stan pivoted his chair sideways and reached down, caressing her arm gently. "Mom, what, or who, could possibly teach *you* a lesson?"

Sophia didn't wish to speak, but Huxley's vile name just had to be purged from her mouth, in someway hoping that would purge the vile deed from her mind and from existence. "Huxley. Archibald Huxley," she spat.

"I knew it!" Stan growled. "What did that animal do, Momma? Please, you must tell me!"

Sophia looked up at Stan, whose face now became clearer—her eyes having adjusted to the darkness. "I can't, Stan. It is far too personal, embarrassing and…oh, I just cannot." Again, her head sank into her hands as her fingers rubbed her watery eyes.

Stan gazed down at her bent knees and legs, which were now revealed; the material of her dress had fallen downward. He couldn't help but notice the black and blue marks on her thighs in the shape of fingers, strong fingers that had evidently grabbed his mother most forcefully. Stan's heart dropped; mortified, petrified. He was old enough to know what wicked deed had befallen his mother, and as he looked back up at her face, her injured expression revealed the carnal crime. She had been barbarically defiled, and spiritually decimated.

Stan began to weep as he snarled viciously, "Momma, what can we do to convict and imprison that deviant bastard?"

Sophia just then realized Stan's observant glance, and now knew her astute son made the connection. Quickly, she pulled up her dress, covering her legs. She grabbed her hair, completely mortified. "Oh, my God! This is a nightmare!"

Sophia crunched over, burdened by yet another layer of pain, knowing that her son now knew of her ghastly ordeal. Wallowing in misery, Sophia screamed internally: *how much more pain can my already tortured heart and soul take, Lord?…if you even exist!*

Stan wiped the tears from his eyes. "I don't understand why God is testing our family so much, Momma. But, it must be for a reason. Every hardship, from my losing a leg, to pa's passing, and now to your ra—" Stan caught himself, not wishing to upset his mother further by voicing that vile word, *"run in* with Huxley, clearly indicates that the Wozniak family has been chosen."

Sophia looked up, shocked and infuriated. *"Chosen!?* How can you say such a thing? Chosen for what? To be punished? If that is the case, after we have been such good, caring people, then all the more I say, this Jesus myth is the most ugly and wicked creation that man ever invented!"

Stan was taken aback, and he shook his head doggedly. "I cannot believe that, Momma. And you're speaking blasphemy!" Stan rubbed his forehead, pained that his mother's words also made sense. However, although he had always focused on the peaceful words of Jesus, Stan now saw no other meaning behind God's actions than that which now filled his mind from the Old Testament. He gazed down at his mother, and said, "I believe we were chosen, Momma, not to be victims, but to eliminate that devil! And, with God's grace, we *will* smite him and triumph over evil!"

Sophia painfully shook her head. "Stan, my dear. You don't seem to grasp what I said earlier. I am beaten. *We* are beaten. Marc is in bed now with a stitched lip after Huxley sent a thug to beat him up and, well, he demonstrated his power again to me tonight. He made it painfully clear that if I, or any of you, attempt to reveal what happened, he would have us all killed. And, believe me, he does have the power to do so."

Stan squinted, he was pained to hear about his brother's misfortune, but his mother's rape and shattered submission was all consuming. "So, you're saying you quit; that we all should just give up? I can't believe I'm hearing this, especially from you, of all people. You have always preached to us that nothing was impossible if we put our minds to it. I detest what he had done to Marc, but I cannot live knowing what he did to you, Momma. Huxley *will* pay for this! And by the will of God, he *must* pay for this!"

As Stan attempted to spin his chair around, Sophia grabbed the wheel, stopping him. "Where are you going?"

"I'm waking up Marc. This will not stand!"

"Stanislaw!" Sophia bellowed. "Please! You cannot do this. You have no idea what we're up against. I have seen Huxley's arsenal and his wicked core. And I know from the look in that man's eyes that he would indeed kill us as easily as he would the dead trophies on his walls. Don't fight me on this. I have personally suffered this evil firsthand, so believe me, this *I* know. You do not!"

Stan's enraged face began to wither into one of utter confusion and severe disappointment. "But, Momma, can't we—"

"*Please!*" Sophia demanded. "End it! For our very survival, we must drop this. Bury it. Like Job, you must maintain that beautiful heart and soul you have, Stan. The Good Book has always offered you solace through all these traumatic events in our lives, so, please, do not abandon it now."

Stan's racing heart simmered to a fairly steady beat; as he gazed wearily down and then back up. "But you no longer believe, Momma."

Sophia rubbed his arm. "That doesn't matter. That you do, does. And my main concern is for my family. Huxley has promised that as long as we remain quiet, he will continue to cultivate Marc's career. He said he sees great things in his future and has already given him a marvelous promotion, so we cannot jeopardize our only hope for survival."

Stan rolled his eyes as he huffed, "But, Momma, how can you trust a satanic snake like Huxley? Especially after what he did to...all of us?"

Sophia took a deep breath and spoke calmly, "Because, I know what Huxley craves—*money*. And Marc *is* a very bright boy and will benefit Huxley Coal, somehow. That is why Huxley had to find out if Marc knew about his crooked past. He needed to know if he was blind to the truth and loyal. Now that he believes so, he will welcome Marc into his inner circle. So, my dear, Marc is our only hope."

Stan listened carefully, trying to make sense of his mother's new mindset and passive strategy. "Yes, I can somewhat understand that, Momma. But Huxley will attempt to mold and own him, just like he does everything else. And although I know Marc is very strong willed, I fear that being under Huxley's constant and corrupt influence might be too much for even him to resist."

Sophia shook her head. "No. I have complete faith in Marc. When I earlier instructed him to destroy Huxley's empire, he, true to his buoyant spirit, had a different plan. Namely, to transform Huxley Coal into a respectable operation that would hire more workers, raise wages, and implement safer working conditions. And after realizing that this dirty coal business is a necessity to our nation, I have come to believe that I was wrong. Marc was right. It isn't the coal business that is ugly; it is Archibald Huxley. And perhaps Marc can succeed where I have failed."

Stan looked down at his mother, quasi disappointed. "In one way, it makes sense, but I still a have problem with letting Huxley off the hook. It doesn't seem right, and it doesn't seem like something my old mom would have condoned. Pa and I always said *love thy enemy*, while you always said *vendetta!* So, I just don't understand this sudden change."

Sophia looked deep into her crippled son's eyes. "Because, you, my dear, and your brothers *are* my life. And before being—" Sophia paused and then choked on the next word, "abused, Huxley told me that if I—" she struggled to find the right word, "complied, he would not kill my family. And the thought now of going against my dark pledge and possibly witnessing you boys being killed off, one by one, would be too much for me to bear. He knew that I would sooner die than witness such a horrible fate. So, I have resigned myself to carrying this cross, which I, and now you, too, must unfortunately bear. So, you cannot mention this to Marc. EVER! Is that clear?"

With a painful nod, Stan now understood his mother's dilemma and vexing curse, which likewise branded Stan's heart and soul, being agonizingly painful and damningly eternal. But he would accept his mother's wishes and somehow try to attain the solace and salvation that Job eventual was granted after so much misery and torment.

Sophia stood up, and caressed her dear son for a long somber moment. She looked into his eyes and assured him— in words that he was most familiar with—that *this, too, shall pass.* She kissed him gently on the forehead and told him to say his prayers and go to bed. As Stan wheeled himself down the hall and turned into his room, Sophia gazed down at her disheveled dress. The ugly memory of what transpired sent a wave of revulsion over her defiled body. Impulsively, she ran to her room, gathered clean clothing, and then ran into the backyard.

Dark, gray clouds loomed in the partially moonlit sky as a dreary, purplish-gray tint bathed the exceedingly small yard, surrounded by a dilapidated wooden fence. Sophia grabbed a bar of soap and began pumping the well, filling a large tin bucket with water. She hauled it into the outhouse and lit the small candle mounted to the wall. With a shiver, she pulled off her clothes and stuffed them into a basket. She would destroy them later.

Curiosity and trepidation filled her tortured soul; she wanted to view the external damage done, yet knew it would be painful. Slowly, her eyes gazed downward, over her manhandled breasts and landing on her violated sanctum. Tears streamed down her face as her blurry eyes struggled to focus. Yet, as they did, her heart stuttered as she saw a nauseating sight—Huxley's dried semen was all over her pubic hairs. Her body shuddered as she wept and feverishly began scrubbing the repulsive fluid off her body. While lathering and rinsing herself, she suddenly stopped. Disturbing thoughts of Huxley's new rubberized protection device entered her mind. Sophia squinted. She had hoped the bizarre new contraceptive would have spared her from the vexing prospect of becoming pregnant, but now, as if being struck by lightning, Sophia fell to the floor—overcome by a hellish torrent of horrific thoughts.

Pulling her hair and gazing upward, she cried, "Please, God, NO!"

9

The Very Dark Next Day

July 2, 1881

At 8:00 a.m. the sun was still unsuccessfully trying to break through the thick clouds, while Sophia pumped the outside well, filling the teakettle with water. Entering the kitchen, she placed it on the cast iron stove and flipped the eggs simmering in the skillet. She had avoided making eye contact with her two sons as much as possible, since the dark, indelible stain on her soul was overbearing. She had hoped that a new day would somehow erase much of the hell she endured—since she had resigned herself to her fate last night—but it had not. She still felt dirty and abused, as well as humiliated and embarrassed.

Twenty minutes later, Marc and Stan finished eating breakfast, and Sophia grabbed their dishes and placed them in the washbasin.

Without looking at Marc, she inquired, "How does your lip feel?"

"A little odd and numb," he said as he patted his swollen lip with his finger, "but I guess okay."

"So, when did Doctor Galton say you could remove the stitches?"

"He said five days should do it."

Sophia continued scrubbing the dishes and cups. "And where is Rusty? He should have been here by now."

Marc's swollen lips twisted. "Well, after last night, perhaps it's best he doesn't stop by."

Sophia turned her head, only slightly. "What do you mean? What else happened last night?"

"Well, Momma, my beating wasn't the only brutal thing that happened last night, but since we got so caught up in that whole mess, I never got around to telling you."

Marc didn't wish to reveal the good news about the carriage his father had built (opting, like his father, to keep it a surprise until it was sold), however, as he explained the ugly lynching of Ying and Rusty's shocking execution of the two perpetrators, Sophia and Stan listened in awe. Just as Marc's long, dark tale was coming to an end, a knock rattled the door.

Stan turned. "I reckon that's Rusty now."

"I really don't know if I want to see him," Marc said dejectedly.

Sophia looked sideways and down at the floor. "Well, we all know that Rusty likes his spirits. Was he drinking last night?"

Marc nodded. "Yes, he and Jack O'Malley were guzzling down their kerosene-flavored moonshine."

Sophia shook her head and stopped scrubbing; knowing that she just had this conversation with Rusty about his drinking, which was one of many, and it sadly appeared to be a lost cause. She resumed scrubbing the dishes. "Listen, Marc, I'm sure the booze helped Rusty make that rash decision last night, but you said the votes were even. So, even though he broke the tie and carried out the sentence, that's not as bad as him doing this without a majority vote. Actually, I think I might have voted against those two murderers myself. After all, you all witnessed that horrible event."

Marc shook his head. "But that's just not how our government works, Momma. You know that."

Sophia stopped scrubbing, looking straight ahead into space. "Marc, there are may things that happen in this world where no rules or laws apply, so we can only make decisions the best we can. Either way, we are only human, and errors and injustices shall always prevail no matter how closely we follow the law. Furthermore, that you all witnessed Ying's lynching seems to be enough to condemn those two villains, despite not being the proper procedure."

Marc stood up to answer the door. "I reckon that's true, but if we break our laws, why even have them?"

Stan nodded. "Yes, Marc, without laws there would indeed be anarchy. But, I think I've come to the realization that some laws contradict others, making things very confusing. After all, our religion tells us to love our enemies, yet our republic tells us to prosecute them."

Sophia uncomfortably began washing the utensils as Marc pondered that paradox while walking over to open the door.

Stan looked up at his mother, who glanced over with a pained smile.

Marc greeted Rusty, and without much discussion, the two rode off to work.

Meanwhile, an hour later, at 9:20 a.m., President Garfield and Secretary of State James Blaine, pulled up in front of the Baltimore & Potomac train station in Washington D.C. As their small coupe rolled to a stop, they spotted Metropolitan police officer Patrick Kearney leaning against a lamppost.

Garfield called out, "Excuse me, Officer. How much time do we have before the train departs?"

Gazing at his watch, Kearney said with his Irish brogue, "Oh, I'd speculate ta say about 10 minutes, Mr. President."

Garfield was eager to escape the brutal summer heat, and looking forward to reuniting with his wife Lucretia for a well-deserved vacation. He had earlier awakened his two teenage sons, James Jr. and Harry, in his typical jovial fashion; a side of him that had been temporarily dormant the past few months due to Lucretia's illness and the strife within his party. But this morning Garfield had been bubbling with excitement as he sung a tune from Gilbert and Sullivan's new comic opera *H.M.S. Pinafore*, while he urged his sons to get dressed.

The boys now arrived at the station in Rutherford B. Hayes' borrowed presidential carriage, right behind Garfield's small coupe. Blaine was not going on vacation, but he didn't feel it was proper for a president to ride alone, so he joined him. Meanwhile, Secretary of War Robert Lincoln and three other cabinet members had arrived at the station several minutes earlier but were standing on another platform, some 100 yards away. Like the president, they, too, were eager to escape the heat and mosquitoes to take their vacations.

As Blaine grabbed Garfield's arm to escort him into the large Victorian station, young James and Harry Garfield followed. The president looked tall and dignified in his top hat and gray leisure suit as he turned toward Blaine. "It appears we need to get Kelley's tariff bill passed, Jim. As much as I loathe Archibald Huxley, this bill will help our coal and iron industries in Pittsburgh."

Blaine nodded. "Sure, but, please, forget about business; focus on Lucretia and enjoying your vacation," he replied as they turned and began to ascend the steps.

Meanwhile, inside, impatiently waiting was Huxley's old peculiar friend, Charles Guiteau. The odd, weaselly little man with big eyes, and appropriately wearing a black suit, had even caught the attention of one of the female attendants. For the past half hour, she had curiously watched the nervous man as he paced back and forth—periodically peering out the window.

Nevertheless, Guiteau had calmly laid out his plans much earlier by composing several letters, some describing how upon fulfilling his mission Vice President Chester A. Arthur would then become president and restore the Stalwarts to power, while other letters portrayed himself as the savior of the republic. However, one letter in particular was addressed to General William Tecumseh Sherman. In this chilling letter, Charles informed Sherman that he had already shot the president, claiming that it was a political necessity. He stated that he was a "Stalwart of the Stalwarts" and that he was going to jail. Therefore, he instructed Sherman to "rally your troops and take possession of the jail at once."

Guiteau had folded and tucked this special letter into his breast pocket, yet had wrapped up all the other letters, and his book, which he had hoped to publish. When he arrived at the train station earlier this morning, he had asked the man who operated the newsstand to hold onto it for a few minutes. The man agreed and had placed the package down, not realizing what it contained.

Content that his historic papers would eventually be discovered after his glorious Stalwart deed, Charles had then gone into the restroom. After making sure it was vacant, he had reached down into his pocket and pulled out his nasty little .44 caliber British Bulldog. After having checked that the trigger operated and having admired its fancy ivory handle, Charles had smiled—visualizing the day when it would be displayed in some museum along with a photo of the hero who saved the Republic.

But the delusional madman had emerged from the restroom minutes ago and was now pacing inside the main lobby, oddly hunched over and with a creepy tilt to his head. Then suddenly, Guiteau's frayed nerves simmered as he peered out the window of the door. He clenched his teeth— Charles' long wait was finally over. There, before his eyes, he saw President Garfield and Secretary Blaine walking up the steps right toward him and the entrance. His heart pumped a beat faster as he wiped his sweaty brow and then lurked into the shadows—waiting to make his strike. His large obsessed eyes barely blinked as they waited and waited, until the door finally began to open. The morning sunlight swept across the floor in an ever-expanding, pie-shaped wedge as the door fully opened. Cascading through the threshold were the president and secretary, who walked arm and arm onto the heavily worn sunlit carpet. No sooner did they walk several steps, did Guiteau emerge out of the shadows and skulk up behind them. Now standing a mere four feet away, Charles wielded his British Bulldog and fired a shot. The bullet tore through the right sleeve of Garfield's jacket, grazing his arm, and then went sailing across the semi-vacant lobby, where it struck the toolbox of a stunned worker, who nervously gazed down at the damaged box.

Garfield lifted his arm, startled, and cried, "My God! What is this?"

Instantly, the president turned his head toward the firecracker sound behind him, only to see Guiteau's calm, familiar face suddenly morph as his wild eyes widened with panic. Evidently, shooting a seemingly inert, clothed figure in the back was not the same as seeing his victim's shocked, and very much alive, eyes peering into his soul. Now racked with fear, Charles nervously squeezed off another shot. This one, however, tore right through Garfield's back. The forceful impact—and internal drag of the .44 caliber chunk of lead burrowing through his body—thrust Garfield forward; as his legs buckled and his body hit the dirty carpet, face down.

Chants of "Catch him!" instantaneously began to reverberate throughout the station, while Garfield's two teenaged sons stood momentarily in shock and then rushed to their fallen father. Garfield was semi-unconscious and began vomiting, while a small puddle of blood formed on the back of his gray suit. Underneath him, however, there was no exit wound. The bullet had fortunately missed his vital organs, but broke two ribs, thus stopping it from exiting his abdomen.

Immediately, Blaine pivoted around and recognized Guiteau; the irritating job seeker that a month earlier he had scolded never to return. Catching Blaine's deadly gaze, Guiteau became frantic as his eyes feverishly scanned the lobby. Yet what they found was not comforting—every shocked and enraged eye in the station was now focused on *him*. In fear, Charles shoved the gun into his pocket, foolishly attempting to conceal his guilt. He then darted toward the door, only to be blocked by a Venezuelan diplomat, named Simon Camacho—who now saw Guiteau's face blanch like that of a corpse. Charles pivoted quickly, and made a dash for the Sixth Street exit, as Blaine charged swiftly after him.

As Guiteau neared the exit, Blaine yelled out, "Bar the doors!"

Pivoting, once again, Charles attempted to flee, when Robert Parke, a ticket agent, grabbed him by the back of the neck and then clamped down hard on his left wrist. "I have him! This is the man!"

Police officer Kearney had already heard the commotion from outside, and now came running in. Spotting Parke holding the assassin, he ran over and forcefully grabbed Guiteau, and began to rattle the scrawny little man.

"You dirty rotten scoundrel!" Kearney snarled as he glanced at Garfield lying on the floor. "Did you do that?"

Guiteau bellowed proudly, "Yes, I did; I am a Stalwart, and Arthur is now president!"

Meanwhile, a group of Negroes had seen the entire tragedy unfold, and began chanting angrily, "Lynch him! Lynch him!..."

One of the porters rushed nervously over to officer Kearney, and advised, "You better get him out of here, quick! Or they *will* string him up; right here and now!"

Kearney looked at the enraged Negroes, and agreed. Pushing Guiteau outside, he began dragging him along the sidewalk, while a flock of enraged citizens followed.

Guiteau was now frantic as the irate crowd shouted threats. Pulling the letter out of his breast pocket, Charles waved it, pleading, "Officer, this letter *must* be delivered to General Sherman!"

Kearney had other things on his mind as the angry mob encircled them.

Charles was now panic-stricken as he yelled, "I want to go to jail! Take me to jail! Quickly!"

"Oh, that's where you'll be a goin', ya dirty little varmint!" Kearney barked, "have no fear of that, laddy!"

Kearney, along with other officers rushing to the scene, pushed Guiteau through the crowd toward a police wagon. Managing to get the assassin out of the deadly clutches of the enraged mob, Kearney set off for police headquarters.

Oddly enough, it was only upon searching Guiteau's pockets at headquarters that Kearney found the .44 caliber pistol in Guiteau's pocket; still loaded with three unused cartridges. With all the confusion, he and his fellow officers had totally forgotten protocol. However, word was spreading like wildfire, and the streets were filling with worried and enraged citizens. The police soon realized it would be safer to bring Guiteau to the District Jail, and immediately did so. Arriving at the jail, they shoved Guiteau into a small, whitewashed, brick cell as Charles sighed— relieved that he was not killed by the hostile mob. It was then that the terrified weasel miraculously morphed back into the calm, valiant hero. Moments later, Charles was gratified to hear that Sherman's troops were indeed arriving at the prison; however, they had come not to laud and rescue the Stalwart hero, but rather to protect the loathsome assassin from being strung up by a mounting lynch mob.

Meanwhile, back at the rail station, Secretary of War Robert Lincoln and the three other cabinet members on the far platform had heard the news, and now came rushing into the station.

Speaker Blaine greeted them, and then shook his head in disbelief. "I cannot believe it! I know the assassin. His name is Charles Guiteau."

Their eyebrows rose in shock, while Lincoln inquired, "Who might this Guiteau fellow be?"

Blaine's face twisted with disgust. "He's an irksome little lunatic who has been pestering me at the State Department, and the president at the White House, for the past few months. The damned maniac boasted of being a Stalwart and even sought a consulship!"

They all turned and gazed at the president; he was still lying on the dirty carpet, but was now being attended to by Dr. Townsend, the District of Columbia's health officer.

Lincoln shook his head. "My God, this is just too chilling. How many hours of sorrow have I endured in this town."

Having stood over his father's deathbed only 16 years ago, watching him also suffer from the bullet of an assassin, Robert was overcome with grief. As he rubbed his forehead, Lincoln now began to recall the odd occurrence that had also taken place at a rail station almost a year before his father was assassinated. He had been standing on the station platform in Jersey City when he lost his balance, just as a train was speeding by. As Robert began to fall into the moving clutches of death, Edwin Booth reached over, grabbed his arm, and saved his life. To Robert's utter shock and horror, a year later he would find out that Edwin's brother, John Wilkes Booth, would be the man that would take his father's life.

Robert shook his head, resolved not to see another president die. He excused himself, and ran outside to his personal carriage, where he instructed his driver to fetch the doctor who had been by his father's side, despite not being successful. Robert was aware that Garfield knew of him, being that he, too, came from Ohio, not far from the Garfield's home.

As the driver received the command, he squinted. "Excuse me, Mr. Lincoln. I reckon you must be frazzled by the commotion, but you said Doctor Doctor Bliss?"

Lincoln's left eyebrow rose. "Yes, that was not a stutter. The doctor has a most unusual name, but I assure you, it is

Dr. Doctor Willard Bliss. Now please go! And return here at once!"

As Robert ran back inside, the crowd was hysterical—some were crying uncontrollably, others looked on in horror, while others tried to push their way closer to gape at the historic nightmare.

Garfield's son Harry stood nervously fending off the crowd, yelling, "Keep back! That my father may have air."

Meanwhile, James Jr. was crouched down by his father, weeping, as Dr. Townsend endeavored to keep the president conscious.

Townsend and several others had rolled the president over, and he now lifted his head slightly. "Mr. President, do you think you can drink this?" he said as he held his concoction of brandy and aromatic spirits of ammonia.

Garfield nodded, and the doctor held the potion up to his lips, pouring, as the president slowly ingested the liquid.

Dr. Townsend wiped his lips and patted his wet beard. "Can you tell me where you feel the most pain?"

Garfield's eyes rolled as he uttered placidly, "Down my legs and feet."

Townsend placed the medical tonic down, and looked up at the train station attendants who were aiding him. "Can you help me roll him on his side?"

As they eagerly complied, with Garfield now lying on his left side, Townsend removed the president's overcoat and lifted his bloodstained shirt. The hole was slightly to the side of his spine, and Townsend decided it was imperative to locate and remove the bullet. Utilizing the standard practices of modern American medicine, he rolled up his sleeve and then stuck his unwashed finger deep into the wound. As Garfield grunted, Townsend continued to probe the wound, digging as deep as his dirty finger could possibly go. Unable to feel the small piece of lead, he removed his finger and stuffed the wound with a piece of cloth.

Townsend looked up around him at the now jam-packed lobby, which was filling up with more and more frantic and worried faces. He gazed back at the station crew. "We really must get the president out of here. It's becoming a madhouse."

A janitor nodded. "Yes, doctor. We have a mattress in the storage room that we can use to transport the president. I'll go get it!"

As he and two others took off, a second doctor arrived at the scene. Dr. Charles Purvis was one of only eight Negro doctors to have served during the Civil War, and he now became the first colored doctor to examine a president of the United States. He got down on his knees and inspected the wound, while discussing with Dr. Townsend what had transpired.

Dr. Purvis then turned and looked up. "I suggest we wrap the president in blankets and keep his legs and feet warm with hot water bottles."

As train attendants scurried around, and others helped to keep the crowd back, Garfield looked up at Purvis and asked, "What chance do I have, doctor?"

Purvis frowned. "I've seen many men fall to gunshot wounds during the war, Mr. President. So, I'm dismayed to say this, but...one chance in a hundred."

Garfield looked up into Purvis' eyes, and replied calmly, "We will take that chance, doctor, and make good use of it."

The room continued to fill with frantic citizens, all chattering nervously about their fallen president.

Robert Lincoln looked down at Garfield and then turned to Blaine. "Would you look at that; everyone in this room is rattled and shaken, yet he is the calmest man in the room!"

Just then the janitor returned with the mattress, stuffed with hay and horsehair, and they gingerly lifted the president and placed him on it. The conductor of the train that Garfield was supposed to be on had now come to assist, and he spread his arms out wide. "Clear a path! Let them through."

The crew lifted the mattress and began carrying Garfield up a winding staircase toward the second floor. As they bumped into walls—juggling the soft and cumbersome mattress, while the president's brawny body twisted—Garfield hardly grunted. His mind was now consumed with only one thing, that of his poor wife Lucretia, who was waiting for him in New Jersey to start their vacation. He gazed up at one of his aides and said, "Please send a telegram to my wife. Tell her that I am seriously hurt and wish for her to come here at once."

As the aide departed, the crew situated Garfield into the second story room. Meanwhile, Dr. Doctor Bliss arrived in Lincoln's carriage and stormed up the stairs.

Bursting into the room, he bellowed demandingly, "Clear the way! And do *not* touch him!"

Doctors Townsend and Purvis had already placed Garfield on his side, inspecting the wound, but now recoiled as Bliss brashly pushed his way forward and set his briefcase down. Peering at Garfield's back, Bliss leaned in for a closer look. His head moved to and fro, and then turned toward the two doctors. "So, have either of you found or retrieved the bullet?"

As both men replied, negative, Bliss haughtily raised his finger. "Ah, yes. Allow me."

He reached down and opened his large briefcase. After digging through his prized collection of bizarre instruments,

Bliss pulled out a long probe with a white porcelain tip. "Yes, let's try this."

Dr. Purvis looked at the long rod and squinted. "Just what exactly does that do?"

Bliss gazed at Purvis, and said condescendingly, "Well, doctor, pay heed! You see, when porcelain comes in contact with bone it leaves no mark whatsoever. However, once it brushes up against lead, the white porcelain will be marred, leaving a dark scratch. Hence, locating the bullet."

With that, Bliss leaned over the president's back and gazed into Garfield's glazed eyes. "Hopefully this won't be too uncomfortable, Mr. President, but it is imperative that I locate the bullet. So I must proceed immediately."

Garfield nodded mechanically. "Whatever you think best, doctor. I'm in your hands."

Bliss smiled. "And good hands they are, Mr. President. They are the best in the country, so you have nothing to fear."

As Doctors Townsend and Purvis rolled their eyes, Bliss leaned back into position. He placed his left hand on Garfield's back and spread the wound open with his unwashed fingers. Then wielding his long, unwashed probe, Bliss plunged it into Garfield's wound and began twisting and jabbing. As Garfield lay courageously still, suppressing his extreme discomfort, Bliss continued his thrusting prods, pushing it further in and moving it in erratic directions. After several agitated jabs, blood began oozing out of Garfield's back. Bliss snarled. He now realized that he had to end the examination. Yet as he began to extract the long probe it suddenly got snagged. Bliss huffed, and began tugging hard on the handle, while Garfield's body jerked with each pull.

Dr. Townsend stepped closer. "What seems to be the problem?"

Bliss glanced irritably at Townsend, and retorted, "It appears the tip has gotten caught between the fractured fragments and the end of the rib."

Refocusing his attention to Garfield's oozing back, Bliss said, "I will need to bear down on your fractured rib in order to remove the probe, Mr. President."

Garfield's eyes rolled sideways, catching Bliss out of the corner of his eye, as he uttered, "Do what you must, doctor. This is your show."

Bliss pressed down on Garfield's fractured rib with is left hand, and began yanking hard on the end of the probe. The gooey-coated rod slid out, dripping with blood and pus, as Garfield grit his teeth and murmured a grunt. Grabbing a cloth, Bliss eagerly wiped the porcelain tip. Yet to his utter disappointment, it was unblemished.

"It appears your probe has found *nothing!*" Dr. Purvis said, indignant.

Bliss glared at Purvis, his eyes radiating contempt. "Your opinion, dear sir, means *nothing!*"

Bliss had already felt secure in the fact that Secretary Lincoln had personally called him to duty, which he somehow believed was condoned by Garfield. As such, he had no intentions of losing this high profile case. Bliss was already having grand visions of the fame this would garner for him and his practice, but better yet, Bliss was already in a state of bliss realizing the bales of money he would soon begin to rake in.

"Step back!" Bliss snarled, "I will not tolerate interference when I'm engaging my patient.

Dr. Purvis gazed over at Dr. Townsend, who now looked at him, surprised. Humiliated, Townsend shrugged his shoulders.

Meanwhile, Bliss was not deterred. He decided to find out just what that obstruction was. Rolling up his sleeve,

Bliss inserted his unwashed pinkie into Garfield's wound and began digging around.

After his brief digital examination, he retracted his hand and wiped off the blood and pus. "Just as I suspected," he said, "I could feel the broken rib and what appeared to be lacerated tissue or comparatively firm coagula, probably the latter."

The two doctors glanced at each other discontentedly, while the small crowd of spectators twitched nervously.

Dr. Townsend then turned toward Bliss, infuriated. "I think that is quite enough, Dr. Bliss. Why don't you simply patch up the wound? I see no need to pester the president with all these probes."

Bliss remained undaunted and indignant. "I will not rest until that bullet is found!"

Dr. Purvis snorted, "Dr. Bliss, I have sewn up many men who had balls of lead lodged in their bodies. Even President Jackson lived to a ripe old age carrying a piece of lead right close to his heart!"

"Those are rare cases," Bliss retorted, "and I shall not place President Garfield's life in danger the way you so eagerly propose! I am an expert, sir. So, stand back!"

Bliss turned and reached into his black leather case once more. Extracting a long, flexible rod made of silver; he began bending the tip, forming an arc.

At this point, Dr. Purvis had seen more than enough, and he pushed his way out of the crowded room. Bliss hunched over and, once again, plunged the probe into Garfield's back, twisting and turning it as he inserted the bent rod ever deeper.

❦

Meanwhile, up in Elberon, New Jersey, Lucretia had received the disturbing telegram. Having collected her belongings, she was about to leave her hotel room when a knock rattled the door. As she opened it, her eyes widened. Standing before her was the former president and general, Ulysses S. Grant.

The First Lady was shocked. Grant had been extremely cold since her husband rose to prominence and took office. Her husband's nomination at the Republican convention and eventual win at the polls, which robbed Grant of a third term, had not sat well with Ulysses. More importantly, Grant had been experiencing financial difficulties and needed the helping hands of his fellow Stalwarts to grease his empty pockets. But despite that disappointment and Garfield's opposing Half-Breed stance, Grant had seen thousands of good men die on the battlefield, not to mention having endured the tumult of Lincoln's assassination, and with his fellow general and Republican now wounded, all past squabbles vaporized.

Grant looked at Lucretia for a long, odd moment, speechless and emotionally paralyzed, when finally he said, "I am most sorry, Mrs. Garfield, to hear of the General's plight."

As Lucretia humbly nodded, Grant continued, "May I assure you that from what I have heard from my sources in Washington, I believe your husband will survive this cowardly and brutal attempt to take his life. And as you well know, James *is* a strong man. He will endure this trial by fire. Mark my words."

Tears welled in Lucretia's eyes. "Thank you, president, or, um, General Grant."

Grant's own eyes were fighting to hold back the surge of tears that began to form in his ducts as he said, "Yes, even in that sense your great husband shares the same titles as I. He is one of our nation's best."

The stoic Lucretia actually managed to squeak out a small smile as Grant added, "The Lord works in mysterious ways, Mrs. Garfield. Where even our own party has been heatedly divided, not to mention our nation by civil discord, I have already come across a number of foes this morning that are mending burnt bridges. At this rate, I believe the nation may very well unite in a way that we have not seen since before the Civil War. So, take solace in the fact that the entire nation's prayers are with you and your family."

A tear streamed down the cheek of the frail and still recuperating First Lady as she thanked Grant, and he respectfully departed. Her aide then bent over and grabbed her luggage, and they headed toward the train station.

Much was on Lucretia's mind as she boarded the special locomotive placed in her service. It was an express train to Washington D.C that the operators made sure would have no delays. As its firebox roared with glowing bituminous coal, the boiler built up pressure and then blew the pistons into motion, thus turning its six large metal wheels. As Lucretia sped southward on the winding rails, she was concerned about her youngest two sons, Irvin and Abe, who were currently on a train heading home to Ohio. Yet, for the time being, at least, she didn't have to worry about them receiving the horrible news while being alone. Word had already been telegraphed to all the train operators and attendants along the line that everything was to remain hush until they arrived home. The heartfelt concern and sympathy of the divided nation was indeed proving to be galvanizing as thousands ran to the nearest rail stations or stretch of tracks to wave and offer their good wishes to the passing trains that carried members of the Garfield family.

❦

Meanwhile, arriving in Manhattan by steamer, Vice President Chester Arthur and his longtime mentor, or rather master, former senator Roscoe Conkling, were just returning from a routine lobbying session up in Albany. The two men were unmistakable—as the extremely vain and meticulously fit Conkling, with his full beard and mustache, strut down the ramp with his canary-yellow vest, while the little spit curl at the center of his large forehead bounced with each step. Meanwhile, Chester looks like a plump walrus with his fleshy face, mustache, and sideburns, which fan out as they extend down to the sides of his exposed cleft chin, looking like two hairy funnels. Chester is also an avid lover of fashion, and now sports a fancy Russet-colored suit with silk bowtie as his leather shoes with spats pound the ramp with each hefty step. Rushing feverishly up to meet him is a messenger, who hands the vice president a telegram.

As Chester's eyes began scanning the message he suddenly blanched. Anxiously, he looked at Conkling, and uttered, "President Garfield has been shot!"

Conkling's scheming eyes widened. "Th…that's astounding," he stammered as the wheels in his head outraced his tongue.

Roscoe quickly pulled out a fancy silk handkerchief from his tailored suit and waved down a taxi, while simultaneously grabbing Arthur by the arm. As the carriage came to a stop, he tactically shoved Chester into the cab— successfully beating the swarm of reporters that were converging on them to needle his protégé.

Chester looked at Roscoe, stunned. "What do I do now?"

"Don't worry," Conkling said firmly, "this is a stroke of fortune no one could have ever imagined. Not even I!"

Conkling's immense power and influence with his crony-based spoils system was only matched by his gargantuan ego. And having been humiliated by Garfield's unexpected win at the Republican convention, compounded by his having made appointments without asking his royal permission, King Conkling had been deeply insulted and politically wounded. Those events had led to his dramatic resignation—which he had expected would win him sympathy and support to get reinstated, while also weakening Garfield and the Half-Breeds—but Roscoe's theatrical power play had backfired miserably. And for the past several months, the self-exiled senator was miserable himself. But now the feisty peacock beamed with thoughts of retribution.

Conkling quickly realized that he had just been handed an unexpected gift, and he was determined to turn this stroke of luck into a major payoff. To do so, he would have to take complete control of the rapidly unfolding events, and such a tyrannical task is just what Roscoe thrived on.

He leaned out the carriage window and yelled up to the driver, "Head directly to the Fifth Avenue Hotel. And don't be shy with the whip!"

As the carriage bucked and thrust forward, Chester gazed at Conkling. "The Hotel? Why your suite? Should I not head to the train station and catch an express down to Washington, or even go home?"

"Shush!" Conkling snapped, "I'm thinking."

As the carriage hobbled over the crowded cobbled streets it finally reached its destination and came to a stop. The two eminent men exited the cab, walking into a wall of anxious and angered people. Updates on the assassination were feverishly being transmitted every few minutes, and the Stock Market was already showing signs of panic as the stocks of several large companies faltered. Amid the din of panic and rage, the two Stalwarts could hear people shouting: "We should lynch the filthy scoundrel!"

"The wretch ought to be hanged, insane or not!"

"If Garfield dies, there will be hell to pay!"

Conkling was flabbergasted. The New York crowd around his main headquarters was a Stalwart stronghold, and to see and hear the unified chants favoring the Half-Breed president and despising this seemingly fortuitous act was disconcerting. As they pushed their way through a throng of people and reporters standing in the hotel's opulent lobby, they finally reached the reception desk. Yet as Conkling signed the register, and Chester gazed anxiously at the rowdy crowd, new and far more devastating rumblings were beginning to reach the two Stalwarts' ears.

From the moment of his arrest, Charles Guiteau had been trumpeting his Stalwart affiliation, having yelled, "I am a Stalwart, and Arthur is now president!" Worse yet, a letter addressed to Chester Arthur had just been found in Guiteau's apartment, whereby Charles instructed Chester on what immediate actions he should take as president. As such, this connection was giving rise to rumors of a deadly political conspiracy, which no longer were confined to discreet whispers.

Nervously, Arthur looked and listened, while Conkling turned toward his minion, and barked, "Chester, follow me!"

As Conkling strode toward the staircase, with a flock of reporters on his heels, Chester remained fixed. Roscoe didn't realize that his pawn was not following him until he heard Arthur's voice some distance behind him. Conkling stopped and turned, shocked and clearly irritated by Chester's insolence. Now curious, Roscoe squinted and listened.

"Can someone please inform me of the latest bulletin regarding the president's health?" Chester bellowed, demonstrating for the second time in his long subservient career his own independence. The first time being when he accepted the position of vice president against Roscoe's wishes.

"As of now," a reporter responded, "we only know that he is being attended to by Doctor Bliss and several other doctors and that his condition is critical. His pulse is 112, and some nausea and vomiting has occurred, once again."

"Thank you," Arthur replied, looking at the reporter. Then gazing broadly over the crowd, he added, "It is with great grief and sympathy that I receive this devastating news. Please know that my most sincere wishes for President Garfield's speedy return to health and to the Executive Office come from the pit of my very soul. This is a time when party and prejudices reveal themselves for what they truly are—petty. I share, most regrettably, your concerns for the president's well being and your fury for this dastardly deed committed by a deranged madman."

Arthur was visibly shaken, and genuinely distraught, and all those present could easily recognize such. However, the rumors of a political coup still continued to reverberate throughout the hotel and, worse yet, all across the nation. One paper railed that it was not the hand of a miserable office-seeker that took a deadly blow at Garfield, but rather the spirit of selfishness and the love of rule as implied by "the machine" and its leader, namely Conkling and his teachings. Even those who did not fully believe that Conkling orchestrated the attempted assassination could not get out of their heads the dismal thought of what lie ahead. Chester Arthur was not presidential material. Even former President Rutherford B. Hayes had already scribbled in his diary his fear of Arthur becoming president, knowing very well "Conkling, the power behind the throne, superior to the throne" would be pulling the strings and exacting his Stalwart revenge. Many feared that the spoils system, which Hayes had at least tried to dismantle, would now be given free reign under a new Arthur Administration.

Voices across the country were largely unanimous in their low opinion of Chester, as one fellow Republican cried, "Chet Arthur? President of the United States? Good God!"

Adding to that, *The New York Times*, which had long been a supporter of Arthur, even during his battle against President Hayes who eventually had him fired on charges of corruption, now found the prospect of Arthur as president to be farcical as they declared, "Arthur is about the last man to be considered eligible to that position."

As Arthur now stood in the crowded lobby of the hotel—being stared down and scrutinized, while others sitting at the bar were already accusing Conkling & Co. of foul play—a wave of discomfort came over him. Nervously, Arthur wiped his sweaty brow, and then dutifully walked over to King Roscoe. Without delay, the two Stalwarts anxiously ascended the stairs to Conkling's Lair.

No sooner did they get settled in the room, did they crack open a bottle of sherry to calm their nerves. As the two sipped down the tonic, one of Conkling's young lackeys came bursting into the suite and handed his boss a telegram. Roscoe nervously unraveled the yellow piece of paper and quickly read the brief message. He looked over at Chester and smiled. "Well, it looks like you have at least one person on your side."

Chester quickly swallowed the sherry in his mouth and asked, "Who is it?"

Roscoe tossed the telegram on the table. "Archibald Huxley."

Chester shook his head. "Christ, that man is a scheming Benedict Arnold. Just recently he rushed to visit Garfield, looking for favors, yet, from what I hear, didn't quite get the reception he expected. Now here it is the president is not even dead yet, and he's already making overtures to me! I never did trust that devious devil, nor will I ever."

"For crying out loud. Stop and think!" Conkling snapped. "Didn't you hear the crowd down stairs? We are losing ground, fast. So, we cannot afford to lose any support, from any source. Huxley has financially supported my efforts in the past, so his money is just as good as a saint's in my book."

Chester chuckled. "The word saint should never be uttered in the same breath as Huxley. Beware, Roscoe! You may instantaneously burst into flames one day."

Roscoe irritably placed his glass down. "Very funny. And come to think of it, you *are* acting rather *funny* lately."

"Why?" Chester snapped, "because I'm starting to think for myself."

Roscoe cackled, "Don't kid yourself, Chet. You have no experience at it."

Chester rolled his eyes and walked irritably to the window. Anxiously, he gazed down at the news bulletin board across the street.

Meanwhile, Roscoe was getting a bit unnerved. With the hostile rumblings downstairs and outside only growing in magnitude, and hearing rumors about lynch mobs—not only for Guiteau, but for Conkling & Co. as well—Roscoe anxiously turned toward his young lackey, who had still been standing nearby awaiting orders. He instructed him to tell his fellow cronies down at police headquarters to have his hotel suite protected with guards. With a dutiful nod, the messenger quickly departed.

It was clear that the pulse of the nation was changing rapidly, and both men, now pensive, began to reevaluate the shifting world around them. Yet where Conkling was simply seeking new angles to obtain his selfish, ultimate goal, Arthur was searching his soul for answers.

10

A Time of Transition & Trauma

July 3, 1881 – March 26, 1882

Sitting in New York City with misty eyes, Chester Arthur was torn. He had accepted his appointment of vice president, as he had his previous position as customs collector in New York, for the simple reason that both positions required very little effort. Arthur had been well known for arriving at the Customs House in the afternoon and leaving early so he could hook up with his elite friends at their exclusive social clubs. Sitting in opulent rooms with rich, mahogany paneled walls, billiards tables, exquisite artifacts, and fine art, they would enjoy lavish cuisine, drinks and conversations amid a pungent fog of cigar smoke. Plainly put, Chester was no workhorse. As one person said, "Arthur never did today what he could put off until tomorrow!"

Arthur was also well accustomed to making a handsome salary. While most Americans struggled to earn

$500 a year Chester was raking in $10,000 plus kickbacks. However, after the Panic of 1873, which caused a long depression, people were beginning to question these overpaid positions and the spoils system that catered to cronyism rather than merit. With a crack down on corruption and the Boss Tweed ring, many of these plum jobs were being targeted, hence why President Hayes had ousted Arthur from his lucrative seat. Despite both men being Republicans, their Stalwart/Half-Breed division had become as fierce a conflict as that waged by their archenemy, the Democrats.

This transition of reform, which Garfield had pledged to continue upon taking office, clearly posed a threat to Conkling's fracturing empire. And now with the president lying on his deathbed, the public's outcry intensified, demanding an end to Conkling's crooked machine, and even suspecting it of having some degree of complicity in Garfield's assassination plot. This put Arthur in a most uncomfortable position. Chester never had any intentions of being president, but with the realization that, at any moment, Garfield could breathe his last breath, making him president, this shook the slothful *bon vivant* to the core. Arthur could clearly sense that the American people would expect him to continue the crusade of eliminating corruption, but that meant turning his back on his longtime friend and master. Fortunately, Roscoe's empire had already started to crumble, but he knew war with a man like Conkling would not be pretty. Therefore, Chester now prayed as much for Garfield's genuine recovery as for sparing him from being thrust into the unenviable position of becoming president, for that would force him to either support or combat his old boss. Either way, Arthur was going to stir up a hornet's nest and create enemies.

Having received a telegram from Secretary of State Blaine, stating that he should come down to Washington immediately to allay the public's fears of anarchy, Chester hopped on an express train and arrived in the Capital on the morning of July 4th. However, despite this being a day of national celebration, the mood was justifiably gloomy.

Arthur anxiously arrived at the White House only to walk into the brick wall of Dr. Bliss. Standing vigilantly on guard, Bliss sternly prohibited Chester from seeing the president. The arrogant and paranoid doctor had assumed complete control over all operations at the White House. Worse yet, he did so without the express approval of the president or the First Lady, who had experienced her own tale of woe on her journey home.

Lucretia's specially outfitted locomotive had blown a connecting rod, chewing up railroad ties and battering the sides of the train, whereby almost derailing the speeding locomotive. According to railroad personnel, it was a miracle the train stopped safely and avoided a disaster, one that would have surely killed the First Lady and all onboard. Nevertheless, Dr. Bliss, who had become Doctor Despot, rebuffed even Lucretia when she had suggested that her own physician, Dr. Susan Edson, be allowed to examine her husband and offer her own prognosis. Attempting to keep the pigmies pacified, Bliss did allow Edson and a small handful of doctors to act as his mere assistants.

Chester gloomily roamed the halls of the White House, being seen by several aides, who all noticed that the vice president was genuinely grief-stricken, particularly when he expressed his sympathies to the First Lady with tear-filled eyes. The exchange was brief, and Arthur promptly left the building, whereby taking up temporary residence at a friend's house on Capitol Hill. Once there, Chester severed himself from the public. He closed the drapes and sulked in solitude for days. Adding to his distress were the two additional telegrams from Huxley. Arthur gazed at the two folded pieces of paper and, with a grunt, tossed them in the trash without even reading them.

Meanwhile, President Garfield had entered what would only be the beginning of a long and horrifying nightmare—his body transitioning from a strong and healthy specimen into an emaciated and bacteria-infested cavity. But although the great man would be stripped of his weight and physical vitality, he would never lose his wit and disposition. For two-and-a-half long and grueling months, Garfield would suffer; yet never once lose his patience or jovial nature, while his body slowly deteriorated, succumbing to the ravages of infection.

Dr. Bliss had adamantly rejected the sage advice of Joseph Lister, the British surgeon who had tried many times to educate the American medical field about the importance of antisepsis. Unfortunately, Bliss, like many doctors his age, who were of the old school, all refused to believe Lister's nonsensical theory that small microorganisms exist and could cause fatal consequences. After all, they postulated, how can anyone take seriously that which cannot be seen? As far as Bliss and his fellow old crows were concerned, Lister was just a lame, limey lunatic. Meanwhile, many younger doctors in America had been open-minded enough to test Lister's procedure—whereby washing instruments and their hands with carbolic acid—but their pleas were likewise ignored. Bliss believed himself to be the best doctor in the nation, and no one was about to tell him how to treat his patient, who happened to be the most important man in the nation.

Americans from all walks of life had been deeply rattled by the president's condition, and thousands wrote heartfelt letters offering their good wishes or advice about any number of remedies for his vomiting and discomfort. Some even recommended ways to locate the bullet lodged in his body. While most were harebrained schemes, with one being more ludicrous than the next, one man did offer a lucid suggestion. He stated that his new Induction Balance device would make an electrical clicking sound once his instrument passed over the piece of lead. However, he requested that he should perform the examination on the president himself. The man's name was Alexander Graham Bell.

However, Dr. Bliss refused to allow the inventor to personally conduct the examination. Bliss, the omnipotent medical maven, would do so himself. This was for two reasons: First, Bliss had already made a public announcement that he, quite brilliantly, knew where the bullet was lodged, yet simply could not reach far enough in to extract it. Therefore, Bliss did not want Bell scanning Garfield's abdomen anywhere else, for if it was found elsewhere, it would indeed make the famous Dr. Bliss look like an incompetent sap. Second, if Bell's new metal-detection device proved to be successful, Bliss would want credit for finding the bullet.

However, to the dismay of all, the first test failed. As did the second test days later, which Bell was allowed to conduct himself, yet, again, only where Bliss instructed him to look. The failure was a disheartening blow, and Garfield's health continued to decline. With large lumps filled with infectious pus growing on the president's back and arms, not to mention the unseen mass of toxic germs that was consuming the inside of his body, Garfield was forced to endure weeks of agony. Yet, true to form, rarely did the president whine or complain.

Bliss continued his debauchery by probing the wound and lacerating all the contaminated blisters as they appeared. However, what was painfully evident to all was that

Garfield was losing weight rapidly. He had been eating less and was clearly dehydrating. As such, Bliss began a process of rectal feeding, inserting tubes up the president's rectum with a nutritious concoction of his own making. Bliss's daily routine was a ghastly shop of horrors not to be wished on a dog, yet Garfield somehow managed to endure the agonizing torture.

The other doctors who were present, all of whom had been humiliatingly reduced to nurses, said Garfield was a "wonderfully patient sufferer," while even the hapless Dr. Bliss was taken aback by the president's perpetual optimism and endurance for pain.

However, the unbearable summer heat in Washington had further tormented the ailing president. Despite inventive methods by the navy corps of engineers to create what amounted to be an air conditioner—by installing huge blocks of ice in a tin box in the next room filled with damp sheets and a fan that blew the cool air through metal ducts—Garfield insisted that he be moved to a cooler climate, near the sea. Apparently the president could sadly sense the end was approaching. His strapping 210-pound body had withered to a frail 120 pounds, and now Garfield wanted to at least be able to view the sea, which had always enamored him from his days as a canal boy.

Rich tycoons offered up their seaside homes to Garfield, as even Huxley offered his mansion on Long Island, slyly looking to hedge his bets on the still surviving president, but Garfield wisely opted for a wealthy New Yorker's summer home in Long Branch, New Jersey. It idyllically overlooked the Atlantic Ocean, and preparations were made. A special train was outfitted with thick carpeting to cushion the ride and baffle the sound as well as with heavy drapes and tightly sealed windows to keep out as much dust and soot as possible. The special locomotive, which used only clean-burning anthracite in lieu of dirty bituminous coal, was likewise placed in the service of the dying president, and Huxley made sure he at least supplied the anthracite.

On September 5, 1881, Garfield's weak and skeletal body was carried onboard the presidential train, and off it went, chugging along the tracks from the Baltimore & Ohio station in D.C. to the Elberon station in Long Branch. However, upon their arrival they faced a dilemma. More than a half-mile of tracks had been laid down by thousands of people the day before for the express purpose of channeling the president's train from the Elberon station up to the hill where the Franklyn Cottage sat. To the dismay of all, the locomotive was unable to climb the steep pitch of the hill. Undaunted, the welcoming party unlatched the president's passenger cars, and with miraculous will and spirit, thousands of hands gripped the sides of the wooden trains and pushed them up the hill.

The medical team setup shop and Garfield was situated near a window overlooking the ocean. However, Bliss refused to admit that the president was dying and fed reporters absurd bulletins that Garfield was showing signs of improvement, so much so, that Bliss felt that even the dismissal of the other doctors who had tagged along was now warranted.

Sadly, Garfield would enjoy the vista of the Atlantic Ocean for only two weeks. At one point, Garfield gazed up at Bliss with his lifeless eyes and gaunt face, and said, "Your anxious watching will soon be over."

On September 19th, the president's heart began to race. Writhing with pain, Garfield began to gasp uncontrollably.

Lucretia rushed to his side, then turned toward Dr. Bliss, trembling with fear. "Oh my God! What is the matter?"

For the first time, Bliss realized his efforts had all been in vain. "Mrs. Garfield, the president is dying. There is nothing more anyone on earth can do."

At 10:35 p.m. Garfield took his last breath, finally being released from the hellish torture that he was forced to endure at the hands of Dr. Bliss, hands that were both unwashed and inept—an appalling, germ-infested nightmare that persisted for over two and a half months.

❦

The news of Garfield's death struck Americans hard, being not only painful but disturbing. In their eyes, Garfield was a good man who, by an ugly twist of fate, became an innocent victim. His assassination was at the hands of a lunatic job seeker, hence, being utterly senseless. Meanwhile, Lincoln's assassination, although grieved much more profoundly, was at least easier to comprehend. The country had been divided by the Civil War, and Booth's bullet was at least for a larger cause. Guiteau's bullet simply made no sense. The mere thought of the brawny and brilliant Garfield being not only shot, but also forced to suffer for 79 grueling days, moved the country to tears.

However, three men had other things on their mind; namely, Dr. Doctor Bliss, Chester Arthur and Charles Guiteau.

As the president's body was prepped for an autopsy by a team of doctors, all eager to find out where the mysterious bullet lodged itself, Dr. Bliss looked on with trepidation. He already knew his failure to save the president would damage his reputation and practice—which had been completely neglected during this protracted affair—yet that he never located the bullet, even with the aid of Bell's new device, had disturbed him deeply. It had become public knowledge that Bliss only permitted the examination to be performed in the area he surmised; yet what the autopsy team was now poised to uncover would tell the world, once and for all, if Bliss's calculations were right or wrong.

The president's body laid cold and stiff on a makeshift table in the Franklyn Cottage. As the surgeon's scalpel sliced open Garfield's emaciated body, the team of medical spectators gasped and covered their noses. Garfield's abdomen was riddled with infection, and the putrid stench was nauseating. As the surgeon's hands dug through the septic soup, he eventually discovered two disturbing facts. First, the bullet was found not where Dr. Bliss said it should be, but on the exact opposite side, near Garfield's pancreas. Second, although not immediately deciphered, they would soon realize that the large glob of infectious pus—which had festered in a long, narrow canal—was not made by the bullet, but rather by Bliss and company's dirty fingers and unsterilized probes. Needless to say, Dr. Doctor Bliss was not at all blissful. It had become tragically apparent to all that Bliss was the kiss of death. In fact, one surgeon was so appalled at the quack doctor that he railed, "Ignorance is Bliss!"

While Bliss' career took a well-deserved nosedive, Chester Arthur was experiencing heart palpitations. The unthinkable had finally happened; he was now the 21st President of the United States. Despite being genuinely grief stricken for the dead president—and rattled over the past two and a half months by the prospect that this day was going to come—Chester had found some comfort in the unexpected voice of a complete stranger. Not long after Garfield's attack in the train station, Arthur had received a letter from a woman named Julia Sand, whom, unbeknownst to him, was an invalid. It would prove to be the first of many, for Chester's new pen pal had the mystical powers of a muse. Julia's words deeply resonated with the depressed vice president as she said, "Once in a while there comes a crisis which renders miracles feasible...Faith in your better nature forces me to write to you–but not to beg you to resign. Do what is more difficult & more brave. Reform!"

The miracle evidently came true, for Chester Arthur did reform. Right from the start of his administration, Chester expressed his intentions to honor and follow the dead president's noble agenda, and even asked that Garfield's Half-Breed cabinet remain intact.

Meanwhile, the third man most concerned about Garfield's passing was the assassin himself, Charles Guiteau. Having sat in Cell Two on the second floor of the District Jail—in what was termed Murderer's Row—Charles had experienced highs and lows. He was still very much pleased that he had shot Garfield, and didn't really mind that the Half-Breed finally died; yet he was terribly disturbed that General Sherman never rescued him, and that his well-planned coup never materialized. Worse yet, on November 14, 1881, Guiteau would begin what would be a long and frustrating trial. He was, however, fortunate that at least one attorney in the entire country stood up to defend him, namely his brother-in-law. This was not because he believed Charles was innocent, but rather he knew of his mental condition, and didn't wish to see an insane man hang. However, during the trial, Charles disrupted the proceedings numerous times, driving not only the judge and prosecuting attorney mad, but even his own relative.

One day Charles exploded in the courtroom, blasting his familial lawyer, "You are a jackass on the question of cross-examination! I must tell you that right in public, to your face!"

Added to Guiteau's displeasure about how his case was being handled was that two assassination attempts were made on his life. One by a prison guard, who wielded his musket and fired upon the assassin, yet missed. The second was by a farmer who rode up alongside Charles as he was being carted back to prison from the courtroom, and fired a shot. Yet, he, too, failed to kill Guiteau, only managing to graze his coat, leaving Charles rattled.

Huxley had heard about these attempts and decided to discreetly help out his peculiar old buddy—the man who had introduced him to the beautiful concept of free love. Shrewdly avoiding paper trails, Archie sent his thug Blaggo to anonymously deliver envelopes of cash to Charles' brother-in-law's house, marked simply: *For Charles' security and trial expenses*. However, Huxley had other reasons for getting involved. Being a covert part of Guiteau's historic assassination superbly stoked his sinister ego. Moreover, he hadn't forgotten how the know-it-all president belittled him with preachy lectures and reprimanded him in front of Mark Twain. So revenge was very sweet, indeed.

Nevertheless, Guiteau's bizarre trial continued, and he didn't mind too much that he was presented as being insane, for he realized that was his ticket to freedom. However, Charles became irritated with his brother-in-law and took matters into his own hands. He wanted to make it very clear that it had been only temporary insanity and that he was of sound mind beforehand and, most importantly, was so now. The latter being crucial, since Charles now defended himself with a very compelling argument; namely, he confessed to shooting Garfield, but as the papers were reporting, Garfield died by malpractice. Charles charged Dr. Bliss and others with mismanaging his care, since it was revealed that the bullet had not hit any vital organs and, most importantly, would not have been fatal. However, as lucid and factual as that was, the prosecution would not rest until a verdict of guilty was achieved, knowing that the American people would riot and cause national havoc if Guiteau won and evaded capital punishment. With two attempts to snuff out Guiteau already, it was clear they could not set him free, or cater to his plea of temporary insanity. As such, for every professional psychiatrist who claimed Guiteau was insane, the prosecution brought twice as many to say otherwise.

Dr. John Gray, from the New York State Lunatic Asylum, had this to say, "A man may become profoundly depraved and degraded by mental habits and yet not be insane." And in Guiteau's case, Dr. Gray concluded, "It is only depravity!"

Charles Guiteau was indeed a riddle, for he had shown himself to be very lucid at times, positing sound pleas in court with stunning clarity, yet at other times it was just as clear that the man was damaged merchandise.

One psychiatrist said aptly, "All the links in the chain are there, but they are not joined, but rather tossed about hither thither."

Nevertheless, on January 26, 1882, a verdict of guilty, with death by hanging, was firmly voiced in the courtroom to a booming round of cheers and applause.

At this Guiteau snarled, "God will avenge this outrage!"

But God did not.

Two months later, back in Pittsburgh, the news of Guiteau's death sentence, or the earlier death of President Garfield, didn't seem to be as devastating as what Sophia and Stan now faced. It was back in September, shortly after Garfield's death, when Sophia had finally decided to reveal that she was pregnant. Naturally, Marc was ecstatic, having been kept in the dark about his mother's rape, yet Sophia and Stan were about to face the terrifying realization that she might be carrying Huxley's child. Sophia had told Stan that their father could very well have impregnated her, so it had been a matter of waiting anxiously to see what actually brewed inside her once she delivers the baby. That is, of course, *if* the child shows any clear physical traits of either Jedrek or Archibald.

The past nine months had been a living hell for all of them, for besides Sophia and Stan's worries, Marc had been struggling to deal with Huxley at work every day, as having been beat-up by Archie's thug Blaggo had left a visible reminder on Marc's scarred lip of how Huxley operates. Nevertheless, Marc's cool, methodical determination coupled with the Lord's directive to *Love thy enemy* had managed to help him bury the abuses and hatred, and instead focus on the higher goal of making improvements at Huxley Coal that would benefit not just them, but everyone who worked in Huxley's dangerous labyrinth of mines. Only then would Marc turn his attention to Huxley, for, deep down, he knew he hadn't the Biblical strength to truly love his enemy.

However, now, on the morning of March 26, Sophia's water broke, and Marc ran to call Dr. Galton. Arriving with his black leather briefcase, Galton, along with a nurse, made all the necessary arrangements in Sophia's bedroom, while Stan and Marc waited anxiously in the kitchen.

Stan was trembling, trying his best to avoid eye contact with Marc. He had uncomfortably withheld their mother's dark secret for nine long months, but worse yet, any second now he knew their world could be shattered, for if the baby should look like Huxley, it would truly be like opening Pandora's box.

Marc gazed perceptively at his brother. It appeared that something more than just anticipation about the birth was on his mind. "Stan, what's the matter?"

Stan uneasily wiped his forehead as he looked up at his brother. "What do you mean?"

"You look as if you're about to see a ghost rather than our new baby brother." Marc paused as his eyes widened. "Or baby *sister*. Gosh, I keep forgetting. That might be nice for a change, don't you think so?"

Stan's jittery eyes didn't offer much of an answer, but a familiar voice from behind them did, "Yeah! A sister would be grand!" Ted said as he calmly strolled into the kitchen as if nothing ever happened.

Marc and Stan spun around with shocked faces as Marc exclaimed, "Oh, my God! Where have you been?"

Ted smiled as he embraced Marc and then reached out to shake Stan's hand.

Stan, however, remained fixed, glaring at his brother with razor-sharp eyes. "How dare you show up after being gone for nine months! And not a word did we hear from you in all that time!" Rolling his chair backwards, Stan was smoldering, while Ted looked back at Marc for support. "What's his problem? I mean, look, pa died and everyone was busting my balls. So why should I have stuck around to be further abused?"

"That's ridiculous!" Stan bellowed. "We're family, and family doesn't just run away without saying a word. Besides, you ran away with Huxley's horse, which Marc has been paying off! Did you think of that, you selfish bastard!?"

Marc was taken aback, never having heard Stan curse.

Meanwhile, Ted retorted, "I planned on giving you money to pay that rich son-of-a-bitch back. Besides, I'm sure Huxley didn't miss it, he has three stables full of horses."

Stan shook his head. "I see you haven't changed, Ted. You have a knack for deciding what other people should do, or what they must tolerate or endure, so long as you do whatever you darn well please."

Marc cut in, hoping to quell the argument, as he looked at Ted affectionately. "Well, you're home now, so I reckon Huxley will only charge you a fine, once you give his horse back." Marc curiously rubbed his chin. "So how much money did you save to pay him back?"

Ted gazed uncomfortably at the floor, then back up at Marc. "About two dollars. But I really did plan on paying him back. Besides, I'm home now anyhow. He'll get his stupid horse."

Stan laughed and then spat sarcastically, "Pa was right, you'll never change."

"Screw you!" Ted fired back. "Just because you're strapped in a chair doesn't mean you can say whatever you wish! You're not the only one with feelings, Stan. So, if you'd like a broken jaw along with that missing leg, keep it up!"

Stan rolled his chair, smashing into Ted's legs, as he grabbed Ted's arm and dragged his body into his lap. With his muscular arms, Stan pounded Ted with several shots to the ribs as Ted yelped and struggled to get free.

Marc rushed over, and pried Stan's muscular arms off, while Ted sprang up with fists drawn. "Come on, Stan," Ted growled, with saliva spraying from his mouth. "Let's go! I'm not afraid of you!"

"Enough!" Marc bellowed as Stan and Ted continued to glare at each other with fiery eyes. "We are brothers for crying out loud! And is this any way to greet the newest member of our family?"

Stan pivoted his chair, and rolled back to the table, while Ted lowered his fists, and said, "Yeah, so how *is* mom doing?"

Stan turned his head away in disgust as Marc answered, "She is fine, but—" he giggled, "you should see how fat she got!"

As Ted chuckled, Marc continued, "She's in her bedroom with Doctor Galton and a nurse. It should be any minute." Marc paused. It dawned upon him that Ted seemed to know their mother was pregnant when he had walked in the door. Marc squinted. "Wait a second. Did you know momma was going to have a baby?"

Ted smiled. "Yeah, I stopped by Aunt Filomena's vacation house while I was in Ohio. She happened to have a pack of her crazy, women-suffrage friends over." As Marc smiled, glad that his feisty aunt hadn't changed, Ted continued, "They were planning another rally, as usual, but anyhow, she told me mom had written her a letter about the pregnancy." Ted's head and voice lowered, "So, I guess this is gonna be our last gift from pa, huh?"

Stan's eyes began to water as Marc promptly changed the topic. "Yes, it appears so. But, what have you been doing all these months?"

Ted smiled. "I had joined the circus."

"No! You're jesting," Marc replied excitedly. "Are you serious?"

Ted's eyebrows rose. "Yep. I sure did."

"So, what act are you in?" Marc inquired eagerly.

Ted held out his chest, and said comically, "My act is even bigger than Jumbo the elephant's, it's called 'Bowel Movement.'" As his brothers both squinted, Ted added dejectedly, "I shovel shit."

Marc's face withered as Stan shook his head.

Marc looked at Ted sympathetically. "You *are* kidding, right?"

Ted shook his head as he pulled out a chair and sat down. "No. I wish I was. I had hoped to get me a job riding in the horse shows, but Barnum stuck me on crap detail. So, quite plainly, I had enough of his shit! I quit."

"Typical!" Stan snapped, perturbed.

As Ted rolled his heated eyes toward Stan, Marc immediately interjected, "So, what do you plan on doing now? I mean, Huxley would still love to tan your hide. So, I reckon you'll have to find another job."

"Well, Aunt Filomena said you got yourself a big promotion. Aren't you a big banana now? Surely you can get me a desk job, right?"

Stan huffed, "Sure, first you abandon us, then fall on your face, as usual, then you hear Marc has a good job, and now you come running back home to leech off his hard work. Like I said, *typical!*"

Ted glared at Stan with dagger eyes, and spat, "I also came home because mom is having a baby!"

Marc shook his head. "Listen, Ted. I doubt I can get you a job at Huxley Coal. Archie is not the type of fellow to get screwed and then forgive and forget."

Ted's head dropped. "So, you're saying I shouldn't have come home?"

Unexpectedly, Marc smiled. "Not exactly. In fact, I have very good news for all of us."

As Stan and Ted looked up at Marc, he continued, "Actually, I was waiting for momma to give birth to our new brother or sister, so we all could celebrate, but I reckon I might as well tell you now."

"Tell us what?" Stan inquired, curious, as Ted prodded with anticipation, "Come on, buddy boy, let's hear it. What's the big surprise?"

"Hold on one second!" Marc said as he ran into his bedroom. A moment later he returned, proudly holding a bank check in his hand for his brothers to see.

Ted looked at the paper stub and back up at Marc. "What in tarnation is that?"

Marc looked down at the decorative piece of printed-paper and smiled. "You see that number there?"

Ted looked again, and said, "Yes, it says $1,000. But I know what money looks like, Marc. I'm not stupid! That ain't money, it's just a silly piece of fancy paper."

Stan was transfixed, knowing very well what it was, while Marc replied, "Well, this fancy piece of paper happens to be a check, Ted. And the bank is holding those crisp one thousand dollars for me, or rather, us!"

Stan sat upright as his mind reeled and his tongue tried to keep up, "Just what are you saying? How in the world did you get that? From whom? For what? How is it possible?"

Marc laughed as he raised his other hand and patted the air gently. "Hold on! Let me tell you." Pulling out a chair, he sat at the table facing his two brothers. "Now, hold onto your seats, fellows, because this, too, is a gift from the grave from our dear old pa."

As his brothers sat savoring his every word, Marc told them about the exotic carriage their father had built at Pendleton's Iron Works. He explained how he needed to design and build the trunk compartment in order to sell it, yet with work at the mine consuming so much of his time, he only completed the job two months ago. At that time, Pendleton had shown the vehicle to both Andrew Carnegie and Henry Clay Frick, the latter just recently purchasing the deluxe carriage; hence, the check.

"That's fantastic!" Ted bellowed, "we're rich!"

Stan gazed at Ted. "Hold on, circus clown! We're not about to shovel hard-earned cash into the stinky hands of a manure shoveler!"

"Jesus Christ!" Ted blasted. "Don't you ever quit? My whole life you've jumped on my back, riding me!"

"Yes, just like a horse, because you're a horse's ass!" Stan bellowed.

"Very funny, Bible Boy!" Ted carped, "I see how much that stupid book really helped. You haven't changed a damn bit, you mean old monk!"

Stan reached over the table and grabbed Ted's arm.

Marc yelled, "Enough!" as he picked up a spoon and whacked Stan's knuckles. Stan flinched and let go, as Marc stood up, infuriated. "This was supposed to be a wonderful surprise for the entire family! Now you're ruining everything. Why don't you both think about mom in that room, and how we can help *her*, and honor her by acting as loving brothers, rather than a bunch of bickering baboons!"

With that, Marc stuffed the check into his pocket, and stormed out the back door, marching toward the well.

Stan and Ted gazed at each other, their hearts filled with shame and remorse.

"It's ridiculous," Stan said, "that our youngest brother should be the one to guide us like this. But Marc is absolutely right. We're fools. I'm sorry, Ted."

Ted put his hand on Stan's shoulder. "So am I, Stan." He gazed into his older brother's eyes, deeply, seriously. "I might not have ever told you this before, but I always looked up to you, Stan, like a—" Ted's mind searched for an appropriate analogy, while Stan became curious, and prodded, "Well, like a what?"

"Like a baby foal that looks up to his big, donkey brother, and says 'What an Ass!'"

As Ted laughed, Stan chuckled and playfully punched him in the arm. "You really are an imbecile, Ted"

"Maybe so," Ted replied, "but at least I'm a funny and adventurous imbecile!"

Stan giggled. "Yes, and that's why you should definitely head back to the circus!"

As the two hugged and giggled, Marc stepped back into the kitchen, drinking a cup of water. His eyebrows lifted. "So to what miracle do I owe this spectacular sight?"

As his two brothers looked up at him, Stan said, "I reckon *you!* Not only were you right to ball us out, but you're the one who turned pa's dream into a salable piece of merchandise. Thank you."

Ted nodded. "Yeah, we all owe you, Marc."

Stan covered Ted's mouth. "Don't ruin it with a corny joke!"

Marc laughed. "That's okay, we here all know that Ted is a silly knucklehead! But we love him."

Ted rolled his eyes as the three brothers joined together, finally rekindling that bond that had eluded them for many months. As they did, a baby cried, startling them all.

Elated, they each looked at one another, while Marc turned and ran down the hall, his brothers close behind. As they stopped in front of their mother's bedroom door, Marc stood anxiously, shifting his weight from one foot to the other, when suddenly the door opened, but just a crack.

The nurse's head popped out. "Now, you boys must be very careful," she said as she slowly exited the room with the baby tightly wrapped in a blanket. The only thing visible was the baby's little reddish-skinned head with sparse, blondish strands of very fine hair.

As Ted and Stan came up alongside Marc, the three gazed at the tiny bundle in amazement.

Marc looked up at the nurse. "Can I hold him…I mean, what is it?"

The nurse laughed. "Yes, you have another brother."

As the three brothers smiled, looking at their fourth, the nurse gently bent forward and slipped the baby into Marc's arms. "Now, make sure you support his little head, and do *not* make quick, sudden turns."

Marc didn't even look at the nurse as he nodded and kept looking at his little brother with wonder. "My God, he's so small."

In his haste, Stan accidently rolled his chair over Ted's toes. "Let me see!" he said as Ted yelped and tried to squeeze in for a closer look.

Stan's eyes scrutinized the little gnome, trying to discern whose features it had. Nervously he looked at the grayish blue eyes, the little nose and thin lips, yet nothing seemed to jump out at him to say "Huxley" or "Jedrek". However, seeing that his little brother had blondish colored hair, a shiver rattled Stan's crippled back. He turned and tried to look into the bedroom, but the nurse stepped quickly back into the doorway, blocking his vision. "Your mother is," she stammered, "w-well s-she—"

"You can see her in just a moment," Doctor Galton's voice anxiously rang out; followed by a stern command, "Close the door!"

The nurse stepped back into the room and shut the door.

As Marc looked at his new little brother, lost in thought and semi-oblivious to what just transpired, Stan rolled closer, and queried, "Marc, did you hear that?"

Marc looked down at Stan. "Hear what?"

"S-something is *not* right," Stan said, his voice cracking with concern.

As Ted leaned in for a closer look at his new baby brother, not sensing the gravity of Stan's trepidation, Marc inquired, "What's not right? Didn't Dr. Galton just say we could see her in just a moment?"

"Yes, but did you hear the way he said *close the door*? It sounds like something is wrong."

Marc shook his head as he handed Ted the baby. "What could possibly go wrong? Babies are born every day."

Stan grabbed Marc's hand. "Listen, do you know how many women die in childbirth?"

As Marc and Ted squinted, Stan added, "I hear three out of every ten, and it may be higher than that!"

"I thought only babies could die, like our two younger brothers," Marc said, his face now marred with concern. He turned and pounded on the door. "Momma! Are you alright?"

Dr. Galton's voice rang through the door. "Marc, *please*, you boys must be patient. Your mother is having a little difficulty, and—"

Marc burst through the door as the doctor looked up, shocked—his jaw still opened from the unfinished sentence.

The nurse ran to block Marc's view, but he pushed her arm away and stepped closer to his mother. The sight was shocking! Sophia was lying on the bed only partially wrapped in bloodstained sheets.

The doctor quickly threw the blanket over her legs. "Marc, young man, you should be ashamed of yourself. You should *not* be seeing you mother like this. Now, please. *Get out!*"

Sophia's bloodshot eyes rolled lazily down toward Marc, and she feebly raised her hand. "No, no, he can stay," she murmured, exhausted and pale. "Let me see my boys, Doctor, before I—" she stopped. "Send them in," she added, looking at the nurse.

Dr. Galton shook his head. "Sophia, I wanted to at least clean you up."

"Never mind that," she said, her voice weak. "Please, leave us. You did all you possibly could."

The doctor lowered his head and solemnly began collecting his things, while the nurse assisted him. Stan and Ted entered the room just as the nurse and Dr. Galton finished up and exited the room, closing the door behind them.

Marc fell to his knees by his mother's side, grabbing her arm. "What's going on? What's wrong, Momma?"

Tears streamed down Stan's face as Ted just realized the gravity of the situation. Taking a seat on a nearby chair, Ted nervously began cradling his new, little brother.

Sophia gazed at her sons through misty eyes. "It appears I had some complications. Dr. Galton tried to stop the bleeding, but it's internal, and, well, there is simply nothing more he can do."

As the three gazed at the discarded placenta in a nearby bucket, with its foul odor, and then at the stained sheets, saturated with their dying mother's blood, Stan almost collapsed. As Marc leaned over to support him, Ted continued to rock the baby, yet with his eyes pinched closed.

Marc leaned back toward his mother. "Momma, are you sure there isn't something that another doctor could do?"

Sophia shook her head. "No, Marc. I'm afraid not."

"But I can now afford the best doctor in the state," Marc said.

Sophia smiled. "Oh, Marc, my dear. Even a highfalutin doctor like Dr. Bliss failed to keep President Garfield alive, so how could you—"

"Dr. Bliss was a fool!" Marc interjected, "and I can pay for any doctor you need, Momma."

Marc told his mother about the surprise he intended to reveal on this joyous day, yet everything now seemed doomed. Despite his mother's joy at the good news, it pained him that not only did his father get cheated out this gift, but so, too, would his mother. Marc swallowed hard—it was horribly cruel and unfair.

Sophia waved her hand, signaling for them to come together for a last embrace. As they all wrapped their arms around their mother, with tears falling on her still warm skin, she said, "You boys use that money wisely. And do not fight with each other. Do you hear me?"

As they nodded, she gazed at Stan. "You, my first born, you have been a part of my life longer than the rest. I beg you, continue to follow the guided course God has set out for you, and never forget to be a man of your word." As Stan swallowed hard, knowing very well that meant never to tell his brothers about her rape, he lowered his head and began to weep, while his mother patted his head and then looked at Ted. "And you, my middle mystery and wild stallion. I am so pleased that you have returned home and that I am able to see you again." As Ted's eyes welled, she continued, "And, please, *never* give up, and *never* get discouraged. You have talents, Tasso, just like your namesake. You just need to focus on them and chase after your dream. Do you hear me?" Ted nodded as she then turned toward Marc. "And you, my brave and bright little darling. You have already shown signs of great achievements, especially for a bo...man your age, and greater achievements await you. Always keep an eye on our family and never let your father or I down."

Marc leaned in and kissed his mother. "Have no worries, we will all be fine."

As he tightly embraced his mother, he felt her chest deflate. Marc choked as tears streamed down his face. He could feel the warmth in his beloved mother's body turn off, just like a snuffed out Davy lamp, as he passionately hugged the now cold and soulless cadaver. Sophia, or whatever constituted Sophia, was gone.

11

A Turn of the Guard and of Fate

March 26, 1886

Four years had passed, and much had changed. Chester Arthur had taken hold of the Executive Office, and although he graciously assured Garfield's cabinet that he would not replace them, they had begun to resign, one by one, for various reasons. Secretary of State James Blaine had been too close a friend of Garfield and too staunch a Half-Breed to work for a Stalwart president, and duly resigned. Furthermore, Blaine always had his eye set on the presidency, a craving that even annoyed Garfield, and he figured he would have his bid four years later.

Meanwhile, at the start of Chester's term, Roscoe Conkling had eagerly met with his protégé in the White House seeking to be awarded his prize, namely yearning for the appointment of Treasurer. However, Chester had indeed experienced an epiphany, and from the minute he slipped into the role of president, he had shown himself to be a new and reformed man. Arthur was well aware that if he appointed the King of the Stalwarts to his cabinet, especially as Treasurer, that would sound the death knell for his administration, and so Conkling's pleas had been rebuffed. Conklin was humiliated that his malleable underling had become his own man, rising in stature far above himself, and it had become clear to Roscoe that his time in the political arena had soundly ended.

But by the fall of 1882, the Republicans had suffered a startling defeat, losing several seats in Congress as the people continued to clamor for an end to the spoils system. This had prompted Arthur to sign the Pendleton Civil Service Act, which oddly enough contained tougher measures than what even the Jay Commission used to prosecute him while customs collector, which had resulted in his dismissal by President Hayes. Nevertheless, this demanding piece of legislation had been a watershed moment in American politics, for it finally began the process of prohibiting many politicians from appointing cronies to high-paying positions, many requiring little work. Worse yet, those appointees had been required to pay into the Republican machine and vote accordingly, hence ensuring the Republican stronghold that the party enjoyed since the Lincoln administration. This legislation had an impact on the recent presidential election in 1884, when Blaine had finally won the Republican nomination, but lost to Grover Cleveland—handing the White House over to a Democrat for the first time since the end of the Civil War.

It was now March 26, 1886, a year after Grover had taken office, and Chester Arthur—along with his coterie of defeated Republicans and affluent friends—were seated around a long table at the posh Manhattan restaurant Delmonico's. The majestic building sits at the corner of 5th Avenue and 26th Street, and this new brand of dining is the pioneering brainchild of Giovanni and Pietro Del Monico. Their luxurious restaurant has taken dining to its gastronomic climax in a setting that is not only unrivaled, but simply never existed before. It instantly became world renowned not only for its exquisite menu, which premièred their famous Lobster à la Newberg, but it also is the gathering place for powerful politicians and imperialistic tycoons who often rent out entire rooms for their private parties or grand conventions.

Sitting in the back corner of the huge first-floor dining hall, with its tall fresco-decorated ceilings and silver chandeliers, Chester Arthur is decked out in his expensive English tweed suit with silk bow tie, eating the now famous Steak Delmonico with a side order of rosemary seasoned potatoes. Gathered around him at the table are J.P. Morgan, Cornelius Vanderbilt II, John Rockefeller, Andrew Carnegie, several minor politicians, an aspiring author, and the landscape artist Albert Bierstadt.

As they engaged in conversation, Huxley arrived with Marc at his side.

J.P. Morgan looked up. "Ah, Archie, good to see you," then gazing at Marc, he added, "and is this the teenage wonder you had mentioned?"

Archie turned and extended his hand toward Marc. "Yes, this fellow is my new right arm. Meet Marc Wozniak."

The heads at the table all looked at the strappingly built teen, and as they all offered their greetings, Morgan chuckled. "My, my, you certainly look fit, but a tad young to be Huxley's right arm."

Marc smiled. "Well, I *am* seventeen, Mr. Morgan."

Carnegie leaned over and interjected, "Well, from what I have read in the papers, it appears this young lad is the brains responsible for saving Huxley Coal from utter ruin!"

Huxley twitched irritably with envy as the elite crowd shifted their gaze toward Marc, beaming with admiration.

Marc had indeed saved Huxley from near bankruptcy after the two deadly explosions in 1881. And despite Marc's veiled animus for Huxley, he had done well on securing a positive financial outcome for his family and managed to make improvements that started to benefit his co-workers. Over the past five years, Marc had uncovered Paul Jackson's scam of stealing coal shipments and selling them to contacts in Canada. This one bust alone saved Huxley thousands of dollars every month, yet Marc actively sought new avenues of trade, which expanded Huxley's business twofold.

America was entering a new era of expansion, not by conquering new territory but rather by imperial colonization and annexation. Marc had become a voracious reader, like his mom, and realized that, even before the Civil War, President Tyler had expanded the breadth of the Monroe Doctrine to cover the Hawaiian Islands and others located near the center of the Pacific. That trade with China, Japan and the Philippines had been rising it had become clear to Marc that the American government could use this piece of legislation to ensure that harbors at Hawaii and Midway were outfitted with American coaling stations. Huxley had immediately contacted President Arthur, and not only did America begin to take a more aggressive role in the Pacific, but Huxley Coal was awarded the huge contract to supply these depots with the anthracitic fuel needed by American steamers to conduct trade. As such, Huxley quickly recognized Marc's talents and worth, and had taken Marc under his wing, like a son—especially since Huxley had begun denigrating his own son, whom he saw as timid and weak, thus driving Archie Jr. into a psychological cocoon.

As Marc gazed at Huxley's dour expression, he knew that, despite the adulation and pay raises, he could never trust the reckless businessman whose unsafe mine had killed his father and many others, and who also happened to be a lustful bigamist and a depraved conman, among other things. Marc smiled internally. He was committed to remaining on task, and the rewards he received had soothed his appetite for revenge, for he had persuaded Huxley to rehire the workers who were unfairly fired and destitute; he fought tooth-and-nail to have the salaries of many workers raised, albeit slightly; and he managed to create a safer workplace by upgrading the lumber and installing Edison's electrical lighting system throughout most of the mines. Therefore, Marc felt a deep sense of accomplishment, and that the Wozniaks were living a much better lifestyle only helped to convince him that he was, in large measure, following the right path and fulfilling his father and mother's wishes.

Former President Chester Arthur barely finished chewing a mouthful of rib eye as he looked up at the handsome youth, and inquired. "That is fantastic, Marc, that you have shown so much aptitude at such an early age. So, tell me, what university did you attend?"

Marc was still taken aback by the elite company he was now confronted with, and his reply wavered slightly with anxiety, "W-well, Mr. President," Marc paused, his face twitched, "do I still call you president?"

As the men at the table chuckled, a Republican Stalwart sitting at a nearby table heard the exchange and added his two cents, "Well, son, a man who passed the Pendleton Act, causing many Stalwarts, including myself, to lose their jobs, and aided in losing our Republican monopoly to a Democrat, should never be addressed with the title *president*. I think *traitor* is more apropos!"

As some frowned, others erupted in laughter. Chester, however, didn't find the man's comment amusing. He looked at the man, and fired back, "Well, anyone who is disgruntled by what my administration accomplished could only be a dead piece of wood that needed to be removed!"

Embarrassed, the Stalwart meekly turned back to his own table, while Chester looked back at Marc. With a slight smile, he added softly, "As everyone here knows, I, too, had my share of living a quite easy and comfortable life, yet I am very proud of what I accomplished while in office, an office, mind you, that I never had any intentions of ever holding."

"Quite true," Carnegie said as he swallowed a succulent chunk of lobster. "Arthur did a fine job while in office. He surprised us all. And while some may balk about losing their plum jobs, overall, no one can dispute the fact that Arthur presided over a very prosperous time and had run his administration admirably with a 100 million dollar surplus."

"Absolutely," Rockefeller said, "and that Chet had ordered the construction of three, modern steel-armored cruisers, the United States Navy had finally taken its first, small step towards being an active player in world affairs."

"Why, I thank you both, most sincerely!" Chester replied jovially. He then turned his gaze back at Marc, and continued, "But to answer your question, Marc, you may call me Mr. Arthur. For as I stated, I never truly harbored any desire for that lofty title. As such, it was only while in office that I expected to be called president. And that, my dear boy, is the beauty of our republic. We serve our country and then must retreat back to our normal lives; a magnanimous precedent set by George Washington, which he in turn learned from the ancient Roman General Cincinnatus."

Marc had heard that bit of rich history from his mom, but he was still a bit awe-struck and self-conscious about his education, and he nodded timidly. "Very true. And very well, Mr. Arthur it is. But to answer your question, I did not attend any university, sir. I was taught by my parents, but mostly by my mother. She was a very bright woman."

Huxley never liked when Marc mentioned his mother, and now uncomfortable, he changed the subject. "Yes, this young man did not need to be processed by the machine of education, which merely pumps out similar products. Like myself, he is a unique, home-grown dynamo."

As Chester swooshed the potatoes around his palate, savoring the resinous flavor of the rosemary needles, he then pointed at Huxley using his ornate, sterling silver spoon. "Yes, perhaps a few manage to survive without an education, but I do say, Mr. Huxley, look at the facts. I have benefited greatly from my education at Union College, while our dearly departed President Garfield was educated at Williams College, and President Hayes before him graduated valedictorian at Kenyon College, and then attended Harvard Law School. None of us were mere duplicates, and we each made our mark. So, a solid education is a must if one has any notions whatsoever of achieving great things in this life."

Huxley snorted. "Not so, Chester. Not only did I achieve success, but look at the burly man in the White House right now. Grover Cleveland never had a silver spoon in *his* mouth—which, by the way, I see you still happen to wield so deftly—yet he's the salt of the earth, just like myself. The real deal."

Arthur self-consciously lowered his silver spoon as he queried, "Are you saying that you're now a Democrat?"

Huxley smiled as J.P. Morgan interrupted, "Archie is neither Democrat nor Republican, he's a damned chameleon! He would side with anyone, or any *thing*, that had an ounce of power."

As the assemblage laughed, Huxley nodded. "Perhaps you're right, J.P. As I've said many times, life is a sea of change, and I'll gladly ride on whatever raft floats my way.

As long as it's strong enough to get me to the treasure-filled isle I seek."

Chester's eyebrows rose. He recalled how Huxley used his presidential raft to acquire all the coal depots in the Pacific. "So I see," Chester said as he shook his head with a pseudo smile. "Then I am glad my days in politics are over!"

"So are many people," Huxley joked bitingly.

As several men around the table laughed, Chester's smile withered; he never found Huxley's sarcastic humor funny. "But in all seriousness, Huxley, you speak of sailing the political tides, but getting back to one's education, we cannot allow any Tom, Dick or Harry to run the ship of state." Gazing at Cornelius Vanderbilt, he continued, "After all, if Cornelius' grandfather, the Great Commodore, allowed untrained helmsmen to steer all his ships the Vanderbilt fleet and empire would have surely sunk!"

Before Huxley could respond, Vanderbilt interjected, "I'll grant you, Chester, that a fine education by a laudable institution is helpful to many, if not most. However, do consider this; my grandfather became wildly successful and astonishingly wealthy with practically no formal education whatsoever. He was only eleven years old when he quit school, yet he managed to form his own ferry service from Staten Island to Manhattan Island. The rest is history, as they say. Or should I say, a very *rich* history!"

The elite assemblage gazed at one another with polished grins, and then at their former president, who had by now stopped chewing and pensively placed his spoon down on his ornate, cobalt-rimmed porcelain plate.

John Rockefeller nodded. "What Cornelius says is quite true. And come to think of it, I believe many of us in high society have followed similar paths. I myself had only a ten-week business course under my belt before jumping into the capitalistic cauldron. I succeeded more by the burning fire in my belly than those ten weeks of turning type-filled pages."

J.P. Morgan chimed in. "Well, I appear to have fallen in between, for I certainly had more than ten weeks of education, even studying abroad in Switzerland and Germany. However, despite my flair for mathematics, I only emerged with a degree in Art History. Little to prepare me for the ventures my life would soon take." Then turning to Albert Bierstadt, he added, "But I suppose my knowledge of art did allow me to amass the greatest private art collection in America!"

Bierstadt smiled as Huxley simultaneously pointed out the great landscape artist to Marc, knowing he was eager to meet the creator of the huge canvas hanging in his office. Marc gazed at Bierstadt and then at all the prominent men sitting around the table—he was still overwhelmed by this splendid opportunity and quietly sizing up all the players.

Meanwhile, waiters served, and busboys darted back and forth clearing empty plates, as Cornelius glanced at Morgan, then back at Arthur. "You see, Chester, I believe too many men in government have academic foundations but little to no worldly experience. How a businessman overcomes obstacles on a daily basis, and perceptively takes heed of the changing tides around him, is what allows him to steer his ship through the shawls and land safely ashore. Conversely, a statesman who has only read the Constitution and a heaping stack of law books has no practical experience to handle a ship when a storm arises." Vanderbilt paused. He then added, "And after weathering the destructive waves of the Civil War, our nation is still struggling to find its true course. Granted, Garfield's tragic death did unite our country like no living politician or piece of legislation could ever have done, but we still have much to do. So what concerns me more than an academic certificate is that we now have a Pro-Southern Democrat sitting in the Executive Office."

Chester picked up his fork and stabbed another chunk of rib eye. "Yes, Cornelius, I believe we all share your concern about a Democrat in office. But I had certainly done my share of getting our country back on track by continuing the process of rooting out corruption in politics. However, the majority of you are all wealthy industrialists who only know how to complain about government or lobby for handsome contracts or subsidies. Furthermore, with no oversight, when will any of you do what is best for your workers or for this country?" As the assemblage stopped eating and gazed at Chester, he continued, "For example, was it truly in America's best interest that Singer Sewing Machine opened a factory in Scotland? I'm as proud of my Scottish blood as the next man, but pray tell, why give jobs to them rather than good, solid American citizens?"

Marc had listened long enough and now wanted to contribute to the debate as his voice rang out, "I agree, Mr. Arthur. I think as Americans we must put America first." As the dignified assemblage all turned and gazed over at the outspoken youth, Marc continued, "My father instilled in me the importance of being an American. We here all have different heritages from other countries, and must continue to hold those traditions close to our hearts, yet our hearts themselves must become full-blooded American. And it must pump our new American blood throughout our entire body. As such, we should not give our life's blood to foreigners, for to do so would surely jeopardize our own life."

As the elite coterie digested the teen's words along with their meals, a powerful voice boomed from several feet away. "Now that's the kind of talk I like to hear!"

All eyes veered toward the source as a vibrant 28-year-old Theodore Roosevelt marched stridently toward the table. "America comes first at all times!" he said as he adjusted his clip-on glasses. Not having heard the beginning of the conversation about American businesses operating overseas, Roosevelt continued his Pro-American charge, while his energetic eyes scanned the sophisticated gathering, "Americans must fight to protect our country, our way of life. All the great masterful races have been fighting races, and the minute that race loses the hard fighting virtues—no matter what else it may retain, no matter how skilled in commerce and finance, in science or art—it has lost its right to stand as the equal of the best!"

Vanderbilt raised his glass of wine. "I'll drink to that!" he said as several others did the same. Cornelius placed his glass down, and added, "We can never forget that our dear Uncle Sam mascot was based upon meatpacker Samuel Wilson. He patriotically supplied our troops with free food during the War of 1812. I'll also have you know, that when the Civil War broke out, my grandfather donated his merchant ships—which he retrofitted with cannons—to Lincoln's Union army. My point; solid citizens, who in this case happened to be wealthy businessmen, patriotically dug into their own pockets to defend our country, and the same holds true about patriotically protecting our trade and commerce." Turning toward Chester, he added, "And that is why—despite your jibes at us capitalists—I must salute you, Mr. President. Because, in the realm of international affairs, it is imperative that we have a strong navy to ensure that we have a strong voice. And you did start the process of empowering our fleet. Strength ensures success!"

"Yes, my good fellows. It is all a matter of *survival of the fittest*," Roosevelt interjected as he heartily slapped the sides of his stout chest. "In fact, I'm grieved to have missed Herbert Spencer's visit here four years ago. His survivalist maxim resonates deeply within my bosom."

At that Huxley proclaimed proudly, "Well, it was *I* who financed Spencer's voyage to America, and had, in fact, met the man."

Andrew Carnegie turned abruptly and glanced bitterly at Huxley and then at Roosevelt. "Well, I was here at Delmonico's four years ago, and even spent some time on that ocean liner with Mr. Spencer, Theodore. And while I agree that the strong do survive, they often do at the expense of innocent people. It's time we survivalists atone for some of our sins. Just look at what we did to our fellow Indians."

As Huxley rolled his eyes, Roosevelt waved his hand dismissively and retorted, "Balderdash! I've heard all of the apologetic whimpers about the Indians before, and I say not a single one of you have ever seen or felt the wrath of those savages. The expression 'too horrible to mention' is to be taken literally, not figuratively. It applies equally to the fate that has befallen every white man or woman who has fallen into the power of hostile Plains Indians during the last ten or fifteen years. The nature of the wild Indian has not changed. Not one man in a hundred, not a single woman, escapes torments that a civilized man cannot look another in the face and even speak of. Impalement on charred stakes, finger nails split off backwards, finger joints chewed off, eyes burnt out—these tortures can be mentioned, but there are others equally normal and customary for Indians which cannot even be hinted at, especially when women are the victims."

Huxley fervently joined the fray, "And let's never forget how they butchered my dear commander, General Custer! I'd slaughter a wild Indian as easily as I would a wild buffalo! They're animals—both of them!"

Roosevelt turned. "You must be Archibald Huxley?"

Huxley nodded and extended his hand. "Indeed I am, Mr. Roosevelt. How did you fathom that?"

Theodore stepped over and shook Huxley's hand. "I've read an awful lot about you, and even saw one of those nasty little cartoons of you in *Puck* magazine. I can't quite recall what issue, but I believe the artist sketched you with devil's horns, jabbing a pitchfork into the rears of your soot-stained slaves."

Huxley chuckled. "Yes, those damned Brits always seem to portray me as a devil. What the hell do they know?" As Theodore diplomatically offered a pseudo smile, Huxley continued, "Yet I see they treat you rather kindly, Mr. Roosevelt. I had seen the cartoon of you clipping the claws of Tammany Tiger, rendering it harmless. And in the background a few former governors of New York looked on, all wrapped in bandages, unable to tame the beast."

Teddy laughed, his already trademark horse teeth lighting up his young face. "Yes, but that cartoon quite accurately captured the gist of what transpired, Mr. Huxley. So I am rather curious. Are you really a devilish slave driver?"

J.P. Morgan chuckled. "Yep! As sure as the Devil needs Huxley's coal to fire up Hell!"

An aptly sinister grin sliced its way across Huxley's face. He then peered down at Marc. "Now, go on! Tell these rude gentlemen just how wrong they are."

Marc smiled nervously as he gazed at the crowd. "Well, perhaps you're all referring to the old Archibald Huxley." Then turning toward Chester Arthur, he continued, "As we know, some people are indeed capable of changing. They *can* become better men," turning back, he added shrewdly, "especially if they listen to those with sound advice."

Everyone chuckled at the witty teen, knowing very well that it was Marc's sage advice that had doubled Huxley's business. Meanwhile, Huxley's brief smile had withered, not appreciating Marc's thorny, yet true, comment.

Gazing at Marc with clenched teeth, Huxley responded in a creamy voice tainted with pseudo affection, "Now don't let your handsome little head swell too much, Marc. Like a balloon, too much hot air *can* prove fatal."

Marc knew by the steely glint in Huxley's pale green eyes that he meant every word of his deadly analogy. Toying with Huxley's ego was always a risky proposition, especially in public. Yet to Marc's surprise, Archie turned and looked at the dinner guests with a painted grin, seemingly unaffected. He then turned and engaged Morgan in conversation.

Marc took that opportunity to look back at Roosevelt. He liked that, apart from himself, Teddy was the youngest man there. Moreover, he had read a number of articles about the firebrand and his rising career. Marc knew opportunities like this were additional reasons why he tolerated Huxley, and it was time now to boldly step out and start making connections of his own. "Excuse me, but I also recall seeing you in another cartoon, as well. I believe it was in *Harper's Weekly*." As Marc stepped closer, he added, "Oh, yes. Thomas Nast had done a sketch of you and Grover Cleveland, back when he was governor of New York."

Theodore nodded. "Indeed, he did. And it's quite odd, because Nast is often nasty." As Marc chuckled, Roosevelt continued, "But to my delight, he, too, has treated me fairly, at least thus far. That particular cartoon proved quite beneficial, for it confirmed just how well I cooperated with *Gopher* Cleveland and his mangy pack of Democ*rats*.

As Marc burst out laughing, Huxley turned and looked at Theodore, having overheard his remark. "Is it wise to be making jibes now that you're running for mayor?"

Roosevelt shrugged his shoulders. "Well, I *am* among friends." Theodore's face suddenly became irritated. "But I still cannot fathom how this country elected a man like Grover, knowing full-well that he fathered a lovechild!"

Huxley smiled. "You're a bit of a prude, I see."

Theodore stood erect. "Prude, nothing! I am a man of honor and moral fiber, Mr. Huxley, especially when it comes to the sanctity of such pleasures, which are solely reserved for those who are wed. Sexual gratification for anything else can only be called one thing—lust! Which, in my book and the Lord's Good Book, is a degenerative sign of weakness!" Huxley rolled his eyes, the sexual deviant clearly not agreeing with Roosevelt's strict moral code, as Theodore continued, "And as for my mayoral bid, Mr. Huxley, I am not putting too much stock into winning this race. It is just to get my name out there—into the minds of the American public. Actually, I just returned from hunting in the Dakota Territory. There are few sensations I prefer to those of galloping over those rolling limitless prairies, rifle in hand, or winding my way among the barren, fantastic and grimly picturesque deserts of the so-called Badlands."

Huxley's face beamed as he pushed a waiter aside to step closer. "Underneath that prudish exterior I figured you to be a man of my caliber!" Huxley turned toward the waiter, and snapped, "We've been waiting for ten minutes, for Christ's sake. Get us a goddamn table!" As the waiter recoiled and nervously scurried to ready another table, Huxley turned back to Roosevelt. "So what do you hunt?"

"You name it," Teddy said. "Grizzlies, elk, moose, but the greatest exhilaration to ever rattle my body was when I killed my first buffalo. Boy, oh, boy, that day I jumped with so much glee that my partner figured me to be doing an Indian war dance."

As Huxley laughed, Andrew Carnegie looked over at the two hunters and sneered, "Yes, and fools like you are wiping out the buffalo, too!"

Huxley twisted his lips in disgust as he waved Carnegie's comment away like an irksome fly hovering over a hog. The bloodthirsty swine then continued, "I couldn't agree with you more, Theodore." Turning toward Morgan, he added, "In fact, I've been badgering J.P. to join me on a buffalo hunt for several years now."

As the waiter pointed to the table he had setup next to Chester's, Morgan took a sip of his sherry and took a seat as he shook his head. "Sorry, Archie, like I told you, big game hunting isn't the sort of killing I like to do. I'll stick to my big game of finance."

Huxley took a seat next to him, pulled out a cigar, and lit up. Puffing the aromatic smoke out the side of his mouth, he straightened out his formal black suit, which he simply hated to wear, and said, "Listen, J.P., lately I've been hunting in style. You know, gentlemanly and all. In fact, a nattily dressed city-dweller like you could even wear one of these silly suits on one of my special bison runs."

Morgan grinned at Huxley's sarcastic humor, but then squinted. "How on earth can anyone hunt wild buffalo, gentlemanly-like, wearing a suit?"

"Easy," Huxley said as he puffed out another pungent cloud of smoke from the corner of his mouth. "I use one of Robert Harris's locomotives with a Pullman."

Morgan's head jerked back. "A *train!* You mean to say you hunt buffalo from a passenger train?"

Huxley smiled. "Sure, the Northern Pacific Railway runs right through all that great wild territory."

"That doesn't sound too sportsmanlike," Morgan replied. "So, in other words, you ride along and shoot these wild beasts in the comfort and safety of a huge Pullman railcar?"

"I sure do," Huxley said proudly. "Now come off it, I'm sure a cozy ride like that would suit your city-loving hide very nicely. And the views are spectacular, just like one of Bierstadt's stunning canvases."

Overhearing his name, Albert looked over from the other table and winked. "Thank you, Archie!"

Huxley turned and nodded briskly. "My pleasure, Albert. You *are* the greatest! In fact, I might have another commission for you." Archie glanced at Carnegie as he added, "I'd like you to do a painting showing our savage Indian friends slaughtering a buffalo."

Bierstadt scratched his thick, bristly beard. "Interesting idea, Archie. This could be an appropriate subject." He paused and gazed up into space for a moment, his eyes oscillating. "Ah, yes! I can see it—*The Last of the Buffalo.*"

A devilish grin washed over Huxley's face. "Yes, I think our good friend Andrew can see it, too!"

As they chuckled, Carnegie remained unaware, speaking to Rockefeller. Disappointed that his jibe wasn't heard, Huxley turned back toward Morgan. "Oh, yes, as I was saying, the train ride is really something to marvel over. It truly is invigorating to see huge expanses of land untouched by steel, bricks and concrete."

As the waiter took their orders, Morgan took another sip of his sherry, and declared, "Well, as you said, man has already laid steel tracks into that pristine landscape."

"Well, yes, they have," Huxley replied. "In fact, it was our dearly departed President Grant who drove in the last 'golden spike' in Montana, some three years ago."

Vanderbilt leaned over. "Ah, Sam Grant, that poor devil had a rough going his last few years. Didn't he?"

Huxley's face filled with sympathy for his idol. "He sure did. That damned cancer is a battle no one ever beats."

"No, no, not only that," Vanderbilt said as he pushed his chair out to get within better earshot. "I'm referring to the pain he endured for being financially ruined. It crushed the man. You see, his son Buck's brokerage firm had collapsed two years ago. That's when Sam had come to see me for a loan. I had given him $150,000. Naturally, I didn't expect to receive a penny in return. But, lo and behold, a year later, the great man died."

Huxley may have been cold as ice, but when it came to Grant and Custer, he could at least defrost into sleet. Gazing at Vanderbilt, he said poignantly, "Then you were a very fortunate man. I only wish I knew. I would have given Grant twice that amount." Then looking back at Morgan, he said, "And you just spoke about how man has run his steel tracks into that paradise of nature, but know this; we can always count on Yellowstone remaining untouched—as it has been for thousands of years—because President Grant made damn sure of it!"

Roosevelt and Marc had still been standing, engaged in conversation, but Theodore heard Archie's remark and had to respond. "I agree, Mr. Huxley. That, too, is something we all must admire about that puzzle of a man. I fear his scandalous presidency might very well tarnish his great name, but I do hope future generations never forget his stellar military career or his pioneering role in conservation."

Marc interjected, "And let us also not forget that it was Grant who established Christmas Day as a federal holiday!"

Roosevelt smiled. "Yes, Marc. It is hard to fathom that our founders and so many great presidents afterwards never took Jesus' birth seriously enough to make it a holiday. Then again, that early Christians shrewdly recorded Jesus' unknown birthday as being on December 25th, which had long been the ancient Roman's day to celebrate their sun god Mithras, it's quite understandable why even popes did not wish to celebrate that mysterious day." Turning back to Huxley, who was clearly bored by the Christian babble, Theodore continued, "But the great beauties of Mother

Nature must be protected. As I'm sure you know, there are some magnificent architectural structures carved by nature that simply can never be surpassed by mankind, and we must ensure that remains so."

Huxley appreciated Roosevelt's return to Mother Nature, and the avid hunters nodded in agreement. They may have enjoyed ravaging wildlife, while most tycoons ravaged the soil or felled thousands of trees to build factories or cities, but awareness to conservation had already taken root and was showing signs that it would continue.

As the elite crowd engaged in various conversations and ate their exquisite dinners, it had become apparent to Marc and Theodore that they had struck a chord. Taking seats at the far end of Huxley's table, which now filled up with other guests in-between, the two found a bit of privacy, and their conversation became more personal. Marc told his new friend about the devastating losses of both his parents within nine months as well as all the hardships the Wozniaks had to endure. Theodore listened, and then opened up his own tortured soul, telling Marc about the two losses he had suffered just two years ago—both on the same day. It had been on Valentine's Day, of all days, when Theodore's mother died at 3:00 a.m. of typhoid fever. Eleven hours later, his beloved wife Alice died of Bright's disease, two days after giving birth to their daughter of the same name. With a lump in his throat, Roosevelt described how that traumatic day struck him like a thunderbolt to the heart. The two women who meant the world to him were gone. It was unfathomable, unbearable, unacceptable.

As the two commiserated, gaining strength from their shared pain, Theodore told Marc that on that gloomy day he had scratched a big, red cross in his diary. Underneath it, he wrote one simple, but devastating, sentence. "The light has gone out of my life."

Roosevelt encouraged Marc to understand that the light may indeed be gone for days, weeks, or even months but that the sun does shine again. With a huge grin, which revealed his infectious personality, Theodore described in detail the new love in his life, a wonderful woman named Edith Carow. And with great anticipation, he said that they would be married on December 2nd of this year. He asked if Marc would attend. Marc eagerly accepted.

☙ ❦ ❧

Marc arrived home, excited and energized. The trip to New York had been a wonderful experience. He had rubbed shoulders with some of the most powerful men in the nation and, of course, befriended Theodore Roosevelt. He couldn't wait to attend his wedding to see what other new and fascinating people were out there in the world, a world far different than the smog-filled industrial pit known as Pittsburgh.

However, even life in Pittsburgh had changed dramatically, at least for the Wozniaks. Marc's sale of his father's carriage and success at Huxley Coal had paid off in grand fashion, and now he and his brothers no longer lived in the squalid tenement. He had purchased a fairly large house, nestled in a little glen on the outskirts of Pittsburgh. Equipped with indoor plumbing and electric lighting, it was a dream come true, a dream he had hoped to share with his mother, but Marc had four years to partially recoup from that nightmare. What's more, his new friend Theodore had given him another burst of fresh air that inflated his healthy lungs and cleared much of the dark and depressing thoughts out of his head.

Added to this new lifestyle was the addition of Marc's little brother Remus. Upon their mother's death, Stan had told his brothers that their mother had chosen two names if it were a boy, but couldn't decide on which one. True to her love of historical figures, Sophia had put forth the names of Romulus and Remus. Stan told his brothers that, since their mother had tragically died, the name Remus appeared to be more appropriate, being that Remus had likewise met a tragic death. However, although Marc and Ted unwittingly accepted Stan's explanation, Stan had silently yearned for the name Romulus, the strong and fearless founder of Rome. Yet upon seeing the baby's blondish locks, Stan had sensed the dreaded bloodline of Archibald Huxley in their bastard brother's veins and opted for Remus instead. And that little Remus was now 4 years old with long blonde hair and light green eyes, Stan harbored repulsion for what he silently termed *The Demon Seed*.

Meanwhile, Ted had taken on the role of guardian for Remus, even managing to become the handyman around the house, despite his two left thumbs. Having to give up Huxley's Arabian stallion, Mazeppa, four years ago, Ted had been heartbroken, having become very attached to the animal. However, a year later, Marc had surprised his brother by riding Mazeppa home. After making payments to Huxley for the nine months that Ted was away, Marc had decided to buy the spirited stallion along with another horse for himself.

As for Stan, he did his share by helping with the cooking as well as washing the dishes and clothes. Marc, as expected, remained the breadwinner, working long hours at Huxley Coal. He had given up the late night hours at Pendleton's Iron Works, yet maintained an excellent rapport with Calvin, since the benevolent old man had been exceedingly helpful and had many connections. The progress Marc had been making at Huxley Coal, however, came at a price, since it only drew him in deeper, consuming his time. But the financial rewards had transformed a grueling life of drudgery and poverty for him and his brothers into a respectful world of relative comfort and class.

Nevertheless, after four years of raising his little brother, Ted felt it was time to move on. Scampering into the kitchen with dirty shoes and little Remus at his side, Ted looked at Stan, who was scrubbing the clothes on a corrugated metal washboard. "Listen, Stan. We need to talk again, and this time you had better take it seriously." Stan knew the drill and kept washing without even looking as Ted continued, "Like I told you, I have to follow my dream, just like momma said I should."

Stan's face twisted as he gazed down at the dirt they both deposited on the floor, which he had just cleaned. Looking up at only Remus, he blasted, "Take those dirty shoes off, Remy! And get the broom and clean this mess up, right now! Do you hear me?"

As Remus recoiled from the harsh reprimand, Ted stepped in front of him and gazed angrily down at Stan. "Why do you always pick on him? My shoes are dirty, too!"

Stan's eyes remained glued to little Remus', who remained clutched onto the back of Ted's pants, with only his trembling head peering out at the screaming banshee.

"Because," Stan retorted, "Remy is a spoiled little slob!"

"He is not!" Ted fired back, "you never cut him a break. You snap at him worse than how you used to bark at me, and that's pretty damned awful!"

Stan now gazed up at Ted. "Oh, stop it! You were a spoiled brat, too! The two of you belong together. So, if you're so hot to leave this house, then why not take Remus with you?"

"Very funny, Stan," Ted snarled. "You know damned well I can't take a little kid like him along. I plan on joining Buffalo Bill's Wild West Show, riding stunt horses!"

Stan dropped the shirt into the washbasin and irritably dried off his hands. "And just how the hell do you expect *me* to take care of him? Huh? In case you forgot, Mr. Selfish Bastard, I'm a goddamned cripple!"

Ted grit his teeth, and then blasted, "For years, you broke my shoes for being a selfish, lazy troublemaker, but I managed to change! I've pitched in around here for the past four years, doing a damned good job of fixing things that get broken, taking care of our two horses, and raising Remus. When the hell are you going to stop whining? And for that matter, when the hell are you going to stop being such a miserable, brooding bastard?"

Stan peered angrily at Remus—who was still clamped onto Ted's pants—and pointed at his little face. With volcanic rage, he blasted, *"He's* the damned *bastard!"*

Just then Marc walked into the kitchen. He had only heard Stan's last scathing line, but that it was spewed with such deep, unnerving venom, rattled them all. "Stan! How dare you!" Marc yelled as he crouched down and hugged Remus. Brushing the long blonde locks away from Remy's eyes, Marc then gazed up at Stan. "What's this all about?"

Stan just snorted, and began to roll away, when Marc reached over and grabbed the back of the chair, halting him. "I want an answer, Stan. *Now!"* he demanded.

Stan pivoted his chair around abruptly, tearing Marc's hand free, as he spat, "How dare you! Who the hell do you think you are? You forget, Almighty Emperor Marcus, that *I* am the oldest!"

Marc realized the sensitive situation he was getting into and sympathetically suppressed his anger. "I know you are,

Stan. I didn't mean to be so bossy, but I cannot believe how you just cussed out Remus."

Ted chimed in, "Yeah, and the bitter old grump rags on Remy all day long while you're at work. So, this is not something new."

Marc glanced at Ted; quite aware that Stan harped on Remus, but he had no idea it was getting worse or this overbearing. Marc turned and looked at Stan. "Is this so?"

As Remus still stood trembling, Stan rolled his eyes and gazed petulantly into space as he murmured, "There are things you two will just never understand." With that, Stan grabbed the wheels on his chair and propelled himself out of the kitchen, down the hall and into his bedroom.

Marc looked down at Remus. "Are you alright, Remy?"

Little Remus nodded. "Yeah, now that *you* are here."

Ted's feelings were a little ruffled by that remark, yet the reality of the situation was that Remus viewed Ted as a big brother, while Marc had become the father figure. This was not only due to Marc's financial role, but also because his demeanor and sheer size aided that fatherly image. Marc had a growth spurt over the past few years and now stood at six foot two, and had an overall physique that was commanding in stature. His golden brown hair was cut short, still featuring those long strands of hair up front that he swept to one side, and he now sported a well-trimmed mustache. Meanwhile, Ted had remained lean with a slight hunched back from his breaker boy days, had dark brown hair, a scruffy goatee, and he peaked out at five-feet, seven-inches in height.

Nevertheless, Marc was still disturbed at what Stan said and, more importantly, how he said it. He gazed at Ted, and asked him to explain what transpired, and why Stan would say such a thing and in such a cruel manner. Ted's response cleared up the initial argument but wasn't very helpful on the latter. Marc had heard the word bastard used many times in all sorts of conversations and nasty brawls, but he still could not get out of his head the way Stan viciously damned their little brother with that word, coupled with fiery eyes that screamed revulsion. He looked at Ted, with his dark brown hair and brown eyes, and then down at Remus with his blonde locks and light green eyes. He visualized Stan, with his black hair and dark brown eyes, which mirrored their mother's, and then recalled how he looked very much like his father Jedrek, with golden brown hair and blue eyes. Remus' blonde hair was indeed odd, yet overall the family appeared to be evenly split in light and dark traits, and he recalled several friends whose brothers or sisters also looked noticeably different. Besides, Marc knew his mother would never have cheated on their father, and he quickly ejected the silly thought from his head, instead focusing on Ted's request.

"So, tell me Ted, why are you suddenly looking to leave?"

Ted rolled his eyes. "It's not sudden, Marc. I've been here for four years, taking care of Remus and doing my share of chores around here. But I'm twenty years old now! Most guys my age are already married, for Christ's sake."

Marc smiled. "Is there a girl we don't know about?"

"Be serious!" Ted replied. "Haven't you been listening? I'm like a mother hen around here, plus we now live far away from the city *and* women. Our neighbors are half a mile away, and every day it's the same two faces, Stan and Remy's. Besides, you heard what momma said on her deathbed. I should follow my dream. And my dream has always been to ride in Buffalo Bill's show."

Marc gazed at his older brother, and then down at Remus. He realized this was not the sort of conversation

Remus should be listening to and directed him to play outside.

As Remus innocently skipped out the door, Marc looked back at Ted. "Listen, I understand your reasons, Ted. I really do. But think of what would happen if you leave. As you say, Stan harbors some odd hostility for Remus, which I cannot for the life of me figure out. It's just not who Stan is, or was." Marc reached out and placed his hand on Ted's shoulder. "But, think of Remy. If you left now, he'd be here all alone with Stan, and…well, I fear things would not work out well for either of them."

Ted frowned. "So why should I suffer for Stan's shitty attitude? I'm sick of hearing his *woe is me* tale, and I'm sick of this ugly bitterness that has consumed him ever since momma died and Remus was born."

"I understand that," Marc said as he lowered his arm. "You have every reason to be upset about that; as even I cannot fathom what troubles him. But, being the provider of this family, I must ensure that Remy is raised properly, and I must say, this is where you deserve all the credit. Without you, Remy would not have a prayer around here, and for that, I'm truly proud of you."

Ted was not accustomed to getting compliments, and a lump welled in his throat. "Thank you, Marc. I appreciate that." Catching his voice, Ted continued, "It's great that you're concerned about Remy's life and even Stan's, but what about mine? So, basically, I have to keep the peace around here, yet give up my own life in the process. Is that your plan?"

Once again, Marc placed his hand on Ted's shoulder. "Well, even though you're older than I am, that's an unhappy bit of reality that I figured out long ago. We all must make sacrifices, Ted. Especially when it involves family. Do you think for one minute that I enjoy working around the clock ever since I could walk?" As Ted's face twisted, Marc continued, "Yet, my sacrifices have made it possible for you to stay home and care for Remy, and live a life of relative leisure. I even bought you your own stallion."

Ted cracked a slight smile. "Yeah, and Mazeppa is a really great horse. But he, too, is stuck here when we both should be performing with Cody, entertaining people and making their miserable lives happier, at least for an hour or two."

Marc patted Ted's shoulder firmly. "And you shall! You're day will come, Ted. I promise. And I know you'll be a great performer, I've seen some of the stunts you do with Mazeppa. You trained him well. But all I ask is that you share some of the sacrifices with me, just for a few more years until Remy can handle himself."

Ted's lips twisted. "A few more *years!?* Christ, I figured you'd say months. How many years are you talking about?"

Marc's face became stern. "Look, Ted. Like I said, you are not the only one who has been making sacrifices. Just help me out for another four years and I'll even be able to give you more money at that time to start your own life."

Ted looked at Marc, uncertain. "I don't know, Marc. Four years are a long time."

"Oh, stop it! You already did four years in the blink of an eye. Besides, this will give you more time to teach Mazeppa new tricks, so by the time you meet Buffalo Bill, you'll be the greatest stunt rider he had ever seen!"

Ted smiled. "You mean the greatest stunt rider *the world* has ever seen!"

Marc chuckled. "So, we have a deal?"

"Deal!" Ted said, "but I need some money to buy a bull."

Marc squinted. "A bull? For what?"

"To practice roping him, and eventually riding him."

Marc laughed. "You really are nuts!"

The two brothers threw their arms around each other and walked out onto the front porch. Remus was trying to groom Mazeppa with a brush, imitating Ted, yet could only reach up to his knobby knees.

Marc smiled. "You see, if you weren't here, Remy wouldn't have learned that."

Ted chuckled. "Yeah, he'd probably have learned to be a grumpy little bastard like Stan."

As they both laughed, Marc looked at Remus, his mind, once again, irked by that damning term—*bastard*.

Nine months had passed, and Marc now found himself in a tweed suit at Theodore's wedding. It was December 2nd, 1886, and much had changed over those several months. On June 2nd, Grover Cleveland had married Frances Folsom, who happened to be 27 years younger, becoming the first president to get married in the White House. On September 4th, the Indian chief Geronimo had finally surrendered in Arizona after decades of mayhem, thus causing many to sigh with relief. And on October 28th, President Cleveland led a huge procession down the crowded streets of Manhattan and then sailed across New York Harbor to Bedloe's Island, where he presided over the grand opening of the Statue of Liberty. Grover stated that the statue's "stream of light shall pierce the darkness of ignorance and man's oppression until Liberty enlightens the world!"

Despite the many injustices and ignorance that still plagued the young nation—including the maltreatment of Negroes, denying women the right to vote, the exclusion of Chinese, the prejudices against non-Anglo Saxon immigrants, and the near slave status of many laborers—the United

States did have much to offer to its own citizens and the world. In the field of manufacturing, the United States had become a dynamo set to surpass the mighty British Empire. Meanwhile, a staggering flood of ingenious products caused the art of advertising to be truly born. This was due to the fact that crafty Americans wanted their products to be bought, not just by their fellow town's folk but by the entire nation, as well. Borden's condensed their milk into powder whereby increasing shelf life, Campbell's canned its soup, and Black Jack gave millions of Americans a tasty, chewy treat with their flavored gum. Levi Strauss' denim work clothes were worn by the enlarged industrial workforce, while higher wages afforded Americans more leisure time to engage in croquet, stick ball, attend Vaudeville shows, or even take photographs with the new box camera. America was proving to be the most fertile breeding ground for ingenuity in the world, for Edison had already electrified New York City, with other cities following suit; Bell's new telephone was being installed in a growing number of businesses and houses, connecting people in ways never dreamt of before; and the standard of living for many Americans was beginning to rise, along with a sense of pride and purpose that they were ordained for greatness. And that the Washington Monument had finally been completed two years ago, Garfield's idealistic vision of America was looking better each day, being further buttressed by the gargantuan, copper Roman goddess that now held her torch up high in New York Harbor to enlighten the world. The United States of America, like its ancient Roman predecessor, was a vibrant nation that the world could not ignore.

Marc's own status had also risen dramatically, for as he sat at Roosevelt's wedding reception next to a local legislator, and among a crowd of high society, he now marveled over the fact that despite being only 17, he had made friends with some very dynamic and important men. To his surprise, it wasn't to be only men as his eyes beheld a stunning vision of an attractive young woman sitting at a table across the reception hall. As he sat gazing at this paragon of beauty, not hearing a word the legislator next to him was saying, Theodore suddenly stepped in front of him, blocking his view. Marc gazed up.

"Ward," Theodore said.

Marc squinted. "What?"

Meanwhile, the legislator rolled his eyes and directed his conversation to the chap on his other side.

Theodore smiled. "That's the girl's name. Ward, Kathleen Ward."

Marc smiled, embarrassed. "Oh, so you noticed that?"

Roosevelt sat down, placing his glass of bourbon on the table. "How could anyone not!" he said with a smile akin to an older brother's. "Does the name Ward ring a bell?"

Marc glanced at the girl, and back at Theodore. "No. Should it?"

"Well, her father is Aaron Montgomery Ward. He's the ingenious inventor of the world's first mail-order business."

Marc still had no clue what Theodore was referring to. "What do you mean mail-order business?"

Roosevelt laughed. "Well, Marc. The United States is a large country and many people don't have access to all the products that our big cities now offer. Subsequently, since our postal system works so well, Aaron realized that he could ship products to anyone who buys his products, even if they lived on a desolate ranch out in Texas or Arizona. For the past twelve years, he has grown his one-of-a-kind business into a giant shipping industry."

Marc was still perplexed. "But how do people know what he's selling if they can't visit his store?"

Theodore chuckled. "We live in a bold new world, Marc! Ward doesn't need a storefront. All he needs is a huge warehouse to store all his products and a printed catalog, which he mails out to thousands of people."

Marc rubbed his chin. "Interesting concept, but how many products could he actually sell through the mail?"

"Well, believe it or not, he has over 10,000 products. They range from household items, like Sapolio and Ivory soaps, to all sorts of clothing, jewelry, clocks, furniture, games and toys for children, and even guns, rifles, and saddlery—you name it!" Marc's eyes widened as Theodore added, "And his customers call his catalog the Wish Book."

Marc was impressed. "Wow! That's an awful lot of products. But the thing I'd wish for most from Mr. Ward is not in that book!"

Theodore laughed and slapped Marc on the back. "Get up, boy!" he said as he stood up and straightened out his jacket. "I'll introduce you to her."

Marc remained seated and looked up. "Well, I don't know, Teddy. I don't even know her."

"But, you will once I introduce you," he said. "That's the whole point, you jackass!"

Marc laughed his apprehension away as he stood up and followed Theodore, who boldly cut a path through the crowd.

Making the introduction, Theodore shrewdly pardoned himself with the pretext that he had to get back to his lovely bride, Edith. Left standing before Kathleen, her parents, and friends, Marc knew it would be disrespectful to speak to her without first winning the approval of her father. Looking at Kathleen with a cordial smile, he nodded, and then turned toward her father. "So, Mr. Ward, Theodore has told me quite a bit about your business. I think your idea is utterly fascinating."

Aaron Ward put down his fork and wiped his mustache as he looked up. "Well, thank you, Marc. But, do know that many people have called me a lunatic."

As the Ward family and their friends laughed, Marc replied, "I can sort of understand that, sir. The concept *is* rather bizarre. I quite didn't believe it myself when Theodore explained it to me. But, after some consideration, I think it *is* brilliant!"

Aaron smiled gracefully. "Again, I thank you, son, but—" glancing at his daughter, he added, "I hope this flattery is not to gain more than just my appreciation?"

Marc's face turned red as he stammered, "W-why of course not, Mr. Ward. I mean, after all, your success justifies my compliment. Does it not?"

"Indeed it does," Aaron said with a hearty chuckle. "Please, relax and have a seat."

Kathleen's friend Marianne eagerly pushed out a chair, while Marc glanced uncomfortably at each woman as he lowered himself. But somehow his eyes ended up staring at Marianne as he finally made contact with the chair. Marianne's eyes were bewitching. Her features were no match for the perfectly crafted ones of Kathleen's, but her eyes exuded a radiance that gave a tantalizing hint of the fireball of life that was deep within this magnificent creature. Marc suddenly felt intoxicated. Uncomfortably, he glanced back at Kathleen, yet she had already noticed Marc's fascination with her friend, and was not pleased to be in competition. Not only was Marianne of common stock, but Kathleen knew she was more attractive than her, and was utterly befuddled by Marc's long gaping stare.

With a spurious smile and commanding eyes, Kathleen gazed deeply into Marc's jittery orbs as she scooted her chair closer. "Yes, please tell me all about yourself."

Mr. Ward could see the feline pursuit and rivalry that was about to ensue, and tactically cut in, "So, Marc, tell me; what line of work are you in?"

Marc glanced awkwardly at the two smiling ladies and then eagerly looked back at Mr. Ward. "I'm in coal, sir."

Aaron nodded approvingly. "That's a mighty good industry, son. And by looking at your fingernails, I see you don't handle the filthy stuff yourself."

"Oh, no, sir. But I did several years ago. I began working at Huxley Coal when I was only 9 years old."

Aaron's pleasant face withered. "Huxley Coal, huh. I'm not a believer in exploiting young children, nor do I relish the articles in the news about Mr. Huxley. It appears he has no regard for human life, safety, or anything else, for that matter. Except for money, of course. So what exactly do *you* do for Mr. Huxley? Oil his whips? Count his money?"

As tension gripped all those at the table, Marc unexpectedly smiled. "No, Mr. Ward. I am responsible for installing modern DC electrical lighting systems throughout the mines, so our workers can see better and don't have to worry as much about explosions from Davy lamps; and for buying better grade lumber to help eliminate cave-ins; and for setting the precedent of having adequate airshafts to supply our men with air and prevent firedamp buildups. Oh, yes," he said as he continued his dazzling charge, "and for uncovering an employee engaged in fraud, and doubling our business by expanding into the Pacific to supply coal stations on Hawaii and other islands. As such, American steamships can now trade with the Orient, and also show the world that we're a major player that must be reckoned with."

As everyone gazed at Marc in astonishment, with their mouths ajar, Marc, added, "And just to set the record straight, I do not condone those things my boss did, but I am determined to continue making substantial changes at Huxley Coal to erase that bad reputation once and for all."

Aaron smiled. "I am very impressed, Marc. And I hope you did not take my earlier wisecrack to heart."

"No, not at all," Marc said as he paused briefly. "Well, to be honest, I did at first, Mr. Ward. You see, I am well aware of Huxley's bad reputation, but it does become tiresome after awhile when I hear the same attacks over and over again. Especially since I've been working very hard to turn things around. But the good news is, some of his clients are seeing the improvements in service, since we bought 42 new hoppers and can deliver much faster now."

"Yes, it is important for customers to be satisfied," Aaron said. "In fact, my company's motto is 'Satisfaction or your money back.' However, it has brought me much condemnation from business owners of all stripes. They think it is utterly ridiculous to make such a guarantee, not to mention being precarious to my company's solvency."

Marc's eyebrows rose. "Mr. Ward. With all due respect, I am inclined to agree with them. Huxley just sells coal. It is a consistent raw commodity that cannot fail to satisfy. However, those who use that coal to smelt iron into steel and then fashion that into a product inevitably face a very different situation. Their products, like yours, are man-made items that *can* be faulty or defective in some fashion. Therefore, to offer a money-back guarantee for something that is not guaranteed to be free of defects does seem foo—" Marc caught himself a bit late as he corrected, "—risky."

Aaron smiled. "Well, despite those who call me mad or even *foolish*, my business is not like any standard business, Marc. You see, people are buying my products, not by looking at the actual item, but, instead, are making decisions upon a printed image and, more importantly, upon my veracity. Therefore, to allay their fears, this has become somewhat of a necessity to my particular business."

Marc paused as he digested Ward's new type of enterprise and new set of game rules. "Hmm, I never thought of that," Marc said. "It's very interesting. I reckon that's one of the aspects about our progressive nation that makes many businesses fail. One must always be open to change, or suffer the consequences."

Mr. Ward was satisfied. Marc appeared to be a bright youth, working at a good company, and he now allowed his blatantly impatient daughter to engage Marc in conversation.

However, it wasn't long before Kathleen's prickly, tinseled charms deflated Marc's bubbling infatuation, and the astute Marianne seized that opportunity to gain his attention. Caught in between, Marc realized for the first time what his father had always warned him of—namely, despite men having the reputation for being bloviating hunters, it was often the dainty feline prey that were the cunning predators.

As the evening wore on, Marianne injected herself into the conversation with greater frequency and verve, until finally Kathleen relented, turning to speak to her mother in humiliation. Marc and Marianne spoke for hours, and even managed to try out dancing, which neither appeared to have any aptitude for, yet they laughed and carried on just the same.

Marc was growing to like what he saw with each passing minute of this amorous encounter. Marianne had curly, dark-brown hair, electric hazel eyes, and a face that, although plain, exuded great charm, especially when she smiled. But what truly attracted Marc was Marianne's vivacious inner spirit, which animated every part of her body, which Marc was keen to notice was very well shaped.

To Marc, Marianne was an effervescent ball of delightful energy, and he knew already that he wanted to see her, not just again, but again and again! Yet, he was painfully aware that they lived far apart from each other and that fanciful notion was physically impossible. Worse yet, Roosevelt's wedding celebration was now drawing to a close, and he feared that he'd never see her again.

The two sat and listened, while Theodore grabbed the spotlight, as was his nature, and made a long speech of gratitude. He thanked everyone who joined in celebrating his resurrected life with Edith and the life they would now share together. Upon Theodore's final words, the party guests were invited to a last session of dancing, and the small orchestra began playing polkas and waltzes. Marc and Marianne, however, had enough of stepping on each other's toes, and instead walked out onto the veranda. Under a beautifully moonlit sky, they gazed at the Manhattan skyline as the sounds of merriment drifted out into the air and echoed between the chasms of tall buildings.

Marc turned and grabbed her hand. "Marianne, I have really enjoyed myself tonight. I hope you did, too?"

Marianne's face lit up with her winning smile. "Of course I did, Marc. To be honest, the moment I saw you walking toward our table, I knew I had to make sure you would never forget who Marianne Sorvin is."

Marc chuckled. "Well, I'm glad you just told me your last name, because I surely can't remember something I didn't know."

As Marianne giggled, Marc rubbed his chin, and asked curiously, "So tell me, you said just by looking at me that you wanted me to remember you. Correct?" As Marianne nodded, Marc continued, "So, basically, you judged this book by its cover. What I'd like to know is this; over these past few hours, did you enjoy reading the Introduction?"

Marianne laughed. "Of course I did. In fact, I think I've already skimmed a few chapters, and I simply love the story."

Marc smiled. "Well, I certainly hope so, because I must confess. From across the room, I didn't even notice you. My eyes were first attracted to Kathleen."

Marianne's radiant smile painfully withered. "Yes, I noticed. She *is* very beautiful, isn't she? All the boys fall in love with her."

Marc just realized his honest confession was tactless, and now embarrassed, he tried to repair the damage. "Please excuse me, Marianne, I'm an idiot. I didn't mean it in a bad way…I mean, what I'm trying to say is, I never really get the opportunity to talk to women. You see, I work long hours with a bunch of men, and, well—"

"You don't have to explain," Marianne said, her face still unable to hide the hurt.

Marc grabbed her other hand and pulled her close, looking deep into her eyes. "What I meant is; I don't have much experience with women, and I just learned that judging a book by its cover is what's really stupid. Kathleen is nothing compared to *you!* Honestly."

Marianne cracked a smile. "Thank you. So I gather you, too, enjoyed George Eliot's novel *The Mill on the Floss?*"

Marc squinted, totally confused. "George Eliot's novel? I don't quite understand?"

Marianne awkwardly bit her lip. She thought because they were connecting in many ways that Marc shared a similar interest in reading, as well. "I'm sorry, but, you see, Eliot's novel is the source of the popular saying 'Don't judge a book by its cover.'"

Marc's blank face said enough, yet he replied, "Oh, I see. I didn't realize that." He swallowed hard and continued, "Actually, I don't read novels. I enjoy reading books about history, and occasionally newspapers from different cities, you know, to get the gist of what's going on in our country." Realizing Marianne's obvious interest in literature, he added with a smile, "But I'm sure this George Eliot fellow writes very well. In fact, I love his saying!"

Marianne giggled. "Well, actually George is a woman."

Marc's complimentary smile morphed back into one of utter embarrassment. "Gee, I guess you must think I'm a real fool?"

"Of course not," Marianne said, "I know very little about current events in this country or big business and politics. So, I guess *I'm* the fool."

"Not at all," Marc said, "there's nothing wrong with us having different interests. But I do find it odd how so many women nowadays have men's names, like President Cleveland's new wife Frank."

Marianne chuckled. "Well, George Eliot is a pen name, Marc. Her real name is Mary Anne Evans."

Again Marc blushed with embarrassment. "I reckon I've made it abundantly clear that I know very little about the literary world. I feel ridiculous!"

"Actually, I never knew our First Lady's real name was Frank," Marianne said with a pleasant smile. "I thought it was Frances. My God, Frank. Now *that* is truly ridiculous!"

Marc chuckled with relief. "Yes it is. I had read that she was named after her uncle. It was only after becoming Grover's fiancée that she changed it to Frances. But the papers sometimes call her Frankie. Well, I'm glad I finally told you something you didn't know."

"That's not true," she said. "Like I told you, I know very little about business and politics, and you were very impressive at the table when you spoke to Mr. Ward. And that sharp mind of yours is what truly clinched it for me, since the only pretty things I admire without substance are jewelry and clothing."

Marc laughed. "Good answer! And I'd love to shower you with jewelry and expensive clothes forever, because—" Marc caught himself a bit too late. His attraction for Marianne was so sudden and unexpected that his emotions were unbridled and galloping wildly. He knew he had just trampled past his bounds, as Marianne's blushing face clearly indicated, and he now tried to pull back on the reins. "I mean, what I'm trying to say is, I really like you Marianne, and I know we hardly know each other, but I want to know you better."

Marianne's face was beaming. "Thank you, Marc. And you're a book I wish to read from beginning to end— savoring every chapter."

Marc smiled. "Well, being that you're a literary queen, I hope you'll help me write the rest of my book, because it's not yet finished and I would love to include you in all the remaining chapters!"

"Marc Wozniak," Marianne said with a delightful smile, "and you say you don't read novels. Balderdash! You certainly speak like a novelist!"

"Well, my mother enjoyed reading history and novels, so perhaps some of her literary flair wore off on me."

"Oh, that's swell! I'd love to meet her some day. We'd have lots to talk about."

Marc's buoyant spirits sank. "I'm afraid that's impossible. She passed away four years ago in childbirth."

"Oh, my dear," she said, "I'm so sorry."

"That's alright," Marc assured her, "as the Bible says, when one door closes another opens. And my baby brother Remus is just a cute little bundle of joy. So another part of my mom survives."

As they walked to the balcony and gazed at the gardens in the courtyard below, Marianne looked back up into Marc's eyes. "So, does Remus have any of your mother's traits, like you?"

Marc's face became sullen. "Well, obviously, Remus never had the opportunity to know our mother, so I don't really know if those sort of traits get carried over through one's spirit, but he appears to be a pleasant little fellow, despite being badgered by my grumpy, older brother Stan."

"That's a shame," she said. "Why is Stan such a grouch?"

Marc slapped the railing with both hands. "That's a good question."

Once again, Marc was confronted with this perplexing issue. He preferred not to think about it, but here it was again, in his face, and still he had no answer. Marc grabbed the railing tightly, his mind reeling. Opting to avoid the subject, he veered back to discussing her and her plans for the future. Knowing that Marianne was only 17, and lived with a loving and protective family, Marc knew his impulsive desire for her to move to Pittsburgh would be too absurd to even ask. However, he just had to see her again, and promised to visit her in Chicago. Additionally he offered to pay for her rail and coach tickets to come down and visit him in Pittsburgh.

As they returned to the main reception hall, the party guests had already collected their belongings and were now making their way down to the street. The couple followed the crowd and finally reached the street where a long line of carriages awaited. The guests began saying their goodbyes to Theodore and Edith and then hopped in their coaches. Pulling away in random waves, the clopping of hooves echoed down the dark and silent street. Marc had waited with the Ward family, being last in line, and he now finally approached the bride and groom. He gave his new friend a bear hug and extended his love and best wishes. Theodore told Marc that he would see him again in four months after he and Edith returned from their extended honeymoon in Europe. The Roosevelts then gave Marc and Marianne a final hug and rode off in their specially decorated carriage, trailed by long white streamers.

Marc turned and wished the Ward family farewell, yet hated saying goodbye to Marianne. He gently grabbed her hand and kissed it as Marianne's eyes became misty. It was a bittersweet moment, as Marc's heart yearned for him to hold Marianne and never let go; yet his brain knew this was just the beginning of something grand. In fact, the entire evening had been a divine stroke of fate, for not only did he attend the wedding of a new friend and rising dynamo, but he was also graced with an unexpected bonus—a magnificent woman that he somehow knew he would one day marry. Seeing the Wards to their carriage, he then helped Marianne board the vehicle. Yet, as she stepped up, Marc leaned over and kissed her on the cheek. Marianne blushed, but then unexpectedly turned and returned the kiss in kind as she entered the cab and gazed lovingly into his eyes. Marc's heart raced as he shut the carriage door, and then signaled to the driver. With a crack of the whip, the horses snorted, and the carriage bucked forward. As it rolled along the cobbled street, Marianne turned and looked out the rear window. Marc smiled and waved as the new love in his life pulled away.

12

Prosperity & Paybacks

November 15, 1892

Six years had passed, and during that time the United States had elected a new president four years ago. The Republicans had regained control as Benjamin Harrison squeaked past Grover Cleveland by winning the electoral vote, yet losing the popular vote. Harrison and the Republicans had looked forward to a prosperous four-year term, yet some had anxiety right from the start, fearing that Benjamin might fall to the same fate as his grandfather William Henry Harrison. The ninth president had died only one month into his administration, succumbing to pneumonia after foolishly delivering the longest inaugural address in history on a cold, rainy day. Worse yet, he had done so without wearing a hat, heavy clothes, or being protected by an umbrella. The proud old general wished to prove himself a tough warhorse, yet where William had survived bullets and arrows in his heyday, old Tippecanoe proved to be no match for a frigid drenching.

Nevertheless William's grandson Benjamin had served his four years, during which time many changes occurred. Ohio Representative William McKinley managed to pass his McKinley Tariff, which had been shot down by former president Cleveland, and it greatly favored American businesses and the government against foreign traders. As such, some grumbled about the Billion Dollar Congress.

Two years earlier, in 1890, J.P. Morgan's father had died and J.P. inherited immense wealth. He now wielded even greater power as he had begun the process of buying up railroads and steel companies, thus intensifying fears of monopolization, or as the press carped—remorganization. This led to President Harrison signing the Sherman Antitrust Act, which was the first bill of its kind, for it now granted the federal government a modicum of power to interfere with corporate America.

However, President Harrison had just recently lost his second bid this month to Grover Cleveland and would be handing control back to the Democrats in March of next year. Grover's odd nonconsecutive terms would prove to be a stunningly singular occurrence, yet underneath the booming economy, signs of stress were beginning to give some investors on Wall Street cause for concern.

Meanwhile, life in Pittsburgh was simply grand for Marc, as his relationship with Marianne had fully blossomed over that past six years. The two lovers had enjoyed a long and meaningful courtship and finally got married two months ago. It had been a splendid affair, as the Wozniaks' huge rear lawn was decorated with a nuptial altar and lined with flowers. The September weather had been cooperative and comfortable, and Marc and Marianne's families were joined by local guests, including Rusty, Pendleton and Dr. Galton, while Theodore and Edith had made the trek to witness their good friends joining in matrimony.

Also in attendance that day was the Wozniak boys' feisty Aunt Filomena, who had not been happy to hear that Marianne's maiden name, Sorvin, had also been molested upon her parents' arrival in America, for the vowel "o" had been chopped off the end of her Italian name. Nevertheless, she and Marianne's parents had enjoyed talking about the old world they had left behind, along with the new world they adopted. Filomena had been joined by her dear friend, and leading suffragette, Susan B. Anthony, both of whom proudly extolled how four states in the union had given women the right to vote, namely Wyoming, Utah, Colorado and Idaho. The times had indeed been changing, and Filomena had wished that her sister Sophia were still alive to see the initial fruits of their hard labors. Nevertheless, the wedding celebration had been a joyful and resounding success, and family and friends had left that evening in high spirits.

Marc was now 23, and enjoying a new level of prosperity and financial success. Yet he had left Huxley Coal a year ago, feeling that his work there was done. He had improved working conditions and increased Huxley's business to such a point that unemployment in Pittsburgh was at an all time low, and salaries, while still grossly disproportionate, at least allowed families to pay their bills. Moreover, Marc simply believed it had been time for him to move on, since working with Huxley had become strained and difficult. The good press that Huxley Coal had been receiving in the news focused primarily on Marc, and Huxley's ego had reared its ugly head, resenting Marc and denying every new improvement Marc tried to implement. As such, Marc figured that before everything he had worked for fell apart it was best to leave. However, although Marc had taken on an administrative role at Pendleton Iron Works, there had also been some changes at home, which only made matters worse.

Ted had fulfilled part of his promise by hanging around for four years to look after Remus, but two years ago he had saddled up Mazeppa and rode off to join Buffalo Bill's Wild West Show. He had written at least once a month, telling his brothers about his exciting life on the road, performing his wild horse stunts to amazed crowds; however, the letters stopped about six months ago. Worse yet, Ted never showed up at Marc's wedding. Curious, Marc had sent a telegram to Billy Cody inquiring about Ted, but the response was short and uncomfortably vague. "Your brother has great talent, but has been missing a few shows. I'll keep you posted."

Additionally, little Remus had turned 10 years old and had finally decided he was tired of staying home with smoldering Stan and his fiery outbursts. Against Marc's wishes, Remus had become a breaker boy at Huxley Coal about four months ago, and had been telling Marc that things at the mine were not good. Just last week, Remus had shown Marc the headline in the local paper: "HUXLEY RESORTS TO OLD WAYS AS EXPLOSION ROCKS MINE."

Marc was now sitting on the living room sofa next to Marianne, rubbing his head. He was disheartened by the disturbing news at Huxley Coal, but more pressing and perplexing was Ted's mysterious silence.

Gazing once again at Cody's telegram, he said, "I just don't understand what's going on. This telegram causes more concern than comfort."

Marianne grabbed the telegram and placed it on the end table. "Your constant reading of it will not change things, Marc. What is it that you want to do?"

Marc looked at her intently. "I must go to him. I know that between our wedding and getting settled in here it has distracted us, but I must find out just what Cody meant by saying Ted's been missing a few shows. Has he been hurt? Has he found a woman? Is he out gallivanting? What?"

Marianne leaned over and turned on the electric lamp, illuminating the semi-dark room that was still partially lit by the soft glow of twilight. "But you said business has been very busy at the iron shop. Will Pendleton allow you to take off?"

Marc smiled. "Pendleton is not like Huxley. If I tell Calvin that I need to find my brother, he'll probably give me train tickets and extra cash for the trip."

Marianne's lips twisted. "Yes, and that creep Huxley would have docked you a day's pay just for having the audacity to ask such a request!"

As the two chuckled, the door swung open. Remus came barging in, along with a cold gust of November air. With tears in his eyes, he cried, "Jason is dead!"

Marianne sprang up and rushed over to Remus, removing his sooty cap and hugging his trembling body. Meanwhile, Marc had simultaneously darted over and knelt before him. "What happened?"

Remus snorted and wiped his cold, runny nose. "We were playing tag on our break, and...and Jason was running along one of the cross beams, when—" Remus began bawling. Marianne tenderly rubbed his back, while Marc grabbed his raw, red-tipped hands.

Looking into Remus' pale green eyes, Marc said, "Go on, what happened? Did Jason fall?"

Remus closed his eyes and nodded as he managed to squeak out, "Yeah, right into the—" he just couldn't say it.

Remus' little friend Jason was 11 years old. Like most child laborers, they had been throwing coal dust at each other and playing tag inside the large breaker house. The grinding machine below them, which pulverized large chunks of coal down to manageable sizes (suitable for locomotives to burn), kicked up huge, dense plumes of black dust that wafted through the breaker house, thus cutting visibility down to a mere four feet. Coal dust settled on all the rafters and beams, and children often performed their death-defying feats by traversing these sooty beams, foolishly trying to imitate Barnum and Bailey's tightrope walkers. However, Jason lost his footing and fell headlong into the grinding machine 50 feet below, being pulverized into a gooey pulp of blood, flesh and coal.

As Marc and Marianne tried to console Remus, Stan, who had been sitting near the kitchen doorway, rolled in and came to an abrupt stop. "I told you that either you or Jason would get killed! You're a thick stubborn mule, just like Ted, who, once again, had run off and now doesn't write to us anymore."

"Well, the hell with w-writing. Here I am…in t-the flesh!" Ted said as he staggered into the living room, drunk.

Remus' wet, black sooty-face lit up. "Ted!" he exclaimed as he ran and hugged his brother.

Meanwhile, the remaining three looked on in shock as Ted wobbled in Remus' arms.

Marc stood up. "Ted, what in God's name happened to you? We were worried?"

A big silly grin twisted Ted's face like that of a circus clown. "Well, what can I say, except, Buffalo B-Billy boy is just a b-big smelly b-bison chip!" As he patted Remus on the head like a dog, he continued, "I was the b-biggest attraction, and Cody had the n-nerve to cut my pay. Then yesterday, the dirty b-bum fired me!"

Stan smirked. "Sure, *you*, the biggest attraction? More like the biggest distraction! You're soused, you damned drunk!"

Marc gazed angrily at Stan. "Enough! He just walked in the door, for Christ's sake. Save your venom for someone who warrants it!"

"Watch yourself, Marc," Stan retorted, "I know you hate when I say this, but I'm still the oldest, and you're just the runt of the litter!"

Marianne knew where this was going, and she walked Remus into the kitchen. Meanwhile, Marc replied, "Listen, Stan, I've done my best over the past several years to keep the peace in this house, and you have not made it easy. And just what do you mean by calling me the runt of the litter? Ever since Remy was born you seem to ignore the fact that he's our little brother. He has feelings, too!"

Stan snarled, "Oh, does he?"

Marc squinted. "What is that supposed to mean?"

Meanwhile, Ted glared a Stan (who was picking up a log for the fireplace) as he chimed in, "Shit! I see n-nothing has changed. Don't y-you have an ounce of consideration left in that b-bitter old heart of yours?"

Stan threw the log into the fire and spun his chair around, gazing angrily up at Ted. "And I see not much has changed with you, Ted. So, is the bottle you're only friend now? Is that why Bill Cody kicked you out of the show, and why you came running home?"

Ted's face contorted with rage as he lunged at Stan and began choking him. Stan grabbed Ted's wrists and twisted them outward, his strong grip and arms tearing Ted's hands off his neck with ease. Pulling Ted downward with great force, their faces collided, as Stan latched onto Ted's ear with his teeth and growled like a dog, "Make another 'bitter' wisecrack and I'll bite it off!"

Marc rushed over and grabbed Stan's larynx with one hand and his hair with the other as *he* now barked, "Just try to bite it off, Stan, and I'll rip your throat out!"

Stan's brown eyes gazed up angrily at Marc, like a dog holding onto a piece of precious meat. Meanwhile, Ted remained trapped in Stan's deadly grip, while his ensnared ear dripped with Stan's canine saliva.

Stan opened his mouth and pushed Ted backward, who wobbled and fell to the floor. Still gazing at Marc, Stan growled, "If I wasn't condemned to this Godforsaken chair I'd kick your ass!"

As Marc released his killer grip on Stan's throat, Ted rose to his feet, slightly more sober from the adrenaline rush.

Marc never wished to compound Stan's hardship by admonishing his older, crippled brother, but the past 10 years had been hell. Stan was a different person. The once holy, good-natured child of God now appeared to be a young disturbed man, mad at the world. Marc had tried to analyze what it was that had changed Stan, but could never nail it down. Was it the deep sense of loss he felt at the death of their beloved mother, who had spent the most time with Stan while everyone else had been at work? Or did Stan resent Remus, blaming his birth as being the reason their mother died? That Stan never answered these questions made Marc assume that it might be both, but Marc now had enough. Stan's bitterness had also been leveled against Marianne ever since she had moved in after the wedding, and Marc had to put an end to this nonsense once and for all.

"Stan, I know you are the oldest, and I'm sure that if you had never lost your leg that you'd surely be able to kick my ass. But, you wouldn't have! You used to be a man of God, loving and compassionate, despite your handicap. I admired you for how you handled that tragic disaster, for I know I never could have done so as heroically and graciously as you have. But everyone here knows that your whole attitude changed ever since Remus was born, and if this house is to remain unified and strong, we must have answers as to why that is?"

Stan sighed and gazed down at the floor.

Meanwhile, Marianne was still in the kitchen, ignoring the ruckus in the living room, as she prepared a sandwich for Remus. Little Remy, however, kept an ear tuned to his big brothers' conversation.

As Ted and Marc took a seat on the sofa, Stan finally looked up. He peered toward the kitchen and then back at his two brothers. Wheeling himself closer, he said, "Of course I know I've changed. Do you think for one minute I like who I've become?"

Ted and Marc glanced at each other—surprised at Stan's admission—as Ted inquired, "So, w-why is that? Was it because you blame Remus for m-momma's death?"

Stan again looked at the floor, his eyes becoming glazed as his shoulders wilted. "I promised mom that I would keep this a secret, but I know I'm only making things unbearable around here, so I just can't carry this painful burden any longer."

Marc and Ted were now not only shocked, but intrigued, as Marc prompted, "What secret!?"

Stan's head remained down, yet his brown eyes rolled up and peered at Marc. "God, forgive me, but, mom...well, she, she was—" Stan just couldn't say the dreaded word, and changed gears, "or rather...Remus is not...not our blood brother."

Marc and Ted's faces recoiled in shock as Marc shook his head adamantly. "No! No way. Momma never would have had an affair. *Never!*"

Ted chimed in, "Yeah! How d-dare you say such a thing!? You really have gone mad!"

Stan raised his head, his face stern and unflinching. "Of course she never would have! I did *not* say that!"

Ted squinted, not getting the drift of Stan's horrible message, while Marc's face turned ashen as his trembling hand scratched his forehead. His eyebrows furled as his sparkling blue eyes oscillated to the tempest of thoughts that now bludgeoned his brain and harangued his heart.

Ted looked at Stan confused. "I don't g-get it? So how then could Remy not be our brother?"

Marc placed his hand on Ted's knee and gazed at him. "Ted, evidently someone—" Marc could not bring himself to say the vile word either as he continued, "had their way with momma."

Ted's face contorted as he stroked his scruffy goatee. "You mean some dirty son-of-a-bitch t-took his pleasures with—" he choked up and began to cry as Marc looked back at Stan, whose face was now streaked with rivulets of tears.

"WHO!?" Marc bellowed angrily. "Who was it?"

Stan hesitated, and muttered, "I don't know if I should say."

"Why the hell not?" Ted snarled as Marc echoed the same.

Stan peered at both of his enraged brothers. "Because, I do not wish to see bloodshed, or either of you get killed."

"What do you mean either of *us* get killed?" Ted growled, his mind now clear with rage, "I'll be the one doing the killing! I'll kill the dirty pig with my bare hands!"

Marc stared deep into Stan's eyes. "Just what are you saying?"

Stan looked at Ted first, "Calm down! And *you* can't kill anyone, especially a man like—" Stan stopped, and gazed at Marc. "I think it is best that you both forget who it was and just deal with the fact that Remus has a different father than us. That's more than enough to bear."

Meanwhile, Remus heard the shocking news, and choked up, while Marianne unwittingly handed him the sandwich. Standing almost paralyzed, Remus' hands fell to his sides.

"What's the matter, Remy?" Marianne inquired, curious.

Remus hardly glanced at her as he sat down, dropping the sandwich, and plopping his face into his palms. Not wishing to let on what he had just heard, Remus uttered, "I just had another vision of Jason, and—" he began weeping. Marianne pulled up a seat and compassionately wrapped her arm around him.

Meanwhile, back in the living room, Marc was not happy with Stan's evasive proposition. "What do you mean we shouldn't know? How dare you break devastating news like this and not finish the dreaded story. Who the hell was the dirty villain? And why did you say we couldn't retaliate, *especially* against this rotten bastard? Who is he?"

Stan shook his head. "Believe me, Marc. It is best you never know."

"Like hell," Ted blasted, "and that's exactly where this son-of-a-bitch is going—to *Hell!* So, who is he?"

Marc's mind had been analyzing Stan's words and surveying every male in Pittsburgh, trying to make a connection. That Stan said they could not kill a person such as this only brought two people to mind—Blaggo the thug and his immoral master, Archibald Huxley. His memory flashed back to that distant night when Blaggo had beaten him up in the alley, and later that evening when he ran home. He thought about how his mother left Dr. Galton to stitch up his lip and curiously left. Did she run into the thug that night? He certainly could have been waiting nearby, stalking their house. But then Marc recalled the ugly face that he chiseled into his memory that night of the big, pug-faced beast with wild black hair and big black eyes. The features just didn't add up.

Marc's eyes filled with rage as he blurted, "It was Huxley, wasn't it?"

Stan's poker face was off duty as he flinched. "No! Why would you think that?"

Marc looked deep into Stan's now jittery eyes. "Because I know of only two dregs in this town that would possibly do such a thing, and Blaggo seems the type to get more pleasure from beating up people than sexually gratifying himself. Not to mention his black hair and black eyes."

As Ted looked at Marc, smoldering, Stan wheeled his chair backwards. "Now come on, you cannot simply pull a name out of thin air and then accuse them."

"The name didn't come out of nowhere, Stan," Marc fired back, "I happen to know that man better than all of you! And to let you in on a little secret, Huxley has two wives and two families!"

As Stan and Ted looked at Marc in awe, he continued, "His other family lives in Sierra Nevada, nicely tucked away from everyone. And that you said we wouldn't have a chance retaliating against this person could only mean a man with immense power, a man like Archibald Desmond Huxley!"

Ted sprang to his feet. "Of course! It had to be him."

Stan waved his hand nervously. "Calm down! You're both wrong, it wasn't Huxley."

Marc stood up, confident of securing the truth. "Swear to God that it wasn't!"

Stan's face turned pale. "I won't swear to anything!"

Ted's lip twisted. "That's as good as saying yes!"

"I agree," Marc said. "We should decide what course of action to take."

Stan shook his head, the resurrected nightmare overcoming his senses. "Wait! If you two try anything foolish, he *will* kill you, and the rest of us. He's a powerful man. And even if by some miracle you do kill him, you'll both dangle at the end of a rope! Is that worth it?"

Ted snarled, "It sure is! But I *won't* hang. After I kill him, I'll run off!"

Stan frowned. "Sure, running off is what you do best, Ted!"

Ted grit his teeth. "Don't start with me, Stan. The villain is Huxley, not *me!*"

"He's right," Marc said. "Now, let's not get ahead of ourselves. We don't need to kill Huxley, we just need to exact justice."

Ted snickered, "*Justice*—through the courts!? That would never happen against a rich tycoon like Huxley."

Stan shook his head. "Ted's right. Not only would Huxley unleash his powerful attorneys on us, or payoff the judge, but what evidence do we have?"

"Yeah, mom's not alive to accuse him," Ted said, "and we can't subject Remus to a courtroom circus by merely stating that he's Huxley's child. Who on earth would ever believe us?"

Just then Marianne walked in with Remus. As they all turned and looked at Remus, with his pale green eyes and blonde hair, Ted and Marc were struck by the disturbing revelation. The damning evidence had been under their noses all along, yet it just now registered as Marc said, "Oh, I'm sure plenty of people would believe us!"

With that, Ted blurted, "That son-of-a-bitch!" and he dashed out the front door.

Meanwhile, Marianne looked confused, and uttered, "What was that all about?"

Marc commanded, "Never mind! Just stay here and keep a close eye on the window." Turning toward Stan, he said, "You know where my new Winchester is, stand guard, while I go after Ted."

With that, Marc stormed out the door as Marianne gazed at Stan, shocked.

Ted had already hopped on Mazeppa and turned the muscular stallion around. Wielding a pickaxe in his hand, Ted kicked Mazeppa's loins, and bolted past Marc just as he exited the house.

"Damn it, Ted! Get back here!" Marc yelled.

But Ted just rode headlong into the darkness.

Marc buttoned up his coat as a chilly breeze howled in the night air. He jumped on his horse and whipped him with the reins. Marc knew his horse was no match for Mazeppa, but hoped to make up time by taking a shortcut. Dashing through a thicket of trees, with only the orange glimmer of dusk to light his way, Marc barreled through narrow dirt paths as branches smacked his arms and shoulders.

Meanwhile, Ted had already scaled the highest mount of Huxley Hills, and now rode toward the hellish mansion that his mother had visited 11 years earlier. Once again, the lights of Huxley's den illuminated the dark side lawn as the crest of the sun finally slipped behind the distant mountains. Ted gazed up and saw a few other lights come on upstairs, but continued toward the large bay window.

Hopping off Mazeppa, he tied him to the marble patio railing, and then walked unsteadily toward the window, rocking his pickaxe as uncontrollable surges of adrenaline pumped through his alcohol-filled veins.

Peering inside, he saw Huxley smoking a fancy pipe as he sat behind his massive mahogany desk, which was situated near the blazing fireplace. Ted was too preoccupied to even notice Huxley's huge gun rack on the distant wall as he breathed out a fiery grunt of anger—the cold air turning his hot breath to vapor.

Whipping the heavy pickaxe back, Ted then swung the sharp metal tool right through the window, breaking three large panes of glass and splitting the wooden sashes wide open. Huxley recoiled in shock, as Ted jumped through the opening and plod angrily towards him—air blowing out his nostrils with each deadly step.

Ted blasted, "You're a dead man, Huxley!" as he raised the pickaxe swiftly. With a grunt, he swung it down toward Huxley's head, when Rex came charging in and lunged at Ted's arm from behind. With Rex firmly latched onto his arm and flailing, Ted's aim was diverted, and the pickaxe came crashing down on a nearby chair, splitting the arm clear off. As Huxley dropped his pipe and ran to grab the poker by the fireplace, Ted spun around and kneed Rex hard in the chest. As the dog fell to the floor, Ted stepped back and swung just as Rex tried to attack again, this time, however, impaling the snarling boxer right in the neck. Rex shrieked with a dreadful shrill that cut straight through Huxley's bones. Archie gazed down at his beloved canine friend, whose head was now half severed from its body—his blood gushing onto the wooden floorboards as he moaned and gurgled.

Huxley hollered, "You sick bastard!" as he raised the poker—pointing the sharp rod at Ted's face.

Just then Marc rushed in and grabbed Ted and the pickaxe from behind. Startled, Ted furiously spun his head around to see who grabbed him, while Huxley looked at Marc and blasted, "Who the hell is this blaming lunatic?"

Huxley hadn't seen Ted in 10 years, and the scruffy facial hair also obliterated any memory of who he was.

As Marc struggled to restrain Ted, he gazed at his old boss, and replied, "This is my brother, Ted. I advise you to put down that poker, Archie. There is something very important that we need to discuss."

Ted barked, "*Discuss* my ass! Let me go, Marc! I'm gonna kill this filthy bastard!"

Huxley gazed angrily back at Ted. "What the hell is up your ass, son?"

"Never mind what's up *my* ass," Ted growled, "this pickaxe will soon be up *yours*—you slave-driving rapist!"

Huxley squinted, suddenly recalling that lustful evening 11 years ago. That nothing had been said all these years only reinforced his belief that Sophia never mentioned a word about the incident. His mind reeled: *How could they possibly know?*

Just then Penelope came bursting through the door, her eyes now wracked with fear as she spotted Rex's dead body on the floor. "Oh, my God, Archie! What's going on?"

Huxley spun around swiftly. "Penny, *just leave*. I'll handle this."

Penelope caught a glimpse of Marc's face as he stood behind Ted holding him back. "Is that you, Marc?"

Marc leaned his head forward. "Yes, Mrs. Huxley. I think you should—"

"Your husband is a—" Ted cut in furiously, trying to tell her. Yet Marc quickly covered his mouth, and snarled, "Shut up, Ted!"

Huxley again pointed the poker at Ted's face. "Yes, you better shut your trap!" Turning back toward his wife, he added, "He's obviously drunk and a bit mad, my dear. Go on, now. We'll handle this."

Penelope's curiosity was piqued. "But I heard that madman yell that you're a slave-driving rapist. What exactly is he referring to?"

Huxley's face began to turn pale, while Marc wrestled his irate brother to the floor—the two now squirming on the grizzly bear rug. Grabbing one of the furry arms, Marc stuffed Ted's mouth to gag him as he looked up and said, "My brother is very upset that your husband has been resorting to his old slave-driving ways, Mrs. Huxley, raping his workers as he does the soil of coal." Marc continued his white lie, yet included more valid grievances and crimes as he added, "Humans are not disposable commodities, Mrs. Huxley, and our young friend Jason died today. As did my father many years ago and countless others. Their lives could have been saved if better practices were followed, but—" Marc glanced at Huxley, "ever since I left, your husband has resorted to his old reckless ways."

Archie snorted, angry, yet relieved as he looked at Marc and then back at Penelope. "Yes, as I said, Penny, we'll handle this."

Penelope shook her head. "You'll never learn, will you? I've been telling you for years to follow Marc's advice. I'm so sorry he resigned."

Huxley grit his teeth. "Shut up—you nagging bitch! That'll be enough out of you! It's fine that you live in two beautiful mansions though, isn't it?"

With that, Penelope furiously lifted her long dress, spun around, and walked out, slamming the door behind her.

Meanwhile, Marc was still trying to subdue Ted, who wriggled wildly and now broke free. Grabbing the pickaxe, he stood up and looked at Marc, who also sprung to his feet.

Ted blasted, "How could you!? Why didn't you tell her that her filthy husband raped our mother!?"

As Marc, once again, grabbed Ted's arms, Huxley wielded his poker like a sword. "How dare you make such a charge!"

Marc gazed at Huxley, eyes blazing. "Archie, if you plan on lying, I'll let my brother go! And he *will* settle this here and now!"

Huxley glanced at his gun rack, but it was too far away. He also knew the two enraged youths were far faster than he. Unexpectedly, he smiled as he lowered the poker. "Well,

I'll admit that I have had several dalliances in my day, but what makes you think that it was not consensual?"

Ted's nostrils flared. "My mother would never consent to lying under a rock with a snake like *you!*"

Marc's eyes glared at Huxley as he tried his best to contain his rage as well as Ted's—who continued to struggle. Marc found Huxley's lie utterly revolting, just like the deed he committed, as he spat, "Consensual!? That's impossible, Archie, so don't you *dare* make my mother out to be a tramp, or us to be fools! Is that understood?"

Huxley's smile vanished; he could now see that the two wild-eyed knights of honor before him were not stupid, nor adversaries he should provoke. "Very well. But I've only done what plenty of other men in my position have. Besides, that brief encounter happened some eleven years ago. So, why this attack, now?"

"Because we just found out!" Ted growled as he continued to struggle.

"Yes," Marc added angrily, "our crippled brother Stan, who was also a victim of yours, just told us. My mother had confided in him that very night, and worse yet, that brief encounter yielded a child, Archie—you have a son!"

Huxley squinted. "Impossible! I took precautions to avoid such an accident."

As Huxley described the newfangled invention he had used that night, Marc and Ted cringed. The thought of their mother being defiled by this methodical, lecherous beast was too much to bear.

Ted's eyes ignited once more as he blasted, "You son-of-a-bitch, you think you have everything planned, and that you can do whatever you wish, well, let me tell you this; you may be rich and powerful, but you're not untouchable! Just like Frick, I'll hack you up but good! Right here, or in your office. Only I'll make sure I kill you!"

Four months earlier, a disgruntled activist had attacked the Pittsburgh industrialist Henry Clay Frick in his office. The assailant had been enraged that the tycoon hired guards to fire upon his locked-out steelworkers who attempted to stop strikebreakers from entering. Seven were shot dead. Storming into Frick's office with a gun and a sharp metal file, the assailant fired two shots into Frick's neck. Frick and several workers attempted to subdue the assailant, yet he managed to stab Frick in the leg several times. By a miracle, Frick survived the attack, yet powerful tycoons were put on notice—abuses were no longer going to be taken lightly.

As Ted lunged furiously forward, Marc grabbed the pickaxe and pushed him into the dilapidated chair that Ted had slashed earlier. "Ted! If you kill him, you'll have to flee the country or you'll end up at the end of a rope. We cannot settle this revolting matter in that fashion. Now sit down and shut up!"

Seeing that Marc managed to subdue his wild-eyed brother, Huxley threw the poker on his desk. He then reached down and grabbed his hand-carved pipe in the shape of a buffalo's head. As he took a few drags to reignite the smoldering tobacco, pungent smoke rose toward the ceiling in thin, twisting veils. Archie calmly took a seat, and said, "How can you possibly prove that the child is mine?"

Unexpectedly, Marc swung the pickaxe hard into Huxley's desk, making the overconfident man recoil as the sharp tool pierced deep into the pristine surface, splintering the wood and knocking several decorative objects to the floor.

Huxley's face twisted with rage. "What the hell was that for?"

"Just as there's no doubt that my pickaxe pierced and defiled your desk's precious skin, there is no doubt that your disgusting defilement of my mother produced a son!"

"How so?" Huxley snarled as he glanced at his battered desktop.

"I think if a jury took one look at our little brother they'd eagerly agree that he looks hell of a lot like you!"

"Nonsense! Look at you and your brother here. You two look nothing alike."

Ted rolled his brown eyes and stroked his brown goatee as he looked up at his golden-brown haired brother with blue eyes. "That may be so, but he looks like my father and I more like my mother." Ted looked up at the huge portrait of Huxley over the fireplace. He was painted in his Union uniform, sporting his long, Custer-like blonde locks. Ted's lips twisted as he added, "Yet, our brother Remus looks very much like that despicable man up there, with pale green eyes and long blonde hair."

"Yes," Marc concurred, "there is no escaping it, Archie. Remus is your son."

As Huxley replayed that lustful night again in his head the distant recollection of his condom being torn came rushing back into his mind. He gazed at the long phallic pickaxe piercing his desk and now rubbed his forehead in disbelief. He took another drag of his beastly bison pipe, and then gazed slowly up at Marc. "Remus, you say? Ah, yes, I now recall, he's a breaker boy. I would like to talk to him."

"No!" Marc snapped as his face stiffened. "He must never know. If news of this got out, my mother's name would be disgraced. This was *rape*, Archie, not a tryst. Either way, my mother's good name would be destroyed. And I would never allow that. *Never!*"

Huxley nodded as he extinguished his pipe and placed it down. "Of course, I didn't mean to insinuate that we make this public, or even let Remus know. I surely would not care to embarrass my wife and children either. But as his father, I do want to know more about him." Huxley glanced up at his gallant portrait, and added, "So tell me, is Remus a feisty boy?"

Ted shook his head with disgust. "You mean like you? *No!* He's a tough little tyke but he's got a good heart and soul, something you never had!"

Huxley rolled his eyes, and had all to do to keep from jumping over the desk to smash Ted in his gaunt, goat-like face. "I just wish to make sure my son grows up to be a man, and not some namby-pamby sissy." Archie glanced at the photo of his son on the wall as he added, "Archie Jr. is a sad excuse for a man, and I'll be damned if I don't spawn at least one real man in the lot."

Ted snickered, "From what I've heard, you have several lots!"

Ted's wisecracks were really getting on Huxley's nerves as he sneered, "You know something, you talk too much!"

Ted's face twisted. "And you screw around too much!"

Huxley sprang up and grabbed the poker. Smashing it on his desk, he blasted, "You're trying my patience, you mangy little goat! I could easily shoot and stuff you like all these other useless animals here, but the only reason you're still breathing is because I respect your brother."

Marc pulled the pickaxe out of his desk and rocked it menacingly back and forth. "Archie, you have bullied people all your life, and Lord knows how many people have suffered or died under your ruthless reign of error, but the fact is Homer had told me everything before he blew up your mine that day. Or should I say *his* mine!"

Huxley's face flushed as his nostrils flared with each deep breath. "So that old piece of shit *did* squeal. I knew it!" His eyes rolled and then looked back at Marc. "So you knew Homer was going to blow up the tunnel that day, didn't you?"

"No," Marc replied. "I was too young to realize how desperate he was. But that was Homer's way of paying you back, and rightfully so, for all the pain and suffering you caused him, by stealing his mine as well as his daughter and grandchildren."

Archie looked anxiously at the door, fearing Penelope might be in hearing distance.

Huxley's relationships with his two wives were certainly odd in the conventional sense, but he had sound reasons for protecting them. Archie had married Jenifer initially for her passionate lovemaking skills, but more importantly, to use her as a tool to seize her father's mine and sadistically punish him. Meanwhile, despite having grown to loathe Penelope's superior intellect, and irritating disobedience, her stunning beauty and attractive royal fortune were certainly charms worth fighting for.

Huxley gazed fretfully back at Marc, and demanded, "*Quiet!* Those things can *never* be spoken of again. Penny must never know! Do you hear me?"

Ted heatedly sprang up, grabbed his broken chair, and threw it into the fireplace. "You piece of shit!" Pointing to the blaze, he continued, "Do you see that chair? It's *damaged*, just like *you!* So if you don't shut up and listen to my brother, I'll toss your ass right into those flames, too! Do *you* hear *me?*"

Before Huxley could respond, Marc interjected, "He's right Archie. We have enough dirt on you to destroy you. Between your acts of fraud, negligence, bigamy and rape, believe me, you wouldn't stand a chance." Then with a bit of melodrama, he blustered, "And now that I have enough friends in high places, we could rain down on you with so much fire and brimstone that it would make God's wrathful destruction of Sodom and Gomorrah look like this paltry fire right here."

Ted's face blossomed with a vengeful grin as Huxley repeatedly smacked the poker against his open palm. "So, the wise little prodigy thinks he has it all planned out. Is that it, Marc?"

"I didn't plan a thing, Archie. You're the one who left a long trail of sins. My point is this: listen to what I propose or else that flammable trail will become public and set ablaze. And I guarantee this; as indestructible as you think you are, you'll never survive this deadly cauldron. You *will* burn!"

Huxley's face twisted as he angrily threw the poker into the fire. "You see that?" he snarled as his whole demeanor became unnervingly intimidating. "That poker is as strong and solid as I am. It may get hot and lose its temper, but it will *never* be destroyed, especially by the likes of little wiseass punks like you. Now, you both hear me and hear me good. You still have no idea who you're dealing with. Granted, Marc, you are an intelligent young man, but you have always played by the rules. What you have failed to understand is that there are no rules that govern *my* actions. Except, of course, the one guiding rule that I have lived my whole life by—Survival of the Fittest! And I, my dear little friends, am the fittest man you will ever see in your entire lives." Huxley placed both hands on his splintered desktop as he leaned confidently toward them. "So, please—spare me your pathetic little threats!"

As Ted's nerves started to unravel, Marc unexpectedly swung the pickaxe down, smashing it into the desktop and clipping Huxley's left hand. As Huxley recoiled in shock, gazing nervously at his bleeding hand, he stammered, "Are y-you nuts? You almost crippled me, you crazy loon!"

Marc's eyes glowed with rage. "That's just to let you know that I don't always play by the rules, Archie. So, you better take this seriously, or my next swing will nail that cocky head of yours to the desk!"

Huxley had never seen Marc react in such a way, and in an odd way, it thrilled him. A devilish smile washed over his face as he licked his bleeding hand. "I never took you to be unpredictable, Marc. I'm actually quite pleased."

"Listen, Archie, as you now know, I knew all along that you stole the mine from Homer, and continue your seedy life of bigamy, yet I never revealed that information, even after you had your thug Blaggo split my lip. My mother originally wanted me to retaliate and destroy you that dreadful night, yet, instead, I decided to help you build Huxley Coal up to be a respectable business, one that would treat its workers better and improve working conditions. And I did that, and proved to you the type of person I am. So, enough of the games! Let's come to an agreement that we both can live with," Marc said coolly, yet commandingly.

Ted looked at his brother with an uncomfortable mixture of pride and frustration. He realized his brother had a gift for somehow rectifying calamitous situations, yet he just couldn't fathom letting Huxley off the hook, especially now, knowing about his wretched act with their mother.

Marc rested the pickaxe on his shoulder, and turned toward Ted. "Get us some chairs. There's much I need to discuss with our host, so we might as well be comfortable."

Ted frowned—irritated by Marc's civil, attorney-like tone—as he unhappily dragged two chairs over to Huxley's battered desk. As the three men took their seats, Marc handed Ted the pickaxe and began making his case. However, to Ted's further chagrin, Marc's stipulations were not what he expected. Ted was aiming to utterly ruin and humiliate Huxley, yet Marc's demands were that he be made co-president of Huxley Coal and that the company go public, whereby both he and Huxley would each acquire one third of the company's shares, putting the rest on the market. Despite Ted's disappointment, these stipulations were extremely mortifying to Huxley, who angrily wiped his brow, trying his best to maintain his cool. After an hour of Marc utilizing his diplomatic skills, and Huxley fighting each request tooth and nail, the two came to a resolution, which Marc committed to paper. Marc would now be vice president and receive one quarter of the company's shares, while Huxley would be president and own one third of the company's stock.

Marc felt secure that the deal, although appearing to give Huxley complete control, still allowed him enough leverage to make subtle backdoor maneuvers, and they signed the agreement. However, Marc refused to shake hands with his new partner, and instead turned and nudged Ted toward the shattered bay window. As they stepped over Rex's hacked body, Ted looked down and growled, "One day I'll make your rotten master look just like you—*a dead dog!*"

As they exited Huxley's mangled mansion, Archie huffed, while Marc sighed, feeling a sense of fulfillment.

However, as Ted mounted Mazeppa, he turned and finally blew his stack, "What the hell was that all about?"

Marc adjusted his saddle, and began trotting down the dimly lit hill as Ted rode quickly up to his side, and groaned, "Well?"

Marc looked at the dark, shadowy figure beside him. "Ted, I have just performed the first step of our coup."

As they traveled down the main dirt path, bathed in bluish-gray light from the moon above, Ted replied, confused, "Kew? What the hell is that?"

Marc smiled understandingly. "That means *takeover*, Ted. I know you don't understand my methods, but, believe me, things *have* changed this time. I didn't wish to destroy Huxley previously because I saw a better way to make good on his indiscretions, with the hopes of changing his dirty business and even him in some small way. Yet, from what

Remus had told me earlier, it appears Huxley has already resorted back to his old evil ways. And, most importantly, I will never allow him to get away with what he did to mom! I *will* destroy him, believe me!"

Ted shook his head with a frown. "I still don't get it. He chopped your demands down; you're only a vice president with one quarter of the shares. I don't know much about that sort of stuff, but I'm smart enough to know that it takes four quarters to equal one dollar. So, it looks like Huxley still holds most of the cash. Therefore, *he* remains in control." With a peeved growl, he added, "That's not what *I* call destroying him!"

"Ted," Marc said calmly, "the key is that Huxley doesn't know anything at all about publicly traded companies. He has always owned his own private business. Archie is under the impression that just because he has the title of president that he harnesses full control of Huxley Coal." Marc steered his horse around a fallen tree as he continued, "So that I managed to persuade him to maintain only one third of the shares will play to our advantage."

Ted squinted, still confused, as he pulled Mazeppa's reins, steering away from a low branch. "But, you'll only have *one quarter*. So, that's less!"

"Yes, it is, Ted. But once the remaining shares go public, I'll enlist Calvin Pendleton and his rich friends to buy up the rest, giving us a controlling hand in Huxley Coal. And once that happens, Archie will be at our mercy. I'll strip him of his own mine, just like he did to Homer. So, payback time has begun!" Marc excitedly kicked his horse's loins, and said, "Last one home is a rotten egg!"

Ted grinned as he kicked Mazeppa and easily dashed past him, screaming, "You don't have a chance, you silly egghead. I can smell you already!"

13

An Eventful Day at the Columbian Exposition

May 15, 1893

Six months had passed, and although Marc relished his new salary and seat as vice president—which Calvin knew he'd obtain and wildly applauded—his plan of gaining a majority of shares in Huxley Coal had been derailed. Even before going public, J.P. Morgan caught wind of the news and shrewdly swallowed up a 40 percent holding in the company, leaving both Archie and Marc powerless to seize control.

However, during those past several months, Marc had spent time big-game hunting with Theodore, who advised him to join his new Boone & Crockett Club. As Teddy said, the club was formed to "promote manly sport with the rifle," for those who like American large game and, of course, are "men of social standing." And quite fortuitously, J.P. Morgan happened to be a member. As such, Marc readily agreed. Better yet, Teddy had scheduled a special club meeting that would take place at the new Columbian Exposition in Chicago, and felt it would be a great time for the two men to bond.

Built to celebrate the 400th anniversary of Columbus' discovery, the Exposition is a true marvel in design and intent. Gathering the nation's best architects, including Frederick Olmsted and Charles McKim, the majestic pavilions were constructed by Daniel Burnham in a beaux art fashion to evoke the grandeur of ancient Rome. However, the beautiful facades were constructed of wood and plaster, in lieu of expensive marble, to not only cut costs, but also make for easy demolition upon the fair's conclusion. The White City, as it was instantly labeled, is a radiant testament to America's knack for ingenuity and burning new desire to emulate the ancient imperial empire.

Adding further to this visually stunning world's fair are the many groundbreaking debuts and exhibitions that are proudly touting American creativity. Among the list of exhibitors are George Westinghouse and Nikola Tesla who are presenting to the world their revolutionary process of alternating current. The automated paint sprayer is likewise making its premiere, along with a life-sized model of a wooly mammoth. Even the art of amusements is being taken to an all-time high as George Ferris debuts his gargantuan rotating contraption for merriment, the Ferris wheel. Other novelties include a building designed by a woman (honoring women) and the moving sidewalk, which transports visitors who arrive by boat along a lengthy pier right into the fair.

However, amid this dazzling display of modern civilization, with its alabaster structures, man-made lakes, and promenades, is a section nestled to the side that pays homage to the past. And it is here, in this small re-creation of the American wilderness, that Theodore decided to convene his manly meeting.

As Marc rode toward the White City on his trusty steed, he asked a policeman where Hunter's Cabin was located. The policeman pointed, giving him directions to Wooded Island. As Marc approached his destination, he could see the island sitting in the middle of a large lagoon—connected to the mainland by a wooden, arched bridge. As he rode closer, a groundskeeper called out, instructing him to check his horse at a nearby stable, since horses and carriages were not permitted into the fairgrounds.

Marc was eager to meet Teddy and J.P. Morgan, as well as his fellow prominent club members, and his heart raced as he made a dash toward the bridge. The sun was an hour away from setting and its rays shed a warm, golden cast over the white buildings behind him as well as over the dense treetops on Wooded Island. The Old Wilderness section of the Exposition was currently desolate, since Theodore had secured the area for a few days exclusively for his club meeting. In fact, it was Roosevelt's club that funded the construction of the Hunter's Cabin and outfitted the rustic display with various artifacts. However, Marc was unaware of Teddy's camping arrangements, and being that this was his first meeting, he had no idea of what to bring or expect.

As he walked over the bridge, he could see the crudely built log cabin up ahead. Off to the side was an old, beat-up pioneer's wagon from days gone by, and the entire site did a splendid job of re-creating a moment lost to time. Marc stopped in his tracks and spun around, taking in the impressive view of the magnificent White City—with its symbolism of civilization, ingenuity and mankind's sophisticated dreams for the future—and then turned back to the rugged and rustic past that now awaited him.

The sweet smell of hickory logs burning wafted through the air as Marc approached the cabin. But just as he was about to grab the crude, iron door latch, he heard a gunshot.

Turning left, toward the sound, he saw Teddy with a smoking shotgun, yelling, "Yee ha!" and laughing along with two other men.

Roosevelt spotted Marc and called out, "Ah, Marc, my boy! Come and join us."

Marc walked over the small patch of grass and up to the edge of the woods; as Teddy cracked open his shotgun. "Marc, I'd like to introduce you to Owen Wister and Robert Chanler."

As Marc shook their hands, Teddy's eyes curiously scanned him over. "You travel light. I hope you brought a firearm. After all, this club *is* for hunters!"

Marc smiled as he pulled out his pistol. "Well, I didn't bring my Winchester, since I didn't expect to be hunting at a world's fair!"

Theodore smiled. "Naturally I don't expect to find any buffalo or elk on this little island, Marc, but I just shot us a splendid-looking wild turkey." Teddy turned and pointed. "Look over there!"

Marc glanced at the huge dead bird. "That's great, but what do you intend to do with it out here?"

"What else," Teddy said, "cook it!"

Marc squinted. "Cook it?" He turned and glanced around, only seeing the crude fire pit he had smelled on his arrival. "You didn't tell me our cuisine was going to be wild birds roasted on this wild little Wooded Island."

Teddy and his two friends laughed as he slapped another cartridge in his shotgun, and said, "Hell, we can't really get the flavor of roughing it like our ancestors if we don't live a few days like they did. Now can we?"

"So, you're saying we'll be hunting *and* sleeping out here?"

"Naturally!" Teddy said, "I hope you didn't make hotel reservations?"

"Actually, I did, but, hey, this sounds like fun. I'm game!"

"Well, don't say *you're game!*" Teddy jested, "otherwise we'll have to shoot you!"

As the foursome laughed, Teddy grabbed Marc's arm. "Come on, let's take a walk. I'd like to show you the cabin we had built."

As Chanler tended the turkey, the threesome walked to the log cabin and entered. Marc gazed at the clay and dirt floor and laughed. "Gee, did you run out of money?"

Owen chuckled. "I said the same thing. But, no matter, we have a few blankets that we can put down."

Teddy shook his head. "Come on girls, I did say we were going to rough it like our ancestors, correct? So get used to a little dirt."

"Oh, I can handle dirt," Marc said with a giggle. "Hell, I handled dirty coal for how many years! So I'm game—I mean, up for roughing it."

Owen chuckled. "I'm up for it, too. I now actually enjoy camping," he said as he unfolded a blanket. "You see, I used to be in banking, but gave it up. The world appears to be developing way too fast for my liking. Lately, I've been spending a good deal of time scouting the West."

"Yes," Teddy chimed in, "in fact, Owen has written a number of good books on the lives of cowboys. He's doing a swell job of keeping a part of our history alive."

"Oh, please," Owen said, "you are one of the busiest men alive, yet you are writing, what—the third volume of your *Winning of the West* series?" Turning toward Marc, he added, "The man is a living breathing dynamo!"

"I'll agree with that," Marc said, "but I think it's fantastic that you both are documenting our history of the Wild West. After all, everyone writes about our presidents, innovations and capitalistic ventures on the East coast, but the literary territory you're both exploring is as much a frontier as the Wild West was, and still remains to a large extent."

"Well said, Marc," Owen replied. "Perhaps you should take up the pen, too."

Marc smiled, embarrassed. "No, the truth is I only had five years of schooling." His face became sullen. "I certainly disappointed my pa, that's for sure."

"Nonsense!" Teddy exclaimed. "You're a bright young man. Never put yourself down! I'm sure your pa looks down upon you with much pride. It's not every breaker boy who becomes vice president of a coal mine."

Marc smiled as Teddy continued, "Besides, I'm sure you could make a valuable contribution one day, once you learn more about these courageous frontiersmen. Their adventures of discovering the beauties of nature—which no white man had ever seen before, coupled with their valiant fights to defend their expeditions against the hordes of savage Indians who scalped their women and children—are all part of our great Anglo-Saxon history, and it must be recorded. I'm sure you recall our visit to Delmonico's; we already have apologists making an awful fuss. But these great frontiersmen and their tales are inspiring, Marc. They even inspired my artistic friend Frederic Remington, who has done a splendid job illustrating some of my books. And once you get hooked, like Owen and myself, the words just flow, like a raging river."

"I suppose that may be so," Marc said, "but first of all, I'm not a full-blooded Anglo-Saxon, and second, although not a full-blown apologist, at times I wonder if our quest has always been so noble."

Teddy picked up two rifles that were hanging on the roughly cut, logged wall. "You see these two fine pieces of engineering?" Teddy said as he looked admiringly down at them, "one was Daniel Boone's and the other was Davy Crockett's. They'll be part of this exhibition once it is opened to the public." Looking back up at Marc, he continued, "Remember, Marc, the white man has only done what every other race has done at one time or another. Even the Indians, before Columbus arrived here, were at odds with each other, fighting for territory. One Carib tribe were even cannibals! Survival of the fittest has been a natural way of life on this planet, Marc, for *all species*. That the white man has proved himself to be smarter—by not only aiding his endeavors with superior arms, technology, and strategies, but also devising a superior civilization—is no reason to belittle the efforts of courageous men like Boone and Crockett, or the many other great heroes of our past. Nay, we must honor them! Hence, the importance of this Columbian Exposition."

"Well, I agree with that," Marc said, "actually it is the recent events of our history that disturb me. Don't get me wrong, I love my country, but you were born into a wealthy family, while I, well, I've seen too many people of my class being treated like animals. That's why I'm committed to making working conditions better for laborers, establishing wages that are fair, and for God's sake, doing something about child labor. This is no way to treat people who are all an integral part of this nation. Despite a growing middle-class, our country is primarily divided by extremely rich and extremely poor castes, and there is no justification for that. A hard working laborer who uses his muscles should not receive mere pennies, while a shrewd thinking business owner greedily devours millions of dollars."

Teddy nodded. "Although I do come from a position of moderate wealth, I have come to sympathize with those less fortunate, Marc. My fleeing the civilized world of New York to live in the Dakota Territory several years ago exposed me to a whole new world. I befriended some brave and rugged fellows who live hard lives, and I, too, have a growing distaste for the disparity between classes. These are causes men like us should rally behind. But despite how bad you think things are here, let me tell you, Marc, there is no place like the United States of America." As Marc readily agreed on that issue, Teddy continued, "And that we now have 44 stars on our flag, adding nine states to the union since the Civil War, only makes us stronger and more invincible. And in that noble endeavor, we must also fight to expand our horizons."

"Yes, that is true," Owen interjected, "but it appears we have consumed all we possibly can of this continent, so the Expansionist era has now ceased."

Marc rubbed his chin. "Well, we may not be able to expand on this continent, but other horizons have presented themselves. A few years ago I had managed to get Huxley Coal to supply U.S. coal stations out in the Pacific. The Hawaiian Islands and the Philippines have proven to be great outposts for expanding our trade. And a strong world economy would put us in a position that wouldn't even require us to seize those territories."

"Yes," Teddy said, "expanding foreign trade is a necessity, but a vital first step is for America to build an even stronger navy. As we here all know; respect and rewards can only come through strength, and although Chester had begun building a navy, a mere handful of warships is no match for Germany or Japan." Teddy gazed into space. "Actually, I'd truly relish playing some sort of role in the navy one day."

Just then the cabin door swung open, and to Marc's delight, J.P. Morgan stepped in. However, he was not alone. Walking in behind him was Archibald Huxley.

As Morgan walked over to shake Teddy's hand, Huxley gazed over at Marc. "I didn't know you were a member, Marc. Or a big game hunter, for that matter."

Marc was not at all pleased to see Huxley, especially with Morgan. His mission to persuade J.P. to sell some of his shares in Huxley Coal now appeared to be in jeopardy, but at least he was quick enough to put on a poker face, as he chuckled and said, "Well, only recently has Teddy introduced me to big game hunting, so I'm still a novice."

Huxley smiled as he pat Marc firmly on the shoulder, each tap progressively stronger with subtle meaning. However, his words were a bit more direct and threatening. "Well, that's another surprise you have sprung on me lately. I reckon I'll have to keep a sniper's eye on you."

That Huxley's remark was made with a congenial smile no one took him seriously, yet Marc knew otherwise.

Meanwhile, Teddy purposefully guided Morgan over to Marc, and interrupted, "Marc, I'd like you to meet John Morgan."

Marc shook his hand. "Yes, we met briefly several years ago at Delmonico's. I believe it was March of 1886."

Morgan eyed Marc up, his face stoic, and his large, gnarled nose, mauled by acne rosacea, being unnervingly intimidating. "Yes, of course. I recall your conversation with our dearly departed President Arthur. The poor soul died about eight months later." Morgan's eyes focused in on Marc's more intently. "But Archie has told me quite a good deal about you on the way here. So you've managed to become his vice president?"

"Yes, sir."

"Well, you sound like a crafty young man," Morgan said in a somewhat critical tone, "but you better make sure you run a good, profitable business at Huxley Coal, because the shareholders are now watching you!"

Marc smiled with a nervous twitch. "Yes, Archie and I are well aware of our shareholders. So, if we run into any problems, I'll be sure to inform you."

Marc saw that Teddy had tactically engaged Huxley in conversation, and he was pretty sure Archie hadn't heard a word, yet he didn't wish to be too forward with Morgan either, knowing he and Huxley were friends. However, he was also aware that Morgan had recently confided to Teddy that he was a strict businessman who only preferred dealing with men of good character. Being friends with Huxley was one thing, but doing business with him was another, and J.P. now had reservations. As such, Marc wanted to at least open a channel for further communication.

Morgan gazed at Marc, trying to feel him out. "Well, do you foresee any problems, Marc?"

Marc glanced over at Huxley, who was still tied up in conversation, and replied, "One never knows what to expect, Mr. Morgan." His voice lowered, "As you must know Huxley Coal has been getting bad press again ever since I had resigned. But now that I am back onboard, I am fully committed to resolving that. I will eliminate any and all impediments that stand in the way of making progress and higher profits."

Morgan eyed Marc over, once again, trying to read between the lines. That Marc intended to *eliminate any and all impediments* was a strong statement, but Morgan couldn't quite tell if that was just bravado or a subtle implication.

Meanwhile, Marc clearly sensed that J.P. was unsure, and he also knew that he could not change his mind in one brief meeting. Nor was this meeting proving to be the ideal forum with Huxley standing 12 feet away.

Just then Chanler popped his head in the door. "Hey, fellows, the sun has set, and I have a tasty turkey roasting out here."

"That sounds fabulous!" Teddy said. "Let's get a bite to eat, men. I had shot us a nice, plump bird."

The six men stepped out into the serene night air and gathered around the roaring fire. There before them, was the impaled turkey on a makeshift spit made of roughly whittled tree branches. Chanler had done a terrific job of slowly rotating the turkey, its skin being crisply charred all around to perfection. As the elite hunters all gazed at the nicely roasted bird, Chanler pulled out an exquisite bottle of champagne, while Owen pulled out a fine set of Waterford crystal glasses.

Marc laughed. "I thought we were supposed to be roughing it?"

Teddy grinned, his prominent teeth illuminated by the blazing fire. "Yes, I told these two gentlemen hunters that we should be drinking whiskey or beer from a tin cup, yet they outvoted me. Ah, the pangs of democracy!"

As they all laughed, and collected their elegant glasses of pink bubbly, Roosevelt said, "Well, let us toast to this splendid Exposition in honor of Columbus and to the many other great men who have all contributed to making our country not only a vivid reality but also a vibrant leader."

As they clicked rims and took sips of the imported French beverage, Owen inquired, "Have any of you heard the new national pledge that was written to commemorate this event?"

Teddy's face lit up. "Oh, yes! It is called the *Pledge of Allegiance*. Shall I recite it?"

As they nodded, Roosevelt placed his hand over his heart, and advised his club members to do the same. He then recited the new pledge that extolled their flag and their proud nation.

Morgan finished his champagne in one swooping gulp, and said, "This is indeed a great country, Teddy, but speaking about the pangs of democracy. I believe the bankruptcy of the Pennsylvania and Reading Railroad this past February is an ominous harbinger of some very hard times to come."

Roosevelt smirked. "Absolutely. And that Grover managed to crawl back into office with his wily pack of Democrats only heightens the probability of that potential calamity becoming manifest."

Owen took another sip of champagne, and said, "Well, I'm well aware of your growing interest in politics, Teddy, but I'm not so sure this economic slump is solely due to the Democrats. Our Republican friends, Sherman and McKinley, have passed some economic acts that might very well have caused this situation, and I believe it is Grover's intent to reverse them."

Chanler looked at Morgan. "Yes, we also know the growing and immense power of lobbyists, who persuade these Congressmen to enact new laws in an attempt to manipulate the economy. But do these tactics ever work?"

Morgan smiled. "Rarely. Or should I say temporarily. Our finagling of silver and gold markets has caused many fluctuations in the value of the U.S. dollar, and I wouldn't be surprised if Grover comes to me for a bailout."

Chanler chuckled. "J.P's wallet—bigger than the National Bank! How on earth does one man become so damned rich?"

As the club members all looked at Morgan with smiles of admiration, J.P. replied, dead serious, "Well, perhaps it is because I use astrology to help guide my decisions."

As some raised a curious eyebrow and others squinted in disbelief, Marc said, "That's interesting, my mother believed in astrology, too." He glanced at Huxley. "Unfortunately, she died tragically, but—" his eyes veered back to Morgan, "she was a Gemini. And, oh, boy, did she certainly show both sides of her aggressive and loving sign."

As Huxley uncomfortably took a sip of champagne, Morgan, unaware of Marc's covert jibe, replied, "Well, I happen to be an Aries. So I reckon I just rammed my way to the top!"

As the group chuckled, Huxley grumbled, "Well, I'm a damn Scorpio with a mean sting, but I'm just a millionaire. How is it I'm not as rich as you?"

Morgan smiled. "Well, you see, that's exactly what separates us; millionaires don't know how to use astrology, billionaires do!"

As the gathering chuckled, Teddy threw his crystal glass into the fire. "Okay, J.P.," he said as he gazed up at the night sky. "If the astrological stars say it is time to eat, then I would love for us to begin the sacrifice and devour this lovely bird!"

With a hearty round of laughter, Morgan nodded that it indeed was, and the six men sat on the ground and dug into the wild turkey. As they ripped off pieces of meat with their hands, Teddy grabbed a leg and bit into it, happily feeling like an authentic backwoodsman. As they all enjoyed their rustic fireside meal and bubbly drinks in elegant stemware, they each began sharing stories, while also taking in the natural beauty of the serene island.

An hour or so later they walked down to the shoreline and boarded a schooner. Launching out into the lagoon, Morgan took to the helm as they silently sailed through the placid waters—each one marveling over the beautiful sight of the illuminated White City. Morgan, however, was a bit disappointed. In a most rare event, J.P. had lost the bid to fund and build the fair (which he intended to be in New York) to Chicago banker Lyman Gage, not to mention that Westinghouse and Tesla won the bid over Morgan's prized wizard, Thomas Edison, to electrify the Exposition. However, as Morgan now gazed at the dazzling city of lights, he had to concede that there was no doubt—the results were stunning.

Meanwhile, Marc was still fascinated by the juxtaposition of the old and new worlds that now sat on either side of their vessel. To his left, he saw a rustic treelined shore, dotted with hooded mergansers and black-crowned night herons, and to his right, was the glowing promenade, lined with lampposts and a dense crowd of people, with a large backdrop of illuminated buildings. The White City looked like a fantasyland; evoking the dreams, aspirations and ingenuity of mankind.

As the crew began lighting up their cigars and pipes, they could hear the ragtime music of Scott Joplin—being performed by the colored composer himself—enlivening the atmosphere with a jubilant feeling of gaiety, hope and promise.

Marc's foot was tapping to the infectious rhythms as he said, "This music is rather catchy, isn't it?"

Being a lover of the arts, Morgan gazed over. "Indeed. It is far more refined than the honky-tonk that pianists play in seedy saloons. I actually hear traditional European influences in this music that takes it to a whole new level. It's a rather fine combination."

Huxley rolled his eyes as he pulled out his revolver and spun the cylinder. "I'd rather we go hunting, or at least check out Buffalo Bill's Wild West Show. I hear he'll be performing somewhere nearby."

Morgan chuckled as he pushed the tiller and pulled on the rigging. "That's not surprising, Archie! You're a bit too crude to enjoy sophisticated music."

The club members all smiled and puffed out billowing swirls of smoke that trailed off the ship's stern as Morgan added, "But if you boys would like to hear truly refined music, you should join me one evening to hear a first-rate symphony. In fact, I recently ran into a Czechoslovakian composer named Antonín Dvořák in New York. He's been doing a three-year stint here, and he was so impressed with our country that he composed his ninth symphony about America. He calls it *From the New World*. And from what my friends at the philharmonic tell me, it appears to be a masterpiece."

Roosevelt exhaled a stream of smoke and sat upright. "Well, if it's about America, I am most definitely interested in hearing it. When and where is the premiere?"

"It's scheduled for December 16, and will be performed in our good friend Andrew's new concert hall on 57th Street in Manhattan. Would any of you other boys care to join us?"

Marc was elated; with Huxley's dislike for music, here was a splendid opportunity to speak to Morgan alone, with his friend Theodore as support. "Sure, I'd love to go!" Marc said enthusiastically.

Just then explosions shattered the silence as fireworks shot skyward, bursting into fiery umbrellas of colorful sparks and smoke. As the crew gazed up and marveled at the celestial light show, Marc felt that these manmade stars were somehow meant for him. The timing was impeccable. And despite not being real stars or believing in astrology, he still sensed this was a good sign.

As Morgan pulled out his new Kodak camera, featuring rolled film, and began taking photographs of the sparkling lightshow, Marc took a sip of the new soft drink called Coca-Cola and smiled.

It truly was an eventful day.

14

A Visit to Carnegie Hall

December 16, 1893

Seven months had passed, and the situation at the Wozniak household had improved in many ways, yet it was still plagued with disappointments, despite Marc's new position. Although he had managed to promote Remus to a clean office job, being his personal gofer, his aims at helping Ted find employment had come to naught three months ago.

While Marc was at the Columbian Exposition, he had taken the opportunity to attend Buffalo Bill's show, and met Cody afterwards. He had managed to persuade Cody to rehire Ted, only because Marc offered to give him discounted rail tickets to aid with the show's traveling expenses. Marc received discounts from most railroad companies being that Huxley Coal was their main supplier, so it didn't cost Marc a penny. However, that perk had been the bait that Buffalo Bill eagerly bit into. Ted had happily rejoined the show, but it wasn't long before Cody realized that Ted resorted to his old inebriated ways. And only because he didn't wish to give up the discounted rail tickets did Cody tolerate Ted's drunken stupors for four nerve-racking months. It finally came to a head when Ted fell off his horse, landing on top of a man in the audience. The bruised man had obtained a bloody nose and cussed Ted, calling him a drunken fool. At that, Ted had pointed his pistol at the man and threatened to kill him. The man's temper had only flared up more, knowing that the show's stuntmen used blanks, yet Ted aimed and took a shot—the very real bullet tearing through the man's arm and lodging in the wooden bench behind him. The man pressed charges, and Cody washed his hands of the mess for good. Marc had to pay Ted's legal fees, as well as the man's medical expenses, not to mention the plea-bargained fines the judge set to keep Ted out of prison.

As such, Ted had been sitting at home the last three months like a lost drunken soul, getting into brawls at the local saloons. Although his drinking had started years earlier while carousing with a bad group of showmen at Buffalo Bill's show, it was now quite apparent that Ted's recent binges were the result of his finding out about his mother's rape. Bad enough his mother suffered Huxley's abuse but that she died giving birth to his son was the real kicker. Ted hated Huxley. And he found it harder and harder to even look at Remus. As far as Ted was concerned, Huxley's son was equally guilty of murdering his mother. Adding insult to injury, Ted had hoped Marc would retaliate with force and kill or at least financially destroy Huxley, yet instead, Marc had become Archie's junior partner. Sure, Marc had told Ted on numerous occasions to be patient, and that Huxley's day would come, yet, as far as Ted was concerned, the past seven months seemed like a God-awful eternity. And to see Huxley walking the streets of Pittsburgh made Ted even more enraged. Worse yet, where Ted used to be a harmless, happy drunk, he had now become a nasty and violent dreg. The utter revulsion, pain, and vengeance that Ted harbored for Huxley was like cancer, eating away at him day after day, drink after drink, and brawl after brawl.

Counterbalancing these sad and disturbing events was the miraculous change in Stan. It appeared that after divulging the horrid secret his soul was somehow purged, as well. Marc and Marianne were grateful for this transformation, knowing very well that Remus would have never survived if both his brothers were filled with animus at the same time. Unfortunately, Ted had always been little Remy's best buddy, so the flip-flopping of his brother's affections, from love to hate, was extremely hard for him to process or cope with.

However, the tender and compassionate presence of Marianne had been a welcomed godsend, as Remus, never knowing the joys of a mother's love, had now found the closest thing to it in Marianne.

Marianne even had a cathartic effect on Stan as they both shared their collections of books and thoughts, sometimes discussing and debating issues well into the night. Moreover, both Stan and Marianne had taken on the roles of being teachers for Remus, which had brought the family closer together than it ever had been since Sophia's death.

However, December 16th had finally arrived, and Marc's rail journey to New York City to catch his first-ever concert just reached its destination. Excited, Marc disembarked at Grand Central Depot and pushed his way through the crowded lobby out to the street. Decked out in a charcoal-gray, Merino wool suit, with a blue silk tie that complimented his electric blue eyes, and a large top hat, Marc cut a striking figure as he strolled along the busy streets of Manhattan on his way to Carnegie Hall. The winter air was brisk, and a light, powdery snow speckled the air, ground and parked carriages that lined the curbs. Marc pulled out his gold pocket watch from his vest and gazed down at the time. He had 26 minutes before the performance began, and calmly, he snapped it shut.

Arriving at the handsome new concert hall, Marc spotted J.P. and Teddy in the main lobby.

Teddy turned and smiled. "Ah, Marc, good to see you."

Marc pulled off his gloves and smacked them against his open palm as he greeted them both.

As Roosevelt dug into his pocket for his wallet, he inquired, "So, how was your trip?"

"Mighty fine," Marc replied. "These newer locomotives nowadays can really move, especially the ones running on anthracite."

Morgan's gnarled, cauliflower nose wrinkled as he cracked a smile. "Yes, I love locomotives so much that I just had to buy up several railroads!"

Marc took off his top hat and shook the snowflakes off it. "And I'd love to supply the fuel for *all* those locomotives, Mr. Morgan. I see our competitors supply a few of those new railways you just acquired. So how, may I ask, can Huxley Coal get those accounts?"

Morgan's smile withered. "Don't worry, Mr. Wozniak, I'm sure Archie will contact me about that, he always has. Moreover, that I own a 40 percent stake in Huxley Coal, I trust the price *will* be excellent."

Marc knew he blew his introduction, but he wasn't quite sure why. Did he push too soon, or was it a topic that he never should have brought up in the first place? Nervously, Marc smiled. "Yes, I'm sure we'll come up with a price that will be excellent, Mr. Morgan."

Teddy decided it was best to leave them alone, and as he left to purchase their tickets, Morgan replied, "Well, as a major shareholder, I must tell you, Mr. Wozniak, that your prices are not good. Not good at all! In fact, ever since you took on the role of vice president, your prices have risen."

Marc began to perspire. "Mr. Morgan, that is only because Archie had neglected to keep what I had earlier installed up to date. During my absence much had fallen into disrepair. But since my return, I've had to reinvest in machinery and ventilators. So, this current rise in pricing *will* go down, once I get things back on track."

Morgan shook his head. "From what Archie has told me, it appears you're steering Huxley Coal off the track. *You*, my dear fellow, spend too much money. There is a thing called overkill, Mr. Wozniak. Additionally, you pay your workers far too much. You can never be competitive if you overpay your employees."

"Mr. Morgan, our miners work extremely hard and put in 14-hour work days. I know, I've been there," Marc said, his passion beginning to rise. "And even though we pay them more than what our competitors do, it still is not sufficient. I know what it was like when my father and I made pennies an hour, struggling to put food on the table and clothes on our backs. That is no way for people to live, no way to treat people, especially people who toil extremely hard and for so long."

Morgan snorted. "Huh! Good intentions don't always prevail in the business world, Mr. Wozniak. Survival, often times, demands harsh actions. This economic depression we are in, which, mind you, I predicted last I saw you in Chicago, is because too many companies do not know how to operate. Such as these railroads I've been acquiring lately; their owners, like you, also had good intentions of serving our country and the people by connecting distant locations with the swift transportation of their railways. Yet too many lines have emerged, and too few people are using them; hence their slump in profits and eventual bankruptcies.

People may balk that I am a heartless monster by gobbling up these enterprises, yet they must be consolidated in order to survive."

"Well, did you ever think that if more Americans made better salaries that they would be able to utilize all these railways?" Marc retorted, now throwing caution to the wind and operating purely on principle.

Morgan's gnarly face smirked. The titan, born into great wealth and never knowing poverty, was beginning to realize that Marc was not riding on the same luxurious tracks as he. He gazed at the young idealist and shook his head. "Mr. Wozniak, you are too young to understand how the world operates. The problem with these railroads is not that their customers cannot afford to ride them, but that these companies lay tracks alongside their competitors trying to steal the same clientele. Added to that, they have their own proprietary locomotives and cars made at different gauges. This way their trains cannot be used on other tracks in the event their company is taken over. This is a waste of resources, bad business, and has proven to be disastrous. The entire rail system must be standardized."

"I can understand standardizing the entire system to a common gauge, Mr. Morgan, but that it must be controlled, or rather monopolized, by one man is entirely unnecessary, not to mention, unfair and un-American. Our nation is a republic that grants fairness to all. Not a plutocracy that rewards a mere handful of rich tycoons."

It was now clear that the two men were on opposite sides of the proverbial tracks, and fortunately Theodore derailed the escalating conflict before it truly crashed and burned when he returned holding up their tickets. "Here we go, boys! Free admission and prime seats. Shall we enter?"

Marc and J.P. gazed at Teddy's jovial face and managed to nod with amicable smiles. Entering their friend's classily decorated hall, with its horseshoe-shaped mezzanines floating above an orchestra of seats, the three men arrived at their row, while Morgan made sure Roosevelt sat in the middle as a buffer.

The stage was crowded with a full symphony orchestra, and its members began warming up their instruments. Some were making dissonant squeals or soothing sighs with their cellos and violins, while others burped and belched with their assortment of brass horns.

Morgan noticed Antonín Dvořák sitting in the audience and pointed him out to Teddy and Marc. The Czech composer, who had spent the last three years in America as the head of the National Conservatory of Music in New York, had visited many parts of the New World and was deeply impressed. This symphony, which he entitled *From the New World,* was composed in four sections, each offering a different impression of the America he had experienced.

The lights dimmed, and the conductor promptly took to the stage and raised his arms, signaling for quiet. With the audience's rumblings hushed to near silence, he gently waved his baton. With an ever so subtle murmur in the string section, the symphony was launched. Teddy rubbed his mustache, a bit curious. He was expecting his bold nation to be represented with far more bravado than this. Yet, to his surprise, the orchestra unexpectedly erupted with a powerful and rugged melody that not only captivated Roosevelt and his two friends, but the entire audience. About 12 minutes later, on the conclusion of the first movement, the audience erupted with applause, a practice not condoned in the stately world of classical music, yet their enthusiasm could not be contained.

Teddy looked at his two buddies and exclaimed, "My God! For a Czech, this Dvořák fellow has really captured the majestic grandeur of our Wild West."

Marc's face was beaming. "Yes, even though I have never been out west, I have seen Albert Bierstadt's painting of it, and it's interesting how Dvořák recreates that scene in sound."

Morgan continued to clap, in full agreement.

However, the conductor did not appreciate the interruption. The symphony's four movements are to be played in their entirety, with silent pauses in between, and this distraction broke the continuity he strove to attain. Angrily, he turned, and scolded, "Please! Hold your applause until the end."

With that, he turned around and once again waited for silence. Upon regaining tranquility and his concentration, he launched the slow, pastoral second movement. The beautiful melody charmed the audience, which obediently remained quiet at its conclusion. The jovial third and concluding fourth movements were likewise performed without interruption, and as the work reached its conclusion, the audience gave a rousing, standing ovation.

The conductor turned and bowed, contented. Then turning toward the composer in the audience, he said in a booming voice, "Please, stand up. This applause is for *you!* I have merely directed what you have brilliantly created. And what you have created is a masterpiece."

Dvořák stood up and humbly bowed as the crowd showered him with an even greater round of enthusiastic applause.

As the conductor left the stage, the audience simmered down, and the lights went on. During intermission, Marc opened the playbill and began flipping through the pages, when suddenly he stopped. Excitedly, he gazed at Teddy. "I can't believe this; the next work is *Tasso*, by Franz Liszt."

Teddy squinted. "I'm not familiar with it. What is it?"

"It's a symphonic poem about the poet Torquato Tasso. My mother named my brother Tasso after him."

"Tasso?" Teddy inquired, confused, "I thought your brother's name was Ted?"

"Well, we Anglicized it, but I am most curious to hear Liszt's impression of this great poet."

Morgan leaned forward to catch Marc's line of vision. "Yes, Tasso wrote *Jerusalem Delivered*. It's a great epic about the Crusades. Delacroix, Boucher, Poussin, as well as a few other French artists, have painted scenes from it, which naturally have attracted my attention."

Teddy laughed. "Yes, I'm sure they have. After all, I know of no private collector of fine art in America like you!"

Morgan grinned. "Well, Teddy, you love the great outdoors, politics and writing, while I have a love for business and the arts."

"Very true," Roosevelt replied, "I only hope that one day I will be as successful in my endeavors as your are in yours!"

As they chuckled, the conductor took to the stage once again. The crowd obediently hushed to a silence and the lights dimmed.

Marc's knees bobbed in anticipation as his eyes scanned the musicians readying their instruments. Before today, Marc had never heard music other than the coarse offerings that emanated out of local taverns or the folk tunes that towns people sang. As such, not only did he find this whole experience today fascinating, but this particular work had truly piqued his interest. With all the tales about Tasso that his mother had so often spoken about, and, of course, its direct link to his troubled brother, Marc was dying to hear what this work sounded like.

With a wave of the conductor's baton, the cellos and bass launched the work with a deep, somber tone, the timber of which was so thick and emotionally moving that it vibrated every heart and touched every soul in the hall.

Liszt's symphonic poems had been a revolutionary new art form that portrayed a poem or expressed some sort of story, thus breaking with the long tradition of the symphony, which, by and large, was pure abstract music. As such, Liszt's music many times portrayed the psychological characteristics of his source, and here Tasso's tragic life was astonishingly brought to life in a variety of tones. The Italian Renaissance poet had become famous in his day; yet had fallen to the intrigues of rival courts, thus having a profound impact on his mental and physical health. Tasso fell into bouts of melancholy and was prone to violent outbursts, which eventually led to his being admitted to an asylum. Even after being released, it was clear that Tasso's artistic genius had suffered along with his mental health, and the last 20 years of his life were, unfortunately, spent in further decline, illness and depression.

As such, the gloomy melody that Marc was listening to now perfectly captured Tasso's tragic life as the lush sounds of the orchestra resonated throughout the hall. But quite unexpectedly, the somber melody was interrupted by a violent outburst, when the strings, horns and cymbals soared into a frenzied rage, mirroring another facet of the troubled poet. Balancing out the work, the second half of the symphonic poem transforms into a brighter and more pleasant melody, depicting Tasso's healthy productive years. This upbeat melody then leads straight into a rousingly triumphant coda, with blaring horns and pounding timpani, which celebrate the poet's genius and concludes the work on a thunderously uplifting note. In ecstasy, the audience burst into cheers.

Marc and his two partners stood and applauded, while Teddy bellowed, "My Lord, never have I heard such a booming and triumphant melody like that before! Now *that's* what I call a whopper of a finale!"

Morgan nodded. "Indeed! It truly lifts the spirit. But I rather enjoyed the entire piece."

Marc was still clapping wildly. "So did I. I never realized that music could have this kind of emotional impact."

Teddy slipped on his woolen overcoat. "Well, I must confess, gentlemen; I truly enjoyed the second half of Liszt's character portrait. However, all that heavy brooding at the outset was a bit much for my taste. I suppose after enduring much pain and misery in my own life, I prefer to bury and forget such lugubrious times."

"Well, I can sort of understand that," Marc said. "But this was not a frolicking polka or pretty waltz, Teddy. It was a tragic and triumphant story in music. So judging Liszt's work on what he strived to achieve, I must say, this new art form of his was sheer genius. All the emotions perfectly depicted the life of Torquato Tasso." As he buttoned up his coat, he added, "After all, Tasso's life *was* tragic and mournful, as well as pleasant and powerfully uplifting."

"I suppose you have a point there," Teddy replied as the hall suddenly illuminated.

The crowd simmered down, and the three men began to make their way toward the exit. As they took half steps in line, Marc gazed solemnly into space. He couldn't get over how Liszt's symphonic poem not only portrayed Tasso so perfectly, but also, quite disturbingly, his brother Ted. He pondered the tragic appropriateness of his mother naming her son Tasso, who was now suffering his own bouts of melancholy and violent outbursts of rage. Yet, what bothered Marc most was that the Italian poet at least had his moment of glory in the sun, being hailed a great poet in his day and enjoying a current revival throughout all of Europe.

He realized that Liszt had taken artistic liberty by not ending the work tragically, as Tasso's life had, but rather triumphantly, to honor his genius, yet that did not take away from the fact that Tasso had earned and deserved admiration. Meanwhile, Ted never had a moment of success or recognition, and a lump welled in Marc's throat as he exited the hall, stepping out into the dark, chilly air.

Breaking Marc out of his gloomy daydream was Roosevelt's reedy voice, "Well, gentlemen, I'm famished. Shall we go somewhere for a bite to eat?"

"Sure," Morgan replied as he slipped on his imported leather gloves. "In fact, I'm throwing a dinner party at Delmonico's with about twenty guests, so come and join us."

"Sounds splendid," Roosevelt replied, while Marc pulled up his coat collar and nodded agreeably.

As the cold wind whistled down the 57th street corridor, Morgan waved for his personal carriage. As the deluxe coach came to a stop, trimmed in gold leaf with a heavy-duty suspension system and a plush leather interior, Roosevelt's eyes bulged. "My Lord. How do you manage to buy and maintain such a vehicle like this?"

Morgan smiled. "If you have to ask you can't afford it."

As Teddy looked at Marc and raised his eyebrows, Morgan entered the carriage and waved them in. "Come on boys, it's cold. Let's get a move on!"

Hopping in, they were driven through the snow-covered streets of Manhattan down to Delmonico's. Meeting up with Morgan's elite dining party, Marc and Teddy eagerly dug into an extravagant meal as they engaged in stimulating conversations with the financier's prominent guests. One guest was a medical professor, and he happened to relay a bizarre bit of news. Evidently, during the Columbian Exposition he had met a doctor by the name of H.H. Holmes. Holmes had been selling human skeleton models to various medical schools, and the professor bought one. However, it turned out that Dr. Holmes was not a doctor at all, but rather a diabolical psychopath. He had lured young women from the fair to his hotel, where he asphyxiated them and then dumped their bodies in the basement. There they were dismembered or cremated, while others were gutted and stripped clean so that he could sell their skeletons for profit. The professor told Marc and Theodore that the deranged serial killer had not yet been apprehended but that it is suspected that Holmes' tally—quite shockingly—might very well surpass that of Jack the Ripper's.

As the professor took his leave, Marc and Theodore glanced at each other with long faces. They had lost their appetites, and couldn't believe that such depraved and barbaric men still existed in this enlightened and progressive age. It was a hard blow to realize that some things never change. Worse yet, this particular madman had been conducting his deranged business right under their very noses at the Exposition.

"I wish I had run into that crazy doctor when I shot that bird for dinner," Teddy groaned. "I would have shot and gutted him, too!"

The two decided to purge the morbid thoughts from their heads, and opted to discuss the other side of the coin. They rehashed the incredible exhibitions they had seen at the Exposition and the inventiveness that was transforming America into a new world. The old Wild West that Theodore loved so much was rapidly fading right before his eyes as a new mechanical world of gadgets and automation was taking center stage and transforming the lives of everyday, common folks. Bicycling had become wildly popular, allowing people who could not afford a horse a means of transportation or recreation, while just three months ago,

Charles Duryea introduced his one-cylinder motor wagon; the first successful gas-powered motor vehicle.

Dessert and coffee was served, and other guests joined Marc and Teddy, lightening the mood further as trivial conversation ensued and even jokes were told. Amid the laughter and tunes of the piano player who had recently begun his set of evening entertainment, Marc gazed down at his watch. Three hours had passed, and it was time for him to catch his train. Marc thanked Morgan and Theodore for a delightful evening and said his goodbyes to the other guests.

Exiting Delmonico's, Marc hailed a taxi and stepped onboard. The carriage plowed through the snow-covered streets and returned him to Grand Central Depot. Hopping on a train to Pittsburgh, Marc took a seat, and gazed out the frosted window, thinking about his frosty reception with J.P. Morgan. His plans to covertly undermine and oust Huxley, by either befriending Morgan or convincing him to sell some of his shares, had blatantly hit a brick wall. Dejected, Marc gazed down, spotting the Playbill in his hand. With a sigh, Marc's head fell limp against the cold, frosty window as the train noisily chugged along. His troubled mind began to rehash the day's events, reaching a depressing conclusion—his trip to Carnegie Hall was a failure. Despite the enlightening and enjoyable experience of listening to two great symphonic works, the sad, haunting melody of Liszt's tone poem now began humming in his head and tormenting his soul, reminding him of his brother's painfully similar plight. With a heavy heart, the world around him fell silent as Marc could only hear the mournful dirge; no triumphant horns would be sounded for his brother Tasso.

War with Spain

February 15, 1898

Five years had passed, and Marc, now 29 years old, had continued to butt heads with Huxley. It was apparent that Archie's friend, J.P. Morgan, condoned or turned a blind eye to his friend's threadbare policy of cutting salaries, hiring more Chinese workers, and limiting expenses for new equipment and maintenance. The past five years had seen a spike in cave-ins, explosions, and deaths, yet Huxley was firmly attached to Morgan's rich, protective hip, and didn't mind the bad press. After all, he had never received good press—save for the few articles in years past that applauded Marc's input—and he had always managed to make money, so why should he care or change?

Meanwhile, Ted was also receiving bad press, yet on a local level. Marc's attempts to get Ted back to work had continued to meet one failure after another. Ted's mood swings of depression and rage, bolstered by the volatile alcohol in his veins, had made his name a slur throughout

Pittsburgh. Even the goodhearted Calvin Pendleton had politely asked Marc to spare him the agony of having to deal with Ted. Almost every shop owner had either hired and fired Ted at one point or had heard of his escapades and tirades and refused to even entertain the thought of hiring him.

Marc was beside himself with grief. He had never forgotten his mother and father's pleas to care for his troubled brother. Yet he also recalled those fateful last words that his father had regretted to even utter, namely that Ted might very well be a lost cause.

However, on February 15, 1898, Marc's eyes caught the shocking headline in the papers. This time it wasn't about Huxley or his brother, but rather the sinking of the *USS Maine* in Havana Harbor. Evidently there was a mysterious explosion, and Hearst and Pulitzer's newspapers fanned the flames for war. The nation had a new president, and William McKinley had previously sent the battleship *Maine* into Cuban waters with the intentions of rescuing Americans in Cuba who may have been in harm's way. This was due to an earlier uprising, which had led to hostilities between Cubans and their Spanish overlords. However, despite this horrific explosion, and the deaths of 266 American sailors, President McKinley cautioned for prudence. He immediately ordered an investigation, despite the fact that the public was already stirred to war to defend American honor. And perhaps no one epitomized that sentiment more than his hawkish Assistant Secretary of the Navy Theodore Roosevelt.

Wasting no time, Roosevelt ordered American war ships to sail to key locations, including Manila Bay in the Philippines, which was also under Spanish control. A month later, when the naval investigation made available its report—stating that the explosion was from an external source—the clamor for war reached fever pitch. Unable to restrain the rising tide any longer, Congress drafted a resolution that authorized the president to use any means of force he saw fit to expel Spain from Cuba and aid the Cubans in attaining independence. It likewise stated that America would not conquer or annex the territory. President McKinley signed the resolution on April 20, 1898, and immediately sent war ships to form a blockade.

Meanwhile, Marc was sitting in his living room with Marianne when their recently installed telephone rang. Still not familiar with the loud ring, they both jumped in their seats.

Marc chuckled. "I'll get it."

Placing the newspaper on the coffee table, he walked over and picked up the receiver. As the operator plugged his call through, he heard the high pitch of his old friend's voice as Teddy said, "Marc, I reckon you heard the good news?"

Marc smiled. "Yes, McKinley's declaration of war now gives you an excellent opportunity to shine as assistant secretary of the navy."

"No, Marc," Teddy's voice responded, "I resigned from the navy. I am—"

"What?" Marc cut in, shocked. "Why? What on earth happened?"

"No, no, my friend, calm down," Teddy said, "that is a good thing. I am amassing a cavalry regiment, and I would be delighted if you and your brother Ted ride with me."

Marc gasped. "*My brother!?* I mean, surely *I* will, Teddy. But, well, my brother is—"

"You said he was a stunt rider for Buffalo Bill's show, correct?" Teddy interjected.

"Well, yes, but that was some time ago, and—"

"And I need the best equestrians I can find, Marc. So, he seems like a natural. Yes?"

Marc was silent for an odd moment. His mind raced; *Dear God, should I take the chance? What if Ted causes men to die and disgraces Roosevelt's bid for national honor?* Marc blinked hard. *Then again, when will Ted ever get a chance to prove himself again? Christ, Ted destroyed every connection and burnt every bridge in Pittsburgh, and his melancholy and angst has only gotten worse.* Marc rubbed his chin. *If I don't offer Ted this rare opportunity now, he'll surely spiral further into a psychosis that will either land him in an asylum, like his namesake, or get him deeper into trouble. Or, God forbid, he'll even end up dead!*

Intuitively, Marc blurted, "*Yes!* Ted is the best horseman in all of Pittsburgh. And, as I said, for a time he *was* Cody's star attraction. So, he—" Marc's conscience suddenly rattled his head, as he paused, and then somberly confessed, "actually, I must warn you, Teddy. My brother has a bit of a drinking problem. So, I will not lie to you, or put your great name in jeopardy."

Marc awaited a response, but heard nothing. He pressed his ear to the receiver, but still only heard the slight buzz of the electrical telephone line. His forehead began to moisten with sweat as he thought: *What the hell am I doing? I should have declined and never said a word about any of this.*

Suddenly, Roosevelt's voice responded, "That's okay, Marc. I still want him."

Marc's face twitched uncomfortably. "Teddy, are you sure?"

"Yes, as long as you think you can handle the situation. I'll be aiding in the task of commanding over 1,000 men, so I'm confident you can handle one fellow, who happens to be your brother. Fair enough?"

Marc smiled. "Fair enough, sir...or, what rank are you, Teddy?"

TR laughed. "They made me a lieutenant-colonel. Actually I conceded command of the regiment to Colonel

Leonard Wood, for he has far more military experience. But as second in command, this should be a gallant mission and a splendid opportunity, Marc. And being that I am the man who first placed a big game rifle in your hands, I feel it is my duty to call you to arms for the good of our nation. So, I would be delighted to have you and your brother gallop into history by my side."

Marc swallowed hard as he said loudly and proudly, "On behalf of my brother and myself, we would be honored, Lieutenant-Colonel!"

"Very well," TR said. "We only have a month to train, since we plan on sailing off the coast of Florida at the end of May. It's imperative that we beat the malaria season down there; it gets mighty ugly you know. And I'll be damned if I die in the swamps of Florida or the jungles of Cuba from a stupid disease! So, hop on the first train you can catch and head down to our training camp in San Antonio, Texas. I'll have someone meet you."

"Sure thing," Marc said, "I know of a train that can get us there in three days. I'll see you then!"

As Marc hung up the telephone, he gazed at Marianne. She had been sitting and listening to his conversation with dread and humiliation. "So, just like that, you and your brother are running off to war?" she huffed.

"Marianne, when a good friend, who happens to have been assistant secretary of the navy, and is now a lieutenant-colonel, asks you to join him in battle, that is not something a man can turn down. Besides, I really think this may be good for Ted."

"Oh, sure! I imagine war will solve all of Ted's problems, once and for all—once he is carted home in a box, that is. And I pray to God you don't come home the same way. How could you, without even consulting me? Or Ted for that matter?"

"Marianne, I have a good feeling about this."

"Sure, just like the good feeling you had after coming home from the Columbian Exposition," Marianne snapped. "Do you remember how that sparkling sign in the sky— which was supposed to firm up your relationship with Morgan at Carnegie Hall and solve all your problems— backfired? It blew up just like the fireworks that night, not to mention how it also fizzled, once again, after you met J.P. at the concert!"

Marc shook his head heatedly. "I will not cave in after a few setbacks, Marianne! Those traits are for quitters, and I will *not* take that path, *ever!* My friend and country need me, and despite your fears, I believe this really might be the last chance Ted may ever have of regaining some confidence and dignity. He was always the best horseman in town, and one of Cody's star performers."

Marianne's face mellowed. "Fine, I understand your needs, but I still think this is a drastic mistake to drag Ted along. He hasn't been in any condition to take on a task like this for several years."

Just then Ted walked into the room, his eyes glazed and a glass of Jack Daniel's in his hand. "Drag me along where?" he asked, looking at Marc. Then turning toward Marianne, he added, "And in no condition for what?"

Marianne gazed uncomfortably at the floor as Marc replied, "I have great news, Ted. I think I found a job that you'll excel at."

Ted took a swig of whiskey and offered his rote query, "What is it this time, and how much does it pay?"

Marc rubbed his mustache and smiled. "Well, you'll be riding a horse. And this time you can even shoot people."

Ted's head recoiled. "What are you saying? Do you want me to be an outlaw, like Billy the Kid or Jesse James? Hell, they both ended up *dead!*"

Marc laughed. "No, no! The law will allow you to shoot people on this job. I'm talking about going to war—with me and Theodore Roosevelt, in a cavalry regiment."

Ted shook his head and chuckled. "So, you're asking me to work for nothing?"

"Not exactly," Marc said, "you'll get a nice uniform, firearms, and be fed, but you stand to gain a hell of a lot more than that, Ted. This is a chance to show everyone just how good of a rider you are, and ride into history. And being that you've already shot one man, you even have more practice than I in that endeavor."

Ted laughed. "Yes, but I only wounded the poor devil."

"Well, this time you will not be drunk, Ted," Marc said dead serious. "Roosevelt said your sobriety rests upon my shoulders, so you must throw away the bottle. Because, believe me, if I do find you nipping a drink, I will shoot you! Is that understood?"

Ted rolled his eyes. "Fine," he said as he turned and threw his glass into the fireplace. As the flames flared up, he added, "But I will only go under one condition. I must ride Mazeppa."

Marc frowned. "Ted, we have to be in Texas in three days. Besides, this is not a Wild West show. The federal government will supply us with horses, uniforms and training."

"Forget it," Ted huffed. "Then I'm not going."

"Ted, don't be a petulant little scamp, we don't have time to dawdle over childish matters like this!"

"Listen, Marc, I'm not trying to be a whining, little baby. Mazeppa and I are like those two coupling dragonflies I see flying around the yard."

Marc and Marianne glanced at each other and smiled, knowing Ted was going to give them one of his colorful analogies as Ted continued, "We pivot and turn just like those horny devils—together, *in unison*. So, you see, I must have Mazeppa, we're a team."

Marianne looked up at Ted, affectionately; knowing his love for the stallion had been a saving grace in his troubled life. "But, Ted, there is no way you can ride Mazeppa all the way down to Texas in three days."

Marc's eyebrows rose. "Ah! Not to worry. I can have Mazeppa put on a freight car. Besides, there's no need to tire him out unnecessarily." Turning toward Ted, he added, "So, pack your things, we need to catch a train!"

Ted cracked a smile and darted with a stagger to his room. Marianne walked over and embraced Marc. Her hug was exceptionally firm, and Marc eased her back slightly to see her face. Her eyes were glazed over with a layer of tears, yet there appeared to be something beyond not wanting to part.

"What is it?" Marc asked.

Marianne blinked hard and suppressed the tears. "N-nothing," she stammered. "I just can't b-bear the thought of you going to war. What if you…you—"

"Don't think like that," Marc said. He crouched lower to stare straight into her misty eyes. "Are you sure that's all it is?"

Marianne hesitated, then answered, "Yes, that's all. Isn't that enough?"

"Yes, it sure is. But, please, have no fear. I have every intention of coming back. I feel good about this, I really do. So, please, relax. I love you, you silly worry wart!" Eliciting a smile, Marc kissed her, and she responded in kind. After a long, emotional embrace, they parted.

Joining his brother, the two warriors gathered their gear and headed to the train depot.

Three days later, Marc and Ted arrived in Texas, as scheduled, and were escorted to the training camp. Roosevelt outfitted his volunteer regiment with blue flannel shirts, brown trousers and dashing slouch hats. He also made sure his motley team of volunteers had better arms, supplying them with government-issued, Krag-Jorgensen repeating bolt-action carbines, along with Colt .45 pistols, and Bowie knives for good measure.

The call for the First Volunteer Cavalry had brought together an odd mixture of primarily southwestern cowboys, along with a few reservation Indians, and a handful of northeastern collegiate athletes who sought adventure. TR especially liked the southwesterners, who he said were "tall and sinewy, with resolute, weather-beaten faces, and eyes that looked a man straight in the face without flinching."

Roosevelt had been eager to meet Marc's brother, and as he handed Ted his Norwegian-made Krag-Jorgensen rifle, he said, "Here's your lifesaver, Ted. We'll be doing drills demonstrating how Colonel Wood intends you boys to use them while on horseback."

Ted excitedly grabbed the carbine, and cocked the bolt, while TR added, "So, your brother had told me that you were quite a rider in Buffalo Bill's shows."

Ted's enthusiasm fizzled as his shoulders sank. "Well, I reckon that was in my heyday."

Roosevelt laughed. "*Heyday!?* My God, son, your brother tells me that you are only thirty-one. I'm nearly forty, for Christ's sake, and I would never use such a prehistoric word as heyday, at least not for another thirty years or so."

Ted cracked a smile. "Well, I suppose you're right, sir, cause I can still ride circles around anybody I know."

"Now that's more like it, Ted!"

Encouraged by Roosevelt's words, Ted now felt more relaxed and self-confident. "Actually, those days with Cody were the best of times. I put on one hell of a show with my fellow Rough Riders."

Roosevelt's eyebrows lifted. *"Rough Riders!?* Yes, of course!"

"Of course, what?" Ted inquired, confused.

"Well, Ted. I've been looking for a catchy name for my regiment that would make it stand out from the rest of the pack. And Rough Riders is absolutely perfect!"

Ted smiled. "Well, I must agree. It certainly is more appropriate for this fighting regiment than Cody's harmless variety show."

"Indeed it is," TR said as he slapped Ted on the back. "Well, I'm glad to have you aboard, Ted." Roosevelt was about to leave, when he added, "But take it easy on the sauce!"

Ted's sanguine smile vanished as he mumbled with embarrassment, "I will, sir."

"Ah, listen, Ted, don't worry yourself silly," TR said, "no one else needs to know. Besides, always remember that our great General Grant had a liking for the bottle, too. The key is not to make it your master. Control *it* like you do your horse. Grab your bottle and your life by the reins, Ted, and gallop into the future, a future where *you* decide where *you* want to go!"

Ted's chest expanded, and his head, once again, rose with confidence. "I will! Thank you, sir!"

The next four weeks were spent doing various drills, tactical maneuvers and studying cavalry strategies on downtime. Ted found it hard to keep from having a drink, but a few in the ragtag regiment appeared no better as some snuck out at night to local saloons and raised hell. However, Marc kept a tight rein on his brother, and Ted actually enjoyed learning how to shoot a carbine while riding horseback. He took to practicing with a renewed vigor that he hadn't experienced since the old days, when he rode Mazeppa day and night, practicing for Buffalo Bill's show.

The training session breezed by, and the day finally arrived to be transported. Boarding a long line of passenger and freight trains, the Rough Riders traveled to Tampa, Florida and prepared for their departure to Cuba. However, due to some ham-fisted logistical maneuvers by Major General Shafter, not only were they delayed in Florida for a week, but once they did ship out, only eight of the 12 companies set sail. Worse yet, most of the horses and some of the food supplies were left behind. Fortunately for Ted, Mazeppa was allowed to make the voyage, largely due to Marc's insistence and Roosevelt's clout.

As they sailed across the Gulf, Roosevelt vented his utter dissatisfaction with Shafter's botch job, which was compounded by another deadly issue. A fair number of his men had already become sick or had died from malaria or yellow fever. And with summer approaching, their window of opportunity was closing fast. Roosevelt was now saddled with trained cavalrymen, most now without horses, who had no training for traveling on foot, especially in hot, humid weather or in dense bug-infested jungles. The start to their glorious invasion was now looking painfully bleak. However, TR was consoled by the fact that his men had trained hard enough to operate as a team, and he was additionally pleased to see that Lieutenant John Parker had brought along four Gatling guns.

As TR stood on the bow of his ship (accompanied by a small armada of 48 other vessels carrying regulars), he was well aware that this mission was America's first blazing step toward an imperial worldwide movement. It would be the make or break event to prove America's mettle on the world stage, and set the stage for a more aggressive American presence in world affairs. Bolstering that mighty sense of American pride was the blaring marine band behind him playing the *Star Spangled Banner*.

As the ship sliced through the Gulf, TR breathed in deep, putting one arm around Marc and the other around Ted. "I know a regiment cannot be made in a week, or in our case a month, but these men are in it because they want to be in it. And that, my friends, gives us a respectable edge."

Marc and Ted nodded as they turned and gazed confidently at the mighty U.S. fleet that was steaming its way into history.

Their landing on Cuba, however, soon proved to be less than perfect. Despite the earlier bombardment by U.S. warships, which left the beach undefended, the soldiers and remaining horses were forced to jump off their vessels and swim ashore, as the large ships could not get close enough to the beach. Taking to the rolling seas, several men and horses drowned in the confusion. Nevertheless, the volunteer regiments and regulars finally managed to make landfall.

No sooner did they land, than the order came to attack and seize the key city of Santiago. To do so, however, they would need to march 15 miles inland and then scale the surrounding hills, called San Juan Heights. Once captured, they expected a quick and decisive victory.

As they marched into the dense jungle, the 15-mile trek became a sweltering nightmare, especially for the volunteer cowboys, whom, without their horses, were like grounded flies that just had their wings pulled off. Traveling by foot under a scorching sun, and breathing thick, humid air was grueling enough, but their equipment added to their malady. With each man hauling a heavy carbine, 100 rounds of ammunition, a poncho, blanket, tent, canteen and food rations, many began discarding their load, keeping only the bare essentials. They camped for the night, only to be drenched in a heavy downpour, which left many peeved that they had ditched their ponchos.

When the sun rose, they continued their journey, trudging through a stifling pass in a dense valley, eventually arriving at Las Guasimas. The enemy was hunkered down on the ridge, and shots immediately rained down, forcing the Rough Riders to scatter. Compounding being targeted from above was that the Spaniards used German Mausers with smokeless powder. Meanwhile, their Norwegian carbines used black powder, which billowed when ignited, thus precariously revealing their locations. The dense, surrounding jungle only added to the confusion as bullets buzzed through the leaves from unknown directions.

As several Rough Riders entered a thicket on foot, TR gazed back at the remaining pack, which was frozen with indecision. Intent on spurring them into action, he yelled, "Come on boys, let's show these damned Spaniards what Americans are made of!"

TR turned and courageously charged into the thicket on foot as Marc and Ted pulled out their Colts and followed their charismatic leader into the unknown.

Meanwhile, Edward Marshall, a field reporter, pulled out his pen and began jotting down notes, when, suddenly, he heard a thump. An odd sensation tickled his spine. He wobbled and then fell to the ground, as his aide came running to his side. Several yards away, an American soldier mistook Marshall as being the Rough Rider's leader, Colonel Wood, and he ran to inform TR that Wood was dead. Upon receiving the grave news, Roosevelt assumed command and led a vigorous charge. Within two hours, TR and company subdued the enemy and won a small but rousing victory.

Yet as the Rough Riders began to regroup, they were horrified—swarms of vultures had already swooped down and began feeding on their dead comrades. The sight was nauseating—as the winged carnivores often pecked at the eyeballs first, as if a delicacy. Several Rough Riders keeled over and began vomiting, while others stormed after the scavengers and began shooing them away. The filthy birds lifted their bloodstained beaks from their ravaged meals and took to the skies, yet the soldiers were further repulsed by what they saw next. Rings of huge land crabs had also surrounded their fallen cavalrymen, and they, too, were snapping away at the human smorgasbord. The Rough Riders forcefully cleared the area, and then with heavy hearts they buried the dead and solemnly said their prayers.

Moments later, Roosevelt received the shocking news that Colonel Wood had not been killed. What's more, Wood had actually been promoted to general, since the brigade commander had been laid low. Now assuming command of the Rough Riders as a full-fledged colonel, TR was in his glory and itching to push onward to engage the enemy. However, General Shafter shafted TR once again, when his latest order arrived to hold their position.

Six days passed in the hot and bug-infested jungle, and TR now stood over a small fire, irritably stirring a can of baked beans. The sun was just about to set, when, out of the corner of his eye, Roosevelt could see the makeshift crosses that marked the graves of his fallen comrades; they were casting long, eerie shadows over the grassy hilltop.

TR gazed deeply into the fire, and moaned, "I better not have come all this way to be denied my hour of glory!"

Marc was chewing bread, when he responded, "D-don't w…orry…Colonel." Clearing his mouth, he added, "You already proved yourself to be a gutsy leader. That journalist, Mr. Marshall, had some great things to say about you."

Roosevelt's face, already glowing from the fire, lit up even more as he inquired, "Did he really?"

Ted was grooming Mazeppa, and chimed in, "Yeah, he had read his report for several of us to hear, and coming from a slimy journalist, I must say, that's pretty darn good."

TR chuckled. "Indeed it is. I used to get good press in years past. But, my God, how fast these maggots chew up a piece of meat once they know it's prime cut!"

As the huddled soldiers all laughed, Marc pulled out a piece of paper from his backpack. Unraveling it, he said, "I made sure to make a copy of it, so there would be no excuse of it not getting published."

"You are indeed a crafty soul and good friend," TR said. "Would you mind reading it?"

Marc nodded. "Sure. Let's see, he writes: 'Perhaps a dozen of Roosevelt's men had passed into the thicket before he did. Then he stepped across the wire himself, and from that instant became the most magnificent soldier I have ever seen.'"

At that, the campsite of soldiers all cheered as TR waved his hand. "Alright, boys, simmer down! I do most heartily appreciate your enthusiasm, but I find this rather hard to believe, particularly coming from a reporter." Turning back to Marc, he said, "Please continue. There just must be some fiendish shred of criticism or sarcasm."

Marc looked down, once again, as he continued, "'It was as if that barbed wire strand had formed a dividing line in his life, and that when he stepped across it, he left behind in the bridle path all those unadmirable and conspicuous traits which have so often caused him to be justly criticized in civic life, and—'"

"Ah!" TR interjected, "there we go! *Unadmirable* and *justly criticized*. I knew a dagger or two had to be in there somewhere."

As the Rough Riders laughed, Marc shouted, "Hold on! I need to finish that line. It continues: 'and he found on the other side of it, in that Cuban thicket, the coolness and calm judgment and towering heroism which made him perhaps the most admired and best loved of all Americans in Cuba.'"

"I'll second that opinion," Ted said as he continued brushing Mazeppa's shiny brown coat.

The troops all sounded off, echoing similar praise, while a few began opening their recently delivered mail.

TR waved his hands. "Alright, enough! None of us can celebrate until we achieve a real victory. What we faced a week ago was a mere skirmish. Capturing San Juan Hill, on the other hand, would be something we can truly blow our horns about. So, put your mail away and get some shuteye, men. Hopefully the red flag will wave tomorrow, and we can charge up that hill like a herd of wild bulls!"

The troops put away their letters and began to lie down on the gnarly ground—stinking from not showering, and tired of waiting. Meanwhile, Ted gazed over at TR with disappointment clearly etched on his face. "I was hoping to ride into battle, Colonel, but marching on foot through this damned jungle has been an utter nuisance."

"I know, Ted," TR replied, "this godforsaken island is not what any of us expected. I myself was not thrilled about charging through brush on foot last week, but hopefully San Juan Hill will offer both of us the opportunity to ride." TR gazed at Mazeppa. "And you should feel lucky; not many of us managed to maintain our horses on this botched-up mission."

Ted glanced up at Mazeppa. "Yeah, he's a great animal. But I certainly hope we can ride up the hill tomorrow, Colonel, because I just might beat you to the top!"

TR looked at Ted, appreciating his enthusiasm. "Well, if the terrain warrants it, I'll certainly look forward to racing you up that hill, Ted. But, unfortunately, we won't know until we get closer."

As the soldiers lay quiet amid the campfire's glow, Marc stood up, and whispered, "Excuse me, Colonel. But Ted is an excellent rider, in both day and night. So perhaps you should have him ride out on a reconnaissance mission to survey the hill. This way you'll know what to expect."

TR looked at Marc and back at Ted, who was now gazing at him excitedly. "Listen, Ted, night reconnaissance in unfamiliar territory is an extremely dangerous prospect. I don't know if I could allow you to—"

"Please, sir!" Ted interjected, "I know I can do it. You can count on me."

"My brother is right on this account," Marc added, "as I said, I know of no one who can ride like him."

Ted nodded. "I can do it, Colonel. Believe me, I can practically make Mazeppa walk on tiptoes!"

TR chuckled. "I bet you could, if he had them."

Marc giggled and added, "Colonel, we both grew up in the mines, so our night vision is as keen as an owl's."

Ted opened his eyes wide, and chirped comically, "Who? Who? Who or what do you want me to find? And I'll find it, Colonel!"

TR and Marc giggled as TR looked at Ted and shook his head. "I must be crazy, but fine. But I want two other cavalrymen to ride several yards behind you."

As Ted and Marc smiled, TR continued, "Make slow, methodical advances, say 50 yards at a clip, and then return half way back to signal your backup team. At that point, you can move them up to the furthest position you had just surveyed, and begin the process again, each time recording your moves and the surrounding environs. Is that clear?"

"Yes, sir!" Ted replied eagerly.

TR turned, and randomly selected Jameson and Keller, two Southerners who were both still awake, and instructed them of their backup roles. As the three men mounted their steeds, Marc patted Ted on the leg, and gazed up at him. "This is your time, Ted. Make it count!"

"I won't let you down," Ted said. Then gazing at Roosevelt, he added, "Nor our regiment."

The two Southerners rolled their eyes, and with that, the three horsemen took off in the general direction of the hill, having only a vague map to guide them. As they weaved through a series of narrow paths they finally came to an opening. Ted turned, and whispered, "We better ride along the tree line. I'll begin the 50 yard procedure now."

Jameson and Keller looked at each other, and then nodded, while Ted pulled the reins and steered Mazeppa quietly down the line. Counting Mazeppa's paces, Ted reached the approximate point. He turned and looked around, completing a full 360-degree sweep. It was extremely dark, but all appeared clear, and he returned half way and waved for them to advance. As they did, they each took mental notes, and Ted repeated the process again. They carried out this procedure seven times when finally Ted could see San Juan Hill in the shimmering moonlight. Jameson and Keller, however, believed they had gone far enough and wanted to turn back, especially since Jameson had something to get off his chest.

"We've seen enough, Ted!" Jameson balked in a raised whisper, "I've heard a buzzin' ear-full about you. You ain't nothin' but a dumb, drunken Yankee, and I ain't gonna put my life on the line a second more!"

Ted's face turned red as he grit his teeth. "I don't give a skunk's smelly ass what you've heard, Dixie Boy! We haven't spotted a single fortification. We must proceed further to find out where the enemy is situated."

"Well, go on!" Jameson snapped. "You can stumble on ahead by your lonesome. Me and Keller will wait right here."

Ted angrily shook his head, and pulled the reins. As he rode another 50 yards ahead, with a row of thick trees to his left, Mazeppa curiously turned his head. Coming to a stop, Mazeppa smacked his front left hoof on the ground and snorted. Ted knew his trusty stallion had heard something, and he quietly dismounted. Tiptoeing into the brush, Ted slowly pushed his way through, trying to keep the leaves and branches from making noise. Up ahead he spotted an abandoned ranch and sugar mill. He scouted around the area and figured it to be a good campsite for the Rough Riders. Ted walked a good mile or so further when he spotted three campsites near the ridge, lined with tents. Surveying the area, he took mental notes, and began backtracking. Already somewhat familiar with the area, Ted made good time breezing back through the woods. Up ahead he could see the dark shadowy figure of Mazeppa, yet two other large figures now stood next to him. Ted's heart began to race. He quickly stopped and squinted, trying to get a better focus on the faint images. Listening carefully, he could hear Jameson's voice, which was well above a whisper, "Where in hell did that danged Yankee go?"

"Beats me," Keller replied. "But knowing that drunken fool, he probably found himself a bottle of Bodegas Riojanas and is sleeping it off somewhere."

As the two chuckled, Ted could now begin to see his two sarcastic buddies come into view as they sat upon their steeds. Ted sighed, and began walking to meet them when suddenly a blurry figure jumped out of the brush and lunged up at Jameson. Keller spun around, losing control of his horse, as the assailant dragged Jameson to the ground. As the Spaniard raised a dagger to impale his victim, Ted ran up behind him, pulled out his Bowie knife, and rammed it down into his back, near his neck. As the Spaniard yelped with a gurgle, Ted quickly covered his mouth to silence him.

The man struggled and tried to scream, but Ted yanked the sharp, scallop-edged knife out and then thrust it back in again—this time near the center of his back, aiming for his heart. Ted's hand wavered as the blade cut through layers of flesh and muscle, slicing the beating organ in half and promptly terminating its life-giving function. The Spaniard keeled over, while Jameson sat trembling with bulging eyes.

Keller dismounted, and ran to help Jameson up to his feet. "You all right?" he inquired, nervous and shaking.

Jameson nodded mechanically. "Where in hell did that damned Dago come from?"

"Never mind that," Ted said. "Let's get out of here!"

"But what about the body?" Keller asked anxiously.

Ted turned and gazed down at the bloody cadaver. "He was just a lone scout. But I suppose you're right, we can't leave him here. Help me get him onto my horse."

Hoisting the dead body onto Mazeppa's muscular hindquarters, Ted then hopped up into the saddle. Not thrilled with his Southern partners, Ted kicked Mazeppa's flanks and made a dash back toward camp, while they frantically trailed behind. Galloping along the winding path, Ted rode headlong into camp and slid in front of TR's smoldering fire, the bloodied body falling to the ground.

TR, and the now awakened troops, looked on with astonished eyes as Ted hopped off his horse and walked over to his backpack. Ripping it open, he pulled out a bottle of whiskey, popped the top, and took a hefty swig.

Marc stepped over and grabbed the bottle. "What the hell are you doing? I told you about drinking this poison. Didn't I?"

"Shut up, Marc!" Ted snapped. "You're not my father."

Just then Jameson and Keller came scrambling in and slid to a stop. Jameson quickly dismounted, and pleaded, "Ted, I do apologize. I owe you my life!"

Ted's heated eyes only glanced at Jameson, and returned back to Marc. "This guy called me a drunken Yankee. I wonder where he heard that, *Marc?*"

"Hold on," Marc fired back, "don't blame this on me!"

TR stepped over the dead body, stopping in front of Ted. "I'm sure your brother would never utter such a foolish thing, Ted." Turning toward Jameson, he added, "So, tell me, soldier, where in tarnation did you hear this ridiculous slander?"

Jameson looked nervously at TR, and then sheepishly at Keller.

TR turned his stern gaze at Keller. "So, am I to understand that *you* concocted this injurious slur?"

Keller nervously wiped his sweaty forehead. "Sir, it was not m-me, per se. I simply heard it f-from a fellow rider at training camp, back in Texas."

"And whom might this rider be?" TR demanded.

Keller stammered, "It was F-Forbes, sir. But, he died of m-malaria in Florida, so—"

"Never mind," TR huffed as he turned toward Jameson. "You said Ted saved your life. Is that true, son?"

Jameson nodded. "Yes, sir. He killed that Dago with his Bowie, just like a savage Indian; all stealth like." Turning toward Ted, he added, "I really am rightly sorry, Ted."

Ted looked at the ground as TR turned and gazed at the corpse. "It appears you're a bit of a hero, Ted." Looking back up at Ted, he continued, "So, tell me, what happened out there?"

Ted looked up and offered Jameson a conciliatory nod, and then divulged to his commander all he had learned. TR and Marc proudly listened, while Jameson and Keller dug a grave and buried the dead Spaniard.

Taking advantage of Ted's reconnaissance, TR gathered his troops and moved stealthily forward under the darkness of night to the defunct ranch, where his men found some shelter. No sooner did they nestle themselves in on the barren floor, when Marc gazed at Ted and pulled a letter out of his backpack.

Ted squinted to see the object in the dark. "What is it?"

Marc whispered. "It's a letter from Marianne. We didn't get a chance to open our letters before, and I can't wait."

"Well don't just sit there, open it!" Ted said excitedly as he leaned over and lit a small candle.

Eagerly, Marc ripped it open and began to read, while Ted impatiently looked on. Marc's eyes oscillated left and right when suddenly his face lit up with a grin.

"Well, what did she say?" Ted inquired.

"I'm going to be a father!" Marc blurted with glee.

His fellow Rough Riders smiled and quietly offered their congratulations as Marc turned and nodded his thanks.

Looking back at Ted, Marc whispered, "I knew when I left that she was holding back something. The poor dear didn't want to burden me; knowing I'd be out here risking my life, and, well, you know, may not ever get to see it."

Ted smiled, but then scratched his goatee. "I don't get it. So, why did she tell you now?"

"Actually, the thought of me dying is what made her change her mind. She said she couldn't live with herself if I died and never knew."

"Well, that makes sense," Ted said as his face turned sullen. "Actually, this is pretty morbid talk." He then smiled. "But on the bright side, what do you think it will be?"

Marc shrugged his shoulders. "Don't know. But somehow I feel the Wozniak family is due to have a girl."

"I reckon we are," Ted said happily as he stretched out his arms and yawned. "Well, congratulations, Marc—I mean Pa! And gee, I guess that will make me a monkey's uncle!"

Marc laughed at the new Darwinian phrase that was sweeping the nation. "Thanks, and I'm sure you'll make a great uncle, you silly baboon!"

As Ted chuckled, Marc folded the letter and placed it back in his pouch. Ted leaned over and blew out the candle. The room went dark. Only the tossing and turning of the troops could be heard, along with a few snores. As Marc's eyes adjusted to the darkness he noticed a faint beam of moonlight coming through the broken window of the abandoned ranch. He turned and gazed out at the speckled array of stars in the night sky. He counted off the next nine months in his head, figuring that his baby would probably be born under the sign Aquarius. He didn't really believe in astrology, but had to admit that many of the character traits the ancient's predicted for these signs were unnervingly true; it certainly was for his mother (the twin personality Gemini), or Huxley (the deadly stinging Scorpio), and Morgan (the relentless Aries ram). Nevertheless, Marc's mind quickly diverted to the Lord. The miracle of birth was just that, a miracle. And as far as he was concerned, no stars or theory of monkey evolution could explain that. His beliefs had wavered over the years, but oddly enough, like the North Star, he found the true guiding light in his life, and he thanked the Lord for this blessing. But then suddenly his mind was rattled by a horrific thought; what if he died in battle? It could be tomorrow, for all he knew. An unsettling wave rattled his body. Marc closed his eyes tightly, and prayed: *I cannot die. Do you hear me, Lord? I must return home.*

Catching a few hours of shut-eye, the Rough Riders awoke to a warm and humid sunrise, with buzzing insects and the rank smell of mold that covered the abandoned paraphernalia inside the ranch. TR hadn't slept much, making sure his sentries kept a vigilant watch, not to mention his growing impatience to engage battle.

Meanwhile, his men were getting ornery—having jettisoned portions of their rations and cigarettes, which some relied on for the nicotine buzz to calm their nerves. Added to this was the depressing news that they would be taking a respite for several days, until the strategy was nailed down.

A scruffy looking Southerner gazed at TR, and balked, "Damn strategy! I ain't never read about it, but I'm gettin' bloomin' tired of hearin' about it. There is Santiago and the Dagoes, and here we is. And the shortest distance between two points is a straight line; which is somethin' everybody knows, and don't have to have strategy to find out. So, I'm in favor of goin' up there and beatin' the faces off them damn Dagoes, and then let the war correspondents make up their stupid strategy later. As they seem to be the only ones frettin' about it!"

"That is not how a sophisticated operation works, son," TR replied. "But hold on to that grit, boy. You'll get your chance to pummel some Dagoes soon enough. I promise!"

As TR scanned the surrounding area, he realized that they were camped on El Pozo hill. He could see the circle of lofty tree-covered mountains, spotted with palms, which hemmed in the sprawling plain below. Running through that plain was the rather shallow San Juan River.

Unfortunately, the next several days were worse than if they did engage battle, since down time only made the men think even more about death. No one seemed to be more disturbed by the delay than Marc. Each passing day was another day to think *what if I never get to see my child?*

Finally, the order came to move forward and ford the river, and TR excitedly gathered his men into formation. As he rode along the stream, his men jogged behind, with only Ted, Keller and Jameson on horseback.

As they began to ford the river, Marc yelled out, "Commander, look up!"

TR was plodding through the stream on his horse as he turned and gazed up. His eyes bulged and his lips twisted with fury. "Those goddamned idiots!"

Overhead was an American reconnaissance balloon being dragged along by a ground team of regulars. As they tightly held onto the long rope and pulled, the manned balloon was clearly giving away their own positions. In an instant, artillery fire broke out from the adjacent hilltop, called Kettle Hill. As shells and bullets rained down on them, the Rough Riders ran for cover in the high grass that lined the river. Meanwhile, those who were still crossing the river were drilled with lead—sinking in crimson-colored swirls of water, as small air bubbles popped on the surface, releasing their last dying breaths.

As they held their position, TR was fuming and growing even more impatient. "When the hell will General Shafter stop wasting time with aerial reconnaissance and give us the order to charge!?"

Spanish snipers began shooting down, picking off stragglers, when TR turned to his men and yelled, "Spot those vermin and shoot them!"

The minutes rolled slowly by, and Roosevelt's patience further eroded. His eyes oscillated, scanning the bullet-infested terrain, when he spotted a messenger. The soldier ran hunchbacked, holding his hat, and stopped in front of him. "Colonel Roosevelt," he said breathing heavily, "you have been authorized to move forward and support the regulars on those hills just in front of us."

TR was elated; his moment had arrived. He interpreted *support* the regulars as free license to *charge* the enemy, and planned on doing just that. Yet as he advanced into position, he came across the lead regiment of regulars, who were lying down in the grass blocking their way. TR quickly scanned for the commander, but only saw a captain.

Looking back up at the hilltop and seeing the enemy firing down, he knew their only option was to storm the hill.

Taking command, TR barked, "Let's go, men. Ready your weapons, and let's charge the hill!"

The captain of the regulars, who was idly cleaning his rifle, gazed up at Roosevelt, and retorted, "You, sir, are a commander of *volunteers*. I will *not* move my troops!"

TR gazed down from his saddle, clenched his large teeth, and barked, "Then if you don't wish to move forward, you danged poltroon, let my men pass!"

The captain flushed from the insult, while his men grimaced at his impotence. Meanwhile, a group of Negro American soldiers, who had been separated from their unit, came running, eyes wide, and ducking from enemy fire.

TR turned immediately, and yelled out to Marc, "You are now a lieutenant. I will lead the charge up this hill, while you take the left flank and order the others to charge up the right." Turning to his regiment, he yelled, "Fall in!"

As the troops huddled together, TR growled, "You boys had better not abandon me on that hill!" Then gazing over at the nervous Negros, he barked, "And that goes for you men, too! If I see any of you run, I promise, I *will* shoot you!"

As the Negro soldiers looked nervously at each other and back up at TR, a Rough Rider yelled, "And Colonel Roosevelt always keeps his promise!"

With that, the Rough Riders pushed their way through the regulars and began to run up the hill. As they did, the regulars gazed at their hapless captain and were shamed into following. As the randomly united unit charged up the hill, shells from above continued to rain down. Trees were blasted to pieces and dirt blew skyward as some men were pelted with bullets, while others were shredded by sharp bits of brass. Evidently, the Spaniards were using German-made shells that were coated with the shiny metal. As the projectiles buzzed through the air their brass coatings split open, flying off into a deadly spray of razor-sharp shards that sliced flesh and bone as easily as a tiger's claw. That these splitting shells also made a peculiar whirring sound added to the uneasiness of the advancing American troops, particularly when they saw one small speck hit TR in the arm.

As men began to scatter, TR turned and yelled, "By God, it's only a flesh wound. Get back in formation! We *will* take this hill. But you men must stay together and support each other!"

One teenager squealed as he watched his buddy's face explode wide open by a bullet, his limp body collapsing. In horror, he turned and ran for cover in the nearby brush.

TR's face twisted as he saw others begin to flee towards the thicket. "Are you men afraid to stand up when I am on horseback?"

Roosevelt's words were painfully true; mounted atop his high horse, he was an easy target, yet he boldly turned his steed and began charging up the hill. As he galloped up the rocky slope, he pulled out his Colt .45 and popped a Spaniard, who stumbled to the ground. Turning back to his men, he yelled, "You see, that damned Dago fell just like a paper target. Now, come on, Rough Riders…CHARGE!"

As TR gallantly charged up the hill, his men were emboldened by their brave charismatic leader. Abandoning their cover, they charged into the thick of battle, running up behind TR to lend their support and lives to the grand pursuit. As Marc directed the two teams and dodged bullets, Ted came riding up alongside him. "Marc, I'll stay by your side. From my vantage point I can spot the enemy hiding in the grass, and alert you."

"No," Marc shouted as his eyes scanned the hilltop. "Your speed will help to startle the enemy, just like the Colonel is doing. *Charge the hill!*"

Ted leaned forward and yelled toward Mazeppa's ear, "Okay, come on, Zeppy. It's time to shine! Let's go!" With that, Ted prodded Mazeppa, who reared up, and then bolted swiftly up the hill.

Meanwhile, Keller and Jameson were nervously hanging back along the rear line. Evidently, being easy targets was not their cup of tea.

Marc turned, and yelled, "Come on you yellow-bellies! Jameson, take the left flank, and, Keller, the right."

No sooner did Marc finish that sentence than a bullet tear through the upper left side of his torso, twisting his body sideways. Marc dropped his carbine and grabbed his throbbing shoulder, which now went numb.

As Jameson and Keller both blanched, Marc yelled, "Never mind me. Go on! Do as I ordered. *Charge!*"

Gazing at each other with wide, jittery eyes, the two cavalrymen dithered as another round of bullets rained down. Keller received one right to his chest, knocking him off his horse. As the horse ran away from the din of shells and gunfire, Jameson panicked and hopped off his horse. Using the large steed for cover, he crept toward Keller, who was now on his back, moaning.

Once again, Marc yelled out, "Jameson, if you do not mount your horse right now, you *will* be court-martialed!"

As Keller lay dying right before his eyes, with a gapping hole in his chest, Jameson didn't give a mule's ass about any court-martial. He'd rather be standing alive before a military court than dead like his buddy, who just coughed his last breath. With tears streaming down his cheeks, Jameson mounted his horse and made for a speedy retreat.

Marc pulled out his Colt and aimed it at the back of Jameson's receding head. His trigger finger shook nervously, and after a stressful three long seconds, it finally relaxed—the pistol lowering to his side. Marc was troubled by a haunting thought: what if Jameson is also going to be a father?

As Jameson disappeared into the surrounding jungle, Marc shook his head free of the thought, and gazed down at his wound. Pulling off his handkerchief, Marc stuffed the hole, and buttoned his shirt up tight. He grabbed his Colt, and resumed his charge, trying to catch up to the regiment. Yet just as he rejoined the ranks, a terrifying clanking sound startled them. The ominous sound now echoed throughout the entire valley, sending a frightful chill down their spines. Turning around, Marc saw Lieutenant John Parker firing off his four Gatling guns, mowing down the Spanish troops on the peak like clay ducks. He yelled out, "It's the Gatlings, men. *Our Gatlings!* Victory is ours for the taking. *Let's go!"*

Relieved, and now emboldened, the Rough Riders turned and resumed their charge up the hill.

Meanwhile, Ted had already stormed one bunker, trampling over three men as Mazeppa's hooves crushed their skulls and bones, while he used his Colt to start popping off the rest. With fear in the enemies' eyes, they began to run, as Ted charged after them. Running out of bullets, Ted slid the Colt in his holster and pulled out his carbine. As Mazeppa ran like the wind, Ted's hat blew off, yet he kept his sights on his running targets. Pulling the trigger, and rapidly cocking the bolt after each shot, Ted nailed six of the seven, the last fleeing into the woods.

As Ted rode toward the center of the advance he saw Roosevelt charging valiantly toward the summit, while 30 foot soldiers followed. Ted hungrily looked back at the woods. He was still peeved he didn't get that last Spaniard, and his eyes rapidly began to search in-between each tree trunk. Yet he saw nothing. Humiliated, Ted rolled his eyes, which inadvertently scanned the treetops. To his surprise, he spotted the Spaniard, perched on a tree branch, taking aim.

Ted's eyes followed the sniper's line of sight, landing on the target. It was TR! Ted immediately placed the sniper in his sights and pulled the trigger. He missed! Anxiously, Ted raised his head from the carbine to see if the Spaniard heard his shot, but the din of battle had conveniently muffled it. Once again, Ted lowered his head and ran his eye down the barrel. Raising the carbine a bit higher, he held his breath, and pulled the trigger. To his delight, he saw the Spaniard fall from the tree, landing on his head as he hit the ground.

Turning around, Ted saw his brother coming up from behind, holding his shoulder as he fired his Colt pistol. Not only had Marc witnessed Ted's amazing charge, and the shot that just saved TR's life, but so, too, had several others, who all cheered Ted's laudable bravery and marksmanship.

Ted rode over to join the horseless Rough Riders, and, in a state of elation, they charged up the hill to meet up with their fearless leader. Roosevelt had by now dismounted his horse and hopped over a wire fence in order to scale the peak of Kettle Hill.

Looking down at his approaching band of brothers, TR cheered, "We did it boys! We did it!"

As the Rough Riders began to reach the summit at different intervals, TR looked eagerly over at the adjacent peak of San Juan Hill. He could see the Spanish fortification across the way that was still raining down deadly gunfire at the regulars below. Pulling out his Colt, TR began to run, calling for his men to follow. But with the din of exploding shells and cannon fire, only a handful heard the command. After running 100 yards, TR realized, to his embarrassment, that his order was not heard. He ran back and started the charge once again, this time followed by his gutsy and loyal troops. As they approached San Juan Hill, many of the Spaniards had already abandoned their posts, having seen the horrifying destruction caused by the advancing Rough

Riders and the regulars, not to mention the merciless, mechanical annihilation caused by the American's sinister Gatlings.

TR and his Rough Riders finished off the remaining stragglers, and cheered. Gathering his regiment together, TR led them in a rousing rendition of the *Star Spangled Banner*.

As the sun began to touch the treetops on the distance horizon, Roosevelt addressed his men, "Today is a pivotal moment in history, boys, and you all are a part of it. It marks the beginning of not only our war with Spain, but also the beginning of the new role that America will mightily seize on the world stage. Know this, a masterful race is a fighting race. And we have just proven to be both!"

Cheers burst out as the men fired their weapons into the twilight sky.

It was a glorious day for Theodore Roosevelt, his valiant Rough Riders, and America. The war with Spain was certainly not over, but the start was so impressive and overwhelming, that every Spaniard that day retreated swallowing a lump of dread, while every American relished the taste of victory.

As the Rough Riders celebrated, Marc looked at his brother with a great sense of pride. Ted had proven himself a man of great ability and courage, and the medal that Roosevelt said Ted would receive only added to the joyous moment. Marc smiled and shook his head as he reflected on the young boy who was frail in health and often scared underneath his tough skin, who in recent years had fallen into a drunken slump. But here it was, Ted had become a war hero. A tear welled in Marc's eye as he watched his brother being congratulated with slaps on the back and water from canteens being spilt on his head. His decision to help his troubled brother had paid off. And better yet, he and his brother survived. He would be going home to soon be a father and Ted an uncle. Life was simply grand!

⁘

Marc and Ted arrived in Pittsburgh by rail, and were greeted by an enthusiastic wave of applause and congratulatory cheers at the train station. Marc had telegraphed ahead of time to make sure the news of Ted's heroism hit the papers, and even Ted's past disgruntled employers came to cheer their town's hero.

Rusty eagerly unloaded Mazeppa from the freight car and proudly walked him over to his old friends. As Ted hopped up into the saddle, Rusty noticed Marc's bandaged shoulder. Marc reassured him that it was nothing serious, but Mulvaney helped the wounded veteran get on the horse anyhow. With big grins, Ted and Marc rode through the city streets as people lined the curbs, throwing confetti and cheering. As they hit dirt, Ted broke Mazeppa into a gallop and charged impatiently homeward.

As they rode up the long, gravel driveway, Remus ran toward them, while Marianne and Stan waited eagerly on the front porch. The three brothers hugged as Marc then walked up the front steps and embraced Marianne. While he inquired about the pregnancy, she asked about his wound.

Meanwhile, they all found Ted's reversal of spirit miraculous. His stride was erect and confident, while even his old corny humor returned. Ted's high spirits rose even higher when two weeks later the family visited Washington D.C. to watch him receive his two medals, which were pinned on his proud chest by TR himself. A tear welled in Marc's eye; his brother now had a triumph worthy of being lauded just like Tasso. Marc knew their mother and father were gazing proudly down on this moment, and he sighed. All was good—very good, as he uttered, "Thank you, Lord!"

The next nine months seemed to breeze by, as the Wozniak household bonded ever closer. Ted and Stan both nurtured Remus, who was now 14 and currently working at Pendleton Iron Works, under Marc's strict advice. Not only didn't Marc like Remus being around his sleazy, no-good father, but Marc was still struggling and suffering himself with Huxley. The day-to-day grind of working side-by-side with the lecherous beast that raped his mother was starting to become a burden he was less willing to tolerate, especially now that Marianne gave birth to a beautiful little girl that they named Sophia.

Additionally, Ted and Stan also had moments of venting their anger, as one day Ted chided Marc, "When the hell are you going to destroy that mangy dog?"

Although Marc managed to pacify them, saying that it would be soon, soon never seemed to come. But Marc reminded himself to have patience, and he kept his sanity by mentally recanting *every dog has his day*. Regardless of his mental anguish, Marc did a fine job of making life very comfortable for his family as he had the Wozniak estate totally renovated. Having called in Huxley's old architect, Charles McKim, who was now wildly famous with his two partners as McKim, Mead & White, Marc had them redesign the entire house, adding on two huge extensions, along with an elaborate garden with a swimming pool and fountains. And with the economy booming once again, the ugly Huxley virus that plagued all their minds was at least somewhat concealed by a luxurious façade.

Pride & Pain at the
Pan-American
Exposition

September 6, 1901

The victorious conclusion of the Spanish-American War three years earlier had jettisoned the once internally preoccupied nation into a world power. Sitting at the helm during this grand transformation, was President William McKinley. He had won a second term last November, and his new vice president was the war hero who most captured the hearts and minds of Americans—Theodore Roosevelt.

However, the two heads of state had become well aware of the risks that came with their nation's rise to power. After defeating Spain at Manila Bay in the Philippines, Admiral Dewey had expressed his concerns about America's new global position. While putting down the revolt of the Filipinos, Germany and Japan had both tried to meddle in U.S. affairs, thus giving the admiral strong indications that America could soon be at war with either belligerent nation in the near future. Even before the war, Germany had attempted to establish coal stations in Haiti and had also offered to purchase Cuba from Spain. Meanwhile, Japan had made direct attempts to seize Hawaii for its strategic location.

Nevertheless, Americans, unaware of such subtle intrigues, were bloated with pride and bursting with bravado. And, now, recognizing the importance of foreign relations, especially with their Northern and Southern American neighbors, the Pan-American Exposition had been built to laud new innovations and hopefully galvanize commercial interaction in the Western hemisphere.

Constructed in Buffalo, New York, at the sizable cost of seven million dollars, the 350 acres of fairgrounds were meticulously landscaped and decorated with a dazzling array of architectural buildings. However, unlike its Columbian predecessor, with its city of white buildings, the Pan-American Exposition features a vibrant array of multicolored structures. As such, it was dubbed "Rainbow City." The centerpiece of this glittering metropolis being the Electric Tower building, which stands almost 400 feet tall and is painted deep green, with details in cream, white, blue and gold.

Marc was certainly eager to see these architectural wonders, however, what interested him most were two things: First was to meet the electrical wizard Nikola Tesla, whom Marc had earlier corresponded with regarding revamping Edison's DC system at Huxley Coal with Tesla's superior AC system. Second was to visit the Mines Building at the Exposition to see the latest advances concerning metallurgy and mining ore.

Marc arrived in Buffalo late last night, on September 5th, and had marveled over Tesla's dazzling electrical extravaganza, for Nikola had once again been awarded the task of lighting an Exposition, as he had the Columbian. Every building was outlined with strings of light bulbs that illuminated the entire pseudo city, which, like its predecessor, had been fabricated out of wood and plaster. The magical wonderland was not only a feast for the eyes, but, more importantly, it personified and electrified the American spirit.

Marc didn't get a chance to meet Tesla last night, and now, as the morning sunlight illuminated the colorful city with its full spectrum of hues, he eagerly looked forward to spending some time with the electrical super-genius. As he impatiently weaved through a leisurely crowd of men sporting straw boaters and women in long dresses with tight corsets, a young boy bumped into him. The lad was decked out in knickerbockers and wearing a plaid, newsboy cap, tilted to one side.

"Excuse me, sir," the boy said as he ran off.

Meanwhile, the boy's little brother (outfitted in a mini sailor suit) chased him in a game of tag as he chewed a new, tasty treat called a Tootsie-Roll. Marc smiled as the boys sped away, running off the paved path onto the dewy lawn. Marc paused for a moment, recalling how different his games of tag were when he was younger. Boys in his neighborhood could only play tag at work, either in the dark, filthy mines or in the breaker house, where so many of them fell to their deaths. He was happy to see that some children no longer had to labor like he and so many others had, for the country was indeed changing as leisure and games were becoming more prevalent. From the founding of Parker Brothers with their board games 13 years ago to George Tilyou creating the first amusement park at Coney Island four years ago, America was truly looking more and more like a wonderland. However, Marc was painfully aware that the battle to protect children with fair and sensible labor laws was still far from won, yet he at least found comfort in knowing that he was actively funding lobbyists to continue the cause.

Marc shook his head and resumed his journey; passing a variety of buildings, each dedicated to a specific field, from Agriculture to the Arts and Sciences. Just up ahead, Marc spotted Nikola Tesla, who aptly stood in front of the Electricity Building.

Tesla is tall, thin, and impeccably dressed, with short black hair and clean-shaven, save for his mustache. In fact, Tesla looks more like a debonair aristocrat than a mad scientist, which some reporters claimed after visiting his laboratory. Tesla's lab was filled with the wildest gadgets and futuristic electrical devices, which some feared were the alchemic workings of the devil. Yet, Tesla is simply a misunderstood genius and a bit of an obsessive-compulsive fanatic.

Marc reached out to shake his hand as Tesla tentatively extended his own.

As the two shook hands, Marc said, "It's an honor to meet you, Mr. Tesla. I know you're a very busy man, so I appreciate your time."

Tesla smiled as he placed his hand behind his back. "Yes, as you can see, Mr. Wozniak, electrifying an exposition of such a magnitude was no small task. However, that Mr. Westinghouse and myself were the first ever to electrify a world's fair, some eight years ago, did make this endeavor much easier."

"I imagine so," Marc replied, "I had gone to the Columbian Exposition. It, too, was magnificent."

"Thank you," Tesla said. "Come, allow me to show you the marvelous apparatus inside this building."

As they began walking toward the entrance of the Electricity Building, Tesla discreetly washed his soiled hand with a handkerchief and tossed the germ-infested cloth into the trash bin. Entering the great hall, Tesla pointed proudly to a massive, metal machine, which was buzzing and vibrating the floorboards. "This transformer generates a whopping 5,000 horsepower!" he said, "and is converting high amperage electricity (which happens to be sent all the way from our power plant at Niagara Falls) down to a low, utilitarian amperage, which is extremely suitable and safe."

Marc looked at the humming monstrosity with wonder. "So, is this powering all the lights here?"

"It sure is," Tesla said. "And I foresee the day when my alternating current will completely lay waste Edison's inferior direct current."

"Yes, I've read about your 'War of the Currents' with Mr. Edison. It has been highly publicized."

"Well, I had worked for Thomas at one time, I'll have you know, but just had to leave. Mr. Edison certainly has talent, Mr. Wozniak, but he is an insufferably untidy man." Tesla pulled and straightened his sleeves to exact lengths as he continued, "But, most importantly, Mr. Edison is a shrewd businessman, and sometimes business can, unfortunately, trump, or rather stump, progress. Meanwhile, I...well, I am an inventor, Mr. Wozniak, pure and simple. For me, science comes first. But that our country's most powerful businessman, J.P. Morgan, funded Edison to electrify cities with his inferior DC system has only caused more problems, by wasting precious time, labor and money. Those vast networks all need to be rewired for AC, which I had tried to explain to him years ago. Yet due to business reasons, they refused to cooperate."

Marc smirked. "Well, I'm very acquainted with J.P. Morgan's power management skills. Not only does he own a large share of Huxley Coal, but he also bought Carnegie Steel, and now owns a third of all our railroads. So, I imagine you cannot fully blame Edison, for he is merely one of Morgan's many puppets."

"I suppose so," Tesla said as he shook his head, disappointed. "In fact, I am a bit surprised that Morgan has recently funded my radio transmitter station in Shoreham, Long Island. I believe radio waves are the future, Mr. Wozniak. I foresee not only being able to transmit the voice, but also visual displays, all without wires. Radio transmissions will eventually make wires obsolete."

Marc laughed. "No offense, Mr. Tesla, but that sounds preposterous. We have only just begun to develop wired electricity. How can you make such an outlandish claim?"

"Marc—may I call you Marc?" As Marc nodded, Tesla continued, "Well, Marc, men of vision can see things most cannot. Just as Jules Verne envisioned a metal vessel that could sail completely submerged underwater thirty years ago, which President McKinley has recently made a reality by ordering five submarines, I foresee a day when radio waves will reign supreme. Once my tower is completed, the world will be like one huge brain, all interconnected. People from all over the world will be able to communicate with one another as quickly as electricity flows through a wire."

Marc gazed at Tesla pensively. "Well, I still think this sounds too much like a fantasy tale, but if J.P. Morgan invested in it, I'm sure there must be at least a kernel of validity to it."

"Yes, but as I said, Marc, Mr. Morgan is a businessman. He does not take sides. In fact, he sometimes pits one side against another, and then hovers like a vulture to consume the loser. Unfortunately, J.P. only sees numbers, or more plainly—dollars and cents. And I know he, Edison, Carnegie and others have already financed this Italian fellow named

Marconi. So, if Marconi proves to be a businessman, like Edison, I fear he, too, may sail into history as the man who invented wireless radio transmissions."

"Capitalism," Marc said, "it has its good points and bad points, does it not?"

"Indeed," Tesla said, "that's why this country has squabbling factions of socialists, communists and anarchists, each clamoring for a more fair system."

Marc, however, was still intrigued by Tesla's futuristic conversation as he said, "But if I may, Mr. Tesla, you had mentioned Jules Verne's *Nautilus*, and that reminds me; I heard that at the time of the sinking of the *USS Maine* you held a demonstration at Madison Square Garden. I believe you premiered what the papers called a radio controlled toy boat." Marc rubbed his chin. "I don't mean to be rude, but I, along with everyone else I know, found such a device to be impossible. So is there some sort of trickery to what you do, you know, like this magician fellow, Harry Houdini?"

Tesla chuckled. "No, Marc. I assure you. Anything I present to the public, universities, or to investors is not trickery. And, yes, I did craft a three-foot long model boat that I controlled by wireless transmissions. It was the first teleautomation in the world, for not only was it controlled by wireless communications, but the mechanisms inside that steered the vessel were the first robotics demonstration of its kind."

Marc's eyes widened. "So, how is it that the navy didn't fund you to develop it further?"

A pained look washed over Tesla's face. "Ah! This is precisely what I mean, Marc. The common businessman or government official often times has little to no vision. If they cannot see past the rudimentary model, or see an immediate payback, they lose interest and invest their money elsewhere. And in this case, the war department feared that the frequency to control the ship could have easily been deciphered and then used by enemy saboteurs to destroy it, as well as a host of other silly concerns, which could have been easily remedied if properly funded." Tesla heatedly shook his head. "But it is exactly these people who control the purse strings that repulse me, Marc. They lack vision! And the world suffers because of it. We have a capitalistic system where the top handful of wealthy people controls far too much. And although they might be adept at managing money—which the lion's share of those profits always seem to go into their own pockets—they are not always qualified to manage grand, farsighted decisions, such as this."

As people walked past, looking at the displays of various electrical components and gadgets nearby, Tesla took several steps away, while Marc followed.

Tesla lowered his voice. "As I said, some twenty years ago, Morgan had funded Edison to install a DC electric system all over New York City, just because he didn't own the rights to my AC system. But years later, after realizing that their DC system was flawed and dangerous, they had no alternative but to get off their high horse and renegotiate, because the city was literally burning with electrical fires."

Marc looked at Tesla, perplexed. "Why was that?"

"Well, Marc, the DC system works fine with light bulbs that all require the same voltage to operate. But with the advent of modern appliances, such as electric fans, for example, a variable current is required. Otherwise, an appliance that needs only 9 volts yet receives 100 volts will begin to overheat and burn. And that sadly proves my point. Capitalism does not always allow the best product to hit the market, Marc. It is what the few masters at the top decide. And many times those masters are masterfully dense or just plain greedy."

Marc shook his head, irritated, as he huffed, "I reckon it's like what Mark Twain said about robber barons," referring to Twain's famous line: 'Get money. Get it quickly. Get it in abundance. Get it dishonestly, if you can, honestly, if you must.'

"Yes, it is, and Twain happens to be a very good friend of mine. And who could possibly disagree with Samuel's observation?"

"Certainly not I," Marc said, "in fact, he did a splendid job of summing up my senior partner, Archibald Huxley."

Tesla nodded. "It appears so. From what you had told me over the telephone and from what I have read in the papers, Huxley is indeed one of the worst robber barons this nation has produced. But I am glad you managed to persuade him to buy our AC generator and lighting system. It was about time Huxley got into the twentieth century!"

Marc laughed. "Yes, but I needed to drag the darn caveman by his ears!"

Tesla chuckled but then turned serious. "But these men at the top have great power, Marc, power that extends beyond the world of commerce, for they are now buying our heads of state and manipulating policy. President McKinley appears to be a good man, but that Rockefeller and Morgan had both donated $250,000 each, and the meatpacking industry poured another $400,000 into his campaign, only indicates that capitalism is heading towards a plutocracy. So, the America that our founders crafted is undergoing a significant mutation, one that hardly anyone seems to notice."

As Marc stood stunned, mulling over the huge dollar figures that were, in effect, funding propaganda campaigns to sway American voters and essentially buy the presidency, Tesla pulled out his pocket watch and checked the time. "Oh, my! You must excuse me. I have a presentation to give in exactly twelve minutes and thirty-seven seconds!"

"Uh, sure," Marc replied as he awoke from his disturbing foray.

Tesla snapped his pocket watch shut and slipped it neatly back into his vest pocket. Quickly, he began walking toward the exit. "Anyhow, I am most pleased that you purchased my AC system, Mr. Wozniak."

Marc ran to catch up. "So am I. But if we have any problems installing or running your AC system, do you offer a guarantee?"

Tesla looked at Marc and smiled. "Yes, I fully guarantee that it is superior to the old DC system you currently have!"

With that, Tesla said goodbye, and disappeared into the bustling crowd.

Marc shook his head as he turned and began walking toward the Mines Building. As he weaved between meandering men and women, and children dragging their parents by the hand to buy them the new cotton-like candy called Fairy Floss, he came across a billboard. The decorative signage announced that President McKinley would be making a speech. Marc's eyes gazed eagerly down to see where and when, but then they blinked and rolled with disappointed—the speech was yesterday. Marc's shoulders slumped. Despite just learning that McKinley was being financially manipulated, he also knew he was a man of integrity and would not totally sell out. McKinley was actively confronting some of the ills of capitalism by proposing provocative reforms, such as the taxation of corporations and eight-hour workdays for federal employees. More importantly, Marc had been craftily utilizing Roosevelt to prod McKinley to tackle unfair wages, worker safety issues and child labor laws, with some success.

As Marc turned and started to continue his journey, a woman carrying a violin case noticed his discontent, and said, "Excuse me, sir."

Marc stopped and turned. "Yes, Madame. Can I help you?"

"Oh, no," she said, "but I think I might be able to help *you.*"

"Marc squinted. "How so?"

"Well, I don't mean to intrude, but I noticed you had an interest in that sign."

Marc glanced back at the billboard. "Yes, but, unfortunately, I missed the president's speech."

"Yes, you did, but he is returning today to do a meet-and-greet at the Temple of Music building. I believe he will be there at 3:30."

"Thank you," Marc said as he gazed down at her violin case. "So I reckon you'll be playing there?"

"Yes, we'll be performing a nice assortment of works. I hope you'll come and listen to a few."

"Perhaps I will," Marc said. "What's on the program?"

The woman smiled, eager to share the high art she and her fellow musicians strived so hard to perform to perfection. "Well, we have some old imperial music with Beethoven's *Emperor Concerto,* some modern watery impressions with Ravel's *Jeux d'eau,* and a thrilling horse ride with Liszt's *Mazeppa.*"

Marc laughed.

The woman's pleasant smile faded. "What's so funny? These are all magnificent pieces of music, nay, fine works of art."

"I'm sure they are," Marc said, "it's just that my brother named his horse Mazeppa, and he himself was named Tasso by my mother."

The woman smiled, relieved. "Oh, I see your family likes Franz Liszt. That is very interesting and good to hear. For a moment, I thought you were a typical, simpleminded

American who wishes us to perform such banal melodies as *Home on the Range*."

Marc shrugged. "Well, I must admit, I happen to like Brewster Higley's song. You see, only in recent years have I had the opportunity to listen to a professional orchestra. The fact is, not every town has an elegant concert hall, Madame, nor do most common folk have the money, breeding or patience to hear anything more complicated than what's sung on the streets or in taverns. So I think simple folk tunes will carry the day for a very long time."

The woman's face betrayed her disappointment. "Well, that may be true, but it is a sad prospect. Comparing a folk song to a symphony is like comparing that simple signage you just read to a novel by Tolstoy or Dickens. One may convey a simple and direct message, but the other is a profound journey that stimulates the mind, heart and soul. And it is only because of such lofty undertakings that our civilization resides at the summit."

Marc nodded. "I reckon that is very true, Madame. But, unfortunately, I believe that the majority of people simply don't have the mental capacity or desire for such taxing endeavors. Making a living to put food on the table, or enjoying leisure time that offers quick and easy gratification is all they seek." Marc's face grew pensive as he added, "I think that also explains why our capitalistic system came into being and why it has been successful. It is the select few with ambition and ideas that advance civilization for the masses. However, our system does have serious flaws. It suppresses too many people that have the ability to do more. I have long believed that far more than a mere handful has the ability to be innovative and productive, and that needs to change." Recalling Tesla's words, Marc added, "And the same holds true for these tycoons manipulating government with campaign contributions. Changes must be made. That is why I am now more eager than ever to meet President McKinley."

The woman was impressed. "I'm inclined to agree with you, and I'm glad you will have another chance to meet the president. So, perhaps I shall see you there."

"You can count on that, Madame. And I'll even be delighted to listen to all those refined pieces of music you'll be performing."

Marc bowed his head as the woman politely curtsied and went on her way.

The sun was now directly overhead, and the Rainbow City was glowing with color and excitement. The smell of grilled sausages and frankfurters filled the air, while tubas belched alongside drums that beat out a series of tunes by John Philip Sousa. Marc turned and looked at the row of pavilions, all meticulously arranged amid a series of lagoons with bridges, and, once again, he resumed his journey. Curiously, he entered the Mines Building, and spent several hours speaking with presenters about new equipment and engaging engineers in technical discussions about their latest findings. Afterwards, he took a long stroll to explore the fairgrounds, visiting other pavilions and finally stopping to eat lunch. Checking the time, he saw that it was 3:40. Swallowing his frankfurter and wiping the mustard off his lips, Marc headed for the Temple of Music.

As he approached the edifice, Marc looked up at what many believed to be the most beautiful pavilion at the Expo. It was modeled after the Roman Pantheon, yet was painted a stunning pale yellow with a pale blue dome. It was also ornately accented with Italian Baroque and French Rocco trimmings that were meticulously painted in gold and red. Just as beautiful was the spacious interior. As Marc entered the large octagonal auditorium, his eyes scanned the eight huge arches around the perimeter that housed eight large alcoves.

Most were filled with neatly arranged chairs, yet one nook contained the largest organ ever built in America. Sitting at the massive keyboard was an organist, who filled the hall with the soft strains of Schumann's *Träumerei*.

The Temple was beginning to fill up as people eagerly pushed their way through the entrance to get a chance to shake hands with the president. McKinley was standing in the far corner with his secretary, George Cortelyou, who was helping to keep the interactions with the president brief and the line moving along. George had not been thrilled with the president's insistence on coming back to the Exposition to do this meet-and-greet, since he felt his speech yesterday was sufficient. What's more, Cortelyou felt that personal contact like this was an unnecessary security risk. He had advised McKinley to cancel this event twice, but the president replied, "Why should I? No one would wish to hurt me." With that, a small security detail was hovering in the auditorium, yet essentially enjoying the beauty of the Temple's interior and the soft, lulling organ music that now enveloped the chamber.

Marc moved his way up the line and then stopped as it came to a halt. Gazing down the line, he saw President McKinley smiling and speaking to a man and his wife. Their conversation lasted less than two minutes, but the woman in front of Marc turned around, and huffed, "I do hope those rude people will shut their traps and move along! Look how long this line is getting. My Lord, we don't have all day."

Marc replied politely, "Yes, the line *is* growing, Madame, but it is understandable that many people want a moment of his time. In fact, I'd like to speak briefly with him about some serious issues."

The woman rolled her eyes, and huffed, "This is a meet-and-greet, not a meeting!" She turned abruptly and looked forward as she continued mumbling under her breath.

Marc shrugged his shoulders, and turned to see who was behind him. It was a thin man, with short, dark blonde hair, who stood at a peculiar angle with his right hand buried in his jacket pocket. The man's blank face didn't give Marc any indication that this fellow's attitude would be any different than the grouch in front of him, but he offered up conversation just the same. "Hello. How do you do, sir?"

The man's eyes seemed to wander elsewhere as he hesitated, and then uttered, "Hello," in his Polish accent. His eyes uncomfortably darted to the floor.

"Ah, you must be Polish," Marc said with a smile.

The man's eyes finally glanced up, his face still stone cold. "Yeah. I reckon you are, too."

"Yes, I'm Polish and Italian. The name is Wozniak, Marc Wozniak."

Leon Czolgosz didn't bother to respond.

Marc was not one to pull teeth, but now he was curious. "So, what do you do for work?"

Czolgosz grit his teeth as he now looked straight into Marc's eyes, his voice deep and agitated, "I used to work at the Cleveland Rolling Mill. But after our union told us to go on strike, that piece of dirt, Mr. Chisholm, fired the whole lot of us, and even put us on a blacklist! He basically signed our death warrants. None of us can find work."

Marc's smile disappeared; he didn't expect such a detailed and disturbing response. "I thoroughly understand your grievances, I—"

"Oh, do you?" Leon interrupted, "this country is nothing but a huge, slave-driving machine operated by a handful of greedy devils at the top."

"Well, yes," Marc replied, "in some instances, it is. But, as I was about to say, I truly do understand. You see, I worked as a miner from the early age of nine. So I know the pitfalls, and I happen to be very interested in getting legislation passed to curb corporate abuses."

Czolgosz frowned. "Laws alone will not solve our problem. It is this crummy capitalistic system. Karl Marx had the right idea, and the Russians are already moving in that direction. Socialism or communism has to be better than this stinking hell. But any true humanitarian, in my book, can only be an Anarchist."

Marc's back stiffened; he pulled out more garbage from this disgruntled hermit than he cared to hear, and he retorted, "Look, sir, I fully agree that capitalism has its flaws, but it is still the best system that mankind has yet created. The American economy is now booming at a level that even our Founders could never have imagined. And they say our industrial manufacturing capacity is on the verge of surpassing England's. So, it's only a matter of time before we surpass the greatest empire on earth."

"Yeah, but at what expense?" Leon moaned. "Capitalism breeds injustice as the wealthy enrich themselves by exploiting the poor. *So what* if America becomes a world power, we lowly citizens are penniless and powerless!"

As the line began to move, Leon once again sank into his own gloomy world, gazing at the ground. Marc shook his head, annoyed that some of his grievances had validity. He turned around and stepped forward. The woman in front of him was now speaking to the president, and quite oddly, chattering away as if the only visitor in the hall. Marc crossed his arms, waiting and waiting. After 10 minutes had passed, he cleared his throat, "Heh humm!"

The woman glanced irritably back with reproachful eyes, and then turned back to the president to resume her plea. Oddly enough, McKinley had a well-perfected system of shaking peoples hands and then quickly grabbing their elbow with his other hand to escort them along. However, this woman had slyly derailed McKinley's machinelike stride by showing him an old photo she had of him and her husband from the Civil War. Her husband was a factory worker who had recently been fired, and she was now seeking some position for her husband in McKinley's administration. McKinley's secretary, George, also had enough of her pestering pleas as he stepped forward and snapped, "Excuse me, Madame, but the president runs the country, not a factory. Your time is up! So please move along so that others may greet the president."

The woman huffed, "How utterly uncouth! Well, I never—"

"Please, come this way," George said as he grabbed her elbow and gently escorted her toward the exit.

Marc looked at President McKinley, who smiled and said, "Come on, step up. The clucking hen is gone!"

Marc chuckled and stepped forward. As they shook hands, McKinley grabbed Marc's elbow—trying to resume his gear-driven production line—yet Marc stood firm, becoming another wrench in the machine. "It is an honor to meet you Mr. President. My name is Mark Wozniak, and I happen to be the vice president of Huxley Coal as well as a good friend of your vice president, Teddy Roosevelt."

McKinley relaxed his grip and smiled. "Ah, TR is a firecracker, and Huxley Coal is a most valuable company. You service a healthy part of our nation, Mr. Wozniak, and I hear Hawaii and Midway, as well. Actually, I have recently taken an interest in your company, since these two outposts are extremely important to our future."

"Yes, they are," Marc said, "I can see how they'll be strategic stepping stones for us to expand trade."

"Not only trade, Mr. Wozniak, but also our influence. Germany and Japan have been very aggressive in those parts of the world, and if we let the Filipinos fall to either of those belligerent regimes, we will have only allowed ourselves to fall into a most precarious situation. Our security and survival rests upon these actions, which some high-minded critics have scorned as being imperialistic. Believe me, we have no desire to conquer or oppress, but rather uplift these people to a higher standard of living by trading with us, and to be free of tyrannical overlords."

"Teddy and I fully agree with you, Mr. President. But there are other serious issues that concern me; namely, workers rights, safety regulations, and a big lament of mine, child labor issues. I imagine you must think I'm part of the problem, but I assure you, I came into this company from the bottom and worked my way up. So, I know the practices that must be eliminated, regulated or completely changed. I just hope TR made you aware of them, sir?"

McKinley nodded with a smile. "I believe he informed me of most, but I would be more than happy to receive a detailed list of your concerns and remedial proposals. Just so you know, Mr. Wozniak, I whole heartedly condemn the mad spirit for gain and riches which is so prevalent in American society today, by abusing workers, as well as gambling in stock, and speculation in commodities, by 'corners' and 'margins.' There is much to be addressed, and I hope to fulfill all, or at least most, of those goals now in my second term. So while there is much to do, I have a great deal of confidence and enthusiasm. So I assure you, Mr. Wozniak, greater days lie ahead!"

Marc was happily content. "Well, I know you're a busy man, Mr. President, so I thank you for your time."

The two men looked each other in the eye and shook hands firmly. As Marc stepped away, Leon quickly moved up—pulling his hand out of his pocket and extending it toward the president. However, it was oddly wrapped in a handkerchief. McKinley looked down and squinted, when, suddenly, fire and smoke blasted out of the handkerchief along with two loud pops.

Immediately, Marc spun around to see McKinley grunt and grab his stomach. Marc's eyes darted over to Leon, who was still holding the smoking handkerchief, which now caught fire. Instinctively, Marc belted Czolgosz in the face and immediately grabbed him, while the gun and flaming handkerchief fell to the floor. James Parker, a tall Negro man who was standing behind Leon, instantly stepped forward and also began pounding Czolgosz as two agents rushed over. One grabbed Leon, and yelled to his buddy, "Al, get the gun, get the gun!"

Agent Al Gallagher bent over, but only managed to pick up the burning handkerchief, which he snapped wildly, to extinguish.

Meanwhile, Marc bent over and picked up the .32 caliber pistol. Yet, a military guard pushed his way through the hysterical crowd and seized it from his hands.

Pandemonium ensued as panic-stricken citizens screamed and began running in different directions, some crying, others covering their dropped jaws in shock, and others remained frozen—paralyzed with disbelief.

Meanwhile, a mob of angry citizens converged on Czolgosz and began pummeling him with shots to the head and stomach.

McKinley looked over and said calmly, "Now, now, go easy on him boys."

Agents elbowed their way into the brawl and forcefully dragged Czolgosz away, while another team vigilantly grabbed the president and ushered him to the rudimentary hospital at the Exposition.

The shooting had occurred at 4:07 p.m. and the sun was already in decline. Oddly enough, the Rainbow City, which was decorated with thousands of lights, had none inside the hospital room. Evidently, no one had wished to waste wattage and electricity on a room that hardly anyone would see, for it was the electrical extravaganza outside that was meant to dazzle the masses. As such, candlelight was all the hospital room offered. However, with McKinley lying on a table, grunting in pain, the doctor had to administer ether to sedate him, therefore candles could not be lit amid the flammable gas. As such, several men scurried to collect silver trays, and then held them on an angle near the windows to reflect light into the ever-darkening room.

The doctor immediately noticed that one bullet had deflected off McKinley's rib cage, being only a minor wound. However, the other evidently had pierced through his stomach, kidney and pancreas, and lodged somewhere near the president's back. Unable to locate exactly where the bullet was, they decided it was best to stitch McKinley up. Oddly enough, the new invention called an X-Ray machine was on display at the Exposition, which Tesla had also made contributions to, yet the doctors' fears of radiation prevented its use.

Meanwhile, Marc was still in the Temple of Music, surrounded by a throng of weeping and anxious people, all exchanging their version of the assassination attempt. Marc and James Parker could not believe that the disgruntled assassin had stood right between them.

Parker seethed in his Georgian accent, "I'm madder than a bull I didn't see that ninnyhammer's gun."

"So am I. But who could have guessed what was in his pocket?" Marc shook his head. "I could kick myself. I even talked to that madman." Distressed, Marc rubbed his forehead. "I simply cannot believe another president has been shot. I just pray to God that McKinley will survive."

"Amen to that," Parker said. "This country is a mighty dangerous place to live, ain't it?"

"I reckon it is," Marc said, half dazed.

Marc had always believed that America was the greatest and most civilized nation on earth. But with the assassinations of Lincoln, Garfield and now possibly McKinley, he was having serious doubts. Also flashing back into his mind was the deranged serial killer Dr. H.H. Holmes and, of course, the nefarious murderer and rapist Archibald Huxley. The more he contemplated it the more he realized that throughout time mankind has strived to deceive itself that it has risen above the animal kingdom. However, that America was indeed one of the most civilized nations on earth, yet still plagued with an ugly undercurrent of vicious and depraved animals, came as an unsettling revelation. Sadly, Marc concluded, mankind can advance technologically, but not intrinsically.

Meanwhile, some 300 miles due east, Vice President Theodore Roosevelt was attending a luncheon in Vermont when he received word of the shooting. Immediately catching a train, TR arrived in Buffalo the next day. Being greeted at the train station by a group of officials, Teddy was quickly ushered to the Temple of Music.

As Roosevelt walked in, escorted by two agents, he came upon Marc, who had been anxiously waiting for his arrival. "So, Marc, I've been told that you heroically defended the president yesterday?"

Marc gazed solemnly at TR as they shook hands. "No, not really. It would have been heroic if I stopped the lunatic before he fired off two shots."

Teddy put his arm around his dear friend, and eyed the agents to give them space. As the agents retreated, TR walked Marc over to a row of chairs and they sat down.

Roosevelt looked around the hall and then lowered his head. "I am utterly thunderstruck. I never believed I'd live to see another shooting of a president. Did I ever tell you that I saw Lincoln's procession?"

Marc looked at Teddy and shook his head, no, as TR continued, "Well, I did. I was just a young lad, but I will never forget that day. I was in New York City peering out a window, looking in disbelief as the gloomy yet majestic funeral procession passed. Lincoln's casket, dressed in black, was pulled by 16 horses. It was a most dismal occasion, just as James Garfield's procession had been." He shook his head. "My God, what has happened to this country?"

"I don't know," Marc said somberly. "But I pray the Lord spares McKinley's life. And if the worst possible happens, then I reckon it is God's way of saying it is your time to serve the nation, Teddy."

Roosevelt gazed heavenward, only to see the beautifully decorated dome above in this magnificent, yet temporary, pavilion that was sadly destined to be demolished. The correlation was poignant, yet inspiring. "I, too, certainly hope the Lord saves McKinley's life, Marc. Despite my not being an admirer of the man, no president should ever be subjected to this." TR's eyes continued to scan the beautiful dome and the ornately detailed arches all around him. "Yet, like this grand edifice, we all must realize that our time here is transitory. Nothing lasts forever." His eyes lowered to connect with Marc's. "That is why it is crucial to labor hard, every moment of every day. The endeavor is to always strive to achieve greatness, Marc. Just like this magnificent building and our magnificent nation— despite the obstacles or even tragedies that come our way. So, whatever is God's will, I am prepared to fight."

"Yes, you always are!" Marc said with relief. "And thank God for that."

❦

Eight days later, McKinley was still lying in bed at the home of the Exposition's president, John Milburn. Initial reports had declared that the president would make a full recovery, yet a few days later his health nose-dived as fever wracked his body. Gangrene quickly surrounded his wounds, and an internal maelstrom broke loose. Doctors tried to pump him up with adrenaline and oxygen, but his temperature soared.

McKinley now realized their efforts were futile. "It is useless, gentlemen, I think we ought to have prayer."

President William McKinley expired at 2:15 a.m. on September 14. He was the last of the Civil War presidents to server, the last president of the 19th century, and the first of the twentieth century. He laid the groundwork for antitrust legislation and workers rights, and had bolstered the US Navy by building the largest and most substantial fleet the nation had ever seen, a fleet that would be crucial in the precarious years ahead.

As for Leon Czolgosz, unlike the prolonged and theatrical trial of Charles Guiteau, Leon remained practically mute throughout his entire trial, and on October 29, 1901, the publically derided anarchist found himself in a chair powered by Westinghouse and Tesla, which proved more shocking—at least for him—than McKinley's death.

Meanwhile, Marc's good friend, Theodore Roosevelt, had been sworn in as the 26th President of the United States. Having heard that Czolgosz was a card-carrying Anarchist, TR made this public statement, "When compared with the suppression of anarchy, every other question sinks into insignificance."

17

A New President for a New Century

December 12, 1901

Theodore Roosevelt was now three months into his administration as he sat behind his desk in the White House. The transition had been a bit disorienting, as the sudden thrust from the shadows (being the invisible and essentially useless vice president) into the blaring spotlight of the grandest stage in America was enough to becloud even a man like TR. Especially since he now held the title of being the youngest president in U.S. history, with only 42 years under his belt. However, TR had already crammed 80 years into those 42, and now looked forward to getting down to business. He had privately made his feelings known about his predecessor; even stating that McKinley had a spine like an eclair, but now it was time for him to prove his mettle, and being that TR had a spine like metal, he knew he could.

Roosevelt dashed off several orders to his aides, all of whom took mental notes or jotted them down on pads, and then he scooted them out. Returning to the pile of papers before him, TR scanned each page, making notes in the margins for two, solid hours, and then pushed his chair back. He peeled off his round spectacles and placed them on the desk. Rubbing his weary eyes, TR leaned back in his chair and spun around. Looking out the window, he saw the snow-covered presidential lawn as snow flurries wafted on the breeze. Meanwhile, in the distance stood the majestic snow-caped Washington Monument. TR shook his head, finding the moment unreal; like a winter's fairyland where Saint Nicholas just handed him his long awaited gift—the Presidency. Roosevelt had for some time believed this day would come, yet he never imagined it would come this soon or in this fashion. However, gazing out at the snow, he recalled how the blizzard many years ago killed all his cattle on his Dakota ranch, nearly ruining him—and that was even after suffering the loss of his mother and first wife. Yet it was precisely those hellish trials that enabled TR to learn how to weather the storms of life. He was resilient, and always managed to spring back on his feet. He felt good, and his restless mind felt even better. Sitting in this particular chair, he knew far more could now be accomplished.

TR leaned forward, picked up the telephone, and rang Marc.

After waiting for the operator to connect the call, Marc's tinny voice finally came out of the receiver, "Hello?"

"Marc, this is Theodore."

"Ah! You mean *the president*. I guess congratulations are in order."

TR's lips twisted, furling his mustache, as he leaned back and rubbed his forehead. "Well, Marc, it's a dreadful thing to come into the Presidency this way. But it would be a far worse thing to be morbid about it. Here is the task, and I have got to do it to the best of my ability; and that is all there is about it."

"Very true," Marc replied. "So, how can I help you?"

Roosevelt chuckled. "Well, I do believe you can help me, Marc, but not by doing any favor. In fact, allow me to extend the favor to *you* by offering you the position of secretary of the interior."

"Teddy, I mean Mr. President, I'm honored...but...I can't."

TR sat upright in his chair. "What in blazes do you mean? For years, you have been bellyaching about how difficult it is to work under that repulsive rodent, Archibald Huxley. So, here's your chance, Marc. I'm throwing you a lifejacket."

"I deeply appreciate the offer, Mr. President, but—"

"Stop calling me Mr. President!" TR bellowed, "you are my dear friend, you damned fool. After all, who introduced you to your lovely wife?"

Marc's laughter rattled the receiver as he replied, "Well, technically, you introduced me to Kathleen Ward, if you'll recall."

TR chuckled. "I stand corrected. You see, I need sharp men like you on my team. Please, come join me."

"Again, Teddy, thank you, but you'd really help me by passing some legislation that would force Huxley to protect our workers and stop him from hiring children. Morgan and our executive board have backed every move he makes, and I'm at my wits' end. I don't know if you've heard, but we recently had another explosion, and I'll be damned, he killed another six people, two of which were kids. This is criminal, Teddy, downright criminal! I see no difference than if he took a gun and shot those poor slobs right in the head. Tell me, am I wrong?"

"No, Marc, of course not," Roosevelt said, his voice reeking with disdain. "This has been a problem that has plagued our country for far too long. But as you know, there are many who will not tolerate even the mere mention of legislation that will allow the government to butt into private industry. As they say, it's a slippery slope."

"Well, the slippery slope here caused another cave-in, and a hell of a lot of grief. The only profiteer here is the damned undertaker! So, something must be done."

TR assertively reached over and grabbed his glasses. Slipping them back on, he said, "I promise, Marc, that I will put up the good fight. I am only at the starting gate, but it will be a long race, one that all predators of wealth—who grow fat by oppressing wageworkers, avoid safety issues, unfairly crush competition, or defraud the public—will eventually learn that they must abide by our new set of rules, or be ejected from the game. But, as I say, this will be a long and difficult battle. So have no illusions. This will not happen overnight, or any time soon."

"I understand, Teddy. I know you have many other things to contend with, but I appreciate your vow to continue the causes that mean so much to me. And please know that I truly appreciate your generous offer. I hope my refusal was not taken personally, because as you know, I do have a very personal issue to contend with myself, right here at Huxley Coal."

TR nodded, sympathetic yet disappointed. "Yes, I know Marc, and if you ever change your mind, please, do call me. Is that understood?"

"Understood," Marc said. "Oh! By the way, did you hear that Marconi transmitted the first radio wave signal across the Atlantic Ocean today?"

"Yes, I have. Isn't that fantastic?"

"Indeed it is. However, I don't think Mr. Tesla will be too thrilled."

"Oh, yes," TR said, "you had told me about Tesla's concerns. But from what I hear, Marconi has been very active on this crusade of his. He's a man of energy as well as ingenuity, and sometimes the former is more crucial than the latter." As TR gazed at the African safari book on his desk, he added, "It appears even the brightest of mankind are relegated to the jungle in a feisty game of survival!"

"I reckon they are. And you, too, best be careful treading through *your* jungle of political panthers and lobbying lizards!"

TR chuckled. "I will, Marc, I will. And you keep an eye on that burrowing beast you have over there!"

As Marc's laughter came through the receiver, TR added, "And if you need a high-powered rifle to rid yourself of that ruthless rhino, just let me know?"

"Yes, I will, Teddy," Marc replied with a chuckle. His jovial voice plummeted, now dead serious. "But I'm fully committed to rectifying this situation in a civilized fashion. I don't want it to escalate into an ugly blood war, like the Hatfields and McCoys, which it easily could have if I didn't keep a cool head. My brother Ted wants blood, but I must believe that our system can provide justice in a peaceful fashion. Besides, you are now the president, Teddy, and you shouldn't say such things, even in jest. You may slip one day in public and scare the hell out of our fellow Americans."

"Well, Marc, I've already said many things that scare the hell out of some Americans, a few already belittling me as a danged cowboy!" As Marc laughed, TR continued, "But I said this to *you*, my good friend, in private, unlike my friend William Hearst, who publishes whatever crosses his sizzling mind."

William Randolph Hearst had published an article in his *NY Journal*, stating: 'If bad institutions and bad men can be got rid of only by killing, then the killing must be done!' That Hearst's crass and deadly comment had preceded McKinley's assassination only exacerbated the issue, causing many to think that such comments can spur others to commit malicious actions.

Roosevelt gazed at his calendar. "And speaking of your brother and rifles, I had invited Ted out to my Sagamore Hill home on Long Island to do some duck hunting, yet we never settled on a date. Christmas is coming soon, so how does Saturday, January 18, in the New Year work for him?"

"One second," Marc said.

TR could hear Marc calling out to his brother through the tinny receiver, but couldn't make out their conversation. A moment later, Marc responded, "Yes, Ted said he'll meet you around noon. Does that work?"

"That's swell," TR said as his mind switched tracks. "But as for you, Marc, I haven't forgotten your predicament. I know you haven't told me everything about your troubles with Huxley, but why don't you let the judicial system work—drag Archie's corrupt ass into court!"

"That wouldn't work for my particular situation, Teddy. It's complicated. There are some personal matters that would be revealed which I could never allow to be made public."

"Well, listen, Marc. Don't let that Huxley fellow get you down. I know your dealings with J.P. Morgan didn't work out as you planned, but perhaps there is another avenue you can pursue."

"Yes, I've been hoping Morgan would sell some of his shares for far too long now, Teddy. The only consolation I have is that I've been making tons of money in the Stock Market and investing in companies that manufacture safety equipment. So at least our workers are better equipped." Marc paused; then impulsively, he blurted, "I don't know, perhaps I should form a labor union here."

Roosevelt rubbed his chin. "I imagine establishing a miners union at Huxley Coal will not be easy with a tyrant like Archibald."

"No, you're right, it certainly wouldn't. That silly idea just slipped out. Archie has no loyalty whatsoever and would fire the entire crew, and then hire all cheap Chinese workers. He also has Morgan and the executive board supporting him, who all despise unions. So I reckon I'll have to look for another way to fight this madness. But as I said, I am at my wits' end, because, I must tell you; Ted has been dabbling in booze again. His hatred for Huxley sets him off into drinking binges and fits of rage, so I really need to do something quick."

"Well, I'll try to relieve Ted's nerves, Marc," TR said as he swiveled around and looked at his Remington sculpture of a cowboy. "In fact, I think shooting some ducks just might be the perfect release valve for Ted to blow off some steam."

Marc's chuckle came through the receiver as he said, "Well, it might at that. Now you have a Merry Christmas and a jolly New Year, Teddy. And I hope you two boys have a good weekend shooting some ducks. Take care, and give my love to Edith and the family."

"The same to you and yours, my friend," TR said with a smile as he leaned over and hung up the telephone.

18

Hunting on Long Island

January 18, 1902

Ted, as usual, missed his train, but finally arrived at Roosevelt's Sagamore Hill home in Oyster Bay, Long Island at 3:30 p.m. He had Mazeppa carted along, and he now rode his trusty old stallion onto the front lawn of Roosevelt's estate. The weather was brisk, but bearable at 40 degrees, and most of the snow that had fallen three days ago had melted; yet a thin dusting of flakes still covered the white terrain.

TR expected Ted to be tardy, and was now standing on his deck holding two shotguns, one under each arm as he said, "Tasso, glad to see you, and your Rough Rider steed!"

Ted, oblivious to his habitually rude delinquency, smiled as he tied up Mazeppa. "Yeah, he's an old man now, but still has a little spunk left. And gees, I haven't been called Tasso ever since I was a teen. In fact, I didn't realize that you even knew my real name."

Ted ascended the stairs and shook Roosevelt's hand as TR said, "Well, your brother had told me. It was some time ago at Carnegie Hall. We had heard Liszt's symphonic poem by the same name."

Ted laughed. "Yeah, it seems everyone else heard that work except me."

"Well, you really should try to catch a performance of it, Ted. The triumphant ending of that work truly lifts the spirit and inspires a man," TR subtly advised. He then gazed down at his rifle. "Now look here." TR showed Ted his new Winchester M97 pump-action shotgun. "This is my new toy. It can pump out 5 rounds faster than a duck can blink."

As Ted admiringly scrutinized the weapon, TR swung the other rifle out from under his arm. "And this baby is my trusty old double-barreled 12 gauge. You'll be using this one. She has two triggers, so it may take a minute or two to get used to it. Here, give it a try. Shoot those targets I setup."

Ted grabbed the shotgun, checked the two barrels and then swung it towards the seven paper targets with red bull's eyes. Aiming at one, Ted pulled the first trigger. The rifle recoiled, and a spray of buckshot blew half of the target away. Ted aimed at the next target, and pulled the second trigger, blasting the target dead center and knocking it over.

"Well done!" TR said. "That was quick. But after seeing you on Kettle Hill, I knew you'd get the knack of it."

Roosevelt raised his Winchester, and quickly pumped out five rounds of buckshot as four of the five remaining targets were pulverized.

Ted's eyes widened. "Wow! That is some dandy of a rifle you got yourself! It's almost as deadly as those Gatlings Parker had in Cuba, which also did a fine job of deafening us." As Roosevelt chuckled, Ted added, "But won't these rifles mutilate the ducks?"

TR shook his head. "No, no. These cartridges are buckshot with large loads. I just wanted you to get the feel of a healthy kickback. We'll be using small birdshot tomorrow, which also has a much smaller load. Besides, those paper targets are much closer than the ducks we'll be shooting at. So, have no fear, you will be able to eat whatever we shoot."

Ted spun around. "It sure is beautiful out here. Nice location. So, I reckon we'll need to march along the shore tomorrow to find these ducks?"

TR laughed. "Ted, we are not hunting Spaniards anymore, so we won't be marching anywhere. I have a flat-bottomed boat that we will sail into the marshes and then sit and take cover."

Ted's head recoiled as he chuckled. "Take cover? From little harmless ducks?"

TR smiled. "Well, yes. I know, it certainly is nothing like hunting a charging buffalo or a wild grizzly, but there is no sport in shooting, pardon the expression, a sitting duck! Therefore, we shall hide and then wait for them to take flight. That's what makes it a challenge—trying to hit these babies in flight."

Ted nodded. "Yes, I found popping off those running Dagoes much harder to hit than that bastard sitting in a tree trying to pop you off."

TR smiled and patted Ted on the shoulder. "Yes, and I owe you my life for that, Ted. That's why I felt the least I could do, beyond recommending you for those well deserved medals, was to start taking you with me on some of my hunting trips."

"I'm much obliged, Mr. President."

"Out here, in God's country, you don't need to call me Mr. President, Ted. Relax, and just enjoy the beauty of nature. I used to come out here when I was a young boy with my family. But several years ago I bought 155 acres of land and had the architects Lamb & Rich design this Queen Anne home. It has 22 rooms. Come, let me show you."

As they walked toward the door, TR turned and said, "Maybe we will take a walk later and shoot some raccoons for practice." TR pointed to the rifle scabbard he had for Ted's shotgun. "Why don't you strap that on your horse."

Ted picked it up and walked over to Mazeppa. He slipped the double-barreled shotgun into the scabbard with some difficulty, due to the girth of the two barrels, and then strapped it on Mazeppa. Securing it into place, he placed a box of cartridges in the pouch next to it, and then joined TR, who escorted him into the house. As they made their way from room to room, Ted met TR's wife, Edith, and their five children (Alice, from TR's first marriage, was away—the independent and spirited young woman was already beginning to feel her oats).

TR finally ushered Ted into his favorite room, the den. As Ted walked in, his skin rippled with goose bumps. It was astonishingly similar to Huxley's. It featured a cathedral ceiling and was all clad in rich wood, with wooden pilasters, ornately designed carpeting, a bear rug, and a sprawling array of mounted animal heads hanging on the walls.

TR noticed Ted's expression. "What is it? You don't like it?"

Ted turned and looked at his host anxiously. "Oh, no, not at all. It's splendid, really."

TR adjusted his glasses. "Well, I dare say, you look like you just saw a ghost."

Ted smiled. "No, not quite. I'm sorry, it's just that Archibald Huxley has a den very similar to this."

Roosevelt took off his glasses and placed them on his desk. "Ah, yes. I know you Wozniaks have had some bad dealings with that man. I sense Marc has not revealed everything to me about Huxley, but I've heard enough to be of the same opinion—that man is a damned weasel!"

Ted sighed heavily. "Believe me, you really don't know the half of it." Ted continued to scan the den with its array of hunting gear and dead animals as he said, "I hear Huxley has another mansion out here somewhere. It's supposed to be grander than his main residence in Pittsburgh."

"Yes, it is," TR said, "it is only eight miles from here and sits right on the hilly coastline of Lloyd Neck. That coal tycoon of yours built himself one hell of a massive estate, he did. In fact, Huxley started the ostentatious ball rolling out here as the Vanderbilts and others are following his lead."

Just then little 12-year old Kermit strolled in with his pet dog Jack by his side. "Excuse me, Pa, but momma told me to bring you these beers."

As they turned, TR at first hesitated, being conscious of Ted's drinking problem. However, that beer was low in alcohol, and that Ted appeared as if he could use a mug of suds to calm his nerves, TR waved his son in. "Sure, Kermit. Bring them over."

As Kermit handed each of them their mug of beer, Jack ran over and started smelling Ted's leg. Ted smiled as he reached down and began petting the spunky black dog. "He's a good looking fella, you have here."

"Thank you," Kermit replied. "But he can do some neat tricks, too."

TR took a gulp of beer, and said, "Go on, Kermit, show Ted what Jack can do."

Kermit commanded Jack to sit, roll over, and give him his paw, which he did promptly and happily.

Ted cheered, "That's fantastic!" as he took another slug of beer. Wiping the foam off his mouth, he added, "That reminds me of the tricks my fellow Rough Riders used to have their dogs do at Buffalo Bill's Wild West shows."

Kermit's eyes lit up. "*You* rode in Buffalo Bill's shows?"

"I sure did," Ted said, "but that was a very long time ago."

Eager to prove that Jack was a star talent, Kermit then explained how Jack also retrieved balls and the dead birds that his father shot.

TR smiled. "Well, Jack won't be coming with Ted and I tomorrow morning, Kermit. But—"

Just then Edith called out for Kermit to help her in the kitchen. TR waved his hand, and said, "Go on, and give your mother a hand."

Kermit pouted. "But that's girly work. Ethel should help mom with that sort of stuff, not me."

"That is not true, Kermit," his father said. "The best chefs in the world happen to be men."

"Yeah, sure," Kermit groaned, "but they wear silly, white mushroom hats and girly aprons!"

Ted laughed as TR shook his head. "Okay, you have a point there, Kermit. But go and help your mother anyhow."

As Kermit grudgingly left the room, Jack happily followed; especially since he secretly stole TR's glove, which dangled from his mouth as his little tail wagged.

Ted looked at TR, and said, "Cute kid. He reminds me of me a little when I was young."

"Yes, Kermit is a very spirited little boy, and I imagine he'll make a good solider like you one day. Yet, like you, I sense—" TR stopped.

Ted had taken a swig of his beer, downing half of it in one gulp as he said, "Sense what?" wiping his lips.

"Oh, nothing," TR said, "let's talk about *you*. Is there anything I can do to help you find employment?"

Ted rolled his eyes. "Well, jobs and me don't go well together. We're kind of like oil and water, if you get my drift."

Roosevelt placed his unfinished beer down on his desk, and walked over to take a seat near the fireplace. "Listen, Ted, I know you honorably serve in the military reserves, but there's nothing for them to do, and I would like to help you get settled down with a real job, you know, something to really sink your teeth into. I believe keeping busy is the key to keeping healthy."

Ted guzzled down the rest of his beer, and sat in the chair across from TR. "So, I reckon my brother has told you I'm not healthy?"

TR shifted in his chair, uneasy. "Your brother is a great man, Ted. He has done his best to help you, and as his friend, I would like to see if I could help you where he has fallen a tad short. You have talent and spirit, Ted. But you have to learn to channel that and apply yourself."

Again, Ted rolled his eyes as he huffed. "I didn't realize I was coming here for a lecture or a job interview. Was this your idea or my brothers?"

"It would do you well not to be so stubborn, Ted. Lord knows, I can be, too, but there are times when you must bend a little, and listen to and learn from others. Did you know that I was granted the command to my Rough Rider's regiment, yet conceded that leadership role to Colonel Wood?"

Ted shook his head, no, as TR continued, "Well, that was because I knew I did not possess the military experience that was necessary to outfit, train, and lead a cavalry unit. It would have been damned reckless of me to have done so, and put thousands of men's lives in danger."

"But, you did end up leading us, and did an excellent job of it at that."

"Yes, but I'm a quick learner, Ted. And from what Marc has told me, you have gone through quite a number of jobs, evidently not learning too many lessons."

Ted stood up, agitated. "I respect you very much, Mr. President, but I will not sit here and suffer this verbal shellacking. The lesson I've learned long ago was not to stick around people who only wish to reprimand and insult me!"

With that, Ted grabbed his coat and marched angrily toward the door.

TR stood up. "If you walk out that door, mister, you will not be welcome here again!"

Ted buttoned up his coat and slipped on his gloves. "Never again, huh? So who's the stubborn one? Oh, yes, it is always only *me*. Good day, sir!"

Roosevelt shook his head as he watched Ted exit and slam the door. Within seconds, Edith came running into the den. "Where did Mr. Wozniak go? He hasn't even had dinner."

"You can remove his place setting," TR huffed, humiliated at both Ted and himself. "Lord knows where he's going. I thought I would try to be the Good Samaritan to help him, but the poor soul has been a troubled young man and a drifter for too many years, Edith. One cannot turn gravel into gold."

Edith looked out the front window and saw Ted ride off into the cold, gray distance. She turned back to her husband. "Shouldn't you go after him?"

"He is no longer a child, Edith. And his brother Marc has told me an encyclopedia's worth of stories about him, and in moments like this, it is best to let him blow off steam and follow his own stubborn path."

Edith shook her head. "Well, that sounds like a recipe for disaster to me. As any recipe that is missing one key ingredient will only yield the same botched dish, over and over again!" Edith put her hands on her hips. "Perhaps you all have just not found that one missing ingredient."

"Edith, for many years, his family has tried to find that elusive ingredient that would turn Ted's life around, and, I assure you, Marc had for a time. But, this troubled young man has fallen back into his own native rut, once again, and there is only so much an outsider can do, especially for a person who is not willing to change. As you know, Edith, God helps those who help themselves."

Edith snorted. "That phrase, Theodore, is *not* from the Christian Bible. It is an ancient Grecian parable that does *not* reflect Jesus' loving message of giving and helping others. I still say you were too quick to turn your back on him. Ted is a human being, not a dog!" Edith turned and marched stormily into the kitchen.

TR sighed, and walked over to his mug of beer. As he gulped it down, his mind blurted, *now I know why men invented alcohol!*

As he wiped his moist mustache, he noticed one of his gloves was missing. He then spotted Jack by the doorway, the shredded glove dangling from his mouth. TR rolled his eyes as he thought; *you're just like Ted, Jack—cute, but a pain in the ass!*

❧

As the sun edged toward twilight, Ted was sitting in a local Oyster Bay tavern downing a few more beers. The tiny stone cottage had a small bar with six stools, eight small round tables with green tablecloths and a lit candle in a Celtic holder at the center of each. The quaint establishment was practically barren, save for the proprietor and two seasoned fishermen, each with ruddy faces, and yellow fingernails from chain-smoking fat stinky cigars. Having heard Ted tell the owner that he was a Rough Rider, the two seamen moved alongside Ted and bought him more rounds. As they told Ted about their oyster and clam digging escapades, Ted hardly listened as his mind reeled deeper and deeper into his own black sea of silt and muck. He didn't know who to be mad at more, his big-mouthed brother Marc or the preachy president. However, it wasn't long before his thoughts dredged up the vilest creature in his dark mucky world of pain and suffering—Archibald Huxley! He had been the thorn in not only his side but in the side of the entire Wozniak family's.

Guzzling down his last foamy slosh of beer, Ted pushed the mug into the stacked wall of 12 empty mugs, and then thanked his fishermen friends and the owner. Staggering out into the cold and brisk air, Ted walked over to Mazeppa and kissed him on the snout. "You're t-the only true b-blue buddy I got! You hear me, Zeppy?"

Mazeppa snorted as two huge streams of vapor blew out of his old nostrils into the frigid air. As Ted moved alongside Mazeppa to mount him, his hand hit the scabbard with TR's double-barreled shotgun. Ted had forgotten he even put it there, and he cracked a sinister smile. *How convenient!*

Ted grabbed the horn of the saddle, slipped his boot in the stirrup, and hauled himself up, almost slipping off the other side. Mazeppa quickly sidestepped, anticipating the potential fall, as Ted righted himself in the saddle. "You see what I m-mean? You're always t-there for me, Zeppy!"

With that, Ted snapped the reins and started down the narrow gravely path. Riding through the tiny village, he passed 10 other small buildings, some sheathed with clapboard and others with cedar shakes. With each step Mazeppa took, his metal shoes made a crackling sound as they crunched the icy gravel. As Ted rode out of the hamlet, he turned east and head toward Cold Spring Harbor. The sun was off in the west, and now sinking toward the horizon, casting a pale golden shimmer over the leafless treetops and the crests of waves that were right before Ted's blurry eyes.

Having reached the shore, Ted looked out at the cold rustling water and barren landscape as gusts of salty frigid air beat against his face. Between the alcohol in his veins and the fiery thoughts of Huxley in his head, Ted didn't feel the slightest bit cold, in fact, he unbuttoned his wool coat and then turned his head into the wind coming from the Long Island Sound. Off in the distance, he could see a small cluster of lights sitting on a cliff, illuminating the beach below it. Ted squinted, but couldn't make out exactly what it was. However, knowing that TR said Huxley's mansion was some eight miles away, and he had already ridden quite a distance from Sagamore Hill, he figured it just had to be Huxley's estate, especially since it was perched on the highest ridge along the shoreline. Ted's heart pounded with a vengeance as he angrily swiveled the reins and kicked Mazeppa's flanks. Riding headlong into the wind and along the beach, Mazeppa's shoes dug up sand and cracked tiny shells, while the sea on their left and trees on their right passed by them in a cascading blur. Hot vapor blew out of Mazeppa's frosty nostrils, while Ted grit his teeth with each kick. As they got closer, Ted pulled back on the reins, slowing Mazeppa down to a saunter.

Ted's wild eyes widened as they viewed the opulent monstrosity that dominated the ridge. A winding marble staircase led up to the rear lawn, and Mazeppa clip-clopped his way up as Ted's line of sight finally saw the rear gardens. Beyond that, he saw the large statue of Neptune holding his trident, and behind that was the massive rear façade of Huxley's Roman-styled mansion. It was lined with a series of arched windows, most illuminated and shedding a warm glow over the snow-covered landscape.

Impatiently, Ted steered Mazeppa up to the towering wall of sculpted boxwoods and entered one of the winding paths. As he rode along, additional pathways branched off. Not sure of which way to go, Ted turned, and followed one path, then turned, and followed another. Yet he soon found himself further away from the mansion. Humiliated, Ted pulled back on the reins and stopped. Spinning his head around, he angrily scanned the garden's hedges and paths. From his high vantage point atop Mazeppa, he now realized that he was stuck in a labyrinth. Frustrated, and now more enraged than before, Ted steered Mazeppa out of the maze, and galloped to the outside edge of the garden. With a clear stretch of snow-covered lawn leading up to the rear corner of the mansion, Ted galloped straight up to the building and then strut along the rear wall on the patio. As Mazeppa slowly clip-clopped along, Ted tried to look in the windows, yet the sheer curtains only hindered his inebriated vision further. As he approached the center of the building, Ted came upon the huge fountain with Neptune surrounded by two horses and dolphins. The basin below was empty, having been drained for the winter, but the entire fountain glowed, being illuminated by the light emanating out the huge rear windows and French doors.

Ted dismounted and slid the double-barreled shotgun out of the scabbard. He then slipped a cartridge in each of the barrels and stuffed two more cartridges in his coat pocket.

Leaning toward Mazeppa, he whispered angrily, "Okay, Zeppy. This won't t-take long. Be a g-good boy and wait here. I have to k-kill me a f-fucking r-rapist!"

Ted walked to the rear door and turned the knob, but it was locked. "Shit!" he bellowed as his voice reverberated. "How r-rude!" Taking a step back, and gazing at all the windows, he yelled, "I'm here to k-kill you Huxley! Open the fucking d-door, or I'll huff and p-puff and blow your head off! Do you hear me, y-you slimy p-pig?!"

Penelope peered anxiously out one of the upstairs windows, while her daughters and son pushed open their curtains to see what the commotion was.

Ted could now see Huxley through the window on the ground floor, yet he was quickly pacing past the rear doors, heading for the den. Ted aimed the shotgun at the double French doors and pulled one trigger. The fiery blast blew the lock off and shattered the glass and wood frame. Slipping another cartridge into the empty barrel, Ted pushed his way through the door and ran unsteadily into the den. Huxley was pulling a rifle off the wall rack, when he heard Ted come in. Quickly, he spun around.

Holding the unloaded rifle in his trembling hands, Huxley's face turned pale. "What the hell are you doing this time, you crazy bastard?"

Ted pointed his double-barrels at Huxley, and slowly stepped closer. "I'm doing what I s-should have done l-last time—f-finishing the job!" His face twisted. "Killing Rex was fun, but it wasn't enough. Now it's time to k-kill *you*—the top dog!"

"You're drunk, Ted, and not very funny," Huxley said nervously. "Put the rifle down. Remember what your brother said last time, you'll hang!"

"That's j-just it, Archie. I don't g-give a s-shit anymore."

Just then Penelope appeared at the entrance of the den, some 10 feet behind Ted. Ted heard her footsteps and turned. Taking a step backward, he now tried to keep both of them in his sights. Huxley, however, had taken that moment to quickly load a shell, and he now tried to raise his rifle. Ted instantly fired off a shot. Huxley's rifle was blown out of his hands as the spray of buckshot hit the barrel and shredded part of his hand. Huxley yelped and quickly grabbed his bloody hand, keeping pressure on the torn flesh. "You crazy bastard! I swear; this is not the end. You—"

"Oh, t-this *is* the end," Ted blasted as he slipped in another cartridge. Looking back at Penelope, who was now holding her hands over her face in shock, Ted said, "I think it's t-time you know a little s-secret about your two-timing, piece-of-shit husband."

Penelope squinted as Huxley yelled, "Don't listen to this drunk! He's a raving lunatic."

Ted cocked both hammers back as he glanced at Huxley. "I m-may be a drunk, but you're a damned bigamist!" Gazing back at Penelope, he added, "Your d-dear husband has a wife and k-kids out in Sierra N-Nevada."

As Huxley edged toward his gun rack, Penelope gazed at him. "Is this true?"

Ted looked back at Huxley, and growled, "Hold still! I don't want to k-kill you j-just yet." Looking back at Penelope, he asked, "Where are your k-kids?"

Penelope gazed nervously at Ted, trembling and bewildered. "Inside. Why? They have done nothing to you. Please, I beg you, don't harm them."

Ted huffed. "I g-got no intentions of s-shooting you or them, Mrs. Huxley."

"I don't understand," Penelope said. "Even if what you say is true, why would you jeopardize your life to kill Archie for something he did to me and his family?"

Just then Huxley's curious 20-year-old son, Archie Jr., and two young daughters crept near the den door and peeked in. Their eyes widened with fear as Ted gazed at them with menacing eyes and said in a bent voice, "Come in and j-join the p-party. I promise I won't s-shoot you."

As they slowly shuffled to their mother's side, Huxley yelled, "Get the kids out of here, Penny! I'll rid us of this deranged madman!"

Ted's temper flared as he looked at Archie and hollered, "Shut up, Huxley!" Gazing back at Penelope, he shouted, "The reason I'm h-here is not b-because of his t-two stinking m-marriages, Madame. I'm here b-because your f-filthy husband r-ra—"

Before Ted could finish the dreaded sentence, Huxley leapt for another rifle on the gun rack, but Ted quickly turned and fired one barrel, blasting a bloody pattern of buckshot into Huxley's lower back. Huxley let out alarming moan and fell to the floor as his wife and children shrieked.

Penelope gazed at Ted with shocked and fiery eyes. "You *are* crazy!"

As her young daughters buried their heads into her dress, screaming uncontrollably with muffled sobs, Archie Jr. held his mother's hand and gazed at Ted with vengeful eyes.

Ted glanced at Huxley, who was now squirming like a slug on the floor, moaning, and then back at the terrified family. "I t-told you I wouldn't s-shoot any of you, and I meant it. But, you s-see, I wanted you all to w-witness your s-shitty father's—and unf-faithful husband's—death." As Ted continued, his voice rose with anger and reeked with vengeance, "My whole f-family has s-suffered, because of *him!* So now it's *y-your* turn to s-suffer!" Ted's body swayed as he unloaded the rest of his vitriol, "My f-father died, and my b-brother l-lost a l-leg, all because of *him!* M-my whole family has endured H-Hell ever since he r-raped m-my mother, all b-because of *him!*" Ted snarled, "So, this *Hellish* p-payback is all b-because of *HIM!*"

As Penelope covered her mouth with her trembling hands, Ted gazed down at Huxley's now motionless body, and he spat, "So do you s-still think *I'm* c-crazy? Or was your dirty r-rotten husband c-crazy?"

Penelope was mortified and remained mute, while Archie Jr. grit his teeth and spat, "*You* are crazy! And you *will* pay for this!"

Ted turned back and gazed at Archie Jr. as he belched out a drunken cackle. "I t-think there is s-something else you s-should know, Junior. The l-last time I had a m-meeting with your p-pa, he called you a namby-pamby s-sissy. Oh, yeah, and a p-poor excuse for a m-man. So I hope t-that adds to the b-baggage *you'll* have to c-carry around for the r-rest of w-what your f-father called—*your w-worthless life!*"

As Archie Jr. looked at his mother, Penelope wrapped her arm around him and pulled him in close. Some years ago, Archie Jr. had revealed his homosexuality to his parents after one of his father's many scathing tirades, where he berated Archie Jr. with similar slurs. However, Huxley had sworn never to reveal his son's secret or bad-mouth him again in public. But now feeling utterly betrayed, Archie Jr. gazed at his father on the floor, seething with animus. But to his surprise, he saw his father's body move!

Ted noticed young Archie's reaction and turned. Huxley was attempting to roll over on his back. Penelope also looked, and then turned toward Archie Jr. "Take the girls upstairs, and call Doctor Thompson, immediately!"

As her emotionally torn son escorted his hysterical sisters out of the room, Penelope started to walk over to her husband.

Ted stepped closer and pointed the shotgun at Huxley's back. Looking at Penelope, he growled, "Why w-would you help a p-piece of s-shit like him? He not only c-cheated on you, and h-has another f-family, but he r-raped m-my m-mother!"

Penelope covered her mouth, trembling, then lowered her hand. "Because although I do suspect you're telling the truth, I must give him the benefit of the doubt. And he *is* the father of my children."

Ted gazed at her, humiliated, as Penelope walked over and wrapped her husband's back with a blanket to control the bleeding. She gently rolled Archie onto his back, while his eyes rolled in lethargic circles. Penelope grabbed his face, but Huxley was drifting in and out of consciousness.

With tears in her eyes, she asked, "Archie, can you hear me?"

Huxley managed to catch Penelope's eyes as he murmured, "Y-Yes. But I c-can't feel my legs, Penny. Not a thing!"

Penelope looked back up at Ted as tears flowed down her alabaster cheeks. "You had better shoot us all, or get out of here this instant!"

Ted blinked hard. "D-did you not h-hear everything I said? Do you really t-think I came here and d-did *this* for *no reason?*"

"Please," Penelope begged, *"just go!"*

Penelope was confused and emotionally shattered. She suspected her reckless and headstrong husband was guilty, but wasn't sure which charges were true. All she knew was that she couldn't bear to see him suffering like this. And after living through the painful hell of seeing three presidents killed by deranged lunatics, she had no idea just how sane Ted really was.

Nervously, she added, "Who's to say you're not mad, like Booth, Guiteau or Czolgosz?"

Ted's face twisted with anger as he growled, "You're c-comparing *m-me* to *them!?*"

"I told you, I don't know what to think, but if you really aren't crazy, you'll leave immediately!"

Ted looked at Penelope and then down at Huxley. To Ted it was a gratifying and long-overdue sight; Archie was now unconscious, and the carpet was saturated with a pool of blood. It would now only be a matter of minutes and this hellish thorn would be gone forever. Ted spun around and ran unsteadily out the back door. Slipping on the snow, Ted fell as the rifle slid and hit the basin of the fountain.

Gazing up at the towering statue of Neptune, Ted barked, "What the hell are *you* looking at?"

With that, Ted picked up the shotgun and fired his last shot, blasting a huge chunk of Neptune's marble head off.

As he turned, he saw Mazeppa wobbling as blood dripped out his nostril. The 25-year-old stallion had lived a long and eventful life but was pushed beyond his capacity. Ted's eyes bulged as he ran and grabbed Mazeppa's head. Gazing into his big, black eyes, he cried, "Oh, God! I'm s-so sorry Zeppy. I never s-should have brought you all t-the way out here."

Mazeppa gazed at his beloved master and tried to step closer, but his body suddenly pitched forward as his front legs buckled. Now resting on his front knees, with his hind legs still trying to maintain balance, Mazeppa snorted, spraying the patio with blood. Ted dropped his rifle and hugged Mazeppa's strong, muscular neck as he began to weep. "It's okay, Zeppy. Just lie down. You're a g-good boy."

As Mazeppa's hind legs slipped on the snow, they finally gave way. His body hit the ground, and he keeled over onto his side. As tears streamed down Ted's face, he reached into the pouch on Mazeppa's back and pulled out two more cartridges. He loaded the double barrels, and uttered, "I'm s-so sorry, Zeppy, but I h-have to do this."

With that, Ted pointed the shotgun at Mazeppa's head, closed his eyes and pulled both triggers. The loud blast reverberated off the marble exterior walls and statues as Mazeppa's blood and skull fragments splattered over the patio, turning the white, snowy crystals red.

With red, bloodshot eyes, Ted reloaded the shotgun with the last two shells from the pouch and ran headlong into the dark, frosty night. As he rounded the corner of the mansion, he saw Huxley's stable some 400 feet away. Running up to the huge double doors, he pointed the shotgun at the lock and pulled the trigger. As fire blew out the nozzle, the lock fell to the ground as the splintered doors swung ajar.

Ted quickly saddled up a horse and then tore into the dark, chilly night. As he headed back toward Manhattan, his drunken mind began reeling about the loss of his loyal old steed. Zeppy had been Ted's partner and crucial other-half for 20 years, and had truly allowed Ted to shine. As Ted kicked the loins of the sluggish and less responsive horse underneath him now, it only drove home that depressing point more as tears froze on his frosty cheeks.

Ted's troubled thoughts then began reflecting, with much frustration, how Mrs. Huxley did not fully believe him. Yet the more he thought about it, he soon found some relief in knowing that with Huxley now dead, his other family *will* come out of seclusion, and the shit *will* hit the fan. What's more, once Penelope lays her eyes upon Remus that, too, will erase any doubts of her husband's other repulsive deed.

Finally reaching the shoreline, Ted dismounted and hopped on a ferry. Ahead of him, he could see the lights of Manhattan through a thin veil of flurries that blew across the East River. Ted turned and leaned against the railing on the stern of the ship—gazing back at Long Island as it receded into the dark chilly mist. As the altercation with Huxley flashed in his inebriated mind, a touch of black humor washed over him: *Well, at least hunting on Long Island was better than I thought!*

19

Aftermath & the Asylum

December 22, 1907

Five years had passed, and the lives of many had changed drastically. Penelope had indeed found out about Archie's other family in the Sierra Nevada, and the two families suffered much emotional trauma and humiliation, particularly since the newspapers flaunted the scandal for several months all across the nation.

Meanwhile, to the shock of all, Huxley had miraculously survived the shooting. However, he had lost all feeling and mobility from the waist down. That Archie would be wheelchair bound for the rest of his life had given many a deep sense that justice had been served.

Life for Ted, however, had been confined first to a jail cell in Auburn Prison in New York for two years. His first trial had been a circus, for it was extremely difficult to select an unbiased jury, since the news of Huxley's bigamy, defrauding Homer of his mine, and recklessness at Huxley Coal (which caused the unnecessary deaths or handicaps of countless miners) tainted the minds of many. That Ted's long record of previous drunken escapades and infractions had arisen at the trial also colored the jury as to whether or not Ted was clearly acting upon his own volition or was temporarily unable to control his actions.

Meanwhile, Marc had made a prompt secret agreement with Penelope to conceal Huxley's rape as not to embarrass the Wozniak family and spare both Huxley families an additional scandal. That had not sat well with Ted, who figured the additional charge of rape would not only have aided his motive for revenge, but would have placed more guilt on Huxley by accentuating his depraved character. However, Marc had Remus' shattered emotions and desire for confidentiality to contend with, in addition to the public shame that would taint their dead mother's name.

Nevertheless, the jury had been presented with so much damaging evidence against Huxley, which was verified by numerous witnesses, that many had felt Ted was somewhat justified in his actions. However, it was hard for them to understand the defense's argument; namely that it was Huxley's reckless disregard of safety measures, which had caused Ted's father's death and the loss of his brother's leg, that had prompted Ted to seek revenge. That those incidents occurred so many years ago somehow didn't add up. It hadn't fulfilled the 'cooling off period' premise, which gave greater leeway to a person who had acted spontaneously against a wrong committed, rather than a person who had a sufficient amount of time to cool off, yet didn't, thus not acting reasonably.

As such, this had given the jury cause to believe it was Ted's drinking problem and, more importantly, his mental instability that enabled this unfortunate crime of aggravated battery to occur. That three of Ted's former Pittsburgh employers had stepped forward to corroborate Ted's violent mood swings, which had gotten him fired, only added to

Ted's guilt—not to mention Ted's shooting of an innocent spectator at Buffalo Bill's Wild West show. As such, the jury had decided that, in lieu of a prison sentence, they would commit Ted to a lunatic asylum.

Consequently, three years ago, Ted had been transferred from Auburn Prison to the Athens Lunatic Asylum in Ohio. The huge and lavish Victorian-styled structure sat imposingly upon a hill, and included its own farm with livestock, a dairy, an orchard, greenhouses and a power plant to generate electricity and steam heat. However, although looking more like a luxurious resort from the outside, the goings on inside were another matter. In the first two years of its operation, which had begun in 1874, the most commonly believed reason for their male patient's insanity was masturbation. The second most reasons were intemperance and dissipation, both of which the jury and hospital staff believed Ted suffered from.

The asylum separated its almost 600 patients by sex, with men occupying the left wing and women the right. The official policy was one of keeping the patients therapeutically busy with work and chores to maintain the building, grounds, livestock, kitchens and washrooms. The regimented schedule was not to Ted's liking, nor was his task. Due to his past experience at Buffalo Bill's and Barnum and Bailey's, Ted had been put on manure detail. Shoveling mounds of cow manure into compost piles, and spreading it over the fields as fertilizer, had become a humiliating punishment, which Ted was finding harder and harder to tolerate. Marc had fought hard over the years to defend Ted, having hired the best attorney he could afford, and even making two appeals, yet it all had been to no avail. This was especially due to Ted's cantankerous behavior, which had gotten worse over the past year.

Just five months ago, Ted had been shoveling dung when one of the doctors was making a round of inspections. The doctor had seen that Ted was dawdling, and he not only scolded Ted, but also had the temerity to strike Ted on the back of the head. Ted had swung around and bashed the doctor in the face with his dung-covered shovel. Dr. Jasper not only had lost six teeth, but the disfiguring gash across his face had taken months to heal as the feces had only infected the wound further, causing painful blisters. As such, no judge or jury was inclined to release Ted.

These setbacks angered Ted, but also plagued Marc, who just now arrived to visit his brother, once again—a trek he had religiously made once a month for the past three years.

Marc walked into the lavish lobby of the Asylum and signed the register. As he turned, he saw Ted being escorted down the stairs by an orderly—shackled in handcuffs.

As they approached, Marc demanded, "What's the meaning of these hand shackles?"

The orderly frowned. "Your lovely brother assaulted another doctor earlier this morning."

Marc looked at Ted, who shrugged his shoulders. "The dirty bastard deserved it!"

"What happened?" Marc pressed.

Ted rolled his eyes. "He walked into Barry's room, next door to me, and caught Barry in the process of pleasuring himself. And for that, he began whacking him in his privates with his riding stick to teach him a lesson."

Marc gazed at the orderly, who added, "Yes, so your brother ripped the riding stick out of Doctor Freedman's hands and began whipping *him* in the genitals!" He glanced at Ted, and snapped, "Your brother Ted is a menace!"

"*Ted* is a menace?" Marc retorted. "Do you mean to tell me your doctors beat patients in the genitals?"

"Mr. Wozniak," the orderly replied, "the unnatural and ungodly practice of masturbation is a clear sign of mental instability. Doctor Freedman, who also happens to be the head doctor at this facility, had every right to punish such lewd and degenerate behavior."

Marc shook his head. "This certainly appears to be an insane asylum alright, but I question if there is anyone here at all that is sane!"

The orderly's face twisted. "You are being most unreasonable and insulting, Mr. Wozniak!"

Marc gazed down at Ted's handcuffs. "*That* is what I call most unreasonable and insulting. Now take them off...*immediately!*"

Doctor Freedman heard the commotion and stepped out of his office. "What seems to be the problem?"

The orderly explained the situation, and Dr. Freedman walked over. "Mr. Wozniak, I know you are an intelligent and wealthy man, but if you are questioning the expertise of the medical profession, then I dare say you are clearly out of your element."

"You, doctor, are clearly out of your mind!" Marc blasted.

Dr. Freedman took off his spectacles and retorted, "Mr. Wozniak, your brother not only struck me repeatedly in the groin, but, as you well know, had also disfigured Dr. Jasper's face with a shovel! It is clearly your brother Ted who is out of his mind! And our policy is that he must remain in these hand shackles until one of our doctors declares it safe to remove them. Is that understood?"

Marc leaned into Freedman's face and growled, "Now hear me, and hear me good, I have had enough of the demented shenanigans around here, and my good friend, President Roosevelt, *will* be contacted about *your* actions, and those of this entire godforsaken facility! Is *that* understood?"

Dr. Freedman's face blanched as he stepped backward and clipped on his round spectacles. Gazing nervously at the orderly, he said, "Take the damned shackles off."

As the orderly took out his keys and began to unlock them, Freedman gazed at Marc with humiliated eyes. "I will release your brother into your care for the extent of your visit. But if he causes any further mischief or harm to anyone, *you* will be held responsible."

"Fine," Marc belched.

"Furthermore," the doctor said, "I am stating in the record that I am making this decision under duress."

Ted smiled as the cuffs came off. "I bet you make all your decisions under a-dress—you damn freak!"

As Marc chuckled, Freedman huffed and stormed back into his office.

Meanwhile, the orderly looked at both brothers with disgust and took his leave.

Marc grabbed Ted's arm and walked him out the front door and down the steps.

Ted looked at Marc. "Do you really intend to call President Roosevelt to help me?"

"Well, you know he was not at all thrilled with what you did with his shotgun," Marc said, "and TR is not the sort of man to forgive easily."

Ted gazed down at the walkway as they strolled along the well-manicured grounds. "Yes, he had even told me that night that if I walked out the door it was for good."

"Yes, I presume that is why he never offered to help us. And, in a way, I can't blame him," Marc said. "Fortunately we managed to keep TR out of this by saying it was your shotgun; otherwise this could have had major repercussions for him. Now that he's president, I dread the thought of getting him mixed up in this mess."

"But Huxley deserved it!" Ted carped. "He's human trash! And if it wasn't for me having the balls to teach him a lesson, you'd still be working for him!"

"That may be true, but—"

"*But*, nothing!" Ted railed, "you were pussyfooting around for years, unable to destroy that bastard! I should be praised as a hero, like at Kettle Hill, for hunting that villain down and ending not only our family's grief, but many people's grief."

"You are, Ted, at least to us and all those who suffered Huxley's wrath. But, many others see it differently. All they see is your long track record for causing mayhem with your drunk and disorderly outbursts, which resulted in numerous fights and two near-fatal shootings." Marc shook his head painfully. "And, Ted, I was *not* pussyfooting around. It's just that I have learned the ways of the world. You cannot run into a man's house drunk and then shoot him in front of witnesses, worse yet, his entire family. I have learned that we must use our *hearts* to defend mom's honor, but our *heads* to know how to go about doing that within the confines of the law. And as TR said, you never seem to learn from your mistakes, Ted. And it is that stubbornness, or lack of using your head, that has been the bane of your existence."

Ted hated these same old boring lectures, and snapped, "Well, my stubbornness to impulsively seek vengeance surely played out pretty well for you and the family though, didn't it? Not only did I cripple Huxley for life and neuter the damn rapist, but I also allowed you to take over Huxley Coal. So, life is pretty darn good for *everyone*—except *me!*"

As Marc veered around a staff member cruelly poking an inmate to pick weeds, he nodded—knowing that, at the time of the trial, he *had* been able to seize full control of Huxley Coal. As news hit the tabloids about Huxley's numerous scandals, J.P. Morgan sold his shares and bought stock in Huxley's next-door neighbor and rival, Pittsburgh Coal Company. As such, Marc had accumulated enough capital to purchase a majority of shares in Huxley Coal, and instructed Pendleton to make a sizable investment, whereby allowing Marc to choose a new board of directors that have made the corporation run smoothly ever since. The capital Marc invested into the mine had not only improved conditions at the site, but also caused an additional surge in business. Three days ago, on December 19, the Pittsburgh Coal Company had the worst explosion in U.S. history at their Darr Mine. Two hundred and thirty nine men and boys, mostly Hungarian immigrants, died in the blast and subsequent cave-in. The company's clients needed their orders fulfilled and turned to Marc. Needless to say, J.P. Morgan was not happy about the explosion and loss of business. Nevertheless, Marc was now pained to see his brother locked up in this *insane*, insane asylum, and to hear his envious and resentful outbursts.

"Ted, you certainly have made things good for us, and I want to tell you that I just renamed the corporation. So even Huxley's name has been erased. It is now Tasso Coal."

Ted was still steaming, but now also peeved that he had to crack a smile. "That's nice, Marc, real nice. I appreciate that." His smile vanished. "Too bad I'll never be able to step foot in Tasso Coal!"

Marc's head dropped as they walked past the orchard and continued to tour the grounds. He gazed back up. "Listen Ted, as I said, I am deeply grateful that you ended a great deal of pain in our family and even in Huxley's two families. It took a few years for them to get over the scandal and public embarrassment, but now that Archie has been abandoned by both families, they have come around to the realization that it was better that his sins were unveiled. They all had been living in a world of lies." Marc paused as his mind dredged up an old memory. He smiled, and continued, "And that reminds me of the tale momma had told us when we were young boys about Plato's *Analogy of the Cave*."

Ted squinted, not recalling the tale. "What cave?"

Marc shook his head. "You see, you never listen!" As Ted did his typical rolling of his eyes, Marc said, "It was about a group of people who were chained inside a cave since birth with their heads facing a blank wall. As such, they could only see the shadows on the wall of the objects that moved behind them, never the real objects themselves. As such, their perceived world of reality was just a world of shadows, so they never knew the truth. And neither of Huxley's families ever knew the truth, either."

Ted nodded, now recalling the story, but sneered, "Yeah, that's just swell! So, like I said, everyone is happy, living their lives in the real world, while I'm stuck here staring into the dark shadows of this wicked madhouse!"

Marc's head dropped, again, as he kicked a rock off the paved path. He knew what Ted had done was not right, but it certainly had rectified quite a few problems that Marc had been unable to resolve for years, problems that had caused innumerable hardships and suffering for their entire family.

Marc scratched his mustache and looked up. "Listen, Ted, life is not fair. We try our best to make laws and rules to eliminate injustices, but we never can manage to get it right."

Ted stopped, and then sat on a bench that overlooked the asylum's farm, while Marc joined him. Ted gazed solemnly at the same rows of wheat he routinely fertilized and then at the cows, whose manure he shoveled every day. Without looking at his brother, he uttered, "My world has gone to shit, Marc. And in this shitty world of mine there are only two ways I know of to settle a matter like this."

"What's that?"

Ted looked into Marc's eyes, his face painfully blank. "Either I escape, or kill myself." A tear welled in Ted's eye as he broke down. "I just can't take it any longer, Marc."

Marc's heart dropped as he put his arm around him. "Don't talk like that, Ted. *Ever!*" Marc gazed up at the asylum on the hill. As he looked at the Victorian structure, it unnervingly began to evoke the aura of a haunted mansion, just like those found in Poe's grisly tales of horror. Marc looked back at his crestfallen brother as a lump welled in his throat. "Listen, Ted, what I said to that jackass, Dr. Freedman, is the truth. I *will* call the president."

Ted's head rose as his grieved face showed a glimmer of hope.

Marc patted Ted's shoulder. "So, this unfair system of ours does offer us another option to settle this matter, Ted. It's called *connections!*"

Ted's face blossomed into a full-blown grin. "But Roosevelt said—"

"Never mind that," Marc interjected, "I had never asked for TR's help because you had told me about his ultimatum that day, and I knew he didn't want his shotgun linked to your shooting. But five years of this madness are enough. I think you served your penance, and I'm sure TR will agree. After all, you did save his life and you *are* a war hero!"

Ted hugged his brother as tears of joy streamed down his cheeks. "This is great, Marc, just great. Thank you!"

A tear blurred Marc's vision, as he gave Ted a tight hug, and then eased him backward. "Alright, let's get something to eat, and then I'll be on my way to get you out of here."

Marc and Ted walked back to the asylum and entered the cafeteria. They each grabbed a sandwich and drink, and then took a seat.

Ted looked at his younger brother, who was now 38 years old. "I can't believe how time has flown, Marc, especially these past five years. Christ, do you realize that I'm forty-one now, that's older than Roosevelt was when we rode with him in Cuba."

Marc nodded as he bit into his ham and Swiss sandwich. "Yes, and I reckon it's time that I fill you in on some of the news and events that you've missed over these past five years."

As Ted bit into his sandwich, Marc said, "Back in 1902, army surgeon Walter Reed discovered that mosquitoes carry Yellow Fever—that horrible disease that killed our fellow Rough Riders in Cuba. So now we can try to find a cure. But, on the downside, Richard Gatling died five years ago."

Ted sighed. "Too bad, his Gatling guns really helped us win San Juan Hill. What a great invention."

"Yes, it was, but let me tell you; the new waves of inventions that are streaming from American ingenuity are simply mindboggling, Ted. These two brothers, named Orville and Wilbur Wright, invented an airplane four years ago. Man can fly! And Henry Ford debuted his first automobile for consumer use, the Model A, that same year."

Ted scratched his head. "That's amazing, alright!"

"It sure is. But I must tell you about some personal victories. Do you remember the strike last year—when a half million miners across the nation walked off, demanding an 8 hour work day, better pay, and safer conditions?" As Ted nodded, Marc continued, "Well, that every other mine in Pennsylvania had gone on strike, except ours, left consumers looking to *us* to fulfill their orders. This has been a record year in sales, and I think our fellow competitors learned a valuable lesson. Running an honorable and ethical business like ours, which treats workers fairly, does pay off, literally!"

"Good for you, Marc!" Ted blurted with glee as he patted his brother on the back. "Your good intentions really *have* paid off."

"Well, after settling their disputes, they did regain most of their old clients. But, yes, I *am* extremely happy that mine owners and workers are making better arrangements and safer working conditions. It has been a long battle, as you know, but I'm really beginning to see the fruits of my labor."

As Ted listened with a mixture of wonder (about all the progress being made) and sorrow (about the five years of his life that were lost), Marc offered up a few tidbits of trivia, such as how the Italian opera sensation, Enrico Caruso, earns a whopping $960.00 per performance, and recently made his first recording. Or how J.P. Morgan proudly hailed the newly rebuilt N.Y. Stock Exchange building, by saying, "The magnificence of our new home is only in keeping with the magnitude of our business." On a final note, Marc explained how a seemingly unhinged Spaniard, called Pablo Picasso, introduced his bizarre and primitive new artwork called Cubism.

Ted shook his head as he sipped his coffee. "Well, it's good to hear that some things out there are just like here— *ass backwards!*"

Marc chuckled, but then raised his finger. "But hold on. I must tell you about TR. He has turned out to be one of the most dynamic presidents I, or the nation, has ever seen. The man is like a raging buffalo in Tiffany's!"

Ted put down his coffee and listened carefully as Marc proudly explained how TR was aggressively attacking corruption in corporate America. He mentioned Roosevelt's bold warning to Americans, namely that he would not allow the country to become a plutocracy, or a Wall Street-syndicate civilization. TR vowed to curb those seeking to rule the nation through wealth, and promote legislation to bust up monopolies. Marc eagerly described TR's attack on the Standard Oil trust, which had caused a stir, and how TR is now being called a traitor to his class. But as Marc pointed out, it was TR's rich class who were the traitors, traitors to the country. Their greed denied competition, while their exploitation of workers denied laborers the nation's most fundamental principles of freedom, especially the pursuit of happiness. Marc then explained that TR had recently read Upton Sinclair's book *The Jungle*, which described the filthy conditions in packinghouses, where diseased animals were slaughtered and packaged with healthy ones, while workers never washed their hands, and rats ran wild. As such, TR passed the Pure Food and Drug Law, which now ensures that sanitary and ethical practices are followed. On the international front, Marc explained how TR boldly gained control over building the technological wonder of the age, the Panama Canal.

"My God," Ted said, "the man *is* a dynamo. I reckon I really was a fool to storm out of his house that day."

"Yes, you can chalk that up as another fine blunder you made!" Marc said with a chuckle.

Normally Ted would have balked, but instead, he laughed. "It's incredible. I can't believe all the things that man has achieved."

"I really don't know where he gets all the energy from myself," Marc said, "but I'll tell you this much; our coal stations in the Hawaiian Islands, Midway and the Philippines will really start to boom once the Panama Canal opens."

It was during the Spanish-American War when the McKinley administration realized how crippling it was not to have quick access to sail U.S. warships from one coast to the other. The long trek around Cape Horn of South America to reach Manila had taken so long that it was apparent a channel at the isthmus of Central America was crucial, not only for military reasons but also trade. And as Marc was astutely aware, once the Panama Canal opens it will increase trade and the number of steam-driven merchant ships that will need coal, Tasso Coal.

"So, you see, Ted, the times are changing, and they're changing faster with each passing year. That's why I have to get you out of here."

"Do you really think Roosevelt can do it?" Ted asked eagerly as he dropped his bland sandwich.

"Haven't you been listening?" Marc said with a smile. "The man is a ball of energy, just like one of Tesla's wireless glowing electric balls."

Ted squinted. "What is that?"

Marc waved his hand. "Oh, forget it, it is just some wild invention by a brilliant wizard." Marc grabbed his lunch tray and stood up. "But getting back to TR; yes, I'm sure he can get you out of here, and when he does, I'll treat you to a real lunch at the new Plaza Grand Luxe Hotel in New York."

Ted returned his lunch tray, and said; "I guess that's another high-falutin' gathering place for high society, right?"

"Right. And, *you*, my dear brother, will be there sometime in the New Year. So count that as your Christmas present."

As they hugged, Ted's voice cracked as he whispered in Marc's ear, "Thanks, Marc. I know I've b-been a lot of trouble, but you have always b-been there for me."

Marc leaned back, and gazed deep into his brother's eyes. "That's what family is all about, Ted. No matter how bad you screw up, I'll be here for you."

"Well, I really appreciate it," Ted said with tears welling in his eyes. "And I appreciate you taking that asshole's name off the business!"

Marc chuckled. "Yes, Tasso Coal has a much better ring to it."

Just then the irksome orderly stepped into the doorway, dangling the handcuffs. Ted glared at him—hate, once again, gleaming in his eyes like daggers.

Marc spotted the exchange and grabbed Ted's arm. "Now you hang in there, Ted, and don't let these bastards unwind you."

Ted remained fixed on the orderly, like a lion sizing up its prey just before lunging to make the deadly strike.

"*Ted!*" Marc grunted. "Remember the Plaza Hotel. Just keep that in mind. Do you hear me?"

Ted cracked his neck, and then gazed at his brother. "Fine. But you better get me out of here early in the New Year. Do you hear me?"

"I will, I mean, *we* will. Remember, you'll now have the President of the United States on your side. So bear that in mind!"

Ted managed to smile as he said, "Yeah, you're right. These quacks don't stand a chance against a seasoned hunter like TR!"

Marc chuckled. "Now *that's* more like it! These idiots don't realize that duck season is about to open."

Ted looked at the orderly and grinned as he spoke out of the corner of his mouth, "And, oh, how I'll enjoy devouring these dead ducks!"

Marc patted Ted on the back. "That's it. Now go on."

Ted walked toward the orderly, who shackled his hands, and nudged him down the corridor. Ted spun his head around and winked, while Marc returned the same. With a heavy heart, Marc watched as they receded down the hallway. The orderly then turned and shoved Ted into his room and locked the door. Turning to look back at Marc, the orderly smacked the keys against his leg, as a sinister grin bent his face.

Fate

December 25, 1907 – April 25, 1908

The days passed, and the Wozniaks looked forward to celebrating Christmas, which had become all the more special for Marc, since he loved the joy and enthusiasm that little Sophia brought to the holiday. Sophia was now 8 years old and had long been in contact with her feisty suffragette relative, Aunt Filomena. They had written letters to each other almost weekly, and when she was allowed to use the telephone, always spoke to her aunt with great passion. Marianne had been a delightful mother, yet her forte was literature, and she instilled in Sophia a love for the written word. Meanwhile, Aunt Filomena fired the spark in little Sophia to fight, in particular for women's rights. This took on the form of not just coordinating rallies to lobby government, but also endeavoring in activities that previously only men enjoyed. And little Sophia already had an interest in the newfangled invention, which ran not on coal, but petroleum—the automobile.

Being one of the first families in Pittsburgh to own a Ford Model A, Marc had allowed Sophia to drive the vehicle with its odd, internal combustion engine. Yet Sophia was not content to just drive the vehicle, she enjoyed opening up the small black hood and fixing the engine whenever it malfunctioned. Often with greasy hands and a dirty face, little Sophia was nothing like her clean and polished mother. She had even read the newspapers with great interest back in June of last year when the Peking-to-Paris automobile race was the grandest endeavor of its kind. The five automobiles had traveled 8,000 miles, crossing the Great Wall of China, the Gobi Desert, the Ural Mountains, Prussia and into France. The roads were only marginally roughed out, most being bumpy horse and cart paths, and the drivers had to endure extremes in temperature, ranging from frigid cold to scorching desert heat. Having an affinity for her grandmother's heritage, Sophia II was elated to see that Prince Borghese from Italy won the race after 62 days of near disasters.

However, that event had spawned the greatest automobile race of all time, the New York to Paris race, which was set to start in the coming New Year on February 12, 1908. For months, Sophia had been wishing that Santa Claus would bring her tickets to travel to New York City to see the historic start of the race, but had been told that her request was too expensive of a gift to ask Santa. Nevertheless, on Christmas morning, Sophia was shocked and overjoyed when she found out that her father was one and the same as Saint Nick and that her wish did come true.

Meanwhile, the Wozniak family celebrated a delightful Christmas as even Rusty and Calvin dropped by for a drink. Marc's mind, however, was elsewhere, namely on his brother Ted. The evening moved along as they ate a hearty meal and enjoyed an array of pastries and home baked pies.

The next few days rolled by, and after the New Year, on January 5th, Marc finally stepped into the den and picked up his new candlestick telephone. Eagerly, he lifted the bell-shaped receiver off the hook and spoke into the cone-shaped mouthpiece. He asked the operator to connect him to the president's personal line, and waited impatiently as he paced back and forth.

Since winning the election for a second term last year, Roosevelt had been busy promoting his Square Deal, which called for railroad and meat inspections, supervision of insurance companies, and child labor laws, which was a personal triumph for Marc, thus validating his resolve, hard work and compassion for a just cause. However, the economy had once again taken a serious downturn (the worst the nation had ever seen, with 20 percent unemployment), and TR's delay in answering the telephone was due to this very critical issue.

A moment later, TR's reedy voice came blaring through the receiver. "Marc, are you there?"

"Yes, Teddy. How was your Christmas and New Years?"

"Hectic, Marc. We had little time for celebrations this year. With the nation ensnared in another financial sinkhole, this one being the absolute nadir, I've been rather busy trying to ensure that we stay on solid ground."

Marc now had trepidations. "Well, I can only imagine the burden you carry, so I truly hate to bother you—" Marc hesitated, "but—"

"But what?" TR said. "Go on, boy, ask away. I live to solve problems. You know that!"

Marc chuckled. "Yes, I know, but I do have a big favor to ask, and perhaps this is not the best time."

"Nonsense!" TR bellowed. "Fire away. I only hope you're not going to ask to be my secretary of the interior,

Marc, because, as you know, I already gave it to James Garfield Jr."

"No, no," Marc said, "I recall your generous offer, and my refusal, which still stands. No, this favor is not for me, but rather for my brother Ted."

There was utter silence. Nervously, Marc rubbed his chin and sat down. Marc now realized that this request was far worse than if he did ask to be secretary of the interior. He shook his head and thought: *what an idiot!*

TR's voice finally sounded, confirming Marc's fears. "Marc, you know I would give you the shirt off my back, but your brother, and that shooting, well, I don't know if that is something I should touch."

Marc swallowed hard. "Listen, Teddy, right from the start I never asked for you to get involved with this matter. But let's face it; this is far from the only shooting that has made the headlines. As much as we pride ourselves on being above such things, we still live in a wild and restless country. You recall what happened to the architect Stanford White, from McKim, Mead and White?"

"Yes, of course. The poor fellow was shot three times in the head by a jealous husband as he sat in Madison Square Garden."

"Exactly," Marc said. "Crimes of passion have been committed by many decent people who have been wronged. And although many have tried to paint my brother as being violent and insane, I assure you, he is not. He had been carrying around a lot of hurt for many years, Teddy, and just because he couldn't restrain himself, like I somehow managed to do, is no reason that he should suffer for the rest of his life in some crazy, insane asylum. And let me tell you, there are some truly *insane* practices that go on there."

As Marc explained some the odd and barbaric events that had taken place at Athens Lunatic Asylum, he could hear TR's moans and sighs on the other end. After giving the president a good earful, TR finally replied, "That is utterly deplorable and unacceptable behavior!"

Marc sat up in his chair. "It is, Teddy, and my brother shouldn't have to tolerate anymore of that abuse. He served five years of his life in both prison and that nut orchard, and we need your help."

TR responded in one of his trademark monologues, "Marc, as you know, I am not a man to ask favors, and I know you aren't either. But I do understand there comes a time when we must reach out to others. As you are well aware, the recent economy is heading toward another major panic, and it has my cabinet and myself in a quandary. There has been so much trickery and dishonesty in high places, Marc, that it's appalling. The recent scandals with Harriman, Rockefeller, Heinze and others, have caused such a genuine shock to people that they have begun to be afraid that every bank really has something rotten in it. But this financial hydra has my back against the wall, and that wall is Wall Street. It galls me to no end that I must seek a 150 million dollar bail out from Morgan, Rockefeller and the like, when I have spent the better part of my presidential career lambasting and battling them. But ask them, I must." TR paused, and finally said, "So if I can ask my adversaries for a favor, I would be grossly remiss if I denied my dear friend a favor."

Marc's face lit up. "That's fantastic, Teddy! I mean your offer to help us, not the 150 million dollar loan or troubled economy, of course."

TR chuckled. "I gathered that."

Marc's knees were bobbing. "I truly appreciate this, Teddy, rather, the entire Wozniak family appreciates this."

"I will contact the asylum right this second," TR said vehemently, "so put your hearts and minds at ease. I never forgot your brother's service to our nation, how he saved my life, or the day I pinned those two medals on his shirt. So in all likelihood, this day should have come sooner."

"Well, as they say, better late than never. Again, we thank you."

"You are all quite welcome, my friend. Be well, and do let me know that everything is settled after I make my call, because if those haughty imbeciles dilly dally, heads *will* roll!"

"I certainly will, Teddy. You're a gem! Take good care, my dear friend."

Marc hung up the telephone and leapt to his feet as he yelled, "Yahoo!"

Marianne, Sophia, and Remus came running into the room, while Stan rolled in behind them.

Sophia looked up and asked, "What's going on, papa?"

Meanwhile, Remus inquired, "Yeah, what are you so happy about?"

Marc grabbed Marianne and pulled her next to him. He kissed her on the cheek, and said to all of them, "Ted will be released sometime soon!"

As they recoiled with excitement and shock, Stan asked, "How did that happen?"

Marianne looked at Marc with an affectionate gaze, knowing, as Marc said, "I just got off the telephone with the president, and he agreed to call the asylum, right now!"

Sophia jumped with joy and hugged her father. "That's great!" But then she squinted. "Actually, I hardly remember him. I just recall him calling me a little monkey."

Marianne smiled. "Yes, you were just a little girl when he left, but those were exciting days alright."

Stan shook his head and chuckled. "Yes, the monkey's uncle sure did bring excitement into our lives, perhaps a bit too much. But thank God. He's finally coming home!"

Meanwhile, Remus had a grin pasted on his face. He was now 21 years old, and after his father's crippling incident and downfall, Remus had left Pendleton Iron Works to return to Tasso Coal. He had never gotten the chance to bond with his father, and he had grown to prefer it that way after learning about his numerous indiscretions and crimes. Having been under Marc's wing for many years, Remus had proven himself to be a smart businessman with scruples, surprising Stan, who had for many years believed that Huxley's tainted bloodline would have had a malevolent effect on Remus somehow. Nevertheless, Remus always had a fondness for Ted, and now eagerly looked forward to his release and return.

Several days passed, and Marc was now concerned that he had not heard from Dr. Freedman or his facility. He was eager to see if they had received the presidential call and pardon, and he picked up the telephone and placed the call with the operator.

A receptionist answered and put him on hold.

Two minutes later, Dr. Freedman answered, "Hello?"

"Dr. Freedman, this is Marc Wozniak."

"Yes, yes, I know," he said in a huff. "I suppose you think you're a big man, having the president call me, huh?"

"Call it what you like, Dr. Freedman, but I recall how you pompously strut your feathers the last time we met. And I *did* tell you this would not stand. So enough of the squawking, it's too damned bad your feathers are ruffled, the bottom line is; when can I pick up my brother?"

Marc could hear Freedman's heated breath melting the mouthpiece at the other end as the doctor finally retorted, "Your chronically sick and demented brother will be release as soon as we fill out all the paperwork!"

"That does not tell me *when*," Marc bellowed. "I want a date!"

"Fine, let's say January 15," Freedman spat.

"The 15th, it is. I look forward to seeing you, Doctor."

No response came as the connection was abruptly terminated.

"That son-of-a-bitch!" Marc vented as he slammed the receiver back onto the candlestick's drop hook.

Marianne had been sitting on the sofa knitting a sweater, when she looked up and smiled. "I suspect Dr. Freedman doesn't like you."

Marc placed the candlestick down on the end table. "Doctors rarely like to be told that they're wrong. After all, they're educated. Yet this buffoon manages an entire ward of mentally sick people. It's scary!"

"Well, calm down," Marianne said, "the 15th is only 10 days away. And you and your brother are the winners, regardless of what that jackass says or thinks."

Marc smiled as he walked over and sat next to her. Leaning over, he kissed her, and said, "I'm glad I married you!"

"You should be!" She said with a playful grin.

Marc shook his head and gazed down at the sweater. "So, who is that for?"

Marianne held it up. "For Ted. You think he'll like it."

"No," Marc said instinctively.

Marianne turned and looked at Marc, concerned. "*No? Do you really think he won't like it?*"

Marc knew the cute little ducks she was knitting into the design looked very decorative, but he wasn't sure if Ted would like being reminded of the Long Island duck hunt that turned dreadfully sour. Then again, he thought, he may be over thinking this. He decided to give her a subtle hint.

"Well, perhaps it would be better to put horses on there instead of Long Island ducks."

"What's wrong with ducks? Look at them. They're so adorable, and—" Marianne got the connection. "Oh, dear! I never thought of that."

"Well, I wasn't sure if I'm being overly conscious or not, because he may very well like them. After all, Ted does have a dark sense of humor."

Marianne chuckled. "He does at that. But I'll change these ducks to horses just to be safe."

"Good idea," Marc said. He then chuckled. "But who knows, is it really better to be a horse's ass than a quack?"

As they both laughed, Marianne began knitting the transformation.

Eight days later, the telephone rang.

Marianne picked up the receiver. "Hello?"

The voice asked, "Is Mr. Wozniak there?"

"Yes, please hold on, I'll get him."

Marianne called out, and Marc walked into the room eating an apple. "Who is it?"

"I don't know, they didn't say."

Marc grabbed the telephone and lifted the receiver to his ear. Speaking into the mouthpiece, he said, "Hello. Who is this?"

"This is Doctor Bannerman from the Athens Lunatic Asylum. Is this Mr. Marc Wozniak?"

"Yes, it is," Marc said, "I hope this call is not to delay the release of my brother, because I will be there in two days to pick him up."

"Well, Mr. Wozniak, that is why I'm calling. You see, there is no need for you to come here, because—"

"What do you mean no need?" Marc said, his voice rising with frustration. "This better not be some foolish attempt to delay his release or test my patience?"

"Please, Mr. Wozniak," the doctor said firmly and coldly, "The reason I said there is no need to come here is because you brother is no longer here. He—"

"Where is he?" Marc interjected.

"Well, allow me tell you, Mr. Wozniak," Bannerman snapped, his voice reeking with condescension. "He has been shipped back to Auburn Prison, pending his trial."

"What the hell do you mean trial?" Marc blasted. "Just what is going on over there?"

"Your brother, Mr. Wozniak, is awaiting trial for murder."

"Now hold on a minute," Marc snapped, "he cannot be retried; he did not kill Archibald Huxley."

"No, he did not," Bannerman said, "he killed Doctor Freedman."

Marc's face went pale as a flash of white light momentarily blurred his vision. "He *what?*"

"Your brother bludgeoned Dr. Freedman to death, Mr. Wozniak. He broke out of his room at 3:00 a.m. this morning, grabbed a cane from one of our old patient's room, and then brutally attacked the doctor without provocation. The man is a dangerous animal, Mr. Wozniak, and he *will* pay for this crime. Of that, I am certain!"

Marc fell back into the chair behind him, while Marianne rushed anxiously over. "What happened?"

As the doctor's voice continued to wheeze out of the tinny receiver, Marc simply hung it back on the drop hook and placed the telephone down. His eyes wandered and then looked up at Marianne. "Ted killed Dr. Freedman. He's back in Auburn Prison, awaiting trial."

Marianne covered her mouth with both hands, trembling. "Oh, my God! No!"

Just then Stan rolled in. "What's all the commotion?"

As they both looked at Stan with their dilated eyes, Stan knew it was bad news, and, as such, figured it must pertain to Ted. "What did he do *now?*"

Marianne sat down next to Marc, gazed at the floor and then back up at Stan. "He murdered Dr. Freedman."

Stan's head fell as he shook his head. "Oh, Christ. He's really done it this time."

Marianne held Marc's hand. "Is there any way we, or the president, can—"

"No!" Marc huffed. "It's all over. He'll fry for this."

"But you said that the last time you were there Dr. Freedman was antagonizing and abusing patients," Marianne said, "I'm sure Ted had a good reason."

Stan snorted. "Are you?"

Marc looked at Stan. "That's not fair. I'm sure that prickly doctor incited this whole mess, but proving it is the problem. We'd be pitting Ted, with his long abysmal record, against the head doctor at a prestigious facility. It would be extremely difficult to make a jury believe that Ted had just cause, especially being a patient at the asylum."

"But it's worth a try," Marianne said. "And would the president—"

"Don't even mention his name," Marc cut in. "I would *never* ask him to get involved in this horrendous mess. As it was, he was good enough to get him released. But now that Ted has a full-fledged murder on his hands, this is not something that I would even dare heap on the president."

"What do you plan on doing now?" Stan asked.

"I need to catch a train and head up to Auburn, N.Y. I'll leave tomorrow morning." Marc rubbed his throbbing head. "I'll leave it up to you and Marianne to break the news to Remus and Sophia. I'm going to bed."

Marc stood up and walked out the living room with his head down and shoulders slouched.

Stan took a deep breath. "Jesus Christ. This is a nightmare."

Marianne nodded and wept.

❦

The next morning Marc caught a train and arrived at Auburn Prison by late afternoon. The meeting was heart wrenching as Marc looked through a set of steel bars at his crestfallen brother in his striped prison uniform. Ted's face was disturbingly gaunt and sallow with lifeless eyes peering out of dark, skeletal eye sockets. In a feeble voice, torn with abuse and hopelessness, Ted explained to Marc how Dr. Freedman had been taunting him and made his life miserable.

The doctor had kept Ted handcuffed, limited his food rations, and antagonized him at every turn. If Ted had even tried to complain, he was punished with hard labor or put in solitary confinement. Dr. Freedman had also experimented with a new therapy that was intended to calm and subdue Ted's aggressive behavior. This involved attaching low voltage wires to his temples, and then passing an electric current through his head. Ted's body had twisted violently with convulsions, since they had no idea how much voltage to administer. Appallingly, the burn marks were still visible.

Marc listened as rage surged through his veins. Sitting with them was the local attorney Marc hired, who jotted down notes. When their time was up, they left Ted's visiting chamber, walking down one of the depressing, brick-walled corridors. The attorney informed Marc that he would do his best, but had to lay it on the line. Between Ted's criminal record, and the fact that the medical society would fully support Freedman's treatments, including the new electro-shock therapy, the prospect of Ted winning any type of plea bargain looked extremely bleak.

Marc telephoned home and relayed the disheartening news. He then asked to speak to Remus and instructed him to manage things for another two weeks, while he stayed on longer to see Ted through the trial, which would begin tomorrow. Marc wasn't pleased that it was slated so quickly, but the attorney said he was ready to move forward.

Remus hung up the telephone, and did his part by managing Tasso Coal, while Marianne and Stan tended to Sophia—who often broke down, not comprehending why her uncle would never come home again.

Marc attended the hearings, and by the end of the first week, Marc called home, his voice riddled with anger, "I have never seen such insanity! The prosecution has presented a series of experts who are all defending Dr. Freedman's long illustrious record and his pioneering use of electro-shock therapy. They're hailing that nut as some kind of medical Messiah!"

"But what about Ted's burn marks?" Marianne replied, "doesn't the jury have eyes?"

"I hate to say it," Marc said, "but I had actually seen four jurors smile when our attorney asked Ted to present them as evidence."

"Dear God! What kind of people are they?" Marianne asked, appalled and infuriated.

"Well, the prosecution had done a splendid job of thoroughly saturating the jury with all of Ted's past misdeeds, Marianne. In fact, they had done such a perfect job of painting him as a warped and drunken derelict that instead of seeing a beautiful portrait by Bouguereau or Sargent, they saw a deranged Picasso." As Marianne listened to Marc, she sat and held her head. Marc filled her in on all the painful details, and then concluded, "I have little faith that Ted will get out of this mess, Marianne. All we can hope for is a life sentence rather than the electric chair."

"Oh, my God!" she blustered. "No!"

"We knew this was inevitable, Marianne. It is what it is. So let's just keep our fingers crossed that they don't send him to the chair."

Another slow, nail-biting week had passed, and Marc called again, this time to say that the trial would be delayed another two weeks, since their attorney sequestered four Rough Riders as character witnesses. Again, Marc asked that Remus hold the fort, while he stayed in Auburn to see the trial through to the end.

Meanwhile, little Sophia had been anxiously waiting for her father to come home so they could travel to New York City to see the Great Automobile Race take off on February 12th. Marianne hadn't told Sophia that her uncle could very well be executed, yet it was troubling for her to hear Sophia talk of automobile racing at a time like this. Yet, she knew how children were, often self-centered, and certainly didn't wish to tell her about the severity of her uncle's situation.

As the grueling two weeks passed, Marianne and Stan had grown deeply concerned. Marc usually called at least once a week, but they hadn't heard a word.

Meanwhile, sitting next to his attorney in Auburn, New York, Ted awaited the jury's decision, while Marc sat behind them, leaning forward with his elbows on the railing that divided them. Behind him, on the opposite side of the aisle, was the Freedman family and members from the asylum.

The judge then summoned the head juror, who slowly stood up.

With a deep and somber voice, the judge asked, "How does the jury find Ted Wozniak?"

The juror glanced at Ted, and then looked up at the judge as he said, "We find Ted Wozniak guilty of first degree murder, Your Honor."

As the Freedman family applauded and released a flurry of sighs, Ted sprang to his feet and turned around, gazing into Marc's empathetic eyes.

Meanwhile, the judge's ominous voice rang out, "By the power invested in me, I hereby sentence you, Ted Wozniak, to death by electrocution."

As the judge continued his lethal sentence, Marc and Ted went numb as they embraced each other. Their bodies were shaking as if the deadly volts were passing through them right now.

The attorney closed his briefcase and gazed at the two entwined brothers. "I'm sorry, but we tried every angle."

Marc waved him away as he patted Ted on the back. Meanwhile, a tear of anguish dripped on his condemned brother's shoulder.

The bailiff grabbed Ted's arm. "Let's go, Ted. I have to take you back."

As Ted held onto his brother's hand, not wanting to let go, he looked at the bailiff, and inquired, "I didn't hear, when, I mean, how much longer do I have?"

"You have a little over two months, Ted," the bailiff said compassionately. "The judge said April 25th."

Ted looked back at Marc as their hands parted. "Is there any way to get a life sen—" Ted's head fell. "Oh, forget it. I can't live like an animal locked in a cell any longer. It's best they—" Ted couldn't say it. He gazed up at his brother. "Can you be there? I mean, I must see you before they—"

"Yes," Marc interjected, with a painful lump in his throat. "Of course I'll be there, Ted. Like I always told you, that's what family is all about. We stick together through thick and thin." As Ted swallowed hard, Marc added, "Now you go, and be brave. Don't let them take your dignity."

Ted chuckled, nervously, "Yeah, they can take my life, but not my dignity."

Marc pushed back his tears and gazed down at the floor, while the bailiff escorted Ted out of the courtroom. Marc sank back into the wooden bench and gazed emptily at the floor for 15 minutes. A wave of nausea washed over him as the unbelievable nightmare stormed through his head. The horrid thought that his brother will be strapped in a chair and electrocuted seemed barbaric. That his life would end on an exact date and at a specific time seemed even more inconceivable. Tears streamed down his face.

Back in Pittsburgh, Marianne finally received the long-anticipated telephone call, yet her worst fears were realized.

Two days later, Marc arrived home to a sullen house as the Wozniak family, minus little Sophia, huddled together and commiserated for hours. The gloomy atmosphere was only broken when Sophia strolled into the room and innocently revived her plea to not miss the Great Race. Marianne had grown awfully tired of hearing it by now, yet it came as a relief to Marc, who couldn't resist the cute expression on his daughter's face.

The days flew by rather quickly as Sophia crossed off each day on her calendar until the day finally arrived. Marc and Sophia had packed their bags, and they now said their goodbyes and rode to the station. Catching a train, Marc actually enjoyed the distraction of his daughter's juvenile conversation, which took his weary mind far away from the hell that waited. Sophia rambled on about the games of croquet and volleyball she played, or the dresses and toys she had seen in Montgomery Ward's catalog. Piquing Marc's interest was how she fixed their Ford's brakes. As the train arrived in New York City, they darted off the platform and headed toward Times Square. As they did, they were swallowed up in the massive crowds that were packing the sidewalks for miles down Broadway. Squeezing their way through, they managed to get near enough to see the starting line, while photographers with huge reflex cameras mounted on tripods stood nearby. The six automobiles in the race were sitting at the starting line; three of which were French, one Italian, one German and one American. With the firing of a blank pistol, the drivers revved their engines and shifted into gear to the thrush of a roaring crowd.

Sophia—wrapped in her heavy wool coat, knitted hat, and mittens—clapped her hands wildly, as the automobiles passed by her. Her little eyes scrutinized every face behind the steering wheels, as well as each decorative line of the international assortment of automobiles. She waved as the Italian Zust car jumped into the lead, followed by the American Thomas car.

She looked up at her father, concerned, "Oh my, I hope we beat the Italian car."

Marc laughed. "Sophia, this race is across the entire planet. They'll be driving 20,000 miles, and the race may last five or six months."

Sophia still didn't quite get it. She had raced Remus (who now had his own Model A) plenty of times before, and whether they raced 200 feet or quarter of a mile, she knew that being in the lead always mattered. Yet, her father explained that, in a race of this great distance, a car could fall behind by several days and still emerge a winner.

Marc was at least glad that Sophia was cheering for the American as he recalled what his father had told him; it was most important to become an American—their Italian and Polish heritage had to come second. Marc realized that the Wozniaks were indeed assimilating right before his eyes, and he gazed heavenward, hoping his father's eyes were seeing the same vision.

Sophia, however, called Marc's attention back down to the race as they watched the tail of the last car skid around the slushy corner. As hordes of spectators excitedly shifted in different directions, Marc grabbed Sophia's hand and began walking through the massive crowd (which had reached a quarter-of-a-million), and headed uptown.

Eventually arriving at the Plaza Hotel, Marc informed the *maître d'* of his prominent friend—namely the former governor of New York, and current president, Teddy Roosevelt—and he was immediately seated in a prime spot by a window overlooking Central Park. As he sat and dinned with his beautiful little daughter, Marc couldn't help but drift off to reflect on this bittersweet moment. He was supposed to be dining here with his brother Ted to celebrate his freedom, yet that day would never come. A dark, gloomy cloud was beginning to muddle his senses when suddenly Sophia's luminous voice and lust for life broke through the mist. As he gazed at her across the table, chattering away like an internal combustion engine, he smiled, finding a ray of consolation. She (along with Remus) was the future of the Wozniak family, and he now found solace in that fact—at least for the moment, but he would take that gleaming moment and enjoy it, for he knew much darker clouds were on the horizon.

April 25th came faster than Marc cared for, yet he could only imagine what his brother Ted had to endure these past two months. The thought of knowing that each day that ticked away brought you closer to the grave had to be the most hellish punishment a mortal could ever endure. And as morbid or cruel as it sounded, Marc couldn't wait for this dreadful day to be over so Ted could lie in peace.

Having arrived at Auburn prison, Marc solemnly approached the entrance to the execution chamber's viewing room. The white-bricked cell was windowless, save for the viewing window that was covered by a drawn curtain. It was only 20 feet deep and 22 feet wide, with seating for about 30 people. As he entered the rear door, he saw only eight people. He recognized Dr. Freedman's wife and two daughters sitting in the front row, and the other five were mere citizens eager to watch a criminal fry. Marc walked in quietly and sat on the opposite side of the room, two rows behind the Freedmans, in an aisle seat. He intended to avoid them, if at all possible, and leave quickly. He preferred not even being a spectator to such a barbaric practice, yet this wasn't about him, this was about his frightened brother Ted, who wanted to see a familiar and loving face before he left this world to enter an eternity of sleep. It was moments like this that always tested Marc's religious beliefs to the maximum, and he was trying awfully hard to keep it together, yet he had to. It would be the ultimate failure in his life if Ted should see him breaking down, when he was looking for strength. Moreover, seeing the Freedman family waiting, with apparently a glimmer of satisfaction on their faces, made it all the more important that Marc was here. But now, 15 minutes had passed, and Marc was beginning to sweat. He pulled out his pocket watch. He only had 10 more minutes to wait—10 more minutes left of Ted's life.

As Marc looked forward, the curtain was drawn open, revealing the execution chamber. Sitting in the center of that death chamber was the all-dreaded and now world-famous Auburn electric chair. It was still empty, yet the wooden contraption—with its metal, helmet-like crown, and leather straps on the arms and front legs—had a long and gruesome history. It was the first electric chair in history ever to be used to kill a human being.

Eighteen years ago, in 1890, William Kemmler was the first man to be honored in this cheaply constructed death throne. They had jolted Kemmler with 1000 volts of electricity for 17 seconds and turned off the switch. The doctor had promptly checked his pulse and declared Kemmler dead. However, several seconds later, a witness had noticed that Kemmler was still breathing. The doctor looked, and cried out, "Turn the current back on, quickly!" Kemmler was zapped with 2000 volts a second time, just to make sure he expired. However, the high voltage had caused the blood vessels under William's skin to explode, and his head had almost caught on fire. The horrid stench of Kemmler's burning flesh and hair had filled the room, gagging the spectators, who later claimed it was the most nauseating odor they had ever smelled.

This famous chair was also where Leon Czolgosz, the assassin of President McKinley, had met his Maker, or, rather, Lucifer.

However, Marc had not heard about the horror story of Kemmler's torturous death, and now waited for this nightmare to end as quickly and painlessly as possible. Finally, two guards escorted his brother into the chamber. Ted's eyes immediately scanned the audience, landing on Marc. It was the most uncomfortable gaze that each had ever experienced. It was excruciating.

As the guards guided Ted into the chair and began strapping his arms, Marc had all to do to even look. He could see the terror in Ted's eyes as they lowered the metal helmet over the top of his head and began attaching the electrodes. Ted's jittery eyes followed every move they made as Marc briefly caught a glimpse of Mrs. Freedman smiling, with a look in her eyes that seemed to say, "Good!"

Meanwhile, Ted gazed up at the guard still attaching the electrode to his head, and then down to the other guard now fastening the leather straps to his legs. Ted twitched with each touch to his skin, but suddenly he noticed the executioner standing by the wall. He was slipping on his thick, rubber gloves. Nearby was the huge throw-switch.

The dreaded death-switch was mounted on a metal panel, surrounded by voltage meters and fuses, and had thick black wires that extended down the wall and ran across the cement floor to his chair.

A priest then stood in front of him, speaking some sort of prayer, yet Ted couldn't hear a word, since the thoughts running through his frightened mind now were that these very thoughts will soon be turned off. He would never think again, feel again, see again. It was all about to end, and there was absolutely nothing he could do about it. He suddenly heard a voice behind him say, "All clear, and ready to go." As the priest stepped aside, Ted's eyes once again connected with his brother's. Ted couldn't hold back any longer, and tears streamed down as he tried to swallow, but he had no saliva left. Just then the warden stepped in front of him and said solemnly, "Do you have any last words?"

Ted's head was strapped tight, yet his eyes rolled up. He was going to curse the warden and the entire flawed system, but instead his eyes veered down toward his brother. "I j-just want to say, I love you Marc. Please t-tell everyone at home I love t-them, too. Okay?" As he saw his brother nod, with misty eyes, the warden gave the signal to gag his mouth and cover his head.

Marc struggled to contain his tears; it was imperative that his brother didn't see him cry. It was excruciating to watch, as they gagged his brother's mouth with a wooden dowel, which Ted would soon be biting down on once the burning current began to fry his body. The executioner then stepped behind Ted and began lowering the black hood. Yet before it passed over Ted's eyes, Marc noticed them widen. It was an odd expression, and Marc didn't know what to make of it. Suddenly, Ted began squirming in the chair and moving his head. The sight was unsettling! Marc wasn't sure if a low voltage current somehow began flowing, or if Ted was just making the last tragic struggle for his life. However, the warden wasn't going to wait for another ugly situation to occur, and he gave the signal to pull the switch.

Before Marc could collect his thoughts, the executioner slammed the toggle switch down as the lights in the chamber alarmingly grew dim and began to flicker.

The hellish electrical storm raged through Ted's body, as he could feel the high voltage boiling his blood and sizzling his skin. He bit down hard on the wooden dowel, as his body rattled and his head numbed and swelled in excruciating pain. Ted felt as if his body was going to explode, as saliva oozed out of his clenched mouth.

Marc had to look away, as Ted's body continued to vibrate violently in the chair. It was the longest 15 seconds in his life, and the last of Ted's. Marc looked back up to see his brother's dead, limp body sitting in the chair. Marc's tears finally broke free and soiled his face as he lowered his head into the palms of his hands. Even more disturbing were the claps coming from the other side of the room and behind him. Marc knew he couldn't tolerate another second in this gruesome shop of horrors, and he stood up, turned, and stepped into the aisle. As he looked toward the rear of the room, his heart almost stopped! Archibald Huxley was clapping wildly in his wheelchair, while 10 feet away stood Blaggo.

Marc was flustered. He now knew what Ted had seen as they were covering his eyes. Marc hadn't seen Huxley ever since the day Ted had shot and crippled him, nor had he seen Blaggo, the ugly pug-faced brute, since his beating and split lip as a young boy. Humiliated and desiring to avoid a confrontation, Marc made a beeline toward the rear door. As he passed and entered the hallway, Huxley came wheeling out after him. Marc didn't bother to turn; yet Huxley was rolling fast and right on his heels.

Huxley bellowed, "It's about time someone killed that scruffy, goat-faced bastard!"

Marc spun around quickly, while Huxley grabbed his wheels and came to a stop. Marc's eyes widened as Huxley pulled out a .32 caliber pistol.

"That little prick crippled me, and *you*, you fucking snake, stole my mine. Now, it's *your turn* to die."

"Go ahead," Marc blasted, "shoot me! Then you'll end up in a new chair—that lovely electrical one inside."

Huxley pulled the hammer back, and snarled, "I don't give a shit! Do you think living like *this* is any sort of life? You two bastards stole everything from me: my families, my business, and even the use of my body. So, you deserve to be with your brother. Good bye, Marc!"

With that, Huxley pulled the trigger. Smoke and fire blew out the nozzle as the pistol recoiled, the bullet violently boring a hole into Marc's chest. Without a thought, Marc instinctively leapt forward, grabbed the revolver, and rammed the barrel into Huxley's mouth—cracking four teeth and splitting both lips. "No, Archie! You're the one taking a trip, and it won't be where Ted or I will be going."

Marc pulled the trigger, blowing the back of Archie's skull out, while brain matter splattered Blaggo, who just arrived. Standing with blood and globular tissue all over his clothes and face, Blaggo looked up at Marc in shock, his ugly face pale.

Marc looked at Blaggo with crazed eyes. "What do you think of your boss now?" Marc growled.

Blaggo remained semi-paralyzed in disbelief as Marc continued, "And, my, I always thought you were a towering giant, but I was just a little kid back then. You're not so big now, are you, tough guy?"

Blaggo wiped the blood off his face and pulled a .45 caliber Colt out of his inner coat pocket. Yet as he went to pull the trigger, Marc slapped the hammer of his revolver with the palm of his hand, firing a shot waist-high into Blaggo's stomach. As Blaggo's upper body keeled forward, his arm moved, and his shot veered toward the floor, the bullet ricocheting off the tile and screaming down the vacant hallway. Just then two prison guards ran up behind Blaggo and grabbed him. Having seen the entire exchange, they asked Marc to hand them the gun, but assured him that he acted in self-defense, and they would stand as witnesses.

The doctor, who had just filled out Ted's death certificate, was summoned, and now walked over and began examining Marc's wound. He was surprised to see that right next to the bleeding bullet hole was a small round scar. Marc looked down and smiled. He told the doctor it was a bullet wound from San Juan Hill. The doctor escorted Marc to the infirmary, and temporarily patched up the wound to stop the bleeding. Using the new X-ray machine, he found that the bullet chipped his clavicle, but otherwise, did no serious damage. He operated immediately, and within an hour had removed the bullet and stitched up the wound.

Four days later, Marc arrived in Pittsburgh. Waiting at the station to drive him home was his darling little daughter Sophia. Marianne knew very well that Sophia was Marc's antidote to any poison that plagued his troubled mind, and she was right to send her. As she drove through the city streets, weaving in and out of pedestrians and the slow horse-drawn carriages in her way, Marc couldn't help but smile inside. His face, however, was still wracked with grief. He hadn't told her yet about her uncle or his wound, and figured he'd wait, especially since she was excitedly chatting away about her number one passion—automobile racing.

"Papa, did I tell you that Aunt Filomena called and told me that they are preparing to schedule the first woman's automobile race?"

Marc gazed at her lovingly. "No, I can't say you have."

As Sophia exited the city and hit the dirt path, the car bounced as they both flew up and landed down hard on the black leather seats. "Well, it will be from New York to Philadelphia, and they want to schedule it at the beginning of next year."

"That's great," Marc said, wanting to smile, but unable.

"Yes, it is," she said as she hit the throttle, snapping their heads back. "Do you think they'll let me enter the race?"

Marc smiled inside, once again, but his face was stern. "First of all, slow down. And, *no!* I will *not* allow you."

Sophia slowed down, with an awful pout on her adorable face. "Why not? I'm a good driver."

"Yes, you *are* a good driver. But you are also too young to be making such a long and dangerous trip. You must focus on school and then college, perhaps engineering."

"But, that means I can race when I get older, right?" Sophia doggedly pressed.

Marc shook his head. "My, oh, my. You do remind me of my mother. You're a feisty girl, Sophia, and, yes, if it means that much to you. Personally, I'd rather see you manage an automobile company one day than drive a racecar. That's why your education must come first. When I was a little boy growing up in Warsaw, Poland, my neighbor was a smart little girl named Marie Skłodowska. And she grew up to be a brilliant scientist, even winning the Nobel Prize for Physics. You probably know her as Madame Curie."

Sophia nodded enthusiastically, while Marc added, "So, you can do great things, Sophia, *if* you learn the proper skills. But if you really wish to race that means you will need to practice, and not with this Ford Model A. I'll have to buy you an Itala car."

Sophia's eyes lit up as she cut the wheel and head up the driveway. "An Itala car! That's what Prince Borghese has. He won the Peking to Paris race with that." As she applied the brake, she squinted. "But that's an Italian-built car. I thought you said we must always put America first?"

Marc placed his hand on her knee. "Yes, my dear, but, in some instances, we must be able to concede that others can do certain things better than we can. Just as the British build better warships than us, or the Swiss build better clocks, when it comes to fast automobiles, I'll put my money on the Italians."

Marianne and Remus came running out to greet them, while Stan sat on the sprawling front porch with Aunt Filomena standing behind him, and Rusty and Calvin flanking him on either side. As Marianne escorted Marc onto the deck, followed by Sophia and Remus, they all embraced. The mood was somber, but the deep camaraderie they shared in this hour of sadness was comforting. No word was mentioned about Marc's final showdown with Huxley or Blaggo, since Marc had decided in Auburn that he wanted to tell Remus about that delicate matter in the morning, face to face, rather than over the telephone or at this gathering. He knew Remus had come to loathe his father, but Marc still felt uncomfortable with the fact that he put a gun in Archie's mouth and literally blew his brains out. As he recollected the bizarre incident, he realized that Huxley had always said Marc was too predictable and always played by the rules. Yet, here it was, Marc had done something that even surprised himself. He didn't like the vexing thought of what he did reappearing in his mind's eye, yet he was also troubled by something else; he had no remorse for doing it. He firmly believed he had finished the heroic half-deed that his brother Ted had done. What's more, that Huxley's life had been shattered in every conceivable way for the past five years also seemed to be just punishment for the life of hell he inflicted on so many people.

As the Wozniak family and their friends ate dinner, they reminisced about Ted's crazy, funny, and stupid antics as well as his talents and heroic actions. Aunt Filomena even brought a book with her, which she said was her sister Sophia's. It was *La Gerusalemme liberata* (Jerusalem Delivered), Torquato Tasso's famous historical poem. She relayed the story of how Sophia choose Tasso for her son's name, particularly for the sake of little Sophia and Remus, who hadn't heard the full story. Yet as she opened the book, her eyes widened as they caught the brief biography of Tasso at the beginning. She hadn't realized it until just now, but Torquato Tasso died on April 25, 1595—the same day as Ted.

Marc couldn't help but expound upon that coincidence, which somehow he now viewed as fate, for his brother's entire life had mirrored the triumphant and tragic life of his namesake. Yet as he thought of Franz Liszt's symphonic poem, which the positive-minded composer altered in order to end Tasso's story on a high, triumphant note, Marc forced himself to view Ted's life the same way—focusing on all the great things he had achieved. Placing a recent recording disc of Liszt's *Tasso* on their new Victor V phonograph, they were all entreated to hearing this passionately mournful and triumphant work, which now appropriately honored their dearly departed relative and friend. Ted's triumphant horns had finally sounded.

Epilogue

November 15, 1912

Four years had passed, and the Wozniaks enjoyed what appeared to be a new era as three more Wozniaks accompanied the clan. Marianne had given birth to twins, Evelyn and Mary, and more recently, Joseph. Marc was elated to see that Sophia had finally decided to go to college for engineering, thus fulfilling another wish of his father's, for although Marc didn't make it to college, the next generation of Wozniaks were indeed stepping up the ladder.

Marc had much to be happy about. He had guided his family through some of the most ugly torments a family could possibly endure, and, with the aid of his brother, finally saw to it that Huxley was destroyed, even gaining full control of his mighty empire. It had been a long and harrowing journey, but Marc had not only fulfilled his promise to his parents, but Huxley's evil spirit, which hung over the family like a dark cloud, had finally been exorcized, and the Wozniaks now basked in the sunshine.

Meanwhile, the nation appeared to be experiencing the end of an era. Back in 1908, Theodore Roosevelt had declined to run for a third term and had backed his friend and secretary of war, William Howard Taft in his bid for the presidency. From Taft's obese and genial outward appearance he seemed like an unlikely candidate to some, yet within that massive frame, William had a wealth of experience under his large belt, having served in a number of roles, including his governorship of the volatile Philippines after the Spanish-American War under President McKinley. Taft had won the election and had taken office in March of 1909.

Days later, TR had felt it was time to get back to nature, and he had planned a ten-months long safari. To allay public criticism of the noted hunter killing more animals for mere sport, TR had craftily enlisted his friend and pacifist, Andrew Carnegie, to fund his *scientific* expedition, of which he had dragged his son Kermit along for the adventure. That enabled TR to bag a rhino, eight elephants, nine lions, 20 zebras and many other wild animals that had been shipped back to Washington's Natural History Museum for scientific research, and some to be put on display.

Meanwhile, Taft's four years in office had demonstrated just how far he had drifted from Roosevelt's progressive agenda, and the Republican convention during 1912 turned ugly. TR had decided to challenge his old friend, now rival, but a discrepancy in votes had arisen, and TR demanded a recount. However, too much rivalry and subterfuge prevailed, and Taft won the nomination. That had made the TR bull madder than a moose, and, in fact, TR had created his own Bull Moose Party to continue the charge.

However, while campaigning in Milwaukee, a would-be assassin attempted to bag the Bull Moose. He had fired a shot—just as TR had been walking toward the podium to make a speech—and the bullet burrowed into Roosevelt's chest. Fortunately, the eyeglass case in TR's breast pocket deflected the bullet just enough to not hit any vital organs.

More shocking still, TR calmed his advisors, boldly stepped up to the podium, and declared, "Friends, I shall ask you to be as quiet as possible. I don't know whether you fully understand that I have just been shot. But it takes more than that to kill a bull moose! The bullet is in me now, so I cannot make a very long speech, but I will try my best."

TR had done more than his best, or anyone's best, and miraculously rambled on for 90 minutes. After which, he had been rushed to a hospital and stitched up—the bullet was to remain in his chest, akin to Andrew Jackson's.

When November finally arrived, TR managed to beat Taft at the polls by gaining a two percent lead, earning 27 percent of the popular vote, yet the three-way race proved a disaster for the Republicans as Woodrow Wilson stole the election by earning a mere 41 percent of the popular vote.

However, the progressive nation had witnessed a transformation, as prohibition was fast becoming a new imperative in many states, being lobbied strongly by women, including Filomena, thus making Rusty and Huxley's old fears manifest. And the old world of static sketches and paintings had been replaced with Edison's moving pictures, which he had recently improved by adding sound. Even Henry Ford improved his automobile by introducing the Model T. The "Tin Lizzie", as it was soon called, fast became the most popular and influential car in history as Ford pumped the Model T out at the mindboggling rate of one every 93 minutes from his trailblazing assembly line. Of equal impact, pilots of the newfangled airplane were flying into history as they broke one record after another. Even women joined the flying circus, when Harriet Quimby became the first American woman to earn a pilot's license on August 1, 1911.

At the same time, the ambitious inventions of gargantuan dreadnoughts and colossal ocean liners literally hit the waves as the unsinkable Titanic struck an iceberg, sinking in the icy North Atlantic and killing 1,595 passengers, thus horrifyingly disproving mankind's invincibility on the high seas. Undaunted, progress continued, as hard learned mistakes engendered superior ships. In the skies, equally gargantuan Zeppelins sailed overhead like floating warships, while the rank smell of world war permeated the European air. German and French scientists mixed odorous chemicals and gases in their laboratories, which in a few years time would be unleashed on the battlefields, killing and maiming thousands. On the flipside, the fields of medicine and technology were advancing at an alarming rate, while commercial airplanes took to the skies. Hence, what had appeared as the Progressive Era had turned out to be only the launching pad for the stellar progress that was about to jettison civilization to astronomical heights.

Meanwhile, the Wozniaks had lived through the preceding gilded and progressive eras that had transformed a broken union into a cohesive whole. It was propelled by a firm belief in the Social Darwinian mantra of "survival of the fittest" and the religious credo of Manifest Destiny, and that had enabled the United States to become not only a world player, but in the decades ahead, the unrivalled superpower and greatest defender of world freedom the world had ever seen. Marc had led his family through these often raw and rusty years from poverty to patrician status, even emulating Carnegie by becoming a philanthropist, thus validating the reality that capitalism, despite its flaws, had proved unequivocally that it was the best system, thus far, for raising the standard of living and the quality of life for more people than any other system proposed by mankind. The hard lessons learned of capitalism's disparate wages, poor working conditions, inherent corruption and greed were all experienced by the Wozniak family and his generation, and continues in varying degrees, yet progress, by nature, is an uphill battle and a never-ending process. And the American grit (which is the key ingredient of American exceptionalism) that pushed these souls and their nation to the forefront of world affairs is a miraculous trait and achievement never equaled by any other people to have walked the earth.

Although initially formed by mostly Anglo-Saxons, America had quickly mutated and experienced its greatest surge forward during these blazing gilded years, for it was this myriad of ethic races that made this magnificent feat possible. Nikola Tesla, whose AC system transformed the nation, was Serbian by birth, while Thomas Edison, the inventive wizard, was Dutch. Herman Hollerith, whose tabulating machine led to the founding of IBM, was German, while Charles Bonaparte, who served under TR's administration and later created the FBI, was Italian. All these men and countless others, all had various old world bloodlines, yet had become full-blooded Americans.

Though proud of their Polish and Italian heritages, the Wozniaks had likewise assimilated and transformed, as had the volatile nation. Being an American citizen took on a higher meaning for the Wozniaks and the waves of millions of immigrants that flooded through Ellis Island (one million in 1905 alone, consisting mostly of Italians and Hungarians) who joined the grand process of becoming Americans. The blazing trail of innovation and progress, which often erupted with blazing explosions, had forged a strong nation, hardening it like steel to become the towering pillar of liberty and ultimate beacon of hope for all mankind. And as Marc repeatedly stressed to his precious brood, it is up to all Americans, old and new alike, to ensure that America continues to blaze into the future as a world leader.

— End —

Acknowledgements

I would like to thank my wife Eileen and family for their love and inspiration.

I also thank my editor and all my dear friends that have supported this endeavor.

I had found it fascinating how the Gilded Age was not only a tremendous burst of blazing talent and blazing progress, but also a blazing time of explosive misconduct and abuse. In addition to the presidential assassinations that marred this period and the abuses by greedy tycoons, were the numerous coalmine explosions that were more often due to negligence than ignorance. I felt these harsh times needed to be illuminated, as well, for the world that many miners and factory workers were forced to endure were of a slave status that modern readers find hard to fathom. Their unsafe work environments, long hours and appalling wages were only compounded by the squalid tenements they were forced to live in. Meanwhile, widows would be striped of their husband's possessions and not even be recognized by a government that had never granted them the right to vote.

Additionally, the political realm was likewise tainted with fraud, strife, and a corrupt spoils system, while capitalists gave birth to the practice of manipulating the presidency with large campaign contributions, all of which were unnervingly the corrupt seedlings that have blossomed into the overgrown mess of weeds we have today.

On the opposite side of the gilded coin, however, the Gilded Age was the major turning point in American history. It was during these tumultuous years that ingenuity burst from the minds of creative thinkers and entrepreneurs, each with different goals, yet all contributing to the advancement of a young and restless nation that began to expand its interests and influence into a global economy. In that noble pursuit, they not only rivaled the leading empire at that time, England, in manufacturing capacity, but also took the first significant step at flexing its military might.

That New York City alone took 200 years to reach a population of 500,000 in 1850, yet by 1900, swelled to 3.4 million, also indicates the immense influx of immigrants that truly helped to bring new ideas to American shores. Along with these ideas came the muscle and sweat of laborers whose paltry pay never compensated nor honored these people properly who had literally built the industrial complexes, and manned them, to produce a vast assortment of newfangled inventions and products to make our lives easier, more productive or just more enjoyable. That these years produced the circus, amusement parks, Ferris wheel, tennis, volleyball, basketball, Coca-Cola, Tootsie Rolls, Aunt Jemima Pancakes, Levi jeans, Macy's, Sears, Montgomery Ward, Parker Brothers games, Kodak film cameras, moving pictures, record players, wireless radios, automobiles, submarines, machine guns, steel-cabled suspension bridges, elevated railroads, subways, electricity, lighting and so many other modern inventions, we must bow our heads to these men in derbies and top hats or women in bonnets who largely shaped our modern world. So, to all the illustrious and well-known heroes, and the millions of unsung heroes, that lived in this blazing Gilded Age, I thank you!

The Domes of the Yosemite by Albert Bierstadt

Niagara Falls by Frederic Church

The Birth of Venus
by William Bouguereau

26103451R00305

Made in the USA
Charleston, SC
24 January 2014